Books by Christopher Valen

The John Santana Novels

White Tombs
The Black Minute
Bad Weeds Never Die
Bone Shadows
Death's Way
The Darkness Hunter
Speak for the Dead

Other Books

All the Fields

Books by Dan Cohen

Non-Fiction

Undefeated
The Spirit of Breck
Anonymous Source

City of
STONES

Conquill Press
387 Bluebird Alcove
St. Paul, MN 55125
www.conquillpress.com

For information about special discounts for bulk purchases, contact
conquillpress@comcast.net

CITY OF STONES

Cover Design: Rebecca Treadway

Library of Congress Control Number: 2019937553
Valen, Christopher, Cohen, Dan
CITY OF STONES: a novel/by Christopher Valen and Dan Cohen—
1st Edition

ISBN: 978-0-9995385-2-4
Conquill Press/September 2019

Printed in the United States of America
10 9 8 7 6 5 4 3 2 1

City of
STONES

Christopher Valen
and
Dan Cohen

Conquill Press
St. Paul, Minnesota

Two people can keep a secret if one of them is dead.
—Old Yiddish Saying

Prologue

Minneapolis
August 31, 1950

The rain is cold and edged with hail as it blows over the faded hotels, flophouses, and rescue missions in the Gateway District. It hammers the neon lights and glass windows of the brightly lit bars and liquor stores, and gusts over the railroad tracks between the Mississippi and the old, gray buildings of Skid Row.

Huddled in the trunk of a car, his clothes soaking wet, his body bruised from a beating, Martin Crenshaw knows it's a one-way ride. The two unmasked men who tossed him in here aren't worried about being identified. The tip of a pointed shovel Crenshaw touches confirms it.

He'll soon be digging his own grave.

His fingernails claw helplessly at the trunk lid. He made a mistake. Trying to help his family. No reason to die over a mistake. He prays the car keeps going. As long as it does, he'll stay alive. But twenty minutes later the driver pulls off the road and kills the engine. He hears the two men get out. One opens the trunk.

The bigger man grabs one of Crenshaw's arms and drags him out. "Walk," he orders.

Crenshaw shuffles his feet, then makes his legs go limp. Dead weight.

A second man, nearly as big as the first, pulls a shovel out of the trunk and slams the lid. "Ditch him here. We'll look for a spot off the road."

The bigger man hauls Crenshaw to the front of the car and leaves him sprawled on the hood, bent at the waist, arms outstretched, his face kissing warm metal.

The two men tromp through the thick, wet vegetation at one thirty in the morning, unconcerned about noise.

"Here," the second man says, pointing to a spot on the ground, thirty yards off the road, in a thicket. "Lots of trees. Rain has stopped. Soft ground."

"Better be," the bigger one says. "Can't take all night. And I ain't diggin' the hole."

"Who said you were?"

The bigger man points toward their car. "How the hell is he gonna dig? He can barely walk."

The second man looks in Crenshaw's direction and shrugs. He sinks the shovel into the soft ground and begins digging. The bigger man watches.

Ribs hurting, legs like Black Jack taffy, Crenshaw knows he's a dead man if he stays here. Probably a dead man no matter what he does, but at least he can try. Rolling off the hood, Crenshaw staggers toward the road.

Leaning on the shovel, breathing hard, the second man says, "There's another shovel in the trunk. Instead of standing there like you've got a lump of coal in your ass, why don't you go get it?"

But the bigger man's eyes are focused on Martin Crenshaw.

The second man follows his partner's gaze. "You were supposed to watch him. Go get him."

"Give me the keys," the bigger man says. "I'll get the other shovel. *You* get Crenshaw." He grabs the keys from the second man.

"Okay," the second man says with a shrug. He drops the shovel beside the hole and goes after Crenshaw.

Crenshaw, reeling toward the road, glances back and sees the second man, walking fast, but not covering much ground.

Crenshaw sucks in cool air, feels a stab of pain in his ribs, and coughs out a foggy breath. *Jesus*, he winces. *Must've broken a rib.* Still, his legs feel sturdier. On the asphalt now, he jogs, heading toward the bridge in the distance, hoping a ride will come along and save his ass.

He can't run well in his dress shoes and suit coat. He stops, kicks off his shoes, and slips out of his coat. Running in his stocking feet now, he picks up the pace, avoiding the rocky dirt shoulder, staying on the smoother asphalt.

"Hey!" the second man yells. Panting, he stops, hands on his hips, bent over, a stitch in his side, trying to catch his breath.

"Shit," the bigger man mutters. He tosses the second shovel back into the trunk and the keys into the front seat, and starts to run.

Crenshaw hears the bigger man's footsteps pounding the pavement. The bigger man can run, and he's gaining ground. Crenshaw kicks it into another gear, ignoring the sharp pain in his side.

"Get the car!" the bigger man calls, sprinting by the second man. "Keys are in the front seat."

Crenshaw is running nearly full out. But the bigger man has long legs and a longer stride. *If he's in shape, he'll run me down. Was a time, when I was running cross-country in high school, the bigger guy wouldn't catch me.*

Struggling to keep his speed, Crenshaw can tell from the sound of the footsteps behind him that the bigger man is closing—and closing fast.

Ahead, the road curves to the right. A steep, grassy hill left of the road leads up to a railroad bridge. Ten years ago, when he was eighteen, hills were his strength. If he can maintain his stride, hold off the larger man till he reaches the hill, he can beat him. But then he hears the car start, the engine roar. No way he can outrun the car. But maybe he won't have to.

Crenshaw runs all out. Sprinting into the curve, off the road and up the hill, he gives it everything he has. The footsteps behind him suddenly stop. Then tires screech, a car door slams, gears grind. The car burns rubber, picks up speed, and races toward him.

Caught in the headlights, Crenshaw legs it to the top of the hill and onto the deck of the railroad bridge, his lungs burning; pain like shards of glass stabs his ribs.

Tires squeal. The headlights go dark. The second man kills the engine. The two men get out and lumber up the hill.

Crenshaw looks to his left and right. He sees two sets of tracks. No trains coming. He's alone. Running again, slower now, he makes it halfway across the bridge before the pain in his ribs stops him. He stumbles to the railing, a queasy feeling in his stomach as he looks down at the dark water far below, his only means of escape. The two men are coming, their heavy footsteps thundering on the wood deck between the tracks. Crenshaw steps over the steel railing, gripping it with two shaking hands.

Ten feet away both men stop. "You won't make it," the second man says, panting.

Trying to catch his breath, Crenshaw says, "What choice do I have?"

"Jump," the bigger man says, his breath coming in spurts. "Saves us the trouble."

The second man gives his partner a look and then faces Crenshaw. "We'll kill you quick. No pain."

Heart thudding in his chest, piss running down his leg, Crenshaw stares once more at the dark water far below. "No, thanks," he says with a shake of his head.

Then he jumps and his scream fades like the whistle of a distant train.

Part One

"... The just man kept his course along
The vale of death ...
Till the villain left the paths of ease
To walk in perilous paths, and drive
The just man into barren climes ..."

—William Blake
"The Marriage of Heaven and Hell: The Argument"

Chapter 1

September 4, 1950

Homicide Detective Lieutenant Jake Cafferty is finishing up his report on a body that washed up on the Minneapolis side of the Mississippi River between the Short Line and Marshall Avenue bridges three days ago. Locals call it the Short Line because the bridge allows trains from Saint Paul to go west out of the city and cross directly into Minneapolis instead of crossing the river near Fort Snelling, significantly cutting the length of the route.

A driver's license found in a wallet ID'd him as twenty-eight-year-old Martin Crenshaw. Crenshaw worked as a stockbroker at Bass, Sterns, and Wheeler, a downtown brokerage firm, and was having money problems. No eyewitnesses saw him leap from the bridge, but his wife and co-workers maintained that he was depressed and had contemplated suicide. He'd disappeared a day before his bloated body turned up.

Seems jumpers are always drawn to bridges in a river city like Minneapolis, Jake thinks. Most believe the myth that it's a romantic way to end your life. Like joining the angels. But Jake knows that when you jump off a bridge, you'll likely die from drowning or from multiple blunt-force injuries, the same way someone dies after being hit by a speeding car.

Only question Jake has about the suicide is the location of Martin Crenshaw's shoes. Uniforms found them, along with a suit coat, a half-mile from the bridge. Why did Crenshaw leave them there instead of on the bridge? And how did he get to the bridge in the first place? It's a long walk from his home. No record of Crenshaw calling a cab. Jake wonders about the fresh skid marks on West River Parkway. Might not have anything to do with Crenshaw's death, but the marks, along with the shoes, bother him.

Jake pulls the completed report out of the typewriter, lights a Camel, and leans back in his squeaky swivel chair. His throat and lips are dry. He rises and walks to the coffee pot and refills his coffee mug.

Antsy, he drinks coffee and checks his watch. It's 8:00 p.m. Four hours before his graveyard shift begins. He came in early to finish his summary report on Martin Crenshaw, but the shoes and suit coat don't fit the picture he's painted in his mind. He sets down his coffee mug and heads for his car and the ten-block "Golden Mile" that runs from the edge of downtown at 18th Street south to 28th Street. It's there, on Park Avenue, that turn-of-the-century industrialists invested their lumber and milling fortunes in the construction of thirty-five stone mansions set on wide elm-shaded boulevards, large lots, and long setbacks.

Douglas Crenshaw, Martin's father, lives in a large Colonial Revival. At the age of 64, he's still one of the most powerful men in Minneapolis. He made his first fortune in the flour milling industry when Minneapolis was known throughout the country as "Mill City." When the industry declined after WWI, Crenshaw went into banking. Jake attempted to talk to him after his son's death, but the old man claimed he was ill and declined an interview. A slender woman opens the heavy wooden door. Jake estimates she's in her late twenties or early thirties. Her brunette hair is styled in a chignon. Indigo blue eyes are shadowed behind cat eyeglasses and match the color of her knit sweater and slacks. She's not wearing lipstick, and if she's wearing makeup, it's perfectly applied. There's no wedding band or any indication that there ever was one, unusual for a woman of her age and station.

"Yes?" she asks with a tilt of her head, her eyes wandering over Jake's face.

Showing her his badge wallet, he says, "I'm here to see Douglas Crenshaw."

"Have an appointment?"

"Didn't know I needed one."

She leans forward and peers at his badge wallet. "Lieutenant Jake Cafferty."

"And you are?"

"Virginia Crenshaw." Her sharp eyes look him over, like she knows something he doesn't. "I'll see if Father is busy," she says, waving him in.

Jake follows her into a large foyer, past the grand staircase outfitted with a stair-lift, and into a walnut-paneled library with large oil paintings of cantankerous-looking men and puritanical women. Virginia Crenshaw directs him to sit on a heavy leather couch in front of an ornate marble fireplace and offers him something to drink.

Jake declines and remains standing.

She waits a beat and then says, "You must be here about my brother, Marty."

"I am."

She takes a deep stuttering breath and lets it out slowly. "Still can't believe he killed himself."

"Were you and your brother close?"

"More so when we were younger. Marty married young and spent more time with his own family."

"Anyone you know might want to harm him?"

Her eyes hold his. "Homicide," she says.

"Beg your pardon?"

"The card in your badge wallet. You're a homicide detective."

"That's right."

"But my brother's death was ruled a suicide."

"Yes, it was."

"Then I don't understand why you're here, unless . . ." A hand momentarily covers her mouth as she sucks in a breath. "My brother was murdered." She says it frankly, her eyes focused on Jake's, searching for anything indicating he's hiding the truth.

"I never said that."

"Will you continue with the investigation, Lieutenant?"

"If it was murder, I'll need a motive."

"Well, I didn't see much of Marty the last few years. He was always a friendly person. A gentleman. I can't imagine anyone wanting to hurt him."

"Then maybe we're right calling it a suicide."

She gives him a tentative smile. "You'll let me know if anything turns up?"

Jake nods.

"All right, then." She turns and strides out of the room.

Jake waits till she leaves and closes the pocket doors behind her. Then he wanders around the library.

Framed black-and-white photos of Douglas Crenshaw's wife and two children, spanning decades, are arranged on the large walnut desk. The Crenshaws must've been in their mid-thirties when the children were born. Jake recalls that Mrs. Crenshaw passed away a number of years ago from cancer. Virginia Crenshaw strongly resembles her mother, Irene.

More family photos hang on the wall behind the desk, along with Martin's and Virginia's high school diplomas from the St. Paul Academy and Summit School and their college diplomas; Martin from the University of Minnesota and Virginia from Radcliffe College in Cambridge, Massachusetts.

To the right of the photos hangs a framed red-white-and-blue membership certificate for the Citizens' Alliance. On either side of the certificate are framed copies of the *Weekly Bulletin*, the CA's primary means of keeping its members informed of important developments, locally and nationally, in the field of labor relations.

Jake is well aware of Douglas Crenshaw's membership in the powerful Citizens' Alliance. The organization first gained notoriety by breaking the 1917-18 trolley strikes. By the 1920s, they had assumed leadership of the Minneapolis business community and kept Minneapolis an open-shop town.

Organized and managed by a network of wealthy bankers, grain millers, and department store owners, the CA once had a permanent and well-paid group of undercover informers—supervised by Douglas Crenshaw—and a membership of eight hundred businessmen. By '34 the CA had successfully broken every major strike in Minneapolis and had attained control over the economy of the city with a monopoly that enabled them to wield immense power. The maintenance of this political and economic power had always been its primary mission.

Jake was a patrolman in '34 when the Teamsters went on strike against the Minneapolis trucking companies, effectively shutting down the Market District, the major Midwest distribution center. The CA—on behalf of the trucking companies—attempted to move goods with nonunion labor. The strike and violence associated with it lasted most of the summer. The worst day was on July 20, known as "Bloody Friday." The MPD shot at strikers, killing two and injuring sixty-seven. Jake suffered a badly bruised left arm in the confrontation. But mostly he remembers how the strike changed Minneapolis.

Thousands of workers in other industries organized. Hated by labor and feared by businessmen who favored a conciliatory attitude toward unions, Douglas Crenshaw and his group of informers and infiltrators struggled to keep member firms united and nonunion. By World War II, the CA's opposition to unions and its control over the Minneapolis business community had weakened.

But the passage of the Taft-Hartley Act of '47, which categorized sympathy strikes, secondary boycotts, and closed shops as "unfair labor practices," and allowed states to pass "right-to-work" laws, strengthened the alliance. Taft-Hartley also required unions to sign affidavits certifying that none of their officers were "Communists," fanning the rising anti-Communist flames ignited by US Senator Joe McCarthy and the CA's contention that Trotskyites controlled unions.

Jake turns as the pocket doors slide open and Douglas Crenshaw, dressed in a brown tweed suit and vest, white shirt, and red patterned tie, rolls across the hardwood floor in a wheelchair. A big, jowly man, he has thinning gray hair combed back on his head, a thick mustache, wire-rimmed glasses, and hairy caterpillar eyebrows. Jake wonders when Crenshaw started using the wheelchair. Last time Jake saw him in public a few months ago, Crenshaw was standing. Maybe his disability has kept him out of the public eye recently.

"Lieutenant Cafferty," Crenshaw says in a deep voice, extending a big hand.

Jake comes forward and shakes. Crenshaw has soft hands, a firm grip, and a commanding presence, despite the wheelchair.

"Take a seat," he says, indicating the leather couch. Crenshaw wheels his chair on the opposite side of the coffee table. When Jake is settled, Crenshaw says, "What's the purpose of your visit, Lieutenant? Certainly not Martin's suicide?"

Jake detects annoyance rather than sadness in the old man's voice. "It was ruled as such, yes."

Crenshaw arches his bushy eyebrows. "Meaning you don't think he killed himself?"

"Was your son suicidal?"

"Aren't we all at some point?"

Not knowing how to respond to that, Jake lets the comment slide. "Let's just say I have no solid evidence indicating it wasn't a suicide. Anyone you know who might have a grudge against your son?"

"Look, Lieutenant. My son's suicide doesn't surprise me. Martin was weak and, unfortunately, not very bright, unlike my daughter. He was also a union sympathizer with Communist leanings."

"Not all union members are Communists, Mr. Crenshaw."

"You're speaking as a member of the Police Federation."

"And you're speaking as a member of the Citizens' Alliance."

"I'm also speaking as a patriot. Law and order must be maintained. Union control of industry will not be tolerated. What the unions call a closed shop is an invasion of the constitutional rights of the American worker. The Citizens' Alliance was formed to protect every man's right to pursue his occupation without union interference and regardless of how he votes or worships."

"And profit margin has nothing to do with it."

"Ah," he says with a dismissive wave of a hand. "Unions are inefficient. They increase the cost of doing business and raise the rent for workers. Costs are less when men are willing to do a full day's work without complaining. Look at me," he says with his arms outstretched and palms up. "My life is an example. When I was a young man at the turn of the century, I chose to be my own boss. I had no capital, but I had ambition. If you're an able-bodied man, you have the same opportunities to succeed. Workers of lower abilities should be paid lower wages."

Jake isn't about to debate the old man. "If what you say about your son is true, that he was a union sympathizer with Communist leanings, then stockbroker seems like an odd choice for a career."

"Martin had difficulty deciding on a career direction. I encouraged him, hoping he could make something of himself, rather than waiting for me to pass and living off an inheritance."

"What about your daughter?"

Crenshaw chuckles. "My daughter has the backbone of a man and the charms of a woman. That's a combination that frightens most men."

"So she's waiting for the inheritance as well?"

"Virginia, unlike her brother, has never been concerned about money."

"Maybe because she doesn't have to be."

"A position all good women deserve to be in, Lieutenant."

Jake moves on. "Were you and your son estranged?"

"We hadn't spoken in a while."

Jake waits, hoping the old man will spill more information. When he doesn't, Jake says, "Your son ever recommend an investment that didn't pay off?"

Crenshaw lets out a long breath. "My personal finances have nothing to do with my son's suicide. And if you continue to pursue this line of investigation, I may be forced to make a phone call."

Jake wonders if the old man has something to hide. "That a threat?"

"Take it any way you like, Lieutenant."

On Jake's way out, Virginia Crenshaw holds open the front door for him. "I appreciate your concern for my brother," she says.

"Just doing my job." Jake wonders how she knew he was ready to leave, unless she was listening at the door.

"Goodbye, Detective Cafferty."

Jake starts to say "Goodbye" and then thinks better of it. He isn't sure why, but he has the feeling that he'll be seeing her again.

Chapter 2

MPD patrolman Nick Cole stands in an alley behind Rex Liquors under a hazy night sky and a sliver of silver moon. He hears the traffic noise along busy Nicollet Avenue and smells the piss in the corners and the strong scent of alcohol from the scattered empty pint bottles and white tile saloons, where customers spit in the tile gutter running parallel to the bar. Air leaking out of the stairwell of a flophouse next to the liquor store is rife with the musty smell of an old building and insecticide. The alley behind the liquor store is a favorite drinking spot known as "Party Alley," where small clusters of men called "bottle gangs" often gather to share some hooch and jackroll one another.

Johnny Rex owns the Victor Hotel, the Sourdough Bar, and the liquor store, where they'll offer to open the bottle of wine you bought. Nick's partner, Joe Briggs, told him that Rex's real name was John Bacich. Nick heard Bacich was a decorated vet and tank captain overseas during the war. First time Nick met him on the beat, he thought Rex carried himself like a soldier. Well liked by the cops that work the area, Rex has booze sellers out every Sunday. When Nick first started on the beat, he was overzealous and arrested the sellers, even though they told him they'd paid for the month. The shit hit the fan. MPD Homicide Captain Avery Arnold chewed him out. MPD Chief of Police William Flanagan read him the riot act. Nick never arrested Johnny Rex's sellers again.

Joe Briggs is working over a guy named Abe Fishman, using a roll of quarters in his gloved fist to pack more power in each punch. Fishman is a bootlegger who sells forty-cent wine for a dollar out of the trunk of one of his cars. He has four different ones to throw off police, though he and his cars are well known to beat cops, especially Joe Briggs.

A big man in his early fifties, Briggs has a large belly that falls over his duty belt like a soft pillow. He uses tight leather gloves and body blows rather than head punches whenever he administers a beating, though from what Nick has learned, none of the brass gives a damn about evidence of beatings when it comes to Jews or Negroes.

Briggs hits Fishman in the stomach again, sending the small man to his knees. "I warned you to stay out of this alley, didn't I, Hymie?" The alley is a place where Briggs regularly expresses his deep-seated hatred of anyone different from him. Kike, Hebe, Hymie, or Sheenie, Briggs' slurs are interchangeable.

Nick has vowed on more than one occasion that he'll intervene the next time Briggs starts beating someone, but then the next time passes and the next, and the beatings continue. Nick isn't afraid of Briggs, though at six feet and at least two hundred twenty pounds, the big man is an inch taller and much heavier. But Nick boxed in the Army as a middleweight and has taken down much bigger men. Plus, he's in far better shape than Briggs, who's sweating and huffing after throwing a few punches.

The sound of muffled voices draws Nick's attention to three men lurking in the shadows between the buildings, the same men who'd scuffled away when he and Briggs showed up to roust Fishman. Nick sees men like these every day in Skid Row, winos and transients shuffling along the sidewalks and passed out in doorways. Those who are nuisances or causing problems are hauled off in the Black Maria, only to return the following day, having paid their fine and sobered up after a night in jail.

"Scram!" Nick shouts.

As the men scuttle off, Briggs kicks Fishman in the side. "I ever see you around here again selling your booze, they'll have to carry you out. You understand?"

Fishman mumbles something that Nick can't hear.

"What'd you say, Sheenie?"

Nick recognizes *that* tone in Briggs' voice and knows it signals an escalating level of violence. This is Nick's last night as a beat cop, and his last night working with Briggs. Nothing is going to screw up his promotion to the Morals Squad. He moves quickly toward his partner.

"Let's go, Joe," he says, stepping in between Briggs and Fishman, who's curled in a fetal position on the ground. "Our shift is nearly over."

Briggs has a glazed, manic look in his eyes, as if he doesn't recognize his partner. Nick wonders if Briggs might throw a punch at him. He slides his rear foot back, giving him balance if he needs to react. But the look fades and Briggs says, "Right." His face breaks into a grin.

Nick glances down at Fishman, into the man's eyes, and in that second something passes between them. *I know this man,* Nick thinks. *But from where?*

Briggs claps Nick on the shoulder. "We got some celebrating to do," he says and steps on Fishman on the way back to their squad.

*   *   *

Nick Cole clocks out, changes into civilian clothes at his locker in the first precinct, and drives to Gluek's Bar, a popular cop hangout in the North Loop, an industrial area and home to a large railroad yard and numerous milling and manufacturing factories and warehouses. Gluek's is noisy and packed with shift workers from the factories and officers from the MPD, having drinks before heading home. With its elaborate woodwork, brick walls, stained-glass windows, and high-arched ceilings, the inside of the bar reminds Nick of the beer halls he saw in Germany at the end of World War II—at least the ones that were still standing.

Socializing with Briggs and other uniforms is something Nick avoids whenever possible. Many of them drink to excess, and some are mean drunks. It doesn't take much alcohol to get Nick high, but not accepting the invitation to celebrate his promotion is a bad departmental move. He never knows when he might need an officer's assistance.

"Hey! It's the soldier boy," Mike Bannister says as Nick approaches a table.

Mike Bannister is a large man with a head of wavy blond hair. He and Briggs came up the ranks together. Neither served in the war, a fact that bothers Bannister more than Briggs. Many senior officers are also angry that MPD vets, like Nick, are given preference in hiring and promotions. Bannister, a member of the Police Federation board, has vowed to do something about it and the stagnant wages he and his fellow officers are paid.

"Sit down," Briggs says, indicting a chair to his right with a cigar he's smoking. "What can I get you?" As Nick sits down, Briggs slips an arm around his shoulders. "This kid is going places, Mike. He's a smart one. Gonna make me proud."

"Beer is fine," Nick says.

Briggs calls to the waitress for three more beers.

"Heard you straightened out some bootlegging kike tonight," Bannister says with a wide grin on his face.

"Not me," Nick says, gesturing at Briggs.

Bannister winks at Briggs. "Soldier boy don't like getting his hands dirty?"

"What's the point?"

Bannister finishes off his glass of beer in one gulp and stares at Nick as if he thinks the younger man is crazy. "The point is, soldier boy, Jews don't belong here."

"I served with some in the war. They fought well."

"Cole was with the 317th Infantry Regiment, part of the Third Army," Briggs says.

Bannister raises his eyebrows. "Third Army. That was Patton's, wasn't it?"

Nick nods. "We liberated twenty-one thousand prisoners, most of 'em Jews, from the Buchenwald concentration camp in April of forty-five." Nick stares into the past. "Embedded in the metal entrance gate was the motto *Jedem das Seine*, or 'To each his own.' The words faced the inside of the camp so that all the prisoners could read it."

"I don't get it," Bannister says.

"To the SS it meant that a superior race had a right to liquidate others."

Briggs shakes his head in disgust. "Never understood how so many Hebes went to the slaughter without putting up a fight."

Though sickened by the inhumanity, Nick's war experiences strengthened his belief that, like animals, only the fittest and the smartest of the species survive. That's why he keeps his head down and his mouth shut. He figures the less he says, the fewer mistakes he'll make.

Bannister says, "Nobody but the godless Nazis thought those concentration camps were a good idea, Cole. Why don't all the Hebes just move to Israel now that they have their own country? They'd be much happier there."

"Makes sense," Briggs says. "Hebes don't want to be around us any more than we want to be around them. They got their own law firms. Soon they'll have their own hospital for Jew doctors when Mt. Sinai opens next year. They have their own way of doing damn near everything, like that whole 'kosher' thing. What the hell is that all about, anyway?"

Bannister says, "Ain't fair that we're on the pad for pennies, while these kikes are making thousands taking bets, selling booze, and running whores."

Briggs nods in agreement.

"You hear a name like Abraham, Joshua, or Simon," Bannister continues, "you know you got yourself a Hebe. Same with last names. Jews didn't even have 'em till a couple hundred years ago. You know that, Cole?"

Nick shakes his head.

"Hebes love money, so they've got names like Goldstein, Rubenstein, and Silverstein. We don't do something soon, the kikes will have all the money."

"If that's the case," Nick says, "why doesn't everyone become a Jew?"

Briggs and Bannister exchange a confused glance. Then Briggs shrugs and says, "Hell, most Jews are Communists. Remember back in '41, Mike? The Socialist Worker's Party ran the Teamsters union. Edited the *Northwest Organizer*, the union's paper. FBI raided their offices in Minneapolis and St. Paul."

Bannister nods. "Nothing but a bunch of Trotskyists accused of plotting to overthrow the government, for Christ's sake. Jew named Goldman acted as their lawyer during the trial. Sixteen of the twenty-nine accused got convicted."

"You know why Jews don't buy Fords?" Briggs asks.

Nick shakes his head again.

"Because they think Henry Ford was an anti-Semite. Can you believe that?"

"Don't make no sense," Bannister says. "Without Fords, there'd be no America."

"Damn right," Briggs says.

During their many shifts together, Briggs spoke openly about his admiration for William Bell Riley, the deceased pastor of First Baptist Church, one of the largest downtown churches in Minneapolis. For forty-five years, Riley defended the Silver

Shirts, a Fascist, white supremacist, anti-Semitic group modeled after the Brown Shirts in Germany and the Black Shirts in Italy. In the early '30s Minneapolis was home to the largest Silver Shirt chapter in the US. Riley openly praised Adolf Hitler from the pulpit before the war began and spoke often about *The Protocols of the Elders of Zion*, an anti-Semitic text claiming to describe the Jewish plan for global domination. Henry Ford funded printing of a half-million copies that were distributed throughout the US in the 1920s, which is why, Nick assumes, Jews don't buy Fords.

Despite Briggs' attitude, he's taken Nick under his wing and taught him the language and rules of the street—and the customs and patterns of those who occupy it—and for that Nick is grateful. But truth be told, Nick feels his future has become too entangled with his partner's and he needs to cut himself free. Lately, he's become more concerned about creating waves, which might hinder his rise through the ranks.

When the waitress arrives with their beers, Briggs offers a toast. "Here's to the new man with the Morals Squad."

Bannister grins. "He's gonna clean up this city."

Briggs laughs. "Gonna rid the city of the Hebes, niggers, and the rest of the riffraff."

Nick swallows a mouthful of beer. It leaves a bitter taste in his mouth.

Chapter 3

Late that night Jake Cafferty is working the graveyard shift out of the Homicide/Sex Division at City Hall. He keeps the squawk box on low in case anything hot comes over the air while he listens to the news on WCCO radio.

The Korean War began in June, and the Commies have pushed the US, United Nations, and Republic of Korea forces nearly to Pusan at the end of the Korean peninsula. President Harry Truman has agreed to a National Security Council plan allowing American troops to cross the 38th parallel into North Korea to reunite the peninsula. Jake figures Truman and MacArthur better do something quick or the war will be over and the good old US of A will be the loser.

Jake sits down in the swivel chair at his desk and picks up a copy of a magazine entitled *Dirty Laundry*. Arthur Hayes was the magazine's first publisher, a Jewish vice crusader who wrote exposés about corruption and gangster rule in the city. When an unidentified assailant gunned him down in March of '39, MPD detectives assigned to the case interviewed witnesses, family members, and the city's leading gangsters. None of the gangsters were eager to help find the perp. No one ever took the fall. Later, Arthur's son, Max Hayes, took over the magazine.

Dirty Laundry

September 6, 1950

MINNEAPOLIS RACKETEERS HAVE INTERESTS IN MIAMI HOTELS

By
Max Hayes

Isadore Blumenfeld, alias Kid Cann, and members of his family own valuable oceanfront property in Miami Beach, Florida. Cann also has a million-dollar investment in a hotel in Miami Beach.

Cann's name first appeared in the records of the Minneapolis Police Department in 1920, when he was arrested for being in a disorderly house and for pickpocketing. He has been charged with such crimes as murder, violation of the National Prohibition Act, assault, and as a suspect in the shooting of two police officers. He was once indicted for conspiracy to kidnap Charles Urschel, a wealthy Oklahoma oilman. This indictment was dismissed.

Kid Cann's brother and his lieutenant, Yiddy Blumenfeld, alias Yiddy Bloom, along with Harry Mitchlin and Harry Joffa, were secretly indicted by a Montana federal grand jury for conspiracy in a large black market operation in liquor. In December 1943, Yiddy Bloom, Harry Mitchlin, Mrs. Verna Bloom, wife of Yiddy, and Mrs. Ray Schneider, sister of Kid Cann, were indicted for illegal distribution of wine. The tax case was settled for $73,000, and fines on the criminal charges amounted to $30,000.

Harry Blumenfeld, alias Harry Bloom, is another brother and lieutenant of Cann. All of the Blumenfelds allegedly are large property owners in the greater Miami area. At least two oceanfront hotels are located on real estate owned by this family.

Kid Cann has also been a suspect in a number of unsolved murders. One of the murder victims was Walter Liggett, who was running a weekly newspaper, the *Midwest American*, and had accused Cann and the police department of controlling and protecting gambling. Liggett had threatened to expose those conditions just before he was killed in a submachine gun drive-by. At Cann's trial, Liggett's wife and the three other witnesses testified that Cann was the triggerman. Shemmin, the barber, and an Artistic Barbershop customer alibied The Kid. Despite the evidence, Cann was acquitted. It's believed that his Syndicate now controls off-sale liquor licenses in the city.

Jake takes a long drag on his cigarette and a sip of black coffee. Local newspapers often refer to Minneapolis and St. Paul as the "Twin Cities." But when it comes to Jews, Jake knows, there's a difference. Jews settled in St. Paul at the same time as Catholics and other immigrants and helped establish the city. Scandinavians and Protestant Anglo-Saxons settled first in Minneapolis and established major industries before the Eastern European Jews came in the late 19th century, leaving Minneapolis Jews like Kid Cann and his brothers with two paths to upward mobility. One was through education. The other was through crime.

Jews hold the monopoly on off-sale liquor licenses in the city. The licenses are strictly limited in number and because of that, very profitable. All licenses in the city are issued by and controlled by the city council, which has the sole power to issue them. They can only be issued within the so-called "patrol limits," the area once patrolled by a cop on horseback during a shift. The restriction was incorporated into the city charter in

1884. Alcohol is now concentrated in the city's twenty-block Gateway District, which is awash in saloons, beer parlors, and liquor stores. On-sale licenses predominate on the North and Northeast sides, where the majority of Catholics live, on the unspoken theory that Catholics like their booze more than Protestants. The city council can issue only one license per person, but one person can have an interest or silent partnership in several establishments.

The Max Hayes article reminds Jake of the time he and his former partner, Russ Krueger, rousted Jack Apple, Cann's enforcer. Apple, a contract killer for the Teamsters, mostly in Chicago, spent his time in Minneapolis shaking down old, rich Jews. Jake remembers when Apple attempted to squeeze a well-known and well-respected Minneapolis businessman who owned coin-operated machines throughout the Midwest. The business brought in thousands of dollars every week. Apple threatened to bust up the man's property and health. Jake and Russ picked up Apple and drove him out to the country. Russ told him what was going to happen if this continued. Apple laughed and said that cops didn't scare him. Later, Russ contacted Yiddy Bloom, Kid Cann's brother. There were no further threats or thefts.

Jake sets down the magazine and glances at the desk beside his, where his partner used to sit. Russ pulled the plug last week after twenty years. Now he's living in Florida. He was the best cop Jake ever knew. Taught him pretty much everything he knows about Homicide. Saved his life by getting him into AA. Homicide Captain Avery Arnold has been pressing Jake about a new partner. Because of Jake's years and experience, Arnold has offered him a choice of qualified candidates, but Jake has stalled. Sooner or later, he'll have to choose—or Arnold will choose for him.

One hour later, Jake is eating chicken lo mein takeout from the Nankin Café on 7th Street when he hears a loud, panicked voice over the squawk box. "Officer down! Thirty twenty-one Bryant Avenue! See the patrolman! Code 3!"

Jake is out of his chair and throwing on his suit coat when the phone rings in the Homicide pen. He snatches it on the first ring. It's the watch commander.

"You got the squawk box on, Jake?"

"I'm on my way."

Chapter 4

Joe Briggs' body is dead-spread on the hardwood floor near the foot of his bed, a halo of blood around the back of his head, his Colt Official Police in the palm of his right hand, all six rounds loaded in the chamber. Two guys from the ID Division are dusting for prints and digging out of the wall the bullet that cored through Briggs' skull.

"We can work with it, Jake," the guy holding the partially damaged round says. "You find the gun, we should be able to match it."

Jake Cafferty shifts his gaze to Harold Jamison, the Hennepin County coroner, squatting beside Briggs' body. Jamison, a slender man with silver hair, rimless glasses, and suspenders, looks up and locks eyes with Jake. "No soot baked into Briggs' forehead. Not a contact or near-contact shot. Briggs was dead before he hit the floor."

Jake notes the reddish-brown powder tattooing of the skin around the entrance wound, indicating an intermediate range gunshot wound, and nods in agreement.

Jamison stands and arches his back to get the kinks out. "Know Briggs well?"

Jake shakes his head. The synapses in his brain are firing like sparklers on the 4th of July. When he caught the 1:30 a.m. squeal, he knew an officer was down, but not which one. Not that it should matter—everyone counts when it comes to homicide—but killing a cop carries a heavier weight than punching the ticket of some lowlife. The whole city will be on alert until the perp, or perps, are found.

Jake steps around the body and peers down at the metal cash box on the bed. The lid is open, the box empty. He stares at it a moment and then lets his eyes rove over the room.

Shards of glass litter the floor under the window on the north side of the house. At first glance, nothing else appears to be damaged or out of order. As his eyes make a second pass, Jake sees it. All the dresser drawers in the corner of the room are slightly open. It's a small clue, but a critical one. When searching a dresser, a professional burglar starts from the bottom, pulls the drawer open, and works his way up. Why waste time closing each drawer? Jake makes a mental note. Then he checks each drawer but comes up empty. Next he searches a small walk-in closet with the same result.

He glances at the cashbox again and wonders where Joe Briggs hid it. Was he stupid enough to hide it in the dresser or sock drawer? Better to hide the money in plain sight, like wrapped in aluminum foil in the refrigerator or in a clean, empty soup can. Just open the can from the bottom, rinse it out, put your items in it, replace the can bottom, and put the can at the bottom of a stack of other canned goods. Even if the burglar goes to the trouble of looking at the cans, he'll notice that the top is still on that particular can. Or maybe Joe Briggs figured he had nothing to worry about. A burglar wouldn't risk hitting a cop's home. But like betting on an inside straight, Briggs made a mistake.

A floorboard creaks as Jake steps out of the bedroom and into the hallway. He searches the bathroom, then, at the opposite end of the hall, a second bedroom that has been converted into a den. He sees a Barcalounger, Firestone Air Chief radio, an empty bottle of Pabst Blue Ribbon beer on a round table, an ashtray littered with cigarette butts, and three armpit slicks: *Argosy*, *True Detective*, and *Adventure* magazine.

Jake follows the narrow hallway into the living room. Framed photos of Briggs and his wife line the wall opposite the Admiral television, but he sees no photos of children or grandchildren. Jake recalls that Briggs' wife died after a long illness.

Outside on the front lawn, his eyes track the barrier of crime scene rope and sawhorses blocking a residential street lined with single-family Craftsman bungalows. A coroner's wagon and four black-and-whites are parked behind the barrier, their cherry lights strobing the houses and flashing against the night sky and the neon haze of the city skyline. Across the street, Jake spots two of the officers he sent out going door-to-door, asking neighbors if they heard or saw anything that might help the investigation. Jake already spoke to the neighbor who called the precinct and reported hearing what he thought was a gunshot. The neighbor was in bed and never saw anyone arriving or leaving Briggs' house after the gunshot.

Sweeping the ground with a flashlight beam, Jake begins circling Briggs' house. Halfway around, he spots something on the ground. He picks it up and shines the light on a Brazama Gold stock certificate. *What the hell is Brazama Gold*? He stares at the certificate for a moment. *Did the robber or robbers drop it on their way out*? *Are there more certificates*? Jake folds it lengthwise, slips it into his suit coat pocket, and continues circling the house till he arrives at the jimmied broken bedroom window on the north side. The flashlight beam reflects off pieces of glass that are scattered among paint chips below the windowsill. He was hoping for impression evidence, maybe a cigarette butt, but the dirt has been swept clean.

He heads to the garage in the alley behind the house. A '48 Chevy Fleetmaster is parked in the one stall. A strong whiskey smell hits him the moment he opens the driver's side door. He searches under the seats and inside the glove compartment, where he finds nothing more than a city map and the car's registration papers. He returns to the house, entering through the back door.

Dirty dishes fill the kitchen sink. The air smells of wet, moldy rags. A pair of black shoes with thick rubber heels rests on a throw rug. Cop shoes. The laces are tied, indicating Briggs slipped them off. Unless Briggs was looking for it, he wouldn't have noticed the jimmied window on the north side of the house, the dislodged paint chips in the grass, the tool marks in the frame.

Jake wonders why Briggs removed his shoes and left them by the back door, unless this was a habit. It wasn't raining. Did Briggs sense something was wrong when he entered the house? Not something he saw, but something he felt. An experienced cop like Briggs develops a sixth sense.

Briggs had a reputation for shaking down retailers and for taking kickbacks on sales of stolen goods. Jake lays odds Briggs had a stash, the only thing of real value in his house, the one thing worth stealing. Briggs must've drawn his gun and rushed into the bedroom—and then what?

Jake walks into the hallway outside the bedroom and steps on the creaking floorboard again. He's guessing the noise is what startled Briggs, causing him to spin around—but it was too late. He was dead before he hit the floor. But why would a burglar kill Briggs? The house wasn't tossed. Someone knew where to look for the dough.

Jake writes his thoughts on his notepad as Homicide Captain Avery Arnold, dressed in a double-breasted brown trench coat and fedora, strides through the open back door and into the hallway outside the bedroom. Arnold has the pale skin and translucent blue eyes of his German ancestry.

His gaze shifts from Briggs' body to Jake's face. "One of our own."

"Who's crazy enough to burgle this house? Everyone in the neighborhood knew Briggs was a cop."

"A window of opportunity," Arnold says, pointing to the broken glass on the floor. As Arnold's eyes settle on Jake once more, his long, narrow face twists in a quizzical expression. "You sleep in your clothes?"

Jake has heard this criticism before from Arnold, a neatnik who always looks like he stepped out of a Montgomery Ward catalog. Jake's annoyed with his small spare tire around his middle that keeps tugging at his shirttails. Silently, he vows for the umpteenth time to rid himself of his paunch and the dreaded nightgown look of an untucked shirt.

Jake steps into the living room; Arnold follows. "What do you think was in the cash box, Cap?"

"I'll tell you what was there," says a big-bellied man in a fedora and plaid sport coat, heading toward them. Nearly everything about Mike Bannister is going soft, except for his stone cold gray eyes, his big hands balled into fists, and his surly personality.

"Easy," Arnold says, moving in front of him.

Bannister stops as his eyes shift off Arnold's and toward the bedroom. "My best friend is dead. I want whoever did this, Captain. Alone in a cell."

"And you shall have him. But Lieutenant Cafferty is in charge of this investigation."

"Found the cash box open on the bed," Jake says to Bannister. "Know what was in it?"

Bannister glares at Jake. "Probably Joe's fuck-you money."

"How much?"

"Must've been more than . . ." Bannister catches himself.

Jake finishes the thought for him. "More than he should have on his salary."

"You would know, Cafferty."

Bannister's accusation doesn't bother him any more than he's bothered by the cardboard boxes filled with bottles of booze, hams, turkeys, steaks, lobster—and oftentimes cash—that miraculously appear on his doorstep every Christmas. An attached note explains what bar and restaurant sent each of the "gifts." It's how business gets done in this town.

"When was the last time you saw Briggs?" Jake asks.

"Early this morning. We had a couple of drinks together at Gluek's. We were celebrating Nick Cole's promotion."

"What time did Briggs leave?"

"Around twelve forty-five."

Bannister steps around Arnold to get to the bedroom, but the captain moves to block him again.

Jake gestures at Bannister. "You're messing up my crime scene."

"I'll mess you up, Cafferty, you don't find out who did this."

Jake waves him off. Bannister is a blowhard and a bully. He looks at Arnold for support.

The captain gets the hint. "Let's go." Arnold puts a hand behind Bannister's elbow and ushers him toward the back door.

"You remember what I said, Cafferty," Bannister calls over his shoulder. "I want whoever did this."

Jake peers at the body on the bedroom floor. He wants whoever did this, too.

Chapter 5

The following morning, detectives from both the Homicide/Sex Division and the Burglary Division, along with the day watch blues going on duty, pack the squad room at City Hall. Homicide Captain Avery Arnold and MPD Chief William Flanagan stand near a lectern and floor microphone. Jake takes a seat in the middle of the first row, facing the lectern. He's wired from only four hours of sleep and too many cups of java.

He looks around till he spots Mike Bannister, in his uniform, sitting in a chair at the far end of the row behind him. Joe Briggs' partner, Nick Cole, dressed in what looks like a brand-new dark suit and tie, sits beside Bannister. Jake recalls hearing that Cole has been promoted to sergeant and will be working as a detective with the Morals Squad.

Arnold steps in front of the microphone. "You all know why we're here this morning. We've lost one of our own, Officer Joe Briggs, in a senseless and brutal attack. And an attack on one of us is an attack on all of us."

A loud grumbling wave washes over the room.

Arnold raises his hands for calm in the room and waits till everyone falls silent once more. "Officer Briggs was two years from retirement. He was shot to death in his own home. This crime is not only unprecedented, but a breach of the unwritten contract we have with the criminal element in this city. A police officer's home is his castle."

Again a wave of anger rises and is silenced by Arnold's hands.

"The fatal bullet came from a .38 caliber revolver. The murder weapon hasn't been recovered. The perpetrator entered through a bedroom window after breaking the glass. The house was dusted for prints, which are currently being analyzed. So far, all we have are rubber glove prints on the windowsill and an open cash box that was found on the bed. We believe a significant amount of cash was taken, so robbery was the obvious motive."

Jake glances at Mike Bannister, who's sitting on the edge of his chair. Their eyes meet for a moment before Bannister's gaze slides away.

"The ground outside the bedroom window was swept to eliminate footprints, which suggests this crime was the work of a professional," Arnold says. "I want every one of you, when you hit the streets, to contact your stoolies. Someone out there knows who's responsible for Officer Briggs' death. Detective Lieutenant Cafferty will be heading the investigation. Any leads should come directly to him."

Jake senses all eyes in the room focused on him. Sweat trickles down his back. The whispers he hears behind him are encouraging.

"We'll get the son of a bitch, Jake. We're with you."

Arnold says, "Chief Flanagan would like a word with all of you."

William Flanagan walks up to the microphone as Arnold steps aside. A stocky, red-haired Irishman, Flanagan says, "All the officers in this room, and all those throughout the department, are looking for swift justice."

Jake and every cop in the room understand the message. Justice for Joe Briggs will not be left up to chance—or to the courts.

*   *   *

At the conclusion of the meeting in the squad room, Jake stops Mike Bannister in the hallway.

"What now, Cafferty?"

"Who else knew about Briggs' cash besides you?"

"What the hell you getting at?"

"Just askin' a question."

"You think I killed Joe and took his cash?"

"Did you?"

Bannister's face twists with rage. He raises a fist and steps toward Jake.

Jake holds his ground. "Lighten up, Bannister. We're on the same side."

Realizing Jake isn't taking the bait, Bannister's face goes slack and his tough-guy act dies fast. "Stay sober," he says, heading for an exit.

Bannister's crack is a cheap shot. Jake hasn't had a drink in five years. He considers going after Bannister and then lets it go.

"Lieutenant."

Jake turns and sees Nick Cole approaching.

"A moment, please."

"Sorry to hear about your partner," Jake says.

"Thanks. I want to help."

"Anyone you remember have a grudge against Briggs?"

"Too many to count," Nick says.

"That a fact?"

"What I mean is, Joe upset some people."

"That was his rep."

"He knew the streets, Lieutenant. He wasn't a bad cop."

Jake lets Cole's comment slide.

"If there's anything I can do, Lieutenant."

"I'll let you know," Jake says.

*   *   *

For the next hour Jake prowls the files in the Burglary Division, looking for porch-climbers and shutter rackets operating in the area near Joe Briggs' house. Nothing jumps out. Jake closes the file cabinet and heads for the street, looking for Teddy Doss, one of his snitches.

Doss, in his mid-thirties, has a record for petty misdemeanors, DWIs, speeding, and third-degree burglary, for which he served three years of a five-year jolt in Stillwater Prison. But Doss has his ear to the ground and usually plays it straight.

Jake begins his search at Augie's Theater Lounge & Bar on Hennepin Avenue. Located between the fancy clubs and restaurants on Eighth Street and the seedy flophouses and bars of the Gateway District, the bar is owned by Sam Ratner, a former professional boxer, who calls himself Augie. Ratner had over one hundred professional fights in his ten-year career as a featherweight and middleweight. After retiring from the ring, he owned a speakeasy called the White Swan during Prohibition before opening Augie's in '43. In his drinking days, Jake liked Augie's, where he could rub shoulders with a mixed crowd of the city's movers and shakers, as well as its racketeers.

"Lieutenant," Augie says with a big smile, squeezing Jake's hand. One look at Augie's flat nose tells you he was once a fighter. "Get you a soda?"

"Thanks, but I'm in a hurry."

"What do ya need?"

"Seen Teddy Doss around?"

Augie shakes his head. "Haven't seen him since he got out of the slammer. Might try Duffy's. Bartender there named Wally is a friend of his."

"Thanks for the tip."

"Any time, Lieutenant."

Jake leaves Augie's and heads for Duffy's, located at the corner of 26th Street and 26th Avenue, on the southeastern edge of the Minneapolis liquor patrol limits. The saloons, bars, and nightclubs clustered in the area called the Hub of Hell draw a rough crowd of thugs, gangsters, and factory workers from the Minneapolis Moline plant.

At Duffy's Jake discovers that Wally, the bartender, has moved on. He spends the next hour traipsing from bar to bar before learning that Teddy Doss has taken a job at the Minneapolis Iron & Steel Company.

At the scrap yard, located northeast of downtown just off Lyndale and Lowry, Jake hangs a left and drives through an open gate. A chain-link fence surrounds the grounds filled with piles of high-grade industrial scrap, copper wire, old appliances, and rusted automobiles.

Fist-size hunks of metal emerge from the shredder, raining down on the shred pile. Ahead of Jake a row of large trucks owned by demolition companies and small pickups driven by scrap peddlers wait to unload. Some of their trucks look not far from being scrap themselves. Sparks fly as employees in coveralls with full-face shields cut metal with oxyacetylene torches. A crane moves the scrap around. Metal is fed to the jaws of a huge hydraulic shearer that resembles a Tyrannosaurus Rex, its teeth ripping bulky metal to pieces. A lone streetcar sits at the far end of the yard. The Korean War has driven up the price of scrap metal. The company has hired extra workers and operates around the clock.

Jake parks in front of a long one-level cinderblock building. The distinctive garlic-like smell from the oxyacetylene hits him as he exits the Ford and stubs out his cigarette. He locates the main office and knocks on the door. A fat man with red suspenders and black hair combed straight back waves him in. Jake recognizes him. "Tony."

"Lieutenant Cafferty."

"You running this place now?"

"Running it and owning it."

Tony Rizzo is a one-time housing inspector. He had a rep-utation as a rigorous enforcer of the housing code and would tag private residences for minor violations of one kind or an-other. The day after he issued the tags, one of his sons would come around with estimates for the repairs. A number of his victims reported Rizzo to the head of the housing department, hoping to put an end to the practice and punish Rizzo. Eventu-ally, Rizzo *was* suspended for five days. Three of the days were over the Fourth of July holiday, which he couldn't be docked for, so he only lost two days' pay.

Rizzo's other son was a sidewalk inspector. He'd go around residential neighborhoods and tag the owners for broken sidewalks, which they'd have to have repaired. A day or two before the scheduled inspection, he'd tell his connec-tion what his schedule was. His connection would then run a heavy truck over the sidewalks, breaking them up, and Riz-zo's son would tag them. The connection would get the repair job, and Rizzo and his son would get the payoff. Worried that his gig had run its course, Rizzo and his sons have moved on.

"I'm looking for Teddy Doss," Jake says.

"He in trouble?"

"Not as far as I know."

"Out front." Rizzo gets on the loudspeaker and calls Doss.

Jake steps out of the plant to meet him.

Doss shuts down his torch, flips up his face shield, and re-moves his heavy cuffed gloves. His brown hair, wet with sweat, is plastered on his scalp as he walks toward Cafferty. His once boyish face is aging fast from too much partying and booze, and from the scar tissue around his eyes. Doss, once a promising featherweight, went ten close but bloody rounds with eventual champions Sandy Saddler and Willie Pep. Because he and

Augie were both fighters, Augie gave Doss a job when the younger man got out of Stillwater prison.

"What's up, Lieutenant?"

"Let's walk." Jake leads Doss to the back side of the plant, which sits on the banks of the Mississippi. "You hear about Joe Briggs?"

Doss nods. "Bad business. Can I bum a cigarette?"

Jake hands him his pack of Camels and a lighter. Doss fires one up, Jake another. He exhales smoke and says, "What'd you hear, Teddy?"

"I'll clue you, Lieutenant, but I'm not sure it's straight up."

"Spill it."

Doss takes a long drag and blows the smoke out through his nostrils. "Word is two Hebes took down Briggs."

"You have names?"

"Ben and Davy Roth."

"Whereabouts?"

Doss takes a long drag on his cigarette and stares at the river as he lets out a cloud of smoke. "Could be in a room upstairs at the Persian Palms."

Jake is familiar with the Persian Palms nightclub. "You sure, Teddy?"

"Guy hears things, Lieutenant. Doesn't mean they're true."

"The boys have family in town?"

"Their old man was a bootlegger who got himself killed back in '33 when his truck slid off an icy road and rolled over into the river. Mother ran off with a gambler when the boys were sixteen. Heard she's back in town living near Waite Park. Boys have been fending for themselves, mostly through B&Es. But you didn't hear any of this from me."

"Why the concern?"

"The Roths are friends of the Kid," Doss says, meaning Kid Cann, head of the Jewish Syndicate in the city.

*　　*　　*

Later that afternoon Jake, along with three squad cars and six uniforms, parks in front of the Persian Palms on Washington Avenue. A large poster on the outside brick wall advertises the current attraction, Divena, a stripper, who performs underwater in a large fish tank. The club features three floor shows nightly and is known for its B-girls and for its whorehouse upstairs, where the Roth brothers are staying—if Teddy Doss' information is correct.

The Palms is located in the heart of Skid Row, twenty square blocks of fifty-cent-a-night flophouses, bars, liquor stores, and rescue missions in downtown Minneapolis. Vagrants, winos, and deviants, most of them old, single white men and former gandy-dancers, who once laid and maintained the tracks for the railroads before machines replaced them, live in tiny rooms constructed of plywood and tin dividers with chicken wire over the top, in what are called "cage hotels."

Jake sends two blues to cover the Palms' back exit and one to watch the fire escape, which runs along the front of the building. When he and the other two uniforms enter the club, Jake nearly runs into Sergeant Nick Cole from the Morals Squad.

"What're you doing here, Cafferty?"

"Looking for the guys who offed Joe Briggs. You?"

"Tailing a pimp wanted on a white slavery beef."

"Maybe we can help each other?"

Cole nods. "Works for me."

They draw their revolvers and climb two flights of stairs. On the third floor, the two uniforms remain at the top of the stairs while Jake and Nick head toward the first door on the right. A door swings open to Jake's left. He and Nick turn quickly and aim at a young woman in a sheer silk robe standing in the doorway, a burning cigarette in her right hand.

Nonchalant, she takes an exaggerated puff and exhales. Behind her, Jake sees a sailor sitting on a bed.

"Two young men," Jake says to her. "What room?"

"The Jews?"

Jake nods.

"Second room on the right." She steps back into the room and closes the door.

Figuring the brothers could start blasting, Jake positions Cole on the opposite side of the door, inside shoulder against the wall. Jake knocks. They wait. Jake knocks again. "Police! Open up!"

When there's no response, Nick gives Jake a questioning look and shrugs. Jake kicks in the door. They enter behind their guns.

No one.

Men's clothes are hanging in the closet and folded in the drawers. They've cleared out in a hurry. Under a pile of underwear in a dresser, Nick finds a Colt Official Police with a 4" barrel.

Why leave the gun behind, especially if it turns out to be the murder weapon? Jake bags the .38 and stuffs it in his coat pocket. Then he and Cole roust the johns in the other rooms, looking for the pimp Cole is after.

As they storm into the last room on the floor, Jake recognizes the stunned face of a man wearing only a cowboy hat. He's sitting on a double bed getting his pole polished by a naked whore on her knees. Everyone freezes for a moment, as if in a photo. Then the man in the cowboy hat scrambles to retrieve his clothes. The hooker remains on her knees, a wide smile on her face, bright red lipstick smeared on her lips.

"Oops. Wrong door," Jake says as he clutches Cole by the arm.

"The hell you doing, Cafferty?" Nick yanks his arm away and holds up his badge. "You're under arrest!"

Jake grabs Cole's arm again and drags him out of the room, pulling the door closed behind him.

"What the hell?" Nick says, breaking Jake's grip.

"You didn't recognize the judge?"

The blood drains from Cole's complexion. "Judge?"

Jake smiles. "Hennepin County. Judge Howard Gunderson."

Nick shakes his head and then laughs. "No shit. Really?"

"Really."

Chapter 6

At the crime lab Jake logs the .38 he found in the room at the Persian Palms and then drives to Waite Park, the furthest northeast neighborhood within Minneapolis, named after former assistant Hennepin County DA and district court judge Edward Foote Waite.

Waite first rose to prominence in 1902 for his investigation into the administration of Albert "Doc" Ames, the corrupt mayor of Minneapolis, whose four terms in office at the turn of the century became known as "The Shame of Minneapolis."

Esther Roth lives in a ramshackle farmhouse near the MPD second precinct. Jake knocks on the front door and waits. When no one answers, he walks along the side of the house to the backyard. A woman wearing a simple, threadbare housedress and apron picks clothes out of a woven basket and hangs them on a rope stretched between two oak trees out back.

"Mrs. Roth?" Jake asks as he approaches.

She faces him, a questioning look in her dark, tired eyes. "Yes?" she says, brushing a strand of graying hair away from her face.

Jake shows her his badge wallet.

Her shoulders slump as her eyes gaze off into the distance and then return to Jake's face. "What have they done now?"

"Not sure."

She lets out a weary breath. "What are they *suspected* of doing?"

"When did you last see them, Mrs. Roth?"

She gives a little shake of her head, realizing Jake won't answer her question. "Week ago. Maybe two. Hard to remember."

Jake looks at the men's and women's clothes on the line flapping in a cool breeze. "They live here with you?"

"Off and on."

"Lived here long?"

"Me or the boys?"

"You."

"Couple years."

"Heard your husband passed."

"Heard that, too."

"You never saw the body?"

"He run off. Heard he drowned in a river. Never found the body."

"Mind if I look inside the house?"

"For what?" she says in a flat voice.

"Something that'll help me find your sons."

"Back door's open. Boys' bedroom is down the hall on the left. Help yourself," she says, turning away and hanging a pair of wet jeans on the line.

Jake pauses a moment, unsure what else he can say. Then he heads for the house, opens the back screen door, and finds his way to the boys' bedroom.

Small room. Two bunk beds. Dresser. Closet. Jake starts there, then moves to the dresser and the beds. No clue as to where the boys might be. Jake peeks out a bedroom window facing the backyard. She's still hanging clothes. He hustles to Mrs. Roth's bedroom at the end of the hallway and looks for a letter with an address or postmark showing where Ben and Davy are staying, but he finds nothing.

In the bottom drawer of the dresser Jake does find a handful of grainy family photographs held together by a rubber band. A signature on the back of one photo, taken on a pier in front of a steamship named the *S.S. Orbita*, identifies the young couple as Esther and Eli Roth, along with a date of 1921.

Jake knows from his own parents' experience that upon arrival in New York City, ships would dock at the Hudson or East River piers. First- and second-class passengers would disembark, pass through Customs at the piers, and then enter the US. Ferries or barges transported steerage and third-class passengers from the piers to Ellis Island, where they underwent a medical and legal inspection. The couple's shabby clothes and tattered suitcases in the photo suggest that, like his own parents, Mr. and Mrs. Roth came through Ellis Island.

When he hears the back screen door slam, Jake quickly replaces the photos, shuts the dresser drawer, and walks out into the hallway toward the kitchen.

"Find what you're looking for?" Esther Roth asks as he steps into the kitchen.

"No," he says, handing her a business card.

She glances at the card. "My boys aren't killers, Lieutenant. If someone told you that, he's a liar."

"Thought you didn't know why I'm here."

"I listen to the news on the radio."

"Call me if you hear from your sons."

"And why should I do that?"

"Because you and I want them captured," Jake says. "Alive."

* * *

That afternoon Max Hayes, the editor of *Dirty Laundry*, is pulling a master stencil from the typewriter on his desk when Jake enters the small storefront office on Washington Avenue.

"Hey, Jake." Max tosses the stencil and copy on his desktop and removes his browline glasses.

With his brown vest over a white shirt, bow tie, chino pants, and brown-and-white Oxford shoes, Max looks like a teenager, Jake thinks. But Max is twenty-two now. Not as wiry as he was in his teens. He has his mother's soft features—and his father's nose for corruption.

Jake glances at the stencil on Max's desk. "What're you working on?"

Max nods at the map on the wall in front of his desk. "A series of articles protesting the continued redlining of districts in and out of the city."

Outlined in red on the map is a large NEGRO section in the city near one of the handful of SLUM sections. Other sections of the city are labeled FOREIGN BORN, WORKING MEN'S HOMES, HOBOHEMIA, and GOLD COAST.

"Banks identify predominantly nonwhite neighborhoods like the ones indicated on the map as declining or risky based on credit risk," Max continues. "New suburban developments, or other places in and out of the city with restrictive covenants, like the area labeled GOLD COAST, limit home ownership to white residents and are identified as good investments. Mortgage applications in the gold coast neighborhoods are treated more favorably, while loans are consistently denied in neighborhoods labeled declining. Bankers can then deny loans based on geography rather than on race."

To emphasize the point, Max points at a page from a mortgage application taped to the wall beside the map. Underlined in red is a paragraph that reads:

> The said premises shall not at any time be sold, conveyed, leased, or sublet to or occupied by any person or persons who are not full bloods of the so-called Caucasian or White race.

"I thought the US Supreme Court outlawed redlining and covenant restrictions in '48, and courts can't enforce them."

Max shakes his head in frustration. "You and most everyone else knows, Jake, that many of the covenants remain in deeds and neighborhood bylaws, and that real estate agents quietly advertise properties as restricted. And Jews are still excluded from Minneapolis civic and government boards and can't join service, athletic, or country clubs. The major businesses, law firms, and law enforcement won't employ us."

Jake knew it was true, but he didn't know what he could do about it, other than to try to protect Max. "Better you write about restrictive covenants than articles on Kid Cann."

"I'm just trying to tell the story of your life, Jake," Max says, half-joking.

"It's dangerous."

"No more dangerous than your job."

"But I carry a piece for protection."

"Not the answer." He stares at Jake for a time. Then he says, "You still working the case?"

"Whenever I can."

"Someone knows who killed my father."

"Sure they do. But they're not talking."

Jake holds up two tickets to Nicollet Field. "The Millers game." Max likes baseball, and the Millers are fighting for first place and a spot in the playoffs.

"How much is it going to cost me?"

"Nothing."

Max lets out a short laugh. "Yeah."

"Okay. Maybe a little something."

"Let's hear it."

"You know Ben and Davy Roth?"

"Should I?"

"Off the record?"

"Okay."

"They're the prime suspects in Joe Briggs' murder."

"Because they're Jewish?"

"No, Max. Because they burgled Briggs' house, stole his cash, and killed him." Jake holds up the baseball tickets again.

"I've got great seats. Dixie Howell is pitching. Remember, he threw a no-hitter against Columbus back in August."

"If I go, then you'll answer some questions I have."

"About what?"

"Kid Cann and the Jewish Syndicate. Something we're both familiar with."

Jake shrugs. He was hoping that he and Max could enjoy at least one evening together without things going sideways.

* * *

Jake leaves the storefront office through the back door. He isn't happy about Max's Skid Row location, but the rent is cheap. As he steps outside, a muffled cry draws his eyes to the alley entrance of the Persian Palms next door, which is under a Grain Belt beer sign. Jake knows that homos often use the door when they visit the small bar behind the main room. A heavy-set man is raining blows on another man who's squatting with his back to the building, his arms crossed above his head, attempting to ward off the blows.

"Hey!" Jake yells.

When the heavy-set man stops and turns around, Jake recognizes Mike Bannister.

"What's going on?"

"None of your business, Cafferty."

But Bannister backs off as Jake walks over and looks at the man who has a bloody nose and bruised cheeks. Jake takes his arm and helps him to his feet. At six feet, he's as tall as Jake and Mike Bannister but much slimmer and less muscular. He's dressed in a white shirt, dark slacks, and sport coat. A long white silk scarf is draped around his neck. "What's your name?"

"Franklin," the man says, holding a handkerchief to his nose. "Franklin Simms."

With his strikingly handsome face, pitch-black hair, and bright blue eyes, he reminds Jake of someone. Then Jake remembers a recent movie poster for *The Black Rose*. *Tyrone Power, the actor. Simms could be his double.*

"What's goin' on?" Jake asks.

Simms' eyes jitter between Bannister and Jake.

"Don't worry about him," Jake says. "Tell me what happened."

"It's a misunderstanding," Bannister growls. "He's my snitch."

Jake gives him his best cop stare. "I'm not asking you, Bannister."

Simms bobs his head. "Yes," he says. "A misunderstanding."

Jake glances at the Palms' back door entrance. Then he lets his eyes rove over both men before they settle again on Mike Bannister. "Your fly's open," Jake says to him as he grabs Simms by the coat collar and hauls him out of the alley.

Chapter 7

Not being much of a cook, Jake eats most of his meals out. Tonight he stops by his place in the Roselle Apartments, a red brick four-story Romanesque Revival in the Elliot Park neighborhood near downtown. It's a typical bachelor flop with a Murphy bed in the living room, a kitchenette, and a bathroom. *Less space, less to clean.*

Jake's eyes linger for a moment on the framed photo of Rachel Wagner on top of the dresser in the living room. The one he'll always remember. He walks over and picks it up. He met Rachel in '28 when he was a 23-year-old rookie walking a beat on Plymouth Avenue in the heart of the Jewish community in North Minneapolis. She was twenty-one and working at her father's delicatessen. With her dark hair, alabaster skin, and long black eyelashes, she was the prettiest woman he'd ever seen. He ate more pastrami and corned beef sandwiches that year than at any time in his life. He brushes away the dust with his shirtsleeve and sets the frame gently on the dresser again.

After a shower, a shave, and a change of clothes, Jake drives to Schiek's Café on South 3rd Street. He likes the dark Victorian interior of the restaurant with its beveled glass and carved bar.

When he's finished with dinner, he decides to try a Friendship Club "Get Acquainted" dance, held on Thursdays, Saturdays, and Sundays at the Radio City Theatre—formerly the Minnesota Theatre—in downtown Minneapolis. The theatre, with its four-story tall lobby, imitation marble columns, velvet drapes, crystal chandeliers, and marble staircase to the mezzanine christened "the stairway to happiness," is modeled after the 13th-century royal chapel at Versailles.

The dance serves coffee, low alcohol 3.2 beers, and cookies. *No cake?* Jake laughs to himself as he considers the architectural elegance. He's sitting alone at a table, realizing quickly that coming here and looking for companionship was a mistake, when he senses a presence behind him, practically leaning into him. Turning, he finds himself looking into the face of Virginia Crenshaw.

"Hello, Lieutenant."

He doesn't recognize her at first. She's all dolled up in a red sheath number with a sash around the waist. No glasses. Jake nearly stumbles getting up from his chair. "Miss Crenshaw. What're you doing here?"

She smiles. "The same thing you are." Virginia Crenshaw gazes at the dance floor and then at Jake again. "Do you dance, Lieutenant?"

"Not anymore."

"Something happen?"

"Long time ago."

She holds his gaze for a time. "I'm sorry."

Jake nods. "I'm afraid I don't belong here. Goodnight, Miss Crenshaw."

Jake exists the theatre and heads up 9th Street to Hennepin. At the corner he spots Nick Cole standing on the sidewalk across the street. He's sure it's Cole, but he doesn't recognize the small, balding man in the gold cardigan sweater talking to him. Jake is about to call out but hesitates, not sure why. The two men start walking in the direction Jake is headed. He follows on the opposite side of the street. Their conversation appears more animated the further they walk. Finally, the small man throws up his hands and walks away. Nick enters the Flame Nightclub, where Jake is heading.

*　　*　　*

Inside the Flame, saxophonist Percy Hughes' ten-piece jazz ensemble is the house band. A smoky haze hangs over the well-dressed crowd that fills nearly every table. Hughes' band is taking a break, and Jake orders a club soda with a twist of lime at the front bar.

He hasn't been to an AA meeting on First Avenue in two weeks. Jake tells himself—as he has in the past—that he can control his drinking, though that's in direct conflict with a main tenet of AA: that he, in fact, has no control over his alcoholism. Putting himself in bars and clubs where liquor is served is like chucking a piece of red meat into a tiger cage. The shiny bottles on the back bar are neon lights, beckoning him. He can smell the liquor, almost taste it. He fingers the bronze sobriety chip he always keeps in his pocket, given to him after his first year of sobriety. As he waits for his club soda, his eyes wander over the room.

Kid Cann is seated at a table closer to the bar, sandwiched by two bottle blondes in white spaghetti-strap dresses. Cann claims his nickname came from boxing when he was young. But rumor has it that he used to hide in the outhouse—the can—whenever guns were drawn. He hates the nickname and denies the story, but Jake uses the moniker whenever possible.

Cann, for some inexplicable reason, prefers to be called "Ferguson" or "Fergie." He favors Parliament cigarettes and flashy clothes. Tonight he's decked out in a maroon suit, maroon suede shoes, and a canary-yellow shirt with matching socks. A sucker for his personal appearance, he visits the Artistic Barber Shop every day for a shave—and maybe for his next alibi. But at age 51, time is catching up to the Kid. A recent magazine article called him "squat and swarthy," with a "sinister stare." The *Minneapolis Daily Tribune* described him as "a little paunchy." Nothing paunchy about Cann's enforcer, Jack Apple, sitting to the right of one of the blondes. Apple's eyes drill right through Jake.

The bartender hands Jake his drink and waves off the five-spot Jake sets on the bar. Jake strolls over to Cann's table.

"I hear you're looking for the Roths," Cann says, filling three tall glasses with Champagne.

"You know the rules," Jake says. "They crossed the line with Briggs."

"I had nothing to do with that."

"You know where they are?"

"If I did, I'd tell you. But those boys ain't murderers, Lieutenant. They didn't snuff Briggs."

"Then tell them to turn themselves in."

"If I knew where they were, I would. Cop killing is bad for business."

"Bad for everyone," Jake says. Out of the corner of his eye, Jake spots Nick Cole alone at a table, gesturing for him to come over. "You be sure to let me know if you hear anything, *Kid*."

Cann's complexion flames red for a second. Then he raises his champagne glass in a toast. "Sure will, Lieutenant."

Jake weaves through the crowded room to Cole's table in a far corner.

"Take a seat," Nick says.

Jake pulls out a chair, sits down, and drops his fedora on the table.

"Saw you talking to Cann."

"Had to ask. He knows where the Roths are hiding out."

"You serious?"

"Cann isn't stupid. He convinces them to turn themselves in, it saves all of us a headache."

"*If* he knows where they are, Lieutenant."

Jake nods. "Cann knows everything that goes on in this town. How was your first day on the job?"

"Still looking for the pimp. But I'll get 'im."

Jake lets his gaze linger on Cole's fine cheekbones, small mouth, and dark hair that's neatly cut and wet-combed, leaving a straight fleshy line through his scalp. He has chestnut brown eyes and cheeks that are slightly sunken.

"I got food between my teeth, Lieutenant?"

Thinking that Cole looks more like a teenager than a cop in his late twenties, Jake shakes his head.

"You want another drink?" Cole asks.

Jake lifts his tall glass. "Still have some club soda."

"Oh, right. Sorry. I didn't mean to—"

"No problem, Cole." Jake considers asking him about the man he was talking to on the sidewalk and then changes his mind. It's none of his business.

Nick downs his Scotch, calls a waiter over, and orders another. Then he leans across the table. "That was something this afternoon, huh? Judge Gunderson with the whore."

Jake can smell the Scotch on Cole's breath and see the boozy mist in his brown eyes. "Best you keep it to yourself."

Nick shrugs and sits back. "He's never gonna turn down our request for a warrant."

Jake thinks the same. But he doesn't know Cole well enough to confide.

"Someday I'd like to get into Homicide, Jake. Maybe work with you now that there's an open slot."

Jake knows he needs to make a decision soon, but Arnold won't be sticking him with thirty-year-old Nick Cole, who has no homicide experience.

"Damn," Cole mutters under his breath.

Jake tracks Cole's gaze. Standing just inside the club's entrance is a tall auburn-haired woman in a black knit dress with a pencil-style skirt and cinched-in waistline. Jake thinks, *A combination of girl-next-door freshness, glamour, and seduction—the Triple Crown.* He's heard Kate Dawson's name batted around City Hall since she became Hennepin County's first woman attorney in the DA's office. Jake shifts his gaze back to Cole. "You know Dawson?"

"We dated."

Jake recognizes the man beside her. Wilson Barlow. "Is she the DA's squeeze now?"

"I don't know," Cole says with an undercurrent of jealousy in his voice.

Percy Hughes and his group return to the bandstand and launch into "She's Funny That Way." Couples hit the raised dance floor.

Jake watches as a waiter leads Wilson Barlow and Kate Dawson to a table with a RESERVED sign on it. Men's heads turn as Dawson breezes by. Jake lights a Camel, leans back in his chair, and listens to Hughes and his jazz band.

A waitress brings Nick Cole's Scotch. Cole tosses back the drink in one swallow and throws a sawbuck on the table. Then he stands and says, "Enjoy your soda, Lieutenant, on me. We'll talk later."

What more do we have to talk about? Jake thinks. He watches Cole glance back at Kate Dawson as he exits the club. Jake tries to concentrate on Percy Hughes' rendition of "Blue and Sentimental," but his eyes keep drifting to Dawson's table. When she catches him staring, she smiles as he averts his eyes. Three numbers later Barlow finishes his drink, stands up, and strides out of the club.

Jake considers going over to Dawson's table and introducing himself—and then quashes the idea. Percy Hughes' warm tenor sax is hitting all the mellow notes of "Someone to Watch Over Me" when Kate Dawson gets to her feet and heads for the exit. Jake tries to think of a catchy line as he rises to follow—then eases himself back in his chair. *Out of my league*, he thinks just as she stops by the door, turns abruptly, and makes a beeline toward him. Jake glances behind him, just to make sure there's a wall there and not another table she's heading for.

* * *

Kate Dawson notices Jake Cafferty's face redden with embarrassment as she approaches. She suppresses a smile. He's been surreptitiously looking at her since she walked in with the DA. Cafferty's not bad looking, she thinks, though a bit rumpled. He has a weathered but kind face. She likes the shock of black hair that falls over his forehead, though his hair is shaggy and needs a comb. Some threads of gray in his hair and mustache suggest that he's in his mid-forties. When she reaches the table she says, "I saw you talking with Nicky."

Jake stands and offers a hand. "Jake Cafferty." She has beautiful hands with long, delicate fingers and a firm handshake.

"I know who you are, Lieutenant. I'm sure you know who I am as well."

"It's Detective Lieutenant."

"I'm impressed."

"No, you're not. Buy you a drink?"

"I'm not looking for a date."

"What *are* you looking for?"

"Information."

Jake gestures at the empty chair to his right. Kate hesitates and then sits down. He lights up another Camel and offers her one. She declines.

Percy Hughes and the boys launch into "I Got It Bad and That Ain't Good."

"How long have you known Nicky?" Kate asks.

"I don't."

"But you two were sitting together."

Jake rests his cigarette in an ashtray and his elbows on the table. "We met briefly today. He saw me tonight and asked me to join him."

A waiter comes to the table and asks Kate what she'd like to drink. "Nothing."

Jake orders another club soda. After the waiter takes off, Jake casually says, "Cole did mention you."

Kate's heartbeat kicks up a notch. "What'd he say?"

"You dated."

"That all?"

Jake nods.

Kate's eyes lock on Jake's. "What'd you say?"

"I asked him if you were the DA's squeeze."

Kate grits her teeth and swallows her displeasure. "Let me tell you a quick story, *Detective Lieutenant* Cafferty. When I was interviewing for legal positions around town, a male attorney at one of the city's most prestigious firms told me that training a woman to be a lawyer is like teaching a dog to walk on his hind legs. You can do it, but why bother?"

Kate stands, slings her purse over her shoulder, and walks out of the club. She doesn't look back.

Chapter 8

The following morning Jake sits at his desk under a bluish cloud of cigarette smoke, drinking bad coffee and typing his reports on Joe Briggs' murder with his index fingers. He re-reads his notes, which refreshes his memory and gives his mind's eye a second and third look at the details of the crime scene.

At 9:00 a.m. Jake meets with Chief William Flanagan and Homicide Captain Avery Arnold in Flanagan's City Hall office. He and Arnold sit in front of the chief's desk.

On the wall behind the desk is a framed photo of Flanagan shaking hands with President Harry Truman, another photo with the governor, Luther Youngdahl, and a third with the mayor, Eric Hoyer, whom Flanagan hopes to eventually replace. When elected in '47, Youngdahl vowed to rid the state of gambling. He started by outlawing slot machines, but gambling continues and slot machines can still be found around town if you bother to look. Something most politicians and police choose not to do.

Flanagan's hazel eyes focus on Arnold before settling on Jake. "You know, it's a funny thing about river towns," Flanagan says, pontificating, as he's prone to doing. "Towns start at a river. Then politicians turn their backs on the river for the next hundred years till they realize it's the greatest asset they've got. So they go back to the river. And they never put their city halls down by the river. Know why that is?" Flanagan asks Jake.

St. Paul's City Hall is near the Mississippi River, Jake thinks. But, going along, he answers, "No."

"It's because there's always a jail in city halls to make it easy on the cops to run these guys up to the courtrooms. They didn't build jails too close to the river because if the crooks ever busted out, it'd be harder to track them than it would be in the center of town."

"Makes sense," Arnold says.

Brown noser, Jake thinks.

"Damn right it does. Why else would the politicians accept a less desirable location for their offices?"

A copy of the *Minneapolis Daily Tribune* sits on Flanagan's desktop. To the right of the newspaper are wanted flyers for Ben and Davy Roth.

Flanagan holds up the newspaper. Jake reads the headline:

KEFAUVER COMMISSION REPORT TARGETS MINNEAPOLIS SYNDICATE

"Kid Cann," Jake says. "The Jewish mob."

Flanagan nods. "The mayor isn't happy. And when he's unhappy, I'm unhappy. This department doesn't need bad publicity." Flanagan's complexion reddens as he slams his palm on the desktop. "I want the kikes who snuffed Joe Briggs!"

"We almost had them yesterday, Chief."

"Almost doesn't count, Cafferty." Flanagan takes a bottle of Pepto-Bismol out of a drawer, removes the cap, and swallows a mouthful.

Jake notes that the bottle is half-empty and understands why. Chief of police is not a civil service slot. You get to be chief because the mayor likes you. You cease to be chief when he ceases to like you, or when he ceases to be mayor. This happens frequently. In Minneapolis, former chiefs of police, who are now serving in various capacities within the department, are lining up their troops and plotting their return to the seat of power. Flanagan figures he's got a shot at being mayor once

Hoyer retires—and nothing can get in his way, especially bad press.

"What about the gun?" Jake asks Flanagan.

"Forensics confirmed a match between the bullet pulled from the wall in Briggs' bedroom and the gun you found at the Persian Palms."

Good news, Jake thinks, and then wonders if it really is.

Arnold says, "Something troubling you, Lieutenant?"

"I checked the rap sheet on the Roths. They've been arrested and charged with petty theft and B&Es. Spent a year in Red Wing at the Minnesota Training School for Boys. Never any weapons charges."

"What's your point?" Flanagan asks.

"The gun bit doesn't play, Chief. Why leave the murder weapon behind when they fled? Better yet, why'd they murder Briggs in the first place?"

Flanagan looks at Arnold, who offers a shrug in response. The chief's gaze returns to Jake. "If they cleared out in a hurry, they didn't have time to retrieve the gun."

Jake figures they would've taken the time, no matter what.

"And as for the Roths being murderers," Flanagan continues, "maybe they shot Briggs after he pulled his gun on them."

"Why would they be armed if it was just a B&E?"

Arnold says, "A murderer's motive may well be beyond our understanding."

"Any prints?"

"Gun was wiped clean."

Jake stands. "Well, we've got the whole force looking for the Roths. No reason for me to be sitting here."

"Leaving the Roths aside for the moment," Arnold says, looking at Flanagan, "there's something else we need to discuss."

"Ah, yes," Flanagan says, putting the Pepto-Bismol bottle back in the drawer. "The matter of the judge. Sit down, Lieutenant."

Jake isn't surprised. He figured the topic would come up. "What judge?" he asks.

"Judge Howard Gunderson. The Hennepin County judge you and Sergeant Cole . . ." the chief pauses, as if searching for the right word, "interrupted yesterday."

"I was never there, Chief."

"Good. Make sure you remember that. This is the House of Whispers."

"What about Cole?"

Flanagan nods at Arnold.

"We'll speak with the sergeant," Arnold says. "No need to alienate members of the judiciary or their families. Our friends on the bench have a difficult enough job blowing off steam as it is."

Flanagan laughs. "Who's to *judge* them?"

"Certainly not us," Arnold adds.

* * *

That afternoon Kate Dawson rises from her chair behind a heavy oak table in a City Hall courtroom in the Municipal Building. On the stand is Ester Levine, Kate's primary witness for the prosecution. Mrs. Levine is a plain-looking woman in her late twenties. She's wearing a simple housedress. Her hands are folded in her lap.

Kate points toward a small, bald, bespectacled man seated at the defense table. Seated next to him is his defense attorney, Joshua Jackson. "Do you recognize the defendant, Mrs. Levine?"

"Yes."

"What's his name?"

"Dr. James Conrad."

"When did you first see him?"

"On August nineteenth, as I remember."

"Where?"

"In his house. On Colfax Avenue."

"And who let you in when you went to the house?"

"A woman dressed as a nurse."

"And do you know her name?"

"She said her name was Mrs. Clayton."

"And did you see the defendant at that time?"

"Yes. The nurse took me into the parlor, and Dr. Conrad came in a few minutes later."

"And what did you say to him?"

"I told him I came to see him because I was in a family way and would like to have an operation performed. I said I have two children and couldn't support another."

"And what did the defendant say to that?"

"He asked me when I would like the operation performed. I told him as soon as possible. He asked if I could come to see him again in two days. I said that would be fine."

"Did Dr. Conrad say anything else?"

"He said to bring a nightgown, and that he would do the operation for one hundred twenty-five dollars. One hundred for himself and twenty-five dollars for the nurse."

"Did you return to Dr. Conrad's house two days later with the money?"

"Yes, I did."

"Was anyone with you?"

"Detective Kelly and Officer Bannister."

Kate glances at the two men sitting in the first row of gallery behind the defense table and the rail. Officer Mike Bannister is big in every way: big body, big voice, big head of wavy blond hair, handsome in a florid way. Sergeant Ray Kelly from the Morals Squad is tall and lean, with a long face and a perpetually smug look. Sitting at the back of the half-empty courtroom are two reporters Kate doesn't recognize.

Kate turns her attention back to the witness stand and Ester Levine. "Did the nurse let you in?"

"Yes."

"Objection," Joshua Jackson, Conrad's defense attorney, says. "Up to this point there is nothing to show that the woman was his nurse. The witness has called her his nurse, but there is no evidence whatever to justify this characterization."

Judge Howard Gunderson raises his eyebrows and stares down at Kate. "Sustained. Witness and prosecutor will refrain from calling the woman a nurse."

Kate sighs. Joshua "Peerless" Jackson is the best Negro attorney in Minneapolis, and maybe the best criminal lawyer in the city. Sweet-natured, bow-tied, rotund, deferential—a winning quality when appearing before the imperious Gunderson—he's an effective pleader with a laser-like ability to focus on the one juror he needs to hold out for an acquittal. The mantra among the most affluent and the most guilty is, "You better be fearless, or you better get Peerless."

Jackson's Jewish father and Negro mother were the head housekeepers at the Sholom Home, the Jewish old folks' residence in St. Paul. Jackson is a major contributor to the place. He grew up surrounded by these elderly Jews. They were all like grandparents to him, reading him stories, giving him small sums of money. One, Hyman Rappaport, left Jackson a legacy that enabled him to pay his law school tuition.

After he graduated from the University of Minnesota in the top third of his class, he began to look for a position at one of the leading Minneapolis firms. During his years at law school, he had developed an interest in banking, particularly as it relates to consumer lending. He sent in his application and received some very encouraging responses. But then came the interview. And the HR reps saw a Negro, a Negro who happened to be Jewish as well. Turns out there were "no openings at this time. But we'll keep your application on file. Thanks for stopping by."

Many times Jackson saw his former classmates scurrying down the hallways of the same firms that had just turned him down, former white classmates. So what was left for him? Low-end, down-and-dirty criminal law.

Joshua "Peerless" Jackson doesn't work with any firm. He doesn't need a firm. He's a sole practitioner that does criminal defense work. That's all he does. If he were at a firm, he'd have to split his fees with his partners. He doesn't want that. He has an inexpensive office a block from the courthouse, and in the morning, if he doesn't have a case, he'll troll outside the court-room of whichever judge is taking the preliminary hearings of the previous night's arrestees. If one of them makes bail, Jackson is waiting in the hallway outside the courtroom, ready to represent him. A brief negotiation about money follows, a deal is cut, and Jackson has a new client. If they can't make bail, he doesn't want them—nor does anyone else—so they get a court-assigned attorney, usually a rookie.

Now, Jackson doesn't do as much trolling as he did in his early years. The thieves and thugs around town have heard of him from their associates, or they have used him in the past.

Kate reframes the question. "Did the same woman who let you in the first time let you in this time?"

"Yes, she did."

"How was she dressed?"

"She had on the uniform of a nurse."

"What happened next?"

"The nurse . . . I mean, woman took me into the parlor."

"Where were Officer Bannister and Sergeant Kelly?"

"Sergeant Kelly waited outside, Officer Bannister in the dining room."

"What happened when you went to the parlor?"

"The woman put a sheet, blanket, and a pillow on an oper-ating table in preparation for, I suppose—"

"Objection," Jackson says. "The witness can't suppose."

"Sustained."

"Very well," Kate says. "But all I asked was what was done."

Judge Gunderson replies, "The witness may state what was done, but not the purpose."

Kate faces Mrs. Levine once more. "What did the woman ask you to do?"

"She had me disrobe and change into my nightgown. She boiled some water. Dr. Conrad came in carrying a black satchel. I asked him if he wanted to see the money now, and he said yes. So I gave him one hundred twenty-five dollars. He asked me to get up on the table. He strapped my ankles, my body, and my legs were doubled up to my chest. Then he took a syringe out of the satchel and used it on me."

"Objection, Your Honor." Rising once again, Jackson says, "I don't understand what the witness means. She says the defendant used the syringe on her. Did he use the syringe on her head or foot, or what part of her body?"

Kate lets out a frustrated breath. "I can't lead her, Your Honor."

Judge Gunderson leans toward the witness chair and says, "We understand that you went there with the knowledge that something was to be performed on you, Mrs. Levine. You cannot claim that any delicacy on your part will prevent your telling the jury exactly what took place. Now tell the jury exactly what happened."

"Dr. Conrad was syringing my womb."

"Continue, Mrs. Levine."

"Well, then I asked the nurse, the woman, I mean, if the operation was over. And she said, 'Wait a moment.'"

"Objection," Jackson says. "The witness is again characterizing this as an *operation*. It's up to the jury to judge whether there was an operation performed or not."

"Sustained," Gunderson says. "The witness is to tell what took place."

Kate bites her tongue. "How long did this syringing process last, Mrs. Levine?"

"Just a few moments."

"What happened next?"

"The doctor took the syringe away and picked up an instrument."

Kate picks up an instrument from the exhibit table and holds it up. "Was this the instrument the doctor had in his hand?"

"Yes."

"And what was the doctor doing with it?"

"He was coming toward me when I called out to Officer Bannister."

Kate pauses for a moment. She knew this was coming. That this was a dog of a case. Why the DA, Wilson Barlow, thought differently, she couldn't imagine.

"Miss Dawson?" Judge Gunderson says.

Kate glances at the judge and then continues. "What did you call out?"

"'I'm ready.' And Officer Bannister heard me and came into the parlor."

"What happened then?"

"Well, I was strapped to the table, and the doctor released the straps, and I got up and went to the bedroom."

Kate says, "No further questions at this time, Your Honor."

"Mr. Jackson," the judge says.

Jackson stands and approaches the witness. "Thank you, Your Honor. Mrs. Levine, when you called out to Officer Bannister, were the words 'I'm ready' prearranged?"

"Yes, sir."

The case is slipping away from Kate, and there's nothing she can do about it.

"What person did you arrange that signal with?"

"Officer Bannister."

"And when you entered the doctor's residence, did you tell Mrs. Clayton that Officer Bannister was your husband?"

"I . . . uh, yes. I said he was my husband."

"And who told you to introduce him as your husband?"

"Sergeant Kelly told me."

Kate rests her head in her hands. Then, quickly realizing how it might look to the jury, she straightens up and focuses her attention on the witness stand once more.

"Who informed you of Sergeant Kelly?" Jackson asks.

"My husband."

"Before you first visited Sergeant Kelly, had you ever heard of the defendant, Dr. Conrad?"

"No, I hadn't."

"Your visit to Dr. Conrad was a sham visit, was it not?"

"Yes, sir."

Kate feels she has to do something. "Objection! That calls for a conclusion. It wasn't a sham."

Jackson looks at her. "Your witness says it was."

Judge Gunderson says, "Well, the question is somewhat inarticulate, Mr. Jackson. According to the witness' testimony, the visit may not have been a sham, though the purpose was. Those are two distinct things. I will sustain the objection."

"Thank you, Your Honor," Kate says.

Jackson continues. "Had you received any money up until that time?"

"No, sir."

"Had you received the promise of any money?"

"Well, my husband had received a promise of money of fifty dollars each from Sergeant Kelly."

"Who furnished you with the information, or the suggestions as to the way in which you were to approach Dr. Conrad?"

"Sergeant Kelly and Officer Bannister."

"Did you have any objection to the lies they asked you to tell?"

"Well, they didn't ask me exactly to tell any lies."

"Not exactly? But they told you to give a wrong name to Dr. Conrad, didn't they?"

"Not that I remember."

"Did you tell any lies to Dr. Conrad, or make any statements that were untrue?"

"Well, yes. Sergeant Kelly told me I should say Officer Bannister was my husband."

Kate has a sick feeling in her stomach.

Jackson holds up a plastic instrument from the table. "This is the instrument that you identified as being in Dr. Conrad's office."

"Yes, sir."

"Now, Mrs. Levine, do you know the name of this instrument?"

"No, sir."

"Miss Dawson and I may agree that it's a speculum, Your Honor. It's used to dilate an orifice or canal in the body to allow inspection."

"Yes, if you agree to it," Judge Gunderson says.

"I concur," Kate says.

"Was the word *abortion* used, Mrs. Levine, during any conversation you had between you and Dr. Conrad?" Jackson asks.

"I don't remember that word being used."

"Did Dr. Conrad ever reach the point of inserting any instrument into you, Mrs. Levine, other than the syringe?"

"No, sir."

"Did Dr. Conrad not mention to you, Mrs. Levine, something about an abscess that you had?"

"He may have. I don't remember."

"You were not under ether or chloroform?"

"No."

"Yet you still don't remember?"

"Objection, Your Honor," Kate says. "Asked and answered."

"Sustained. Move on, Mr. Jackson."

"Now I offer in evidence the speculum identified by the witness and ask to have it marked as defendant's exhibit two. You have stated to the prosecuting attorney that you were pregnant with child when you came to see Dr. Conrad. How did you know that?"

"I knew it from having had my other babies. I don't know how else to explain it."

"No further questions at this time, Your Honor."

Kate stands. "The prosecution calls Officer Mike Bannister to the stand."

Mike Bannister is the only person Kate knows of who manages to lumber and swagger at the same time. There's no mistaking him for anything but what he is: a cop.

When Bannister is sworn in and seated, Kate says. "What did you do when you got inside the parlor with regard to the defendant?"

"I told him I was a Minneapolis police officer and took the speculum out of his hand. Then I placed him under arrest and asked him for the one hundred twenty-five dollars."

"Did Dr. Conrad say anything?"

"He said he was at my service. Then he took the money out of his pocket and handed it to me."

"Had you ever seen those bills before?"

"Yes. We had them marked. Six twenties and one five."

Kate has Bannister ID the articles in the doctor's satchel: syringe, bottle of ether, speculum, placental forceps and uterine dressing forceps, surgical scissors, cervical dilator, gauze, and a tenaculum.

"No further questions."

Jackson stands. "Who was present, Officer Bannister, when the orders or instructions were given to send Mrs. Levine to Dr. Conrad?"

"Mrs. Levine and her husband and Sergeant Kelly."

"Thank you."

Kate calls Dr. Conrad to the stand to explain the purpose of each instrument, in hopes of turning the tide in her favor once again. "Could you repeat the purpose of the tenaculum, Dr. Conrad? I'm not sure everyone heard it."

"The tenaculum is an instrument used for taking hold of the neck of the womb."

"I see." Kate lets the words linger for the jury before asking the next question. "Now, doctor, I ask you whether all these instruments that you have examined are known in the profession as instruments used to produce miscarriages?"

"Objection."

"Sustained, Mr. Jackson."

"Your Honor, am I not permitted to ask the doctor what the general purpose of these instruments is?"

"No, Miss Dawson, because it may be that the act of abortion could be committed without any one of these instruments at all. It does not necessarily follow that abortion can be committed by particular instruments."

Kate senses that this is where the case gets lost. Jackson senses it, too.

He stands, "Your Honor, we move to dismiss the jury on the grounds that the evidence does not show as charged in the indictment that the defendant attempted to commit the crime of abortion or attempted to thrust and insert into the womb or private parts of the woman any instrument for the purpose of procuring an abortion. We also move to dismiss on the grounds that the People have failed to sustain the burden of proof. And we move to dismiss on the grounds that every step taken toward the consummation of the crime was instituted and instigated by the Prosecution, and the initial step was taken by the complainant herself."

One look from Judge Gunderson, and Kate knows how he's going to rule.

Chapter 9

At 6:40 that evening Mike Bannister steps on the gas. He and Sam Witherspoon are in pursuit of a stolen green '48 Hudson Commodore two-door coupe. Witherspoon, one of a handful of Negroes in the department, is manning the radio. Bannister is pissed that he got saddled with a colored partner. He aims to take his objection up with his captain again, but right now he's hoping that the "nigger" won't wet his pants.

Witherspoon describes the make and model of the car for dispatch. Then, trying to keep the excitement out of his voice, he adds, "We're headed west on 36th Street."

"Copy that."

Bannister roars, "Duck!" a moment before an object hits the Ford's windshield, cracking the glass into the shape of a spider's web. Moments later the windshield shatters, scattering shards across the dash and front seat.

Witherspoon uses his left hand as a shield, but slivers sting his face.

"God dammit!" Bannister hollers. "The bastards are shooting at us!" With a fist he knocks the remaining glass out of the windshield, cutting the backs of his fingers and hands. Raindrops stippling the hood from an earlier shower pelt their faces.

"Pull over!" Witherspoon shouts.

"Like hell I will!" Bannister tightens his grip on the steering wheel and glances at Witherspoon. "Give those assholes some of their own medicine."

Witherspoon hesitates. He's only fired at targets before. "A stone broke the windshield, not a bullet."

"They threw it! Could've killed us!"

Witherspoon gauges the menace in Bannister's lowered brow and flared nostrils.

Bannister glances at the road ahead and then at Witherspoon once more. "What the hell you waiting for, boy? An invitation? Fire the damn gun!"

Witherspoon can feel the wind on his face as he draws his Smith & Wesson, sets his gun hand on the dashboard to steady his aim, and fires three shots at the fleeing car ahead.

The Hudson's back window explodes.

"Thatta boy!" Bannister shouts, stepping harder on the gas pedal. "We're gaining on 'em!"

As the Hudson ahead of them screeches into a left turn, Bannister slams the clutch to the floor, downshifts into first, and stomps on the gas pedal. Their Ford lurches forward and quickly picks up speed, the tires squealing as he shifts into second and makes a hard left.

"Suspects turned left on Emerson and are heading south," Witherspoon radios dispatch.

"Roger."

The man in the Hudson's passenger seat looks back, and as he does, Bannister feels a jolt of adrenaline. "It's the Roths!" he yells. "The assholes that snuffed Joe Briggs!"

"You're sure?"

"I ain't blind. I know their faces. Call it in!"

Witherspoon alerts dispatch as the Hudson carrying the Roths skids on the rain-slick streets, makes a sharp right on 39th Street, collides with a parked car, and spins into the middle of the road.

Bannister takes the turn too wide to avoid the Hudson. The Ford hops the curb, slides onto a lawn, and slams trunk first into a telephone pole. The engine conks out. Out of the corner of his eye, Bannister sees the Hudson back up and then race ahead down the street. The Ford's engine whines as he tries the key, but it won't turn over. He bangs his hands against the steering wheel. "God dammit!"

Bannister tries the key again and the engine starts, just as the Hudson turns right at the next corner and disappears.

*   *   *

Jake Cafferty catches the heavy dispatch chatter on his radio while he's driving back to the station after a couple of nothing leads, heading north on Penn Avenue out of Richfield, a post-war suburb on the southern edge of Minneapolis. Cornfields, farms, and new housing construction flank the road. There isn't much traffic, though every squad patrolling the streets has been searching for the Roths since Bannister and Witherspoon first spotted and then lost them.

He considered taking up the chase when it first began but concluded he was too far away. Now, since the Hudson was last seen heading west, Jake's alert. His eyes sweep the side streets that run perpendicular to Penn Avenue, hoping he'll get lucky. He wants the Roths alive, wants answers to the troubling questions surrounding Joe Briggs' death.

As he passes 50th Street he spots the Hudson speeding straight toward his passenger-side door and a black-and-white hugging the Hudson's bumper. Jake hits the gas to avoid a T-bone collision. In his rearview he sees the Hudson hang a left, followed by the squad car, the tires screaming as it burns rubber and races south on Penn Avenue.

Jake slams on his brakes and yanks the steering wheel to the right, sending the Ford into a 180. When the car comes to rest, he hits the siren and lead-foots in the direction he's just come from, the big flathead Mercury V-8 rumbling under the hood of the '49 Ford, the two-way alive with chatter between black-and-whites and dispatch. He hauls ass along one of two paved county roads leading into Richfield. Up ahead he spots red flashing lights on a squad parked on the west side shoulder. Jake roars up behind the black-and-white, skids to a stop, and grabs his keys. As he exits his Ford, he notices the dented trunk on the squad and its missing windshield.

He sees Bannister and Witherspoon running for the cornfield to his right. Witherspoon carries his Military & Police .38 Special, Bannister the 12-gauge shotgun off the rack between the black-and-white's front seats. There's blood on Bannister's right hand.

"Hey!" Jake calls. "Wait for backup!"

Bannister stops and shakes his head. "Bullshit! We're going after those assholes now."

The questioning look on Witherspoon's face tells Jake he doesn't know whom to follow.

Tires skid on the pavement behind Jake and slide onto the dirt shoulder. The Studebaker's driver's side door flies open. Nick Cole jumps out and runs toward him.

"What're you doing here, Cole?"

"Helpin' you out."

Jake smells alcohol on Cole's breath. "You okay?" he asks.

"Damn right!" Cole says, his eyes charged with excitement. "I want in on this."

"It'll be dark soon," Bannister says, glaring at Jake. "Quit dicking around." Bannister points with the shotgun barrel. "They ran into the cornfield right there."

"They armed?"

"They were when they snuffed Briggs."

"There's too much ground to cover," Jake says. "We need more men."

"The hell with that," Bannister says. He turns and runs into the cornfield.

Jake estimates the cornfield is about two acres, or about the size of a football field. They're standing on the east side of it, halfway between the north and south ends. Fifty yards to the west, beyond the field, is a farmhouse with a light in a front window, and thirty yards beyond that, a small barn with fencing and corrals.

"We'll spread out," Jake says, going along. "You're the youngest and probably the fastest, Cole." He points to his left, toward the south end of the field. "Get ahead of them if you can. If the Roths come out, you'll be waiting. Witherspoon will cover Bannister's right flank. I'll cover his left. We might get lucky. But watch out for an ambush. And beware of where we all are, so we don't start shooting at each other."

"Hope they're not headed for the farmhouse with the light in the window, Lieutenant," Cole says.

"You got that right. Let's go!"

The dirt is soft under Jake's feet as he makes his way between the rows that are three feet apart and stalks that must be fourteen feet high. The cool, dusky air is thick with the sugary sweetness of corn ready to harvest. As darkness falls, so do the odds of catching the Roths. They might've already hightailed it out of the cornfield and are looking for the next car to swipe. Maybe they're in the farmhouse and have taken someone hostage. In Jake's experience, hostage situations never turn out well.

He keeps going, slipping between the tall stalks. He's traveled an additional forty yards when he hears someone yell and then the unmistakable crack of a gunshot. The bullet rips through the cornstalks and whizzes by his head. Instinctively, he ducks, knowing it's already too late. A foot to the right and the bullet would've split open his head. He pauses, sucking in deep breaths, before he starts moving again, in a crouch, swallowing his fear, his heart thumping in his chest. He picks up his pace, fighting his way between the stalks. Then he hears a second and third shot. He bats cornstalks away from his face with his left hand and clutches his .38 tightly in his right hand. He's nearing the opposite side of the field when there are two more gunshots in quick succession. A few seconds later, he clears the corn.

Ben and Davy Roth lay chest down in the soft dirt ten yards in front of him. A Colt M1911 semi-automatic pistol lies beside Ben Roth's outstretched right hand.

Sam Witherspoon is standing on the far side of the bodies, holding his gun along his leg, looking confused as he stares at Jake. Nick Cole and Mike Bannister are standing to the left of the bodies. The shotgun is at Bannister's feet. Cole is holding two Colt Official Police revolvers in his hands.

Bannister looks at Jake and says, "I got 'em. I got the Hebes who murdered Joe Briggs."

Chapter 10

Arc lights brighten the far side of the cornfield, where the ID boys are working the scene. Flashlights dart through the corn. Cherry lights flashing atop squads reflect off metal and puddled streets.

Standing in the shadow between the Studebaker's headlights and the pitch-black darkness, Jake looks at Nick Cole and says, "Tell me again what happened."

Head bobbing, one shoe tapping the ground to the beat of some inner rhythm, Nick says, "When I was running along the south side of the field, I spotted the Roths running through the corn. I yelled for them to stop. They fired at someone in the cornfield."

Must've been the bullet that nearly hit me, Jake thinks.

"I fired two rounds that went wide. Then I lost sight of them. Heard two more gunshots a few seconds later. When I got to the far side of the field, Bannister was standing over the bodies. He told me they fired at him and ran. He returned fire and killed 'em both. Since I was senior officer to him, I took Bannister's piece and gave it to you." Nick points to the evidence bag in Jake's hand. "That it?"

Jake nods. "I'll need your gun, too."

Nick gives it to him.

Jake takes it and says, "What about Witherspoon?"

"I don't know what he saw, but he didn't fire. He came out of the cornfield just before you."

"Anything else?"

"Nope. Same account I gave you before."

"Wait for Arnold to get here. And don't talk to Bannister or Witherspoon."

"Got it."

Jake walks back to his Ford, bags Cole's gun, and fills out the collection information on the front. He places both evidence bags in the trunk. Then he opens the driver's side door and slides in. Witherspoon is seated in the passenger seat.

He glances at Jake and then stares out the windshield.

"I checked your weapon, Sam. You shot three rounds."

"That's right. When we were in the squad chasin' the Roths."

"Tell me what you saw and heard in the cornfield."

"Just like the man says."

"You mean Bannister."

"Yeah. Whatever he says."

"I haven't talked to Bannister yet."

"Maybe you should."

"I want to know what *you* saw, Sam."

Witherspoon looks at Jake. Then he turns away and stares out the windshield again. "Nothin'," he says.

"You're sure?"

"Damn sure."

"What'd you hear?"

"Shots."

"How many?"

"Not sure. Five, maybe."

"You talk to Bannister or Cole?"

Witherspoon hesitates and then shakes his head.

Jake takes an evidence bag out of his suit coat pocket. It contains the Colt M1911 semi-automatic pistol that was lying next to Ben Roth's hand.

"Look at me, Sam." Jake waits till Witherspoon's eyes are focused on his. "You recognize this gun?"

Witherspoon nods.

"Found next to Ben Roth's body," Jake says.

"Didn't know which boy had it."

"But you saw Ben Roth fire it at Bannister."

"No," Witherspoon says with a quick shake of his head.

"So he didn't fire at Bannister?"

"That's not what I said, Lieutenant. I said I didn't see nothin'."

"Anything else you didn't see?"

"Told you all I know. I ain't lyin'."

"Never said that."

Witherspoon holds his gaze steady for a time before his eyes slide off Jake's face.

Jake waits, sensing Witherspoon is about to say something else. When he doesn't, Jake says, "You can go. One of the blues will drive you home. But don't talk to Bannister or Cole."

Witherspoon gets out of the Ford without looking at Jake and closes the passenger side door behind him.

Jake sees Bannister standing near his smashed-up squad car, where Jake told him to wait. A cloud of smoke from his cigarette drifts into the cool night air. Jake gets out of his car and approaches. "Kill the cigarette, Bannister. And don't leave it on the ground."

Bannister smirks, extinguishes it on the fender of his squad, and tosses the butt into the front seat. "This isn't a crime scene, Lieutenant."

"Let's hear your version of the shooting."

"Version? Cole and Witherspoon telling you something different?"

"Don't know till I hear it from you." Jake wants to keep Bannister in the dark for the time being. "So what happened?"

"I spotted the kikes hiding at the edge of the corn. They saw me and took off. I gave chase but lost sight of 'em. They shot at me."

"Then what?"

"I heard a couple more shots and fired back."

"How many times?"

"Two. When I ran out of the field, they were both lying chest down. Dead."

"They were shot in the back."

"They were running away. Where else was I supposed to shoot 'em?"

"How far away would you estimate they were when you first fired?"

"Maybe twenty yards."

"So it's sunset. They're running. You're running. Yet you hit them both in nearly the same spot."

"What're you getting at, Cafferty?"

Jake shrugs. "You're a helluva shot."

"Damn right I am."

* * *

It's nearly 11:00 p.m., but there's a light on in a window of the farmhouse when Jake opens the screen door and knocks. He can hear movement behind the front door, so he waits instead of knocking again. The air is cool and breathless, the sky veiled with clouds. Ten seconds later someone flicks on the porch light. The door opens slightly before catching on a safety chain.

Standing in the space between the door and frame is a buxom woman with thick black hair cut short on her neck and wary, dark eyes. She's wearing bedroom slippers, a long over-coat, and an expression of distrust. Her arms are crossed over her chest.

"What do you want?" she asks with a thick Hispanic accent.

Jake holds up his badge and identifies himself. "I know it's late, ma'am, but I'd like to talk with you about the shooting that occurred in the cornfield earlier this evening."

He sees the blood go out of her cheeks, and her eyes dart back and forth. "I did not see or hear anything," she says as her eyes leave his. "I was asleep."

"And what time was that?"

She gazes at him with a look of confusion on her face.

"When you went to bed," he adds.

"At seven thirty. I was tired."

Jake recalls seeing a light on in the farmhouse just before going into the cornfield. Sunset was around 7:30. He doesn't remember seeing the light turn off. "You always leave a light on in the house when you go to bed?"

"When my husband is away, yes. I do not like the dark."

Jake takes out his notebook and pen. "You mind if I come in? I have a few more questions."

"I do mind."

Jake's eyes stay on hers till she looks away. He usually gets more information out of someone if he's in the same room with them, but he backs off. "Okay. Then let's start with your name."

"Ramona Gutierrez."

"And this is your farm?"

"My husband's."

"Is he home?"

"He is in Mexico." She pauses and then adds, "But he will be home soon."

"What's his name?"

"Manny."

"Anyone else living here?"

She shakes her head and says, "I should not be talking to you."

"I'm a police officer."

"You are also a man," she says, shutting the door.

Jake hears the lock turn. He considers knocking again and then changes his mind. He writes his name and phone number in his notebook, tears out the page, and places it between the screen door and frame.

Chapter 11

The next morning, after three hours of restless sleep, a hot shower, and three cups of Joe, Jake heads for the first-floor autopsy suite at Minneapolis General Hospital. When he arrives, the coroner, Harold Jamison, is peering through an x-ray machine. Davy Roth's naked body is lying on its stomach on a porcelain autopsy slab. His blank face and dead eyes are staring at Jake. The strong pickle-like odor of formaldehyde, the sweet copper stench of blood, and a smell like spoiled meat hit him. A printed sign on the wall behind the dissecting table and above the refrigerators reads

"Medicine, to produce health, has to examine disease."
—Plutarch

No amount of medicine is going to improve Davy Roth's health, nor his brother's, Jake thinks. But maybe the coroner can give him some answers.

"Just removed the clothes. Don't like to do that before the x-rays," Jamison says, his blue eyes alight with curiosity as he looks at Jake through the lenses of his wire-rimmed glasses. "Once had a .22 slug that exited the right chest and impacted the lining of the victim's suit coat. It'd lost most of its velocity and fallen into an inside coat pocket. Never would've recovered it if I hadn't seen it on the x-ray." He curls his index finger. "Take a look."

Jake moves to the opposite side of the autopsy table.

Jamison gestures toward the wound in Davy Roth's back. "What do you see?"

Jake takes a moment to observe before speaking. "There's no powder tattooing. So we're not talking intermediate range shot. Could be a distant shot. That's what Bannister claimed."

"Look carefully."

As Jake moves closer, he detects a wide, teardrop zone of powder, soot, and seared, blackened skin above the entrance wound. He knows immediately that the muzzle of the gun was held at an angle to the skin, creating a gap, which allowed gunshot materials exiting the muzzle to produce a teardrop shape.

He straightens up and looks at Jamison. "It's an angled wound."

"Yes, it is, Lieutenant. Now look at the x-ray screen. The fatal gunshot entered the mid-back, right to left, wounding the posterior left ventricle, the pericardium, and lodging in the left anterior fifth rib."

"We have Bannister's gun. It's a Colt Official Police .38 caliber revolver."

Jamison nods. "I'll dig out each bullet and see if we can match them to the gun."

"So what's the skinny, Doc?"

"Both victims were shot at close range. Either shot would cause immediate death."

"Bannister claims he shot them both from about twenty yards. Plus, there's no powder tattooing."

Jamison shakes his head. "Given that the blackened teardrop zone is on one side of the wound with the bullet going the other way, I'd say we're dealing with an angled near-contact wound. The angle of the bullet's trajectory in each of the victims indicates the shooter shot them from a position higher than the victim's head. The trajectory of each bullet was downward."

"So it's clear both victims were shot from the rear."

"That's correct."

"And if the trajectory of each bullet was downward, the shooter would have to be on higher ground."

"That's one theory."

Jake looks at Jamison. "Another theory being they were shot while kneeling or lying face down."

"Could be. And if you shoot someone in the back who's kneeling or face down, Lieutenant . . ." Jamison shrugs.

That could be an execution, Jake thinks.

*   *   *

That afternoon Jake is seated at an oak table upstairs in a crowded wood-paneled room reserved strictly for men at Richards Treat Cafeteria on South Sixth Street in downtown Minneapolis. Homicide Captain Avery Arnold is seated opposite him. Jake often stops here in the morning for a six-cent roll. Buying a roll reduces the cost of his coffee to eight cents.

Lenore Richards and Nola Treat, former economics professors from the University of Minnesota, own and operate the cafeteria, whose décor resembles a tearoom more than a traditional cafeteria, particularly the main dining room with its pewter utensils, china dinnerware, colonial-style furniture, and glowing candles in candelabras. Their motto is "Educated Food for Educated People." For the past twenty-six years, judges, lawyers, and others who work in the Rand Tower, the Soo Line Building, the District Court building, the Builders' Exchange building, and the *Minneapolis Daily Tribune* have gathered daily in the five dining rooms to eat their fresh homemade dishes.

One of the men seated near them at the "Judges Table," as it's known around town, is Howard Gunderson. He's a middle-aged man with wavy white hair and a thick white beard. His strong face and sharp eyes can flash with authority. The last time Jake saw Gunderson, the judge was stark naked in a room at the Persian Palms. Gunderson's eyes are fixed on the other three men around the table. If he notices Jake, he doesn't acknowledge it.

Jake has a chicken potpie and Arnold the ham loaf.

Jake says, "I just came from Ballistics. The two recovered bullets from the Roths' shooting came from Bannister's gun."

"No surprise there," Arnold says. "Bannister shot them."

"Yeah, he did. In the back."

Arnold sips his coffee. "What does it matter where he shot them? They murdered Joe Briggs."

"They weren't shot from some twenty yards as Bannister claims."

"Says who?"

"The coroner. I was there for the autopsy before talking with Ballistics. There's a teardrop zone of powder indicating an angled shot, Cap. And the bullet trajectory was downward in each of the bodies."

"What're you suggesting?"

"The ground around the cornfield is flat. Either Bannister climbed a tree that doesn't exist, or the Roths were on their knees or their faces when they were shot. They could've given up."

Arnold's eyes are focused inward in thought as he sets his coffee cup carefully on the saucer in front of him. He gestures at the file folder under Jake's palm. "That your report, Lieutenant?"

"It is."

Arnold extends an open hand. "I'll take it."

Jake hesitates and then slides the file across the table.

"I'll speak with the coroner as well."

"We can't just write this off, Cap."

Arnold sucks in a breath and lets it out slowly. "You're a good cop, Jake. But, unfortunately, your priorities are sometimes skewed."

"How are my—"

Arnold holds up a hand in a stopping gesture. "Let me finish. The people of this city and all its officers sought justice for the murder of a policeman. Joe Briggs had many friends in the department. His best friend, Mike Bannister, is responsible for meting out the well-deserved justice."

"I'm not sure the Jewish population will see it as justice."

Arnold waves off Jake. "What is it with you and these people, Detective?"

Jake now wishes he hadn't broached the subject. He changes the topic. "Look, Cap, I'm not sure the Roths murdered Joe Briggs."

Arnold sits back in his chair, his eyebrows raised. "You have evidence to the contrary?"

Jake gives a slow shake of his head. "Not yet."

Arnold spreads his hands as if to say, *I thought so*. He leans forward and places his elbows on the table. "You've been a policeman for over twenty years, Jake. We both know the MPD's reputation has suffered in the past. We've worked hard to regain the Jewish community's trust. If what you're suggesting about the Roth shooting is correct, and if this information were to become public . . ." Arnold shrugs. "Well, you know what could happen." He pauses a moment and takes a sip of coffee before speaking again.

"The Jewish population of this city has grown. Along with this growth has come more rights and, frankly, more power. With the Kefauver Commission rattling cages and making waves in nearly every major city across the country, the department cannot afford another scandal, particularly if it involves the deaths of Jews at the hands of the police.

"You're one of the team that brought two murderers to justice," Arnold continues. "As such, the mayor and chief are holding an award ceremony tomorrow at City Hall. Officer Bannister will receive the Medal of Valor and a promotion to sergeant with the Morals Squad. Officer Witherspoon, Sergeant

Cole, and Lieutenant Jake Cafferty will receive a Medal of Commendation."

"No thanks, Cap."

"Perhaps I didn't make myself clear. You will appear at the ceremony, and you will accept your award."

"I don't deserve a medal."

"Not your call. The chief and mayor are in full agreement. And speaking of Sergeant Cole, he'll be your new partner."

"What?"

"Nicholas Cole. Starting tomorrow, he'll be your new partner."

"He was just promoted to the Morals Squad. What experience does he have in homicide?"

"The same amount of experience you had when you transferred."

Jake lets out a frustrated sigh.

"What you have to remember about street work, Lieutenant, is that it's an age thing. Best years for a street cop are between twenty-five and thirty-five, few years either way. Too young, they're too quick tempered. Too old, they're burnouts. That's why twenty and out is best for uniform guys. The first few years they're walking time bombs, and the last few years they're bombed out, period."

"Cole doesn't have a lot of friends in the department. They think he's arrogant."

"Do you even know the man?"

"Not really."

"Then give him a chance. He's a comer. He has potential. Besides, you wouldn't be happy with anyone I partnered you with."

"I worked with the best."

"Russ Krueger was the best. But now that he's retired, you need a partner."

"And I don't have any say in the matter?"

"In this instance, no. Give it some time. You'll see I've made the best decision."

Jake has two choices. Go along with Arnold's decision, or request a transfer out of Homicide.

"Harold Jamison is prepping the Roths for their well-deserved dirt nap," Arnold says. "We have Joe Briggs' killers where we want them. I expect your cooperation and your silence, as well as your participation in the award ceremony. Do we have an understanding?"

Jake exhales and nods his head.

As soon as Arnold leaves the restaurant, Jake hustles downstairs to the pay phone and calls Harold Jamison, the coroner.

"Avery Arnold is on his way to see you," Jake says. "Before he gets there, run me a copy of the autopsy reports on Ben and Davy Roth."

"What's this about, Jake?"

"The fix is in. You need to cover your ass."

Jamison hesitates. Then he says, "Thanks for the heads-up, Jake."

"This is between you and me. I'll be over later to get the copies."

Chapter 12

At Minneapolis General Hospital that evening, Kate Dawson heads for the coroner's office, propelled by speculation from the Minnesota Jewish Council and its executive director, Samuel Scheiner, that the Roths were murdered. She hopes to get a look at the autopsy files for Ben and Davy Roth before they disappear into the ether that is the political bureaucracy. Under her breath, she rehearses the dialogue she's concocted, but when she reaches the coroner's office, a sign on the door indicates that Harold Jamison is gone for the day.

"Dammit," she mutters to herself. Then, as she considers alternatives, she realizes Jamison's absence might be a lucky break. Death never sleeps, so the morgue never closes, which means an attendant is likely on duty. Unlike Jamison, most attendants are young and more likely to cooperate with someone from the DA's office, especially if that someone is an attractive female. Kate opens her purse and compact. Gazing in the mirror, she carefully applies fresh lipstick and a touch of powder. She lets down her hair and combs it out. Then she heads straight for the autopsy lab.

A body lies on the examination table, covered with a sheet. The air is rife with the stench of cold, dead meat, dried blood, and formaldehyde. Frank Sinatra, backed by Tommy Dorsey's orchestra, croons "Let's Get Away from It All" on the radio. Kate looks around. A young morgue attendant sits in a chair with his feet up on an old metal desk, eating a sandwich.

"Hey there," she says, walking toward the desk.

He turns to look at her, does a double take, and then tosses his half-eaten sandwich in the lunchbox on his desk as he scrambles to his feet.

Kate figures he's about her age and not bad looking, but he could use a shave and a shower to wash out the grease in his brown hair and the sour odor of perspiration.

"Ah . . . you're not supposed to be in here, miss."

She extends a hand. "I'm Kate Dawson from the DA's office."

He wipes his hands on his blood-spattered green scrubs and shakes. "Oh, I heard they hired a . . ." He stops and offers her a crooked smile.

"Yeah, I'm the woman. And your name is?"

"Scott."

"Nice to meet you, Scott."

"Likewise," he says with a grin.

"I wonder if you could do me a big favor, Scott?"

"Sure, Miss Dawson," he says, looking into her eyes.

"The DA, Mr. Barlow, sent me over to get copies of the autopsy reports on Ben and Davy Roth." Kate gives him a bright smile.

Scott's brown eyes light up. "Oh, wow. That was something, huh? They killed the cop and then shot it out in the cornfield."

"Sure was."

"Well, Miss Dawson, Dr. Jamison isn't here. And the reports are locked in his office."

Kate nods and revises her plan. "Where are they?"

"You mean the Roths?"

"Yes."

Scott gestures toward the three rows of individual coolers along the wall. "In the coolers."

"I'd like to see the bodies."

Scott looks around nervously. "You would?"

"If you're not allowed to make that decision," Kate says, "I understand. I can come back when Dr. Jamison is here or someone else who has the authority."

"I don't need permission," Scott says, straightening his back.

"Good. Then let's take a look."

His chin bobs up and down, as if he's convinced himself that he's made the right decision.

Kate follows him to the coolers, where Scott opens two side-by-side drawers and pulls out the rolling trays containing the bodies. A sheet covers each body, and toe-tags identify them as Ben and Davy Roth.

"Pull back the sheets," Kate says.

"You sure?"

"I need to see."

Scott pulls back the sheets, revealing their faces.

Kate stifles the urge to look away.

"You okay?"

"Fine," she says as her stomach rumbles. "I need to see the whole body."

He shrugs and removes the sheets.

Immediately she sees the wounds in their chests. Having never seen gunshot wounds before, she says, "Are these entrance or exit wounds?"

"They're exit wounds."

"How can you tell?"

Scott points to the chest wounds. "The ragged skin and tissue damage. You see?"

Kate nods.

"Entrance wounds are usually smaller and more symmetrical, with a reddish-brown zone of abraded skin."

"Turn them on their sides."

"What for?"

"I want to see the entrance wounds."

Scott turns Ben's body on its side first, then Davy's.

"You sure these are entrance wounds?"

Scott smirks. "I've seen plenty of 'em. Shape of the wound depends on the angle between the bullet and the skin."

"How would the shape be different?"

"A bullet striking perpendicular to the skin should produce a concentric abrasion ring. If the bullet penetrates at an angle, the abrasion zone is wider on the side that the bullet came from. Like these wounds."

"So they were both shot in the back and at an angle?"

"Sure were."

"And from a distance."

"Oh, no. Close up."

"How can you tell?"

"See the zone of powder and soot above the entrance wound?"

"Yeah."

"Don't get that from a distant shot." Scott flips each body on its back again. "Need to see anything else?"

Kate shakes her head. "Anyone claim the bodies?"

"Not that I heard."

"What happens if no one claims them?"

"Dr. Jamison can send the bodies to the University of Minnesota for anatomical study, or he can have them buried or cremated, which is cheaper."

"Do me one more favor, Scott."

"You bet, Miss Dawson."

"Let's keep this little visit just between you and me."

"But I thought the DA sent you?"

"I lied."

Scott looks wary. "What?"

"If the DA or Dr. Jamison finds out I was here, I'd be in trouble. But so would you. Understand?"

"But I didn't do anything wrong."

"I don't think you did, Scott. But they might not agree. Why take the chance?"

Scott narrows his eyes. "You set me up."

"And how did I do that?"

"Well, you . . ." He stops abruptly and finishes the thought with a dismissive wave of a hand.

Kate touches him lightly on his arm. "I know I can count on you, Scott, if I need anything else. You're a professional. You'll go places with the right people behind you."

"Like you?" he says sarcastically.

"Don't make the mistake of counting me out."

*   *   *

Late that night Nick Cole bolts awake from the nightmare that has haunted him since the war. Sitting up in bed, his sleeveless T-shirt and boxers wet with sweat, he tucks his hands between his knees to stop them from shaking and gulps deep breaths to calm his racing heart.

Then he shuffles barefoot across the moonlit wood floor of his one-bedroom apartment, fills a tall glass with cold water from the sink, and downs it in one long swallow. Shivering now, he grabs the robe hanging on a hook attached to the inside of the bathroom door and puts it on.

He checks the alarm clock beside the bed. 3:27 a.m. Nick knows that he won't sleep much the rest of the night, so he turns on the gas stove and reheats a pot of coffee. He pours a steaming cup, sits in a cushioned chair, and stares into the darkness.

When Nick first returned from the war, his dreams replayed a confused jumble of his worst wartime experiences. They gradually coalesced into one recurring theme: that he must go back into the Army and back into combat—forever.

In this nightmare two military police appear at his door, hand him his fatigues, and forcibly haul him away. "You're making a mistake!" Nick yells loudly. "I served my time!" Then, in a moment, he finds himself back in combat, a furious fire-fight going on around him, bullets and shrapnel flying. He often wakes up yelling, flailing, screaming, drenched, and panting, his heart pounding. The episode drains him, but he cannot go back to sleep.

Nick's not sure what triggers the nightmares, but he was rereading the copy of the *Intelligencer Journal* of Lancaster, Pennsylvania, before turning in. The newspaper contains a banner headline and article about Nick's family and his exploits in WWII.

Cole's father, Joseph, left Germany with a new wife, Hannah, in 1921, and joined a couple of hundred other Rhinelanders in the fertile, rolling countryside of Lancaster County, Pennsylvania, where he and his wife farmed and raised two girls and one boy.

The Great Depression, which lasted from the end of the First World War until the Second, fell hard upon Lancaster County's farm economy. Nick's father wound up as a guard/custodian in the Lancaster Valley State Institute for the Feeble Minded.

Nick liked athletics. He was good—but not that good. The fall football season was his weakest. As a sophomore he was neither very big nor very fast. He realized he would never be the star quarterback throwing the game-winning pass, or half-back streaking down the sideline to score the winning touch-down in the waning seconds of the big homecoming game. Given his good looks, Nick dated the prettiest and most popular girls, but it wasn't enough. He hated never being picked first when they chose up sides.

He became the kicker, the one slot that, at the high school level, is the product of endless practice and determination. Winter was his best season. He wrestled. In his senior year he was the runner-up in the district 160-pound weight division, having grown taller and considerably stronger in his last year of school. In the spring, he ran cross-country and lettered.

By then, he had an idea of what he wanted to do. His one real talent was art. From the time he was a high school freshman, he'd done the illustrations for the school paper and the yearbook. If there was a poster to be drawn for a school event, he designed it. When he was a senior, the feature columnist for the local paper wrote an article about Nick, which included Nick's rather unflattering caricature of the columnist. Unflattering or not, the columnist incorporated Nick's sketch into the masthead above his column.

There was no money for college, but the owner of the paper, who had originally suggested the column, had established a scholarship fund for worthy students. No one was surprised when Nick received a full scholarship to the Minneapolis School of Art. One year was enough. He didn't have the ability to make a living as a commercial artist. Nick left the School of Art to join the Army in July of 1942, where he found that the rigors of the service appealed to him.

Sent overseas, he was assigned to Company G of the 317th Infantry Regiment, 80th Infantry Division. The Division originally consisted of men mostly from Pennsylvania, Virginia, and West Virginia, and was nicknamed the "Blue Ridge Division." Landing on Utah Beach on August 5, 1944, Nick was a battle-hardened soldier by Christmas Day, when they reached the outskirts of Bastogne to free the besieged 101st Airborne Division.

Then, when his platoon was hit by murderous machine gun crossfire during an advance in the Ardennes, Private First Class Nicholas Cole charged across an open field, firing his M-1 carbine. Though wounded in the left arm and leg, Nick tossed a grenade at the nest and still had the strength to shoot the two remaining German survivors. For his action, he won the Silver Star and his second Purple Heart.

Nick knew from months of experience on the battlefield that he couldn't think *I might get killed*, for to think about the future and the terror of his own death during combat would make it more likely that he *would* get killed. The time for fear was before or after, not during the battle.

Now, the deferred fear of battle waits coiled in his sleep, and he dreads the hours before dawn. The nightmares come more frequently of late, depriving him of sleep and leaving him tense, with a hair-trigger temper and the bizarre sense that his conscious waking life is at peace, but his subconscious mind is still engaged in battle. He left the war, but the war hasn't left him.

Chapter 13

The thing about cops is they don't trust anybody, especially other cops. It's something Nick Cole is acutely aware of as he stands near the podium in the large five-story rotunda at City Hall, waiting for the mayor to speak. Six rows of folding chairs set up on each side of the large "Father of Waters" statue in the center of the rotunda are filled with dignitaries, friends and family members of the honorees, newspaper reporters, and photographers. Television cameras broadcast the awards ceremony.

Starting on the day a man becomes a cop, the process of exclusion under the guise of cohesion begins. Day watch versus swing shift versus dogwatch. Uniforms versus plainclothes. Patrolman versus sergeant versus lieutenant versus captain versus deputy chief versus chief. Homicide vs. Burglary vs. Robbery vs. Fraud/Theft. It breaks down that way real fast. Who you are is who you aren't.

Why become a cop? One guy says, "I want security. I took the exams for postman. I took the exams for fireman. Passed everything. But the waiting list is forever. Took the exams for cops. They need cops. I'm a cop. Civil service mentality. No layoffs. Decent pension. Twenty and out." Other guys want to help people. Other guys like the authority. Other guys like the action.

A young cop can go a couple of ways. He can become a thumper. Every department needs street cops like Joe Briggs, who can handle anything and really like the rough stuff. The trouble is that cops like that rarely know where to draw the line. Even though the brass tries to cover for them, they always seem to be in the shit.

Nick goes the other way. He sees all this but knows where the line is and is careful about crossing it. He has multiple citations for service to the public above and beyond the call of duty. Joe Briggs' record shows a fuckup with an endless capacity for messing up his life and that of everyone around him.

Most cops don't bother to crack the books because opportunities for advancement are few. Nick doesn't wait till deaths and retirements open the list. Instead of spending his time drinking it up with his buds and getting laid, he spends more of it on the books. When openings are posted, he's ready. He hasn't fouled up with any of the guys on the oral exam board, either. He gets the nod.

Nick scans the crowd. When his eyes rest on Kate Dawson, his heart quickens. He hoped she'd be here. Hopes that she sees how far he's come in a few years. Homicide is just the first step up the ladder.

*   *   *

Seated in the last row to the left of the podium, Kate Dawson smells a cover-up as the mayor of Minneapolis lauds the actions of the four police officers that brought the Roths to justice. *No way they were shot from a distance. The bodies prove it!* It irks her that the MPD and mayor are whitewashing the shootings. But what can she do about it?

Her eyes drift from the podium to the "Father of Waters" statue. According to legend, rubbing its big toe brings good luck. Kate figures she can use some. Because she lost her first case, Wilson Barlow, the DA, is not happy with her. But Kate isn't happy with the DA. She had little or no chance of winning. Now Barlow is reluctant to toss her another bone. Kate needs to get back in the DA's good graces—and soon. The cornfield shooting has given her an idea. Maybe there's a way forward. All she needs is a willing accomplice.

Kate shifts her gaze back to the podium, then to the downtown businessmen, city council members, and Chief of Police William Flanagan, seated in a row of chairs on the landing behind the mayor. She recognizes Douglas Crenshaw and recalls that his son, Martin, recently committed suicide by jumping off a bridge. Crenshaw, always a private man with an aversion to the press, has become more reclusive in his later years, shunning the spotlight whenever possible. Kate is surprised to see him at the awards ceremony and wonders why he chose to attend.

Her gaze shifts to the four award recipients standing on the steps behind the mayor, and then to Nick Cole. She feels a pang of regret for breaking off their relationship but knows it was the right thing to do.

She met Nick two weeks after the DA hired her, and two days after she bought the bright blue '47 Packard Clipper, her first decent car. Nick and his partner, Joe Briggs, pulled her over for speeding on Lake Street. She remembers Briggs walking up to the driver's side window and hearing Nick say, "Let me handle this one, Joe." Then seeing the lewd smile on Briggs' jowly face as he stepped away and Nick appeared. He left her his business card instead of a ticket. A week later he called her at her office and invited her to dinner at Charlie's. Afterwards they danced to jazz in the Bamboo Room at the Cassius Bar & Café.

Back then Nick had a sense of humor, despite the trauma of war and the nightmares that frequently interrupted his sleep. Sometimes when he stayed over, Kate would awake in the middle of the night and find him sitting in a chair, staring into the darkness. At first she figured this behavior, too, was all about his war experiences. But later she suspected there was something else in his past that he refused to share. Whatever it was, over the last few months he'd grown more intense, more . . . *clingy*. Kate needed space, needed time to focus on her career.

She picks up the mayor's speech again. He's moved beyond the accolades for the police officers and into full campaign mode.

"There is convincing evidence that organized groups of criminals have been engaged in illegal activities in this city."

No kidding, Kate thinks.

"These organized groups of criminals have large sums of cash and have monopolized commerce by means of violence, bribery, corruption, and intimidation."

Is he really asking the people in this room to believe that he just stumbled upon these "revelations"? Kate tunes out the speech and lets her gaze settle on Jake Cafferty. She recalls the scene at the Flame Café and Cafferty's remark about her being the DA's squeeze. She clenches her jaw. *Goddamn men!* Then she shakes her head to clear her mind and focuses her attention on the mayor once more.

"Whether dealing in narcotics trafficking, prostitution, or gambling, individuals and organizations involved in illicit activities best heed my warning. My administration does not and will not tolerate criminal organizations whose existence in this city has tarnished its reputation."

Applause erupts. The mayor, who with his glasses, slicked-back hair, and slightly receding hairline, reminds Kate of Harry Truman, nods his head, basking in the applause. Kate wonders if he knows anything about the shooting in the cornfield and the rank hypocrisy of the awards ceremony.

"The question is not whether gambling or any other form of illegal activity is morally right or wrong," the mayor continues. "Rather, we must weigh the effects upon society of permitting powerful groups of criminals to consolidate their power through violence and intimidation, corruption and control of local government, and by amassing great wealth through monopolies

and nonpayment of taxes. Those days are over, ladies and gen-
tlemen. I'm charting a new course for this city. From now on,
when people across the country think of Minneapolis, they'll
think of our city as they do the North Star. A shining light that
others look to for guidance."

The guests rise in applause. Smiling, the mayor thanks the
crowd and gestures for everyone to sit down. Then he presents
the medals to each of the four men, shakes their hands, and
poses for photos.

A reporter asks, "What would you consider a success, Mr.
Mayor, in terms of reducing crime?"

"When there isn't any. My job is . . . a police officer's job is
rewarding when you're helping people. It's frustrating, though,
because you're dealing with people who are not having their
finest moments. A lot of them are angry or in a lot of pain or
they're doing bad things. The public, the people who pay our
salaries, they are our customers. We want to treat them with
courtesy and respect, the way anyone would treat their customers. We're going to be nice. We're going to be nice just as
long as we can be nice, until we can't be nice anymore. And
then we'll do whatever it takes to get the job done."

As the crowd disperses, Kate's eyes search for Jake Cafferty.

* * *

Never seeking publicity for doing his job—or for anything
else—Jake bolts for the nearest exit, anxious to get away from
the crowd and well-wishers. He's experienced enough to know
the ceremony wasn't about him. It's all about PR for the chief,
the mayor, and members of the city's elite, who seek the lime-
light whenever it shines favorably on them.

He's nearly clear of the throng when he comes face to face
with Virginia Crenshaw, clad in a navy blue suit that fits her
curves snugly.

"Lieutenant," she says with a closed smile.

"Miss Crenshaw."

"Good to see police officers getting some recognition. You certainly deserve it."

Jake nods and offers a smile. Then, without thinking, he blurts, "Surprised to see you and your father here."

She cocks her head. "Are you?"

"Not something you'd usually attend, is it?"

"My father has always supported the police department."

"Except when they organized as a union."

"That isn't my concern."

"What is?"

"My brother's death. Are you still looking into it?"

"Got a little distracted," he says, gesturing toward the podium. "If something changes, you'll be the first to know."

She nods her head, but the questioning look on her face suggests she doesn't believe it. "Do you have a business card, Lieutenant?"

Jake gives her one. She peers at it for a time and then slips it into her purse. "Nice to see you again."

"One minute," Jake says.

"Yes?"

"Did your brother ever mention Brazama Gold?"

She cocks her head. "What's that?"

"Guess not."

"Does Brazama Gold have something to do with my brother's death?"

"Don't know, Miss Crenshaw."

Douglas Crenshaw wheels his chair beside his daughter. "Wonderful ceremony, Lieutenant. Congratulations on a job well done." He offers a hand. Jake takes it but doesn't reply.

The awkwardness breaks when Virginia Crenshaw says, "Lieutenant Cafferty asked if I'd ever heard of Brazama Gold, Father. Do you know anything about it?"

Douglas Crenshaw shakes his head. "What is it?"

She looks at Jake. "That's what I'd like to know."

"A bad investment?" Jake says.

"Not something we're familiar with," the old man says, indicating his daughter. "We wouldn't be where we are today if we were."

She acknowledges her father's comment with a slight smile and says to Jake, "Sorry we couldn't be of help, Lieutenant."

Jake thanks them for their time and heads for the exit. He's nearly home free when he hears a woman calling his name.

"Lieutenant Cafferty!"

Virginia Crenshaw again? He pretends he doesn't hear and keeps going.

The woman calls out once more, only louder.

Jake turns and looks around, trying to locate where the voice came from. His eyes settle on Kate Dawson.

She waves and heads toward him. "Congratulations, Lieutenant."

Jake looks down at the medal hanging from the ribbon around his neck. In his haste to leave the rotunda, he's forgotten to take it off.

"You must be very proud."

"Thank you," he says, but without much feeling behind it. He removes the medal and stuffs it in a pants pocket.

"You don't sound very excited about your award."

"Two young men died."

"Yes, they did."

He waits for her to continue, but she remains standing in front of him, looking smart in her black wool dress and black wide-brimmed bucket hat.

Finally, she says, "They were shot, Lieutenant."

He's suddenly concerned about her tone and where this conversation is headed.

"From behind," she adds.

"Where'd you hear that?"

"I have my sources."

"Well, you'd better find yourself some reliable sources."

"Is that right?"

Jake peers at his watch.

"You have to be somewhere, Lieutenant?"

"As a matter of fact, I do. So if you'll excuse me, Miss Dawson."

"I'll buy you dinner," she says.

"Huh?"

"At Murray's. Say six o'clock."

"Well, I—"

"Do you have plans?"

"Not exactly."

"I'll see you at six."

Jake's eyes linger on her as she exits City Hall.

*   *   *

Nick Cole is waiting under a cloudy sky as Kate Dawson leaves the building. "Hello, Katie."

She stops, surprised, and looks both ways, as if searching for a way around him. Then she straightens her back, composes her expression, and says, "Hello, Nicky."

Nick has a speech all prepared, but it's suddenly gone all to hell as he stands in front of the woman he loves, heart pounding, like an actor who's forgotten his lines. "I made Homicide," he blurts.

"Congratulations."

"It's more pay."

Kate shakes her head slowly. "It was never about the money."

"But now I can afford to . . ." Nick pauses.

"Take care of me?"

"Not what I was going to say."

"'Course it was. Why is your career more important than mine?"

"Listen to yourself, Katie. You're not making any sense. I know you love me. We love each other. We should get married and have a family."

"And I'll be the understanding woman tending to the children, waiting for her man to come home, never knowing if it'll be in a body bag."

Close to desperation, Nick steps forward and grabs her by the shoulders, maybe a little too roughly. "Katie, please!"

"You're hurting me, Nick."

He backs off quickly. "Sorry. I didn't mean—"

"Listen to me, Nicky." She steels herself. "It's just not enough."

Nick is stunned and takes a step back.

"I'm sorry. I really am." Kate steps around him, brushes a tear off her cheek, and strides down the street.

Nick hopes that she'll look back, that she'll change her mind, that she'll realize she's made the biggest mistake of her life. He's still hoping when a streetcar bell chimes, Kate steps aboard, and the streetcar rolls away.

Chapter 14

Jake arrives at Murray's Restaurant fifteen minutes before 6:00 p.m. He gives his overcoat and fedora to the hat check girl, follows the hostess to a booth, and orders a soda water with a lime. While he waits, he lights up a cigarette. This meeting with Kate Dawson isn't a date. She's buying him dinner, so what does she want?

When a waitress brings his drink, Jake swallows some soda water and thinks of Nick Cole again. He's still upset with Avery Arnold for sticking him with Cole. Outside of their brief partnership at the Persian Palms and their short conversation at the Flame, Jake doesn't know the guy. He'll press Kate Dawson to learn more about the young detective.

She arrives ten minutes late. The hostess leads her toward Jake's booth. She's wearing a slim-fitting emerald green velvet cocktail dress that accentuates her auburn hair and hazel eyes.

"Sorry I'm late," she says, sliding into the booth. "Traffic was heavy. The streetcars slow up everything."

A waitress appears. Kate says, "Vodka martini, please. Dry. Straight up, with an olive."

Jake nods at his cocktail glass. "Another soda and lime on the rocks."

"Thanks for coming," Kate says as the waitress departs.

"Anything for a free meal."

She gives him a tight smile.

Jake takes a drag on his cigarette and lets out a smoke-filled breath. "No sense of humor, huh?"

"I have a wonderful sense of humor, Lieutenant. When something strikes me as funny."

"Look, Miss Dawson, you invited me here because you want something."

"What if I do?"

"The sooner you get to it, the sooner we can be on our way."

A thin vertical line appears between her eyebrows as she scowls at him. "Gonna make this difficult, are you?"

"I don't like to be played."

She smiles. "So much for the polite dinner conversation, huh?"

Jake shrugs. "Classy women like you don't generally ask out men like me."

"No need to sulk about it."

Jake shrugs. "I got over that a long time ago, lady."

When the waitress reappears with their fresh drinks, Kate orders the double Silver Butter Knife Sirloin steak for the two of them.

"That's over eight dollars," Jake says.

"I can afford it."

"Not on your salary."

"My father has an open tab at many of the restaurants in town."

Jake knows that her father is Paul Dawson, senior partner in the second largest law firm in the cities. "He the reason you wanted to be a lawyer?"

Kate shakes her head. "He never forced me to study law. In fact, he advised against it. He thinks I can be a bit headstrong at times."

"I'll bet."

Kate offers a little smile and sips her martini. "Only child?"

"Yes," she says. "Why?"

"I'm guessing you're used to having your way."

"I wasn't given everything, Lieutenant. I had to earn it. I completed my BA at the University of Minnesota in political science and received my law degree from the St. Paul College of Law, graduating summa cum laude. My bar exam score was the highest in the state that year."

"That supposed to impress me?"

"Scare you."

"I'm armed."

"Maybe I am, too."

"Now that scares me."

"You don't think a woman can handle a gun?"

"My sister sure could."

Kate raises her glass. "Here's to your sister."

"Why not work in your father's law firm? Why the first female lawyer in the DA's office?"

"Too easy. Plus, I'd have other problems in his firm."

"Nepotism as well as your sex."

"You're quick on the uptake, Lieutenant—for a man."

"I didn't just crawl out from under a rock."

"Unlike many of your colleagues."

"Your father could protect you."

"Do I look like I need protection?"

"Woman like you. Someone's going to be looking out for you, whether you like it or not."

"I don't need a man to protect me."

"That why you broke off your relationship with Nick Cole?"

"Why bring up Nicky?"

"He's my new partner."

Her jaw drops. "As of when?"

"Yesterday."

"Nicky always wanted Homicide."

"Cole is the boy wonder of the department, but the guys resent him."

"How come?"

"It's more his veteran status rather than his personality. Vets get preferential treatment when it comes to promotions. Older officers don't like that he cut in line."

"Makes sense," she says. "Did you enlist?"

"Navy. Shore Patrol. They gave me a uniform, a baton, and law enforcement training I already had. Spent most of my time riding back and forth between cities, looking at leave passes and making sure sailors, Marines, and Coast Guardsmen on liberty didn't get out of hand."

"So," she says, setting her glass down and folding her hands on the table. "What's your story, Cafferty?"

"Not much to tell," Jake says, crushing out his cigarette in the ashtray on the table. "Good Catholic boy raised in Hibbing, Minnesota. Parents emigrated there from Ireland when the iron ore industry started booming at the turn of the century. My father worked in the mines. I was fourteen when my sister, Lorna, married and moved east to New York with her husband, a banker. She still lives there. Haven't seen her in quite a few years. My older brother, Ethan, was killed during the Normandy invasion."

"I'm sorry," Kate says.

"I'm sorry, too."

"So how does a good Irish Catholic boy get a Jewish name like Jacob?"

"My name isn't Jacob. It's John. Parents called me Jack. Friends called me Jake. I liked Jake, so I stuck with it. Sort of a pet name, like Nicky."

She gives him a little smile and says, "Nicky distinguished himself in the war."

"Tell me about him," Jake says.

"Why don't you ask Nicky?"

"I'd like to hear your take first."

"He doesn't talk much about his past."

"Any idea why?"

"Maybe it wasn't all sunshine and rainbows."

"Did Cole go to college?"

She nods. "Used the GI Bill to attend classes at the University of Minnesota while he worked for the MPD. Got his degree in political science a year ago."

"Sounds like a man on a mission. So why break up with him?"

"Did he tell you I broke up with him?"

"Not in so many words. But when he saw you at the Flame the other night, I could tell he still has the hots for you. And he was jealous you were with the DA."

Kate tries to suppress a smile. "Really?"

"You seem pleased to hear that."

"Nice to know he still has feelings for me."

"What about you?"

"I like Nicky."

Jake smirks. "You must've hurt him. Bad."

"We hurt each other."

"How?"

"I don't think that's any of your business, Lieutenant."

"So what do you want, Miss Dawson?"

The waitress arrives with their dinners. "Anything else?" she asks.

Jake shakes his head.

The waitress looks at Kate. "Miss?"

"I'm fine."

As the waitress leaves, Jake tries cutting his steak with his butter knife. "Hey," he says. "You *can* cut it with a butter knife." Jake tastes his steak. *Delicious.*

"You were skeptical, huh?"

"Comes with the job."

Kate leans forward. "Then you must have doubts about how the Roths were killed. The way the department is smoothing it over."

"Not in the least. They were shot."

"In the back."

Jake pauses for a moment, his fork halfway between his mouth and plate. He's not sure if he should go with a standard response, or let her know how he really feels about the deaths of Ben and Davy Roth. Then he recalls what Avery Arnold told him yesterday. Anything other than a standard response might pique Kate Dawson's interest in the shootings. And given that she works for the DA, his choice is a no-brainer. "Who says?"

"The Jewish Council, for one."

"Speculation."

"Have you seen the autopsy report?"

Jake looks at her for a time, trying to read her face. "Hasn't been released to the public yet."

"You wouldn't lie to me, Lieutenant."

"Sure I would." Jake washes down a piece of steak with a swallow of club soda. "I don't know you from Adam."

They eat in uncomfortable silence for a time before Kate says, "Look, Lieutenant, if you know something about the deaths of Ben and Davy Roth, it's your duty, your . . . obligation to come forward."

"My obligation was to find the perpetrators who killed Joe Briggs. I found them. I would've preferred that they stood trial for their crime, but it wasn't my call."

"Mike Bannister has a terrible reputation."

"You wouldn't be gunning for Bannister because of what happened in the abortion trial?"

"How do you know that?"

"Speculation."

"*Touché*, Lieutenant."

112

"What does Bannister's reputation have to do with the shooting?"

Her hazel eyes stay with Jake's. "I believe you know."

"And why is that?"

"Your reputation as a detective."

"Don't believe everything you hear, Miss Dawson."

Kate's face flushes as she tries a smile. "What do you mean?"

Jake raises his glass. "You know I'm an alcoholic. I've never worked a major case as the lead detective—"

"Until now."

Jake takes a long swallow of soda water. "Kind of strange, isn't it? Why would I get assigned this case?"

"Because the department wants it solved. And you've done that. Congratulations."

Jake finishes his steak and wipes his mouth with a napkin. "Anything else?"

"The Roths. You haven't answered my question."

"Sure I have. You haven't been listening."

"Now is your chance to make a difference, Lieutenant. You might never have the chance again."

"A lot can happen between now and never, Miss Dawson. Thank you for dinner." Jake slides out of the booth and heads for the coat check.

*   *   *

Jake's dinner conversation with Kate Dawson is running through his head like a phonograph needle stuck in a record groove as he leaves Murray's Restaurant. It bothers him that he hasn't been truthful with her, but it bothers him more that he can't act on his suspicion that Mike Bannister murdered the Roths. Well, if he's being honest with himself, *can't* is the wrong choice of words. *Won't* is a better choice. He doubts Kate

Dawson is the only one in the DA's office aware of the cover-up. Jake wonders if she's willing to risk antagonizing Wilson Barlow in an attempt to further her legal career. *That's why she came to me,* Jake thinks. *The brass and the DA are sitting on this. If I continue with the investigation against orders, then I'm the one who'll take the fall if things go south.*

Wind swirls through the alleys along Hennepin Avenue, scattering debris, as Jake lights up a smoke and heads toward Max Hayes' office. Traffic is heavy, and he can hear the sound of streetcar bells and the occasional honking of horns. The odor of car exhaust fumes hangs in the cool, neon-lit air.

The overhead lights in Max Hayes' office are off. The window blinds are closed. Jake opens the door, hits a switch on the wall, and calls out Max's name.

No answer.

Something's wrong.

Jake doubts Max has forgotten they're going to the Millers game this evening, or that he would leave the office door unlocked if he left. Jake heads for the copy room, where his stomach suddenly twists in a tight knot.

Max Hayes is sprawled on his back on the floor in front of the mimeograph machine, arms outflung and legs fully extended. Blood leaks from his misaligned nose and swollen lips and is spattered on his white shirt. His cheeks are bruised and red. His wire glasses lay next to him on the floor. Both lenses are cracked.

Jake kneels beside Max. "Can you hear me, Max?"

Max's eyes blink open. He mumbles something unintelligible.

Jake hands him a handkerchief and rolls him on his side to keep the blood out of his throat. Then he grabs the desk phone and calls for an ambulance. As he hangs up, he spots the drop of blood on a crumpled sheet of paper in the wastebasket.

Chapter 15

Seething, Jake stands near the door to the private room in Minneapolis General, where Max Hayes lies on a bed with bandages covering his broken nose. An emergency room doctor has reset Max's nose and advised Jake to keep Max in the hospital overnight for observation because of a possible concussion.

Sarah Weisman, Max's girlfriend, hovers beside the bed, holding Max's hand. Underneath her belted white box coat, she's wearing a blue, knee-length wrap dress. Her raven hair is worn in a bouffant hairstyle, and her face already has a few fine lines. Jake knows she's older than Max. Maybe in her early thirties. She works for the Minnesota Jewish Council. He suspects she has Communist leanings.

"How you feeling?" Sarah asks, stroking Max's forehead.

"Like I was hit by a truck," he mumbles.

"Are you in any pain?"

"Doc has me pretty drugged up."

"Who did this to you, Max?" Jake demands.

"Let him rest, Jake," Sarah says with more concern than anger in her voice. Her dark brown eyes glisten with tears.

"It's okay," Max says, squeezing her hand. He thinks about Jake's question, then responds, "I don't know who did it."

"You didn't recognize the person or persons?"

Max shakes his head.

"My God," Sarah says.

Jake walks around to the opposite side of the bed from her. "Doc said he might have some dizzy spells for a time."

Sarah peers down at Max. "But you will get better, right?"

Max, seeing the concerned look on her face, nods.

Her dark eyes look up at Jake. "Maybe it was because of the protest."

"What protest?" Jake says.

Sarah exhales. "This afternoon some of us from the Jewish Council were protesting at City Hall."

"About what?"

"Redlining and restrictive covenants. There were men and women taunting us in front of the courthouse. They weren't happy with our signs and protest. One or more of them could've attacked Max in his office. It's not like his face and name aren't known."

"It's possible," Jake says. "But while waiting for the ambulance, I found this." He hands Sarah the crumpled article. She reads it and hands it to Max.

An unidentified group of stockholders hoping to fire President Charles Green and name a new set of directors now holds enough votes to control the Twin City Rapid Transit Company. The group is demanding that the company call a special stockholders' meeting between ten and sixty days, as mandated by state law. The names of the new stockholders who purchased the 19,200 shares of trolley common stock that Green sold have not been revealed. A spokesperson for the unidentified group maintains they are all business or professional men, and not "questionable characters" as Green reported. Green claims he sold his stock to the chairman of the board of directors in the belief the chairman was buying it for Detroit investors. Instead, Green asserted, the stock was transferred to Fred Ossanna and then came into the hands of persons having questionable characters.

Jake isn't sure what, if anything, the TCRT Company and its stockholders have to do with Max's beating. But it's all he has to work with.

Max studies the article and then searches Jake's face. "Where'd you find it?"

"In a wastebasket beside the mimeograph machine. Did you type it?"

"Yeah."

"What do you know about Charles Green and Fred Ossanna?"

Max closes his eyes.

"Don't go to sleep," Sarah says, her voice rising.

Max offers a crooked smile. "I'm thinking." He opens his eyes and focuses on Jake. "Charles Green is a wealthy New York stock promoter. He came to Minneapolis in '48 and bought six thousand shares of Twin City Rapid Transit stock, figuring to make a sizeable profit. Then he found out the TCRT was losing money. So he hired Fred Ossanna to help him take control of the company, which they did in '49."

"Ossanna has a criminal law practice," Jake says.

Max nods. "But he also lobbies for the mob-controlled liquor business in town. He owns office buildings, an expensive house in Florida, and a hundred-acre Minnesota estate." Max pauses and closes his eyes for a moment. "Still a little groggy."

"Take your time," Jake says.

Max smiles and continues. "Ossanna ran for mayor of Minneapolis in '27 but lost. He still has considerable influence on Minnesota politics." Max gestures for the water pitcher. "Pour me a cup of water, would you, Sarah?"

She obliges.

Max sits up, sips some water through a straw, and then lies back again. "Green knew nothing about transit. He was in it strictly to make a profit. So he quit rehabbing equipment and nearly all track maintenance. He cut schedules, hundreds of employees, and eliminated routes that weren't profitable. Then he threatened to cut service to St. Paul altogether, making enemies on Minneapolis and St. Paul city councils, and the local papers."

"Why would Green or Ossanna send someone to beat you up?"

"We don't know that they did."

"Someone is upset enough with you to rough you up. What else are you working on?"

Max shakes his head. "Nothing really, but . . ."

"What?"

Max squints and rubs his forehead. "Head feels as soft as a pumpkin. And I've got a helluva headache."

"You want me to get a nurse?" Sarah asks.

"No. I'm fine. Give me a minute." Finally, Max says, "You know who Leonard Lindquist is?"

Jake thinks. "He's chairman of the State Railroad and Warehouse Commission. They regulate telephone, railroad and truck rates, and supervise public warehouses."

"Right. Lindquist is investigating ownership of TCRT Company. Green says he won't talk to the press, but he'll cooperate with Lindquist and welcomes an investigation by the Senate Committee on Organized Crime."

"I'll bet he does. What do you know about Lindquist?"

"He graduated from the University of Minnesota law school and served in the Navy during World War II. Started his law firm in '46. Has a wife and two sons. By all accounts, he's clean and a man with political ambitions."

"You think organized crime has made inroads into the TCRT Company?"

"It's possible."

"For what ends?"

"Not sure."

Jake considers his next question before asking it. "Maybe you ought to think about selling the paper."

"Can't do that, Jake."

"Well, at least quit writing editorials about the corruption in this city and the mistreatment of Jews."

"Not what my dad would do."

"He'd want you to stay alive."

Max thinks on it. "You don't have to keep making amends, Jake."

"Is that what I'm doing?"

"Not your fault my father was murdered."

Jake wants to say, "We did the best we could to find the perp who killed him," but he believes the department didn't go out of its way to solve the crime. To the department and most of the city's leaders at that time, Arthur Hayes was just another muckraking Jew who signed his own death warrant.

"Quit worrying, Jake. I'll be fine."

"You don't look so fine. This time it was a beating. What's it going to be next time? A bullet like the one that killed your father?"

Sarah gasps.

Max takes her hand to reassure her. Then he says to Jake, "If that ever happens, you won't be responsible."

*   *   *

Jake drives home, strips off his suit, and sleeps in his underwear for a solid six hours, waking at nine a.m. to the sound of rain beating hard against the windows. He sits up in bed, lights a cigarette, and gets Leonard Lindquist's home phone number from the operator, figuring Lindquist won't be working on Saturday.

Lindquist's wife answers the phone. Jake identifies himself, assures her it's not an emergency, and asks to speak to her husband. It takes a minute before Lindquist picks up the phone.

Jake tells him he's interested in information on the TCRT Company. Lindquist says he can spare an hour before his luncheon appointment at one. So Jake dresses and fixes a pot of coffee. After a pan of scrambled eggs and bacon, he grabs his hat and raincoat and heads for Leonard Lindquist's house, a Lowry Hill Tudor near Lake of the Isles and Kenwood Park.

Jake finds it ironic that Leonard Lindquist lives on Lowry Hill, a neighborhood named after the late nineteenth-century real estate magnate and trolley tycoon Thomas Lowry. Lowry was once head of the Minneapolis Street Railway Co., which became part of the Twin City Rapid Transit Co. Lowry's son, Horace, later became president of the TCRT until his death in '31.

Leonard Lindquist opens the door. He wears a white shirt, a black tie, and a black business suit cut to fit his trim frame. He leads Jake through a large foyer under a crystal chandelier, down a wide hallway, and into a dark wooded study at the back of the house.

Jake sits on a thick leather couch in front of the fireplace.

"Something to drink, Detective?"

"I'm fine."

Lindquist sits in a heavy leather chair opposite Jake with his legs crossed and lights up a pipe with a small gold-plated lighter.

Jake scans the study. Shelves filled with thick books, oil paintings on the wall, Oriental rugs on the hardwood floor, a Swedish flag in a glass-framed case above a marble fireplace, and a well-stocked bar. "You've done well for yourself, Mr. Lindquist."

"My father died when I was fifteen. I came up hard, riding freight trains to Montana and Washington looking for work. The value of hard work and giving back to the community comes with being raised Methodist. The law isn't just about making money."

Coming from most fat cats Jake has met in his years as a cop, Lindquist's words would've rung hollow. But from Lindquist it comes off as real.

Lindquist puffs on his pipe and asks with a turn of his head, "Why are you interested in the TCRT Company, Lieutenant?"

Jake looks Lindquist directly in the eyes. "It might have something to do with an investigation."

"I see."

"Do you think certain members of organized crime might be trying to take control of the company?"

"Oh, I believe they already have, Lieutenant. Problem is, brokers are holding large blocks of stock, but the true owners are not listed in the company's offices."

"Can you prove it?"

"One Minneapolis brokerage firm has agreed to furnish the names and addresses of customers now owning common and preferred stock in the company. I had originally sought this data for a three-year period, but now I'm requesting this information only for the period since August 1949."

"Why is that?" Jake asks.

"It covers the time period when Charles Green sold his stock."

"You said *one* Minneapolis brokerage firm has agreed to furnish the names and addresses."

"Five other firms said they wouldn't furnish stock information unless ordered by the courts. I've informed them that I'll prepare subpoenas if they continue to resist."

"So why would organized crime want to take over the TCRT?"

"I suspect they intend to sell off the company," Lindquist says.

"But if it's losing money, what's the angle?"

"The Korean War has driven up the price of steel. The buyers probably intend to dismantle the streetcars and rail and sell off the steel."

"Which is why they don't want their names known."

Lindquist nods and draws on his pipe. "But what does any of this have to do with your investigation?"

"I don't know for sure, Mr. Lindquist. I'll need more time to figure it out."

Chapter 16

Jake spots the four-door light green Cadillac as he's leaving Leonard Lindquist's home. The expensive ride is parked three cars behind Jake's Ford. It's in Jake's rearview as he drives along Lake of the Isles Parkway. He coasts to the curb and cuts the engine. The Cadillac Sixty Special does the same.

Jake gets out of the Ford. The rain has stopped, leaving a layer of gray covering the sky. The air smells of fish, peat, and silt. Jake walks toward the Caddy. Jack Apple, Kid Cann's enforcer, is sitting in the driver's seat, both hands on the wheel. Jake notes the bruises on his knuckles. Apple stares at Jake a moment and then hits a button and the driver's window slides down, a convenience Jake has seen in some newer and fancier cars. Kid Cann is seated on the passenger side of the back seat.

Jake rests his forearms on the car roof and looks down into the dark well of Jack Apple's eyes. "What's with the tail?"

Apple tilts his head toward the Kid.

Cann's lips twitch in a half-smile as he opens the back door and gets out. He's wearing a brown trench coat and fedora. There's a small paper bag in one hand.

"What's in the bag?" Jake asks.

Cann smiles. "It ain't a piece." He opens the bag and tosses breadcrumbs toward a gaggle of geese. "Let's walk, Jake."

As they head for the lake, Jake says, "I don't like being tailed."

Cann jerks his thumb. "Look behind you."

"I'm not talking about geese."

"Who says I'm not house hunting?"

"Good luck with that."

Cann stops and looks up at Jake. "You don't think I can buy around here?" he says with a wave of his arm.

"You don't either, Kid."

"I don't like you calling me that."

Jake shrugs.

"You disrespect me, Jake, yet you expect me to answer your questions."

"You know how things work in this town."

"I know how they *used* to work."

Jake gazes at the lake and then lets his eyes settle on Cann. The Kid has aged considerably in the last few years.

Jake first met Isadore Blumenfeld back in '35 when he was a uniform making $212 a month working the graveyard shift from 12:00 a.m. to 8:00 a.m. on the north side of Minneapolis. Blumenfeld had just been accused of killing journalist Walter Liggett. But Jake had heard of Blumenfeld long before he met him.

Just after the turn of the century, Blumenfeld and his parents and five siblings moved into a Romanian community of crowded, dirty tenements and unskilled laborers in the Phillips and Cedar-Riverside neighborhood. He dropped out of school at fifteen while *still* in fifth grade and sold newspapers downtown on Newspaper Row. He brought prostitutes coffee for tips and resold streetcar transfers that riders dropped on the ground. He was arrested twice at nineteen, once for being in a disorderly house and again for pickpocketing.

By the time he was twenty-four, he was known around town as Kid Cann. In April of that year, Cann got into a fight with two other men over a woman. One of the men pulled a gun. Cann wrestled it away from him. A bystander intervened and was shot. Cann was left holding the gun. He told cops it was an accident. The wounded man died nine days later. Floyd B. Olson was the Hennepin County DA at the time. Olson, who would later become governor, had grown up in north Minneapolis with the Kid and many of his associates. The murder was ruled an accident.

Cann and his brothers, Harry and Yiddy, soon changed their surname from Blumenfeld to Bloom and launched a Prohibition bootlegging operation known as the Syndicate. By 1927, they were buying industrial alcohol though a barber supply outfit they owned called La Pompadour and selling Minnesota 13—a high-quality 139-proof corn liquor moonshine distilled on Stearns County farms—to the Chicago Outfit led by Al Capone for ten bucks a gallon. The Syndicate also smuggled whiskey down from Canada and up from the Gulf of Mexico. They were soon in control of bootlegging, prostitution, and labor racketeering in Minneapolis, with close ties to the Genovese crime family in New York City.

The Kid was charged with operating a still in 1933. Prohibition was repealed in December of '33, just a few months before his sentencing. Cann spent a year in the Hennepin County workhouse. While he served his time, his associates took control of the Minneapolis liquor license office through bribes and payoffs. When Cann was released in '35, no one in the off-sale liquor business could sell booze without the Syndicate's okay. La Pompadour Barber became Chesapeake Brands Liquors, where Cann claimed he was employed as a salesman.

Now Jake believes that Cann is in charge of the entire liquor industry in Minneapolis and that the Syndicate is receiving a kickback of five to twenty grand for every license sold, despite the fact that Cann's criminal record prohibits him from owning a single license.

"Why the visit to see Leonard Lindquist?" Cann asks as they stroll through the park.

"None of your business."

Cann tosses more breadcrumbs to the gaggle of geese behind them, which has doubled in size. "Everything in this town is my business, Jake."

"Like the TCRT?"

Cann sighs. "That what you and Lindquist were talking about?"

"Why the interest?"

"I'm a businessman, Jake. I see an opportunity, I take advantage of it." Cann tosses more breadcrumbs at the honking geese and the quacking ducks that have joined them.

"Suppose you don't know anything about Max Hayes' beating?"

"Who's Max Hayes?"

Jake stops and faces Cann. "You know damn well who he is, Kid. Want to tell me how your boy Jack Apple got those bruises on his knuckles?"

"Sure. Someone who owed me money was delinquent."

"Listen to me, Kid. Stay away from Max Hayes. Anything happens to him, I'll come looking for you."

"Then you'd be looking in the wrong place." Cann tosses the last of the breadcrumbs and then the crumpled bag and heads for his car.

* * *

That afternoon Kate Dawson takes the elevator to the Oak Grill on the 12th floor of Dayton's, the largest department store in Minneapolis. The Oak Grill features dark paneling, dim lights, heavy furniture, an intricately carved oak fireplace, and a cigars-and-brandy ambience.

The short, bald-headed *maître d'* smiles at Kate and says, "You must be looking for the Sky Room on this floor, miss. It's the restaurant for the ladies and has a wonderful view of the city through the floor-to-ceiling windows."

Condescending little prick. It's a strict code that men must accompany all women in the Oak Grill. Kate clears her throat. With a tight smile she says, "I'm meeting my father here, little man."

The *maître d'* adjusts his glasses. "I see. And who might he be?"

"*He* might be Paul Dawson."

The *maître d'*s face reddens. "Ah, yes. Mr. Dawson. One of our best customers." He scans the reservation list and tries a warmer smile.

"Did someone call my name?"

Kate turns and sees her father approaching. With his dark hair, graying at the sideburns and temples, and his pinstriped suit from his favorite men's store, Hubert W. White's on Marquette Avenue, he cuts a striking figure here and in the courtroom. Kate is nearly as tall as her father. Her auburn hair is darker than her mother's. And thank God she doesn't have her mother's freckles.

"Katherine," her father says, giving her a light peck on the cheek.

The *maître d'* holds up two menus. "Right this way, Mr. Dawson."

Kate follows the two men to a table near the flickering three-hundred-year-old fireplace that was shipped from England specifically for this room when it was created in the 1947 Dayton's expansion. Kate sits down. She's the only woman in the room.

The *maître d'* hands her a menu. Her father waves his away. "Tell the waiter I'll have the almond-crusted walleye, Sidney, with a popover."

"Excellent choice, sir."

"And a dry martini."

"Of course." He looks at Kate.

She quickly scans the menu. "I'll have the wild rice soup."

"Something to drink?"

"Coffee. Black."

The *maître d'* collects her menu and glides away.

"Well, Katherine," her father says with a grin.

She hates it when he calls her that, not so much because she dislikes her given name, but because he's always treated her formally, as if she were a distant relative rather than his only child.

"I'm happy that you joined me," he continues. "We haven't seen much of you lately. Your mother and I miss you."

"I've been busy."

"Yes, I heard."

She hears the disappointment in his voice. "The Morals Squad messed up. If they'd done their job correctly, I wouldn't have lost the case."

"Perhaps you shouldn't have taken it."

"What was I supposed to do? Wilson gave it to me. I couldn't turn it down."

"Yes, he did, didn't he?"

"What does that mean?"

"Nothing," her father says with a shrug.

Kate bites her lip as she recalls the sting of losing her first and only case.

"You seem a bit tense."

She lets out a breath. "I can handle the job, Father."

"Of course you can. You're driven. It's a family trait. Ever since you were a child, you never liked coming in second. Whether it was swimming or academics." He leans forward. "But the door is always open if you'd like to come work with me."

"We've been through this before."

"You'd be making considerably more money in corporate law than as a county prosecutor."

"It's not just about the money."

"Easy to say when you're young and hungry. And I don't mean that in a literal sense. If you ever need anything, Mother and I are here to help."

She nods her head without comment, having heard the offer too many times before.

"But there are . . . sacrifices you'll have to make as a prosecuting attorney," her father continues. "Sacrifices beyond the obvious financial ones."

"I'm prepared to make them."

"I hope so. Are you still dating the police officer, Nate?"

"His name is Nick. And no, I'm not."

"Was that your decision?"

"That's not important, but yes, it was."

"It's probably for the best."

"Why do you say that?"

"He's a . . . policeman."

"So?"

"You know what goes on in this city, Katherine."

"Nick isn't on the take."

"How do you know?"

"Because I know."

"Just because he's a war hero, that doesn't make him a good cop."

"And it doesn't make him a bad one either."

"Point taken."

Kate considers the next question before asking it. "What do you know about Lieutenant Jake Cafferty?"

"Why are you interested in him?"

"Indulge me, Father. Tell me what you know."

"Cafferty worked with Russ Krueger."

"Tell me something I don't know."

"I mentioned it because Krueger was clean compared to most of the department. Some of that rubbed off on Cafferty. But now that Krueger has retired, who knows which way he'll go? In the past, Cafferty's been known to . . . look the other way. He's also an alcoholic."

"He doesn't drink now."

"That you know about."

"He drank club soda when we had dinner."

"Is that why you broke it off with Nate?"

"Do you do that deliberately?"

"What?"

"You know what I'm talking about."

"All right. His name is Nick. You're not dating Cafferty now, are you?"

"What if I was?"

"For God's sake, Katherine. He must be twenty years older than you. Your mother would have a heart attack."

"What about you?"

"Well, I certainly wouldn't approve, knowing his history."

"We're not dating."

"Then why the dinner?"

"Information."

"About what?"

"About a case I'm interested in."

The waiter arrives with the black coffee and dry martini. When he departs, her father says, "What case are you talking about?"

"The cornfield killings."

Her father leans forward. "Leave it alone, Katherine."

"What have you heard, Father?"

"Nothing that you haven't heard."

"Everyone knows Mike Bannister is crooked. What if he murdered those young men?"

"You don't know that."

"Why are all the men in this town so afraid of the truth?"

"Nonsense."

"It's far more than that."

He nods his head as if coming to a decision. "If you do this, Katherine, there's no turning back. You'll have to go all the way. Are you prepared to do that?"

"If that's what it takes, yes."

"You were a resourceful child. Remember your Houdini phase."

Kate smiles at the memory. "It wasn't Houdini's magic so much as his ability to escape from seemingly impossible situations."

"Magic can't help you now. Be careful with Wilson Barlow."

"Meaning?"

"All I'm saying is, be careful what you ask for."

"The abortion case," she says.

Her father's hazel eyes stay locked on hers, but he offers no response.

"Wilson knew I wanted that case. He gave it to me."

"Yes, he did."

"He gave the case to me knowing full well that the MPD had entrapped the woman. I had no chance of winning it, did I?"

Her father shakes his head.

His self-contained manner upsets her even more now. "You knew that and didn't tell me?"

"I didn't know it at the time."

Kate sweeps the room with a hand. "Always the men's club."

"Wilson Barlow hired you, Katherine, knowing full well that you'd be the first woman in the DA's office."

Kate has always wondered if she got the job because Barlow has the hots for her or because of her father's reputation. Discussing the first issue with her father would be uncomfortable. She sticks with the second. "Maybe you pressured Wilson into hiring me."

"I did no such thing."

Kate stares at him for a time. She's relieved when she sees no indication that he's lying. "Then why did Wilson sandbag me?"

"I never said that."

"You don't have to."

Chapter 17

Later that afternoon Jake drives to City Hall and walks over to the Fraud/Theft Division.

"What's the shake, Jake?" Detective Frank Morris says with a smile. It's his standard opening line every time he sees Jake. Morris sprawls in a chair, feet on his desk, ankles crossed, fingers laced behind his balding head.

"Brazama Gold."

Morris chuckles.

"Wanna clue me in?"

"Zeno Malkin," Morris says.

Jake takes the empty hardback chair in front of the desk. "Give me the skinny."

Morris plants his feet on the floor, opens the file cabinet behind him, and gives a thick manila folder a yank. He plops the folder on the desk. "Zeno Malkin," he mutters under his breath as he opens it, peruses the first three pages, and then lifts his gaze, so that his hooded brown eyes are the same level as Jake's.

"Zeno Malkin is the son of a shoe salesman and a school nurse and spent the first twenty-nine years of his life with his nose pressed up against the glass. He managed two years at the U of M before he decided he'd had enough. When he turned thirty, he married Shirley Ginsberg, the unmarriageable daughter of an immigrant junk dealer who'd made his fortune when World War II sent the price of scrap metal to the moon."

"Like what's happening now with Korea," Jake says.

Morris nods and continues. "The marriage gave him access to all the money he'd ever need, but not the status. He craved the acceptance of what passed for celebrities in Minneapolis, the bluebloods and the jocks. When a beard was needed, Zeno was the designated hitter. If a payoff had to be made to a greedy pol, Zeno was the bagman. When a charity wanted a fat check, Zeno was happy to oblige. In return, some of the beautiful people accepted Zeno and Shirley's invitations, and a few reciprocated by inviting the Malkins.

"But Zeno is no fool. He knew there would only be scraps unless he could acquire some panache, so he hooked on as a salesman with one of Minneapolis' lesser stock brokerage firms, Bass, Sterns and Wheeler."

That's the firm where the late Martin Crenshaw worked before taking a dive off the Short Line Bridge, Jake thinks.

"Zeno was good at it," Morris continues. "A quick study who earned a piece of the action by snaring a couple of dubious underwritings for the firm. Then he became an author. Or rather, he hired a ghost, and the ghost became the author and Zeno took the bows."

"Why a ghost?"

"He wanted the world to think he actually wrote it, and if you know anything about Malkin, I doubt he could have written *My Summer Vacation* by himself."

"Who's the ghost?"

Morris shakes his head. "Don't know. Anyway, to everyone's surprise, including Zeno's, *Malkin Money*, a loosely knit collection of business homilies and self-help advice, became a best seller. A not-quite-as-successful sequel was stamped out from the same mold, *Malkin the Falcon*. The books generated profitable spinoffs: speeches and motivational films. Zeno's stock brokerage business, which had been mostly a way for him to get out of the house in the morning, thrived in the wake of his celebrity."

"What about Brazama Gold?"

Morris leans back in his chair and plants his heels on the desk again. "Brazama Gold is a penny stock. Name is a combination of 'Brazil' and 'Amazon.' One day Zeno looks up the listing in the pink sheets, where all the brokers who deal in penny stocks list their companies. Brazama has one broker named Fitch & McGuire. They have a dozen of these penny stocks. Zeno goes to their shabby one-room office just off Hennepin Avenue. Fitch and McGuire are sitting around playing gin and waiting for the mail to come in so they can charge brokers, who buy and sell Brazama for their clients, a dime transfer fee for every ownership change on the stock. Zeno plops a bag on the desk. There's fifty thousand dollars cash in it and a clear sealed plastic tube about six inches around and a foot long filled with mud and water."

"A core sample?" Jake asks.

"Right. Zeno holds it up to the light so they can see the little flecks of gold in it. He says, 'A geologist friend of mine got this from your claim on the Amazon. If we can get a dredge upriver, the claim is worth gazillions. I'll give you fifty thousand dollars for an option to buy two million shares of the stock at a dollar a share.' The stock's selling a little higher than usual at the time, about twenty-five cents a share, and here's this guy offering to pay fifty large cash for the right to buy it at a buck. Must be something there. So they go for it. Send out a letter to their shareholders and explain the deal, with a picture of the dredge that looks like a giant cockroach with these cranes sprouting out of it in all directions. The stock goes up. Twenty-five cents. Fifty cents. Seventy-five cents. Zeno sends the Brazama boys the progress reports. They send out more letters to their shareholders. The barge is heading out of Miami down the coast. The barge has entered the mouth of the Amazon. The barge is heading up the tributary chopping its way to the claim. The stock gets to ninety cents. Bam; it turns around and goes down. Bam.

Bam. Bam. We're back where we started. The Brazama broker-age boys press Zeno. What happened? 'Well,' Zeno says,' we tried getting the barge up river, got all tangled up in the weeds, couldn't make it. Sorry. So I guess we won't be exercising our option. But you got fifty grand for your trouble.'"

"What's the hustle?" Jake asks.

"Zeno and a favored few buy the stock at up to twenty-five cents a share, just tons and tons of it. Makes his deal with the Brazama boys, who are clueless. Sells it on the way up at seventy-five cents for a three-bagger, and probably shorts it on the way down. The barge? Some old rust bucket they sent down there so nobody could say they didn't try. All perfectly legal unless we prove fraud, that Zeno never intended to dredge out the claim. The fifty grand for the option was just an expense, like the cost of the nuggets when you're salting a mine. Zeno probably cleared upwards of a million and left two or three hundred people holding the bag. Last I heard the stock was down to a nickel and the Brazilian government was expropriat-ing the claim for non-payment of taxes. The Brazama boys were telling their stockholders to write their congressman. Zeno's firm, however, saw through the whole scam and requested Zeno's letter of resignation. He quit and hung out his own shingle in an office in the Lumber Exchange building."

Jake wonders how much Joe Briggs lost on the Brazama Gold scam, and if he threatened Zeno. Could be a motive for Zeno to murder Briggs. Men have been murdered for far less.

*   *   *

In the Records and Identification section Jake pulls the file on Zeno Malkin. His rap sheet is short but informative. Malkin's been charged with paper hanging and playing the float, both check kiting schemes. Suspended sentences. Probation. No men-tion of Brazama Gold stock. Jake calls Zeno's office and speaks to Zeno's secretary, a grouchy-sounding woman who quickly changes her tune when Jake tells her he's a cop.

When Zeno picks up his phone, Jake asks for a meeting.

"Ah . . . what's this about?"

"I'll tell you when I get there."

"I'm a very busy man."

"Okay then, my office is in City Hall, Mr. Malkin. What time can you be here?"

"Well, I'd rather you come here."

"Fine. I'll be right over."

Jake hangs up and heads for the Lumber Exchange building at the intersection of Hennepin and South Fifth, across the street from the Masonic temple.

Zeno Malkin sits in a high-back leather chair behind a large roll-top desk in his sixth-floor office. He's a small, narrow-faced man with a receding hairline and dark hair styled in a sleek comb-over with a lot of Brylcreem to keep it in place. He's dressed in a dark double-breasted suit that seems too large for him, a white shirt, and a black tie. Behind him is a wall of windows with thick rounded arches offering a panoramic city view. A handful of books occupy a shelf against the brick wall to Jake's right. Near the wall to Jake's left are a large area rug, a couch with pillows, and a long coffee table.

"Detective," he says, coming around the desk. He offers a hand and a smile that shows off his small teeth. It's like shaking hands with a fish. Beads of sweat dot his brow. Malkin gestures toward the cushioned wingback chair in front of his desk. When they're both settled, Malkin says, "What's this about?"

"Joe Briggs. You heard about his murder."

"Of course. It's all over town. But how I can be of any help?"

"You sold Briggs some Brazama Gold stock."

Malkin shrugs. "What's that have to do with his death?"

"Brazama Gold was a scam, and Briggs lost money. Pissed him off."

Malkin clears his throat. "If he was, he never told me."

Jake ignores Malkin's response and continues. "Briggs comes to your office and threatens you. You're worried he might follow through on his threats, and you act first."

Malkin waves it all away. "That's preposterous. Besides, from what I've read and heard, Briggs was killed during a routine burglary. Money was stolen. Do I look like I need any money?"

Jake shifts direction. "What do you know about the TCRT stock and its owners?"

"I don't know anything about the company."

Jake notes the change in Malkin's expression and the sudden rise in the tone of his voice. He presses forward. "You know Charles Green or Fred Ossanna?"

"I may have met them at some time. But I certainly don't know them."

"What about the Kid?"

"Who?"

"You know who I'm talking about."

"I've never met Kid Cann. I don't hang out with hoodlums."

Jake doubts that. He'll ask around.

"How about the Brazama Gold scam?"

"That was not a scam."

"Investors like Briggs lost money."

"There are never any guarantees when it comes to stock. I'm sure Mr. Briggs was aware of the risks."

"But you came out of it okay."

"I lost fifty grand."

"And made a lot more."

"You have to spend money to make money."

"Spoken like a man who wasn't on the losing end of the deal."

* * *

That evening Zeno Malkin broods in the dark in the high-back leather chair behind his office desk. He holds a cold cocktail glass filled with Canadian Club whiskey and ice. He glances at his watch, notes the time is 9:15, and takes another sip of his drink. He's thinking that if he waits a bit longer his wife, Shirley, will be asleep when he arrives home. But what mostly occupies his thoughts is Jake Cafferty's visit this afternoon. Why is the detective still looking into Joe Briggs' death when two other Jews killed the sergeant? And why is Cafferty interested in the TCRT and its ownership?

Though Zeno tried to remain calm while Cafferty was in his office, after the detective left, he downed a full cocktail glass of whiskey to calm his nerves before placing a call. The nosy detective might have to be dealt with in the same manner that the muckraking journalist, Max Hayes, was dealt with. There's too much at stake to leave anything to chance.

His desk phone rings, startling him. *Who's calling me at this time of night?* He picks up the phone. "Hello?"

He receives no reply.

It's not a dead line. He senses the silence is alive. "Who's there?"

He listens for a moment longer and then hears a click.

Zeno places the phone back on the cradle and swallows the last of his drink. His heart pounds. His palms sweat. He pours another half glass from the bottle on his desk and drinks it in one gulp. He thinks he hears a noise in the hallway but dismisses it. Just nerves. Thanks to the goddamn detective. Then the sound of the elevator doors opening startles him. *Who's in the building this late besides me? Perhaps it's the janitor?*

He sets down his empty glass, gets out of his chair, and walks through his open office door, past his secretary's desk to a door that leads to the hallway, where he peers around the corner toward the elevator. Nothing. He checks the opposite direction with the same result before returning to his desk.

He stands gazing through one of the floor-to-ceiling windows at the skyline, a silhouette cutout backlit by bright lights. All his life he's wanted to be a force in the city, a member of the inner circle, but the true powerbrokers have always shut him out. So he's had to go his own way, form alliances with the men in the city that wield control through their shady enterprises. In a way, it's been more satisfying working behind the scenes to achieve his goal. Zeno smiles as he thinks about those he's screwed in the past and those he'll screw in the future. Zeno is still smiling when darkness folds around him like the wings of giant black bird, stifling his startled cry.

He claws at the couch pillow pressed against his face and at the hand that holds it. He's losing consciousness. He makes one last attempt to free himself from the vice-like grip, but the man behind him—and surely it has to be a man—is much too strong, and Zeno goes limp. He feels himself being lifted and thrown like a ragdoll. Glass shatters around him. Then nothing but air and falling, trapped in a nightmare from which he'll never wake up.

Part Two

"... Save me from curious Conscience, that still lords
Its strength for darkness, burrowing like a mole;
Turn the key deftly in oiled wards,
And seal the hushed Casket of my Soul."

—John Keats
"To Sleep"

Chapter 18

September 12, 1950

Nick Cole stands beside his new partner, Jake Cafferty, in Zeno Malkin's office, staring out a shattered window. The dawn sky is a pale violet. Malkin's sheet-covered body lies on the sidewalk six floors below. Crime scene personnel comb the office.

"If you were to commit murder, Cole, how would you do it?"

"The hell you talking about, Cafferty?"

"Humor me."

Nick shrugs. "Depends. If it was a random deal, you know, just for the thrill of it, I'd probably just pick up a hooker, do her with a piece of rope, and toss her in the bushes."

"But what if it were someone we could connect you with?"

"Then it gets a bit more complicated. Where you going with this?"

"Zeno Malkin might've had some assistance in taking the high dive out his office window. It'll be very hard to prove an accident. Forensics is no help. Body's a total mess. Smart lawyer can explain away every tiny scratch."

Nick points to the bottle of Canadian Club on Malkin's desk. "Maybe the booze gave him the courage."

"Could be."

Nick waits while Cafferty rubs his chin, deep in thought.

"I remember a case before the war," Cafferty says at last. "Sidney Cain. Big businessman. He moved into the Foshay

Tower when it was completed in '29. Art Deco architecture modeled after the Washington Monument. Beautiful. A few months later he's up in his lofty perch overlooking the river and the city, when the stock market goes belly up. Cain loses everything and decides to take the leap. But he can't get the damn window open. Finally, he fills up his briefcase with awards and the paperweights he keeps on his desk, knocks out a hole, and walks out the window, still holding the briefcase. When they find him on the sidewalk, he's on his back holding onto his pecker."

"And your point is?"

"Psych consultant says that's not unusual in these cases. Something about, it's the only thing they've got left to hang on-to."

"Sounds to me like an apocryphal story," Nick says.

Jake meets Nick's eyes but doesn't respond.

"That means made up," Nick adds.

"Not having a college degree doesn't make me stupid."

"I know. But Malkin wasn't holding onto anything. And he didn't leave a note. His secretary was gone. Office door was closed and locked. Building was locked."

"Zeno could've opened it to let someone in, or if it was open, they could've just walked in. Then the someone does him, locks the office door, and closes it behind them."

Nick recalls that the building super had to let them in. "You can only lock the office door from the outside. So no burglar trying unlocked doors. No break-in. If someone did Malkin, they locked the office door on the way out, making it look like a suicide. And what about getting into the building after hours? Someone had to have a key."

"Did Zeno's keys turn up?"

"He had them on him."

"Find out from his secretary if Zeno issued building or office keys to anyone else."

Nick makes a note. "Do you like anybody, Lieutenant?"

"Old joke: What's a gold mine? A hole in the ground with a liar on top."

Nick shakes his head. "I don't get it."

"One of Zeno's scams."

"Then we'll need to get a shareholders' list. See who the big losers were."

"Stockholders usually don't kill. They sue. But in this case, it might be worth the time. Any other ideas, Sergeant?"

"The usual. Wife. Girlfriend."

Jake shakes his head. "I don't like the ladies. Don't see them tossing a one-hundred-sixty-pound man through a window. But they could hire someone."

"Agreed."

"Anyone downstairs with security?"

"Night watchman. Old guy. Might've been asleep."

"The perp could've waited outside until the old guy went for a pee. Could've been sitting in the can. Talk with the night watchman. See if the old guy saw or heard anything."

"Motive?"

"If they knew Zeno," Jake says, "they had a motive."

* * *

While Cole talks with security and Zeno's secretary, Jake searches the office, stepping around the boys from the crime lab, and thinking about his conversation with Malkin just hours before concerning the Brazama Gold certificates and Joe Briggs' murder. Maybe Malkin murdered Briggs, and the scam artist decided to take a high dive out the window after Jake questioned him about it. But there's no physical evidence linking Malkin to Briggs' murder. And Malkin doesn't strike Jake as someone who'd carry a gun, much less coldly put a bullet through Briggs' head.

All of this is supposition on Jake's part. And if Arnold or Flanagan discovers that he's still investigating Briggs' murder after the department has publicly announced that the Roths were responsible, Jake could lose his job and his pension. He needs to keep his suspicions to himself.

Jake starts with the drawers in Malkin's office, then the cubbyholes in the desk, where he finds a title and deed for a company called Globe Enterprises in Las Vegas. Jake wonders what the company does and how and why Zeno owns it. He writes the company name in his notebook and moves to the bookshelf, on which are framed photos of Malkin with local and national celebrities. The only books on the shelf are copies of Malkin's books. Jake recalls that Frank Morris in Fraud/Theft believed that someone had "ghosted" the books. On the "Acknowledgments" page of *Malkin Money*, Jake reads a short list of Malkin's friends who inspired him to undertake his literary efforts, including George Mikan. One name jumps out, but it isn't the name of a basketball celebrity.

Franklin Simms.

Simms is the guy Mike Bannister was beating in the alley behind the Persian Palms. Jake checks the "Acknowledgments" page in Malkin's second book, *Malkin The Falcon*, where he again finds Simms' name.

*   *   *

Kate Dawson has been fuming ever since yesterday's lunch with her father, when she concluded that her boss, DA Wilson Barlow, had sandbagged her on the abortion case. She was tempted to confront Barlow when she returned to her City Hall office after lunch but changed her mind. She needed to cool down before saying something she'd regret. Now, the next morning, tired and irritable, she heads down the corridor for her scheduled meeting with Barlow in his office. She should have confronted him sooner. Didn't sleep much. Tossed and turned all night.

As Barlow's secretary ushers Kate into his office, she explains that the DA is in a meeting and will return shortly. Kate declines the offer of coffee or tea. When the door closes, she sits in a tall wingback chair in front of Barlow's big mahogany desk. Barlow's suit coat hangs over the back of his chair. Thick law books line the shelves of the floor-to-ceiling bookshelf to the right of the desk. To the left are three mahogany file cabinets. On the wall to Kate's right is a large framed photo of Governor Luther Youngdahl, and Barlow's framed college diploma and law degree from Harvard. Underneath the frames is a dark brown leather couch with a coffee table in front of it and two side tables with Tiffany lamps. Kate imagines having an office like this someday instead of the windowless, closet-size office she now occupies.

Suddenly aware that her right hand is nervously tapping the desk, she stands and walks to a window overlooking Fifth Street. Through the slats in the wood blinds she sees the blue sky littered with thin, ragged clouds, like pieces of torn paper. Has she made a mistake? Should she let this whole thing go? She turns away from the window and strides toward the door, reaching it just as it opens and Wilson Barlow walks in. They nearly collide.

Surprised and embarrassed, Kate steps back.

"Sorry," Barlow says. "The meeting lasted longer than I anticipated. Were you leaving?"

Kate thinks fast. "I was going to ask your secretary for a cup of coffee."

"Margaret," Barlow calls, "would you bring Miss Dawson a cup of coffee, please?"

"Black," Kate says.

Barlow gestures toward the couch to his right. "Let's sit."

After they're seated—closer than Kate is comfortable with —Margaret brings the coffee. Barlow waits for Margaret to close the door behind her before he says, "So, what did you want to see me about, Kate?" He rests his thick forearms on his knees as he leans forward, close enough that Kate can smell the strong odor of cigarette smoke on his clothes and in his thinning brown hair and walrus mustache.

Kate sips the coffee slowly, organizing her thoughts. Then she sets the cup on the table in front of her. "It's about the abortion trial."

Barlow pats Kate's thigh. "It was your first case. I'm sure you'll win the next."

If there is a next time, Kate thinks. "Why did you assign that case to me, Wilson?"

Barlow sits up and crosses his legs. "You needed the experience."

"Is that all?"

"I thought we had a winner."

"Did you?"

Barlow cocks his head. "What are you suggesting, Kate?"

She takes in a deep breath and exhales slowly. "I think you knew the defense had a strong case of entrapment. Yet you let me prosecute the doctor anyway."

"That's quite an accusation. Why would I do that?"

"I don't know why, Wilson. I'm asking."

"Well," he says with a shake of his head, "I took a chance when I hired you against my colleagues' advice. There would be no point in having you fail the first time you tried a case."

"Other than to teach me a lesson."

Barlow uncrosses his legs and spreads them wide. "I think you'll make a fine lawyer someday, Kate," he says, resting a hand on her shoulder. "But it's going to take time. I'm here to mentor you, to help you improve that fine legal mind. But you have to trust me, trust that I know what I'm doing." He gives her shoulder a little squeeze.

She pulls away. "I want another case. Another chance in the courtroom."

"Of course. As soon as something comes along that I believe fits your talents, I'll let you prosecute."

"How about the cornfield case?"

Barlow leans back. "There is no cornfield case, Kate."

"Really? The Minnesota Jewish Council suspects Mike Bannister murdered the Roths in that cornfield."

Barlow stands, walks to his desk, and sits on a corner, looking down, towering over her, his double chin on prominent display. "There's no evidence to suggest that."

"Come on, Wilson. They were shot in the back at close range and *at an angle.*"

"I think you're mistaken, Kate." Barlow goes behind his desk and pulls a folder from a file cabinet. He walks over to Kate and hands it to her. "Open it."

She does.

"Take a look at the summary on the third page."

Kate finds the page and scans the summary. *Not how it happened according to Scott,* the young morgue attendant she'd tricked into letting her see the bodies. She reads the summary again, as if the wording will be different the second time through. "This isn't right, Wilson," she says, looking up at him.

Standing over her with his hands on his hips, Barlow says, "Despite my . . . admiration for you, Kate, it's not your case. It's no one's now. And that's the way it's going to stay as long as I'm DA."

Chapter 19

Jake and Nick drive to Zeno Malkin's residence to inform Malkin's wife about the death of her husband. After insisting that Zeno had no enemies, she breaks down. Nick calls the wife's sister. They wait till she arrives and then drive to City Hall. Jake sends Nick to the brokerage firm where Malkin used to work to gather a list of names of those who had invested in Brazama Gold stock. Jake searches the crime files and then skims the rap sheet on Franklin Simms.

Three misdemeanor solicitations. Fines paid. Arrested just last week while playing the skin flute in one of the bathroom stalls at the Dugout Bar. Probation. Jake jots down the address from the file photo of Simms' driver's license. Then he drives to Nicollet Island.

The island lies in the middle of the Mississippi, reached by the Hennepin Avenue Bridge connecting downtown and Northeast Minneapolis, and is home to De La Salle, a parochial high school, and the huge neon Grain Belt beer sign erected in the '40s. Mill and lumber titan William Eastman and his relatives and friends built their mansions on Nicollet Island in the late 19th century, leading many of the city's Gilded Age politicians and mill owners to live there as well. When Eastman Flats was built, one on the north side of the island and the other on the south, Eastman figured the pair of three-story stone row houses would attract an upper-middle-class clientele, but the idea never panned out, and in the early 1900s the flats were subdivided into one or more apartments per floor to create cheaper housing. Now the island is a labyrinth of transient hotels, flop houses, saloons, junk metal shops, second-hand stores, and army surplus outlets.

Franklin Simms lives in a second-floor row house apartment in the rapidly declining building on the north side of the island. The door opens a crack. Simms looks over the chain. "I remember you," he says. "What's this about?"

Surprised once again by how much Simms looks like Tyrone Power, Jake shows his badge. "Zeno Malkin is dead."

"I heard."

"Open up."

Simms hesitates and then pops the chain. Jake enters and sits on a worn davenport in the carpeted living room. Bookshelves line one wall. Straight ahead is an archway that leads into the dining room and built-in buffet. The colonial furniture is old but well cared for. Lots of flowers in vases, doilies, and chintz curtains, floral wallpaper, and framed black-and-white photos of Simms with an older woman Jake figures is Simms' mother based on their similar features.

"Is it true how Zeno died?" Simms asks.

Simms' cheek is still bruised from Mike Bannister's pummeling, but the bruise has turned from red to a purplish blueberry. The opposite side of his cheek has what appear to be recent scratches. Jake doesn't recall seeing them.

"Malkin went out his office window."

Simms shakes his head in disbelief. "Such a tragedy."

"Knew him well, did you?"

"I did."

"Was he suicidal?"

Simms shrugs. "Don't know."

"Well, if his death wasn't a suicide . . ."

Simms' eyes jitter as he searches for a response. "You're implying he was murdered."

"Pretty impossible accident if he didn't commit suicide."

"But who would murder him?"

"I'm asking you."

"How would I know?"

"You said you knew Zeno well."

"Yes, I suppose I did."

"No supposition about it." Jake holds up his notebook. "Want me to read what you said a moment ago?"

"That won't be necessary."

"Where were you the night Malkin died?"

"I was home."

"Alone?"

"My mother was home."

"She lives with you?"

He nods.

"I need names, Simms."

"Like who might want Zeno dead?"

"We could start with your name."

"Hey," he says with raised palms. "I had no grudge against Zeno. He and I were . . . partners."

"How is that?"

"I ghosted his two books, for Christ's sake."

"So he was your meal ticket?"

"I wouldn't put it that way."

"But you shared in the profits from the sale of his books."

"Of course."

"Is ghosting what you do for a living, Mr. Simms?"

"It supplements my income."

"What's your background?"

"I majored in English at the U of M. I teach at North High. Coach wrestling. Since Zeno came along, I'm concentrating more on writing."

"Ever written anything for yourself?"

"I'm working on a novel."

"Tell me about Mike Bannister."

Simms' Adam's apple bobs. "What's to tell?"

"Look, Simms, I'm aware of your record. What's your relationship with Bannister?"

Simms hesitates, lets out a long breath, and says, "Sometimes I provide him with . . . information."

"That all?"

"Nothing else."

"How long have you been snitching for Bannister?"

"Couple of years."

"How'd you meet Zeno?"

"He is . . . *was* my broker."

"Was Zeno queer?"

"No."

"You're sure?"

"Definitely."

"How'd you get those scratches on your cheek?"

Simms' hand moves toward his cheek and then abruptly stops. "My cat."

Jake thinks they look more like fingernail scratches. "Really?"

"Yes. We were playing. It was an accident. Oscar is very gentle."

"Where's Oscar now?"

"Around the house somewhere. I don't let him outside."

"Have to be more careful when you play."

Simms' thin smile is as taut as a tightrope.

"Ever hear of a company called Globe Enterprises in Las Vegas, Mr. Simms?"

He shakes his head. "Why?"

"Zeno owned it."

"I don't know anything about it."

"How about Brazama Gold?"

Simms looks away for a moment. "I lost some money on that investment."

"You weren't the only one."

"It wasn't much."

"You mean it wasn't enough to kill Zeno over."

Simms nods.

*　　*　　*

That afternoon Jake and Nick each interview the brokers whose clients lost money on Zeno Malkin's Brazama Gold scheme. One of the men on Jake's list is Martin Crenshaw, the guy who took a dive off the Short Line Bridge. In Jake's first interview with Mrs. Crenshaw regarding her husband's apparent suicide, she never mentioned specific investments, either because she wasn't privy to them or because Jake hadn't asked the right question. Now, when he talks to her again, she reveals that her husband's father, Douglas Crenshaw, lost a considerable amount of money in Zeno Malkin's South American flimflam. Martin never fully recovered emotionally after losing his father's confidence and much of his father's money.

*　　*　　*

Later that afternoon, Jake watches as Harold Jamison, the coroner, examines Zeno Malkin's body, which lies naked—except for a toe tag—on a waist-high porcelain table. A morgue attendant has placed a rubber body block under Malkin's back, causing his chest to protrude outward and his arms and neck to fall back, allowing the maximum exposure of the trunk for the incisions. Classical music plays softly in the background.

Resting on a cart beside the table are the key instruments used for dissection: a scalpel, scissors, "pick ups," better known as forceps, and Jamison's favorite tool, an eighteen-inch-long sharp knife called a "bread knife," used to cut away organs.

Jamison is very protective of the knife and carries it in a leather sheath inside his briefcase.

Bending over the body, his gaze focused on Malkin instead of Jake, Jamison says, "Bloodshot eyes. Some bruising around the nose and mouth as well."

Jake says, "You thinking Malkin was smothered?"

Jamison straightens up and peers across the table at Jake. "Likely. I'll check the blood for high levels of carbon dioxide to confirm it. Some skin under the fingernails as well. Might've scratched the killer."

Jake's eyes drift to a second autopsy table. "Hey, Doc," he says to Jamison, pointing to the still-clothed body on the table, the shirt soaked with blood. "Who's this?"

Jamison looks up. "Guy by the name of Abe Fishman."

"What happened?"

"Stabbed by a gandy dancer on Skid Row."

Jake peers at the man's face again, just to make sure. *No doubt,* he thinks. It's the same guy Nick Cole was talking with outside the Flame Café a week ago.

*   *   *

Late that afternoon Jake and Nick are sitting across the desk from Homicide Captain Avery Arnold. The captain keeps his office as natty as his clothes. Resting on a corner of his desktop is a photo of his three children, a boy and two girls. Jake estimates they're between seven and twelve, all dressed neat as a pin, all three enrolled in excellent private schools, the boy at St. Paul Academy, his two female siblings in the Summit School for girls. There are no photos of Arnold's wife, who divorced him a year ago.

Arnold is the "fixer" for the Minneapolis PD. Every department in the country has one. The wheels of commerce would grind to a halt if professional movers and haulers were expected to obey all dumbass parking and traffic restrictions the city dreams up. For a city to function, there has to be a considerable amount of double-parking, lane blocking, and meter violating.

Most cops understand this, but there are always a few hot dogs, rookies mostly, who regard a parking violation as an impeachable offense. For them there's a cop who straightens things out on these matters, and other less benign offenses that require special attention. Avery Arnold is that man.

His list of Rent-a-Badges is one of the sources of his authority. Lots of cops want to pick up extra bucks off-duty. Arnold rewards those who behave according to his set of rules with off-duty work. Arnold provides off-duty cops as bouncers for Minneapolis' bars and security for sports and entertainment events. Minneapolis is a middle-sized, middle-American, slightly East Coast city. It has a full menu of events and the usual complement of bars for every market niche, so there's plenty of opportunity to pick up extra cash.

Lots of cops work both bars and events, but there's a slightly better odor to the events. For one thing, the venue or event issues the paycheck, not some barkeep that might be operating in violation of the liquor laws or permitting gambling in the back while a cop is checking IDs in the front. For another, bars naturally tend to be rowdier. On those rare occasions when things do get out of hand at a large event, it tends to get really rowdy. Unlike a bar, where it's usually just one customer at a time in need of an attitude adjustment, when you've got a whole crowd of people going berserk, you've got a major problem. Jake knows Nick Cole regularly works off-duty in uniform and for Arnold in plainclothes. He's the captain's birddog, checking whether joints are operating within Arnold's relaxed interpretation of the law and gauging the performance of the badges.

Arnold leans back in his chair and eyes Jake. "Anything from the wife?"

"She claims her husband would never commit suicide. Everyone loved him."

"What do you think, Jake?"

"One of her claims is wrong."

"Would you care to enlighten me?"

Jake recounts Malkin's scams as told to him by Sergeant Frank Morris in the Fraud/Theft Division.

"So not everyone loved Malkin."

"Especially those he screwed, Cap. Like Joe Briggs."

"But Malkin didn't murder Briggs," Nick says. "The Roths did."

Jake lets the comment slide but makes a mental note to remind his new partner to keep his mouth shut unless asked. "All the brokers whose clients lost money on Zeno's scheme had alibis for last night."

"Any alibis strike you as shaky?"

"Eight of the twelve were home with their wives and families."

"And the other four?"

"Baseball game, dinner with partners, and a movie with their kid. We'll verify those, but it looks like the brokerage angle is a dead end."

"What about the fourth name?" Arnold asks.

"It was Martin Crenshaw. He committed suicide."

"Like Malkin?"

"Crenshaw jumped off a bridge before Malkin went out his office window."

"What the hell is it with the suicides?" Flanagan says. "Is it '29 all over again?"

"As to Malkin's suicide," Jake says, "I agree with the wife. He wasn't suicidal. Coroner found indications of suffocation. I checked with the crime lab. They found threads from a pillow in Malkin's office in his hair."

"Any solid suspects?" Arnold asks.

"Too many to count given Malkin's business dealings."

Arnold muses for a moment before he says, "Martin Crenshaw was Douglas Crenshaw's son."

Jake nods. "I spoke with the old man."

"What'd he say?"

"Not much. Other than to back off."

Arnold leans forward. "That's good advice, Jake. He *is* a big contributor and friend to the department. No sense in making him an enemy."

"Still quite a coincidence that Crenshaw committed suicide," Nick says.

Arnold's eyes settle on Nick for a moment and then on Jake. "Any evidence Crenshaw's death was something other than a suicide?"

Jake shakes his head. "Doesn't mean he wasn't murdered."

"Proving it is the trick, Lieutenant. Who had keys to Malkin's office?"

"Secretary had keys," Nick says, "as well as the janitor. But he doesn't come on till eleven. Only other person who might've had a key—the secretary isn't sure—is a guy named Franklin Simms."

"Who's Simms?"

"Don't know," Nick says.

Jake isn't sure how much he should reveal. *As little as possible, without some solid evidence.* But if Simms is somehow involved in Malkin's murder, Jake doesn't want to be on the outside looking in.

"Bannister told me Simms is his snitch," Jake says. "He's got a rap sheet. Charged with misdemeanor solicitation three times. Paid the fines. Last week he was arrested in one of the bathroom stalls at the Dugout Bar."

"Maybe Malkin was queer, too," Arnold says. "Marriage could be a cover. Maybe Simms was blackmailing Malkin for money."

"Possible," Jake says. He decides to keep his interview with Franklin Simms on the QT till he's gathered more information about the Brazama Gold scam. He's not ready to share everything with his new partner—at least not yet.

"Okay, Detectives," Arnold says. "Let's review what we've got. The queer thing may be the reason Simms was there on the sly, did his business and went on his way. But we don't know if Zeno was queer. And while being queer might be a motive to commit murder, it could be merely a reason to meet after hours. And we don't know that Simms was in Malkin's office. The blackmail theory for money is both good and bad. It strengthens the queer possibility, but weakens the motive."

Arnold is quiet for a time and then continues. "We have no motive. We're a little weak on opportunity, since we lack anything but a hunch to put Simms—or anyone else— at the scene. That leaves the means. We believe Zeno was thrown through a window." Arnold looks at Jake. "Could Simms handle Zeno?"

Jake recalls that Simms isn't just an English teacher. He's the wrestling coach. "Well, Simms looks like he's in shape."

Arnold nods. "I'm beginning to like Simms. If he has a key, do you think he's smart enough to get rid of it?"

Jake shrugs. "Who knows?"

"Does Simms have an alibi?"

"Says he was with his mother."

"You check it out, Jake?"

"Planning to."

"What if we send a couple of guys over to see Simms on the sodomy thing at the Dugout Bar?" Nick says. "One guy keeps him busy while the other guy pokes around his apartment."

"I don't want to do anything to spook him," Arnold says. "No cop is going to show face until we know if he's got the key for sure."

"What if it's stashed and not on a key chain?"

"I don't want to breathe the word *key* around Simms until we know if he has a key. And I don't want him leaving town or hanging himself from the shower rod just yet." Arnold's eyes shift from Nick to Jake. "One of you two should get the DA to prepare some kind of bullshit letter about Simms' sodomy bust: 'No charge will be pursued at this time pending further investigation. You will be notified if there's any change, blah, blah.' That way, we can always reactivate it if we need it."

Jake isn't convinced that the key angle leads anywhere, but he nods. He'll send Cole. It'll be good experience for him.

"What if I toss the place, Cap?" Nick asks. "Do it real messy. Maybe I find something. Even if I don't, we see if Simms reports it. If he's too scared to call us, that says he doesn't want anything to do with us."

Arnold shakes his head. "He might be carrying the key around with him, and if we do find it in his apartment, we can't take it. He might spook."

"How about I check out the key chain without Simms knowing about it?" Nick says. "Let's call it plan A. If Plan A doesn't produce, then we go to plan B, toss the place very professionally, he'll never know it, and if I find it, we get the court order."

"You'll need probable cause for a court order," Jake says.

"What's plan A?" Arnold asks Nick.

"I'll tamper with his car. Make sure he has to leave it at a garage. That way I can check his keychain."

"If he leaves it with the car," Jake says.

"Okay," Arnold says to Nick. "I approve Plan A. But Simms can't know you were in his place. You'll have to search it when the mother is out. Check with her about Simms' alibi, but be careful. We don't want her covering for her son with a lie."

"If this Simms thing goes off the rails, Captain," Jake says, "we'll need the court order to cover our asses."

"Cover *your* asses," Arnold says. "My ass is covering this chair."

Chapter 20

Franklin Simms is too upset to notice that his car is being followed. The windshield of his dark blue '46 Chevy Fleetmaster Sport Coupe has been smashed by a heavy object, leaving a massive, nearly opaque blot of splintered glass directly atop the drivers' sightline. Simms creeps along the side streets, cursing the vandals who did it.

He pulls into a Chevy dealership, calls his insurance company, makes arrangements to pick up the car later, hands his keys to the attendant at the service desk, and heads for the streetcar stop.

Thirty minutes later, Nick Cole arrives. After he identifies himself to the attendant, he consults a clipboard that has a stolen vehicle flyer with a description of the Chevy Fleetmaster on it and says, "I got an anonymous tip about an hour ago, saying you guys might be servicing stolen cars here. I've got to check out licenses and registrations."

A short, chubby, bald man wearing a light green, checkered blazer with "Dennis" laminated on a nametag pulls a fat stub of cigar from his mouth and says, "We don't have no stolen vehicles here, Detective."

"Mind if I take a look around?"

Dennis points to the service department with what's left of his cigar. "Follow me."

Inside the service area Nick says, "What about that dark blue Chevy Sport Coupe over there with the broken windshield?"

"Fellow brought that in about a half hour ago. Never seen him before. He just walked off, heading east. Said he'd be back around closing time."

"You have the keys?"

Dennis cocks his head and says, "Sure."

"Get 'em."

While he waits for the keys, Nick checks out the inside of the Fleetmaster. Under the seats. Inside the glove compartment. Nothing.

Dennis returns with Simms' keychain. Three keys on the chain. One for the car. The others, Nick guesses, are Simms' house key and the key to the school building. Probably took his schoolroom key with him.

"I'll need to confiscate the keys."

"But what happens when the guy shows up?"

Simms is teaching school. Nick will return the keys before school lets out. He'll explain to Dennis that there's been a mistake. The car wasn't stolen after all. "The guy probably won't show up. But if you're worried about anything, or if he does show, just try and stall him and give me a call. Here's my card."

"It says Detective Cole. Homicide."

"That's my old card. I can still be reached at the same number." Nick leans in and in a soft voice says, "I wouldn't mention our little visit to any of your other customers. Might make them nervous, not want to do business here."

* * *

Nick uses the phone at the car dealership to call Simms' residence. When no one answers, he figures Simms' mother is out. He drives to the row house apartment on Nicollet Island and uses the house key to enter. He groans when he sees the bookshelves. He needn't have. Simms has hidden the key in the standard place for hiding keys, taped under a dresser drawer.

Nick checks the pattern against the office key on Zeno's chain to make sure it's the same and leaves Simms' key where he found it, undisturbed.

His first homicide case, and he's cracking it. Alone. Without Cafferty or his blessing. He smiles to himself and scans the books on the shelves, looking for any queer material. Then he randomly checks under a dozen or so dust jackets. The only books of interest are signed copies of Zeno's books, with inscriptions thanking Simms for his "wise counsel and inspiration," his "friendship and loyal support." From the absence of any queer material, Nick gathers that Simms probably wants nothing openly visible on the premises that can compromise him. Certainly nothing that his mother could see.

A professional burglar never takes more than seven minutes. Cole takes twenty. He gets out and locks up.

*   *   *

Minneapolis is the epicenter of the sports betting world thanks to Leo Hirschfield, who runs a company called Athletic Publications, Inc. The company sets the lines in all sports and distributes them to bookies across the country via telephone and telegraph. Leo also publishes schedules for all the games in the country and distributes several publications that provide sports information intended to help bookies make a better line and for bettors to be able to spot weak numbers. The most popular of these publications is called *The Green Sheet*. The whole operation has only eighteen full-time employees, but it grosses nearly $10 million a year.

Jake has placed bets and played poker with Leo since he first set up his operation in the mid-'30s. He's always treated Jake honestly and fairly. While most of Leo's thousands of customers are illegal bookmakers, his business is purely legit. He has a team of handicappers that analyze each game for the upcoming week and set the lines during Monday morning roundtable discussions. Leo pays airplane pilots and cleanup crews for a collection of newspapers from around the country that his staff uses to formulate just about every point spread. He sends his publication to colleges for free, and in return he receives information about player injuries and illnesses, and anything else that might affect the outcome of the game.

Leo's office is on the 12th and top floor of the Nicollet Hotel, adjacent to Gateway Park and at the intersections of Hennepin, Washington, and Nicollet Avenues, and South 4th Street. The mayor has declared the office to be off limits for the MPD, but Jake—and many others in the department—pay no attention to the directive.

"Jake, my boy!" Leo gives him a big smile and a hug.

Hirschfield is a gray-haired man in his mid-fifties, who lost the hearing in his right ear after a bout with influenza in the Marine Corps during World War II. He has a knack for numbers and knows instinctively when a wrong line is set, though he doesn't have anything to do with the actual handicapping of the games. He stays clear of shady associations and proudly points out that he's a member of the tony Oak Ridge Country Club, which he considers "the finest Jewish country club." He fails to mention that Oak Ridge in Hopkins is one of only two Jewish country clubs, the Brookview Country Club in Golden Valley being the other. Jews aren't allowed in any country clubs in and around the city, so if they wanted to golf and mingle, they needed to purchase their own course.

Because of Leo's hearing loss in his right ear, Jake stands slightly to Leo's left when he speaks. "How you doing, Leo?"

"Not so good."

"How so?"

"It's the damn Kefauver Commission," he says with a shake of his head. "They think all gambling is immoral. Now Congress is considering two anti-gambling laws. Bookies would have to buy a fifty-dollar federal wagering stamp and pay a ten percent tax on all bets. Most bookies won't buy the stamp or pay the tax. It's a joke."

"Then what's the concern?"

"We run an honest operation. So we'd pay. And once Congress starts passing anti-gambling laws, they won't stop. They're talking about outlawing gambling across state lines. If that happens, we're out of business. Plus, we've got to worry about Las Vegas, where gambling is legal, despite being run by the mob." He shakes his head in frustration. "But you didn't come here to listen to my problems."

"No. I've got problems of my own."

"Sit down. We'll talk."

Hirschfield ushers Jake to a chair near a cluttered desk and the tickertape machines that are used to contact bookies in New York, Vegas, and other major cities.

After Hirschfield is seated in a chair behind his desk, he says, "How can I help?"

"You've got contacts in Vegas."

"I do."

"I need information on a company called Global Enterprises."

"I'll ask around. Give me an hour."

Jake nods and heads for lunch at Jax Café on 20th and University. The place is crowded, so Jake eats his lunch at the bar. Sixty-five minutes later, he's back at Leo's office. "Anything?" he asks.

"Global Enterprises is housed in the same building as a number of companies." Leo slides a piece of paper across his desktop. "That's the Las Vegas address. It's in an area otherwise occupied by bail bonds offices and liquor stores. Guy who owns the building is named Dominic Cozens."

"Ever heard of him?"

Leo nods. "Comes into town now and then. He's an ex-con who did time for a P&D stock swindle."

"What's a P&D?"

"Pump-and-dump. It's a form of securities fraud. Basically, it involves artificially inflating the price of an owned stock through false and misleading positive statements in order to sell the cheaply purchased stock at a higher price. Once the operators of the scheme 'dump' sell their overvalued shares, the price falls and investors lose their money."

Jake thinks the P&D sounds a lot like the Brazama Gold scam Zeno Malkin ran. "You said Global Enterprises is housed in the same building as a number of companies."

"Probably a shell company—those with no employees, no assets, and no real business to speak of."

"For what purpose?"

"To move money without it being traced back to them. Say a politician takes a bribe, or a company pulls off a tax scam or pump-and-dump stock swindle. You can pretty much guarantee that a shell firm was used to move the dirty money and to cover the trail."

"Why Nevada?"

"Lax rules on business incorporations. Doesn't matter who you are or what business you're in. The city bills itself as the Delaware of the West."

"Meaning?"

"Similar set-up in both states. Lots of ways to hide cash, and because of their secrecy laws, real difficult to find out who actually owns what. And here's the cherry on top of this shit sandwich, Jake. There's no need to actually go to Nevada to form the company. The whole process can be done over the phone in about fifteen minutes. Cost is cheap. Just need to provide the name of a contact person."

Like Zeno Malkin, Jake thinks. *But who was he fronting for?*

"If you want to keep your name hidden, oftentimes the contact person is a lawyer," Leo says. "That way you're protected by attorney-client privilege, or it might be a trusted bagman.

You'd still control the company, but your name won't appear anywhere in public records. I'd layer my network by setting up a firm in one place and subsidiaries of it elsewhere. After that, I might open a foreign bank account that would be very hard for the IRS or law enforcement to trace. You might have to look around a little, but you'd be able to find a foreign banker who'd open an account for you."

"And I could do it all without leaving home?"

"Absolutely."

"Do me another favor, Leo. Let me know when Dominic Cozens is in town."

"Will do."

*   *   *

Nick Cole sits in a booth across from Homicide Captain Avery Arnold at the Market Bar-B-Que in Minneapolis, on First Avenue North and 6th Street. The table is covered with a red-and-white checkered cloth, and the walls with posters of touring Broadway shows and photos of celebrities who've dined on the Market's pit-smoked ribs and brisket.

Willard and Sam Polski, two Jewish brothers, opened the restaurant in '46. The dining spot quickly became one of the most popular in the city. Even the most hard-bitten anti-Semitic cops manage to set aside their attitude about Jews like the Polskis when it comes to the Market's world class ribs and the twenty percent discount the restaurant gives them. In return, the department turns a blind eye to the gambling operation upstairs.

Arnold points a half-eaten rib bone at Nick. A napkin is tucked like a bib under his shirt collar. "Good work on Simms, Cole."

"Thanks." The ribs are delicious, but Nick isn't hungry. He's excited about his first homicide case and the possibility that he's going to get sole credit for solving it.

"Let's bring Simms in on Saturday," Arnold says. "Try and pick him up when he's out. Tell him the DA wants us clear up some things. Real low key. Just you. Drive an unmarked, not a squad. If Simms balks, explain that we're being nice, so we don't embarrass him. We can always wait till Monday and arrest him at school in front of his whole class. He'll come along. Let him think it's just a bullshit thing, and he's still in control. While this is going on, have a couple of the boys paste the judge's order on Simms' front door. Then go in messy and bring back the key. Make sure there's some other stuff, anything else that looks interesting. Now let me see that warrant."

Cole hands him the draft of the search warrant and waits while Arnold looks it over.

"Good. Put a dummy key in Simms' apartment after you take the key. If we have to release him, I don't want him to know we've got it till we decide to tell him."

"What about Jake? He should be in on this."

"I'll let him know. But you do the interview. Alone. Show me what you've got. We'll watch. We got means, we got opportunity, and we got motive, kind of—some queer thing, or money thing, probably. Let's see what you can pry loose. What we don't have is proof. No proof whatsoever. No weapon. No nothing. So if this is going to go down, you've got to find a way to make Simms give it up."

*   *   *

That evening Jake sees the notice in the Variety section of the *Minneapolis Daily Tribune*. The Calhoun Beach Club is hosting a party in celebration of Douglas Crenshaw's sixty-fifth birthday. Construction that began in 1928 was delayed due to the Great Depression, the war, and financial difficulties. The members-only club finally opened after WWII. It sits across West Lake Street on the north side of Lake Calhoun. Originally named *Bde Maka Ska* by the Dakota Indians, the lake's name was changed in 1839 to honor John C. Calhoun. Jake wonders why he hasn't received an invitation to the party and then laughs at his joke.

He showers and shaves and puts on his best suit before driving to the club. Leaving his car with a valet, he notes the plaque near the club's front entrance.

NO JEWS, PEDDLERS, OR DOGS ALLOWED

As he opens the entrance door, Jake takes a last drag on his cigarette and crushes the butt under his shoe.

The social hour and celebratory dinner are over. Men in tuxes and women in gowns are mingling and dancing to the big band sound of an old Tommy Dorsey tune, "I'm Getting Sentimental Over You." Jake scans the ballroom, searching for Douglas Crenshaw. *Shouldn't be hard to find,* Jake figures, *given he's likely the only one in a wheelchair.* He spots Wilson Barlow, the DA, Captain Avery Arnold, and Chief William Flanagan conversing at a table. Then, out of the corner of his eye, he sees another familiar face approaching in a sharp-looking suit and tie.

"What're you doing here, Cafferty?" Mike Bannister asks.

"Could ask you the same." Jake looks him over. "Nice suit. That a rental?"

"I bought it."

"Been savin' your pennies, huh?"

"Lose the fedora, trench coat, and cheap suit. You might fit in."

"Give me the name of your tailor."

"Hey, I'm workin' security here, Cafferty. What's your excuse?"

"Douglas Crenshaw. Where is he?"

"Got an invite?"

"My badge."

"Don't think so. You can leave now, or I can throw you out."

"You're gonna need help."

Bannister's mouth curls in an ugly grin. "That so?"

"Lieutenant Cafferty."

Jake turns and spots Virginia Crenshaw walking toward him. She wears a black thigh-split satin gown that clings to her curves. "Miss Crenshaw," he says, tipping his hat.

"We got a problem," Bannister says to her. "The lieutenant here wants to crash the party."

"Not exactly what I had in mind," Jake says to her.

"I'm sure Lieutenant Cafferty is here for another reason."

"I'm looking for your father," Jake says.

"I can help you with that," she says with a warm smile.

"Don't think your father wants to be disturbed," Bannister says to her.

She glares at Bannister, her indigo eyes darkening. She takes Jake's elbow and leads him toward the French doors and onto the terrace overlooking the moonlit lake.

"What do you know about Mike Bannister?" Jake asks her.

"He's one of the cops we hire to work security for our parties."

"Know him well?"

She shakes her head. "He makes my skin crawl. But my father likes him."

Douglas Crenshaw is seated in his wheelchair near the railing, enjoying a cigar and conversing in low tones with that greaseball Tony Rizzo, who owns Minneapolis Iron and Steel. Rizzo looks uncomfortable in a tux.

"I need to speak to your father . . . alone," Jake says quietly to her.

"Wait here," she says.

It's a beautiful fall evening. Leaves turning, air crisp and clean. For just a moment Jake remembers a similar night years ago. *Rachel*. Then the memory is gone like a wisp of smoke.

Jake watches as Virginia Crenshaw speaks with her father. As she talks, Rizzo, standing beside Douglas Crenshaw, gives Jake a crooked smile, nods at Douglas Crenshaw, and strolls down the terrace, a hand trailing off the railing as he moves out of earshot. Virginia Crenshaw waves Jake over.

"Sorry to bother you, Mr. Crenshaw."

Crenshaw stares at Jake. "I doubt you're sorry, Lieutenant. And you certainly didn't come here to wish me happy birthday."

"No, sir, I didn't." Jake turns to Virginia Crenshaw. "If you wouldn't mind, Miss Crenshaw."

"Oh, but I would mind, Lieutenant."

"Anything you have to say to me, you can say to my daughter," the old man says.

Jake shrugs. "All right. You lied to me, Mr. Crenshaw."

The old man isn't taken aback by the accusation. "How exactly?"

"You said you knew nothing about Brazama Gold. But your late son's wife told me you lost a bundle on Zeno Malkin's scam."

"And how would she know that?"

"Martin told her. It's the reason you and your son were estranged."

"You seem to know a great deal about my family all of a sudden, Lieutenant."

Jake ignores the comment. "Lying piques my curiosity, Mr. Crenshaw. Suggests to me that you've got something to hide."

"It's time for the lieutenant to leave, Virginia. Please see him out. Goodnight, Detective Cafferty." With that, the old man rolls away.

Virginia Crenshaw takes Jake by the hand. "This way, Lieutenant."

Inside the clubhouse again, she leads him to the door to the ballroom. The orchestra is playing Glenn Miller's "Moonlight Serenade." A couple wave to her as they dance to the music.

"Friends of yours?" Jake asks.

"From my college days at Radcliffe."

Jake recalls seeing her diploma in Douglas Crenshaw's study. "Expensive college."

She looks into his eyes. "I spent four years at Radcliffe. We had private rooms, cleaned by Irish maids. Our clothes were washed and ironed every week. We ate off china plates in our own dining room. We had our own newspaper, our own literary magazine, clubs, and student government, and we had wonderful conversations about what we'd do once we graduated. But," she says with a wistful smile, "we all knew that the real power and money were across Cambridge Common at Harvard."

Jake clearly hears the sarcasm in her voice. Hoping to avoid any conflicts, he says, "Thanks for your time, Miss Crenshaw."

"You can't leave."

"Why not?"

She smiles. "We haven't danced yet. I'd be awfully hurt if you turned me down again."

"Again?"

"Yes. Remember the 'Get Acquainted' dance?"

Jake shrugs. "It was nothing personal."

"Of course not," she says, taking him by the hand again.

The band is playing a Harry James tune, "You Made Me Love You." Jake is a little rusty, but once on the dance floor he remembers the steps for the foxtrot. It helps that Virginia Crenshaw dances well, gliding across the floor as if she's floating.

Leaning closer to him, she whispers in his ear, "This isn't so tough, now is it?"

She smells good. Feels even better. They dance two more tunes before he leads her back to a table.

"Are you going to sit with me awhile?"

"Miss Crenshaw—"

"Call me Ginny."

Jake gives her a lopsided smile. "I was on my way out."

"Going home?"

He nods. "That's the plan."

"How 'bout my place for a drink?"

"I don't drink . . . anymore."

"I'm sure I can find something non-alcoholic."

"Look, Miss Crenshaw . . . Ginny, I appreciate the offer, but I'll take a rain check."

She shrugs it off. "All right then, Jake. Do you mind if I call you Jake?"

He shakes his head. She has beautiful eyes. It's been a long time since he's been with a woman. Too long.

She smiles and runs the palm of her hand across his cheek. "Another time then. You take care, Jake." With that she turns and strolls away, her dress clinging to her curves like a silk stocking.

Chapter 21

The following afternoon, when Franklin Simms is settled in an uncomfortable, scarred-up chair in one of the interrogation rooms, Nick Cole takes a seat on the opposite side of the narrow table. He knows that Jake Cafferty and Avery Arnold are watching from the other side of the one-way glass, and his armpits are damp with nervous sweat. He needs to break Simms down, and he believes he knows how to do it, thanks to the interview observations and studies he's read ever since he joined the force.

Nick has assured Simms that it's merely a routine interview, but he can see that the man is anxious. Beads of sweat dot his forehead. He constantly taps his right foot. His eyes dart around the small, enclosed room like flies trapped in a glass jar. Nick is certain that anxiety is a characteristic of lying. Therefore, interviewing involves watching for signs of anxiety and occasionally causing it. Whether or not Simms breaks eye contact, whether he's fidgety, whether he crosses his legs or folds his arms—all are signs of deception.

"I told the police before that nothing happened at the Dugout Bar," Simms says. "It was all a misunderstanding. I wouldn't do something like that. I'm not queer."

"I'm sure we can clear this up, Mr. Simms."

"I could lose my teaching job. And my mother would be so upset. She would kill me if she thought I was . . ." He ends the sentence with a helpless shrug.

"No one wants to hurt you."

"I thought this was all over. I got this letter from the city attorney. He said they weren't prosecuting. They said they made a mistake. It was all over. If there was any change, they'd let me know."

"I have a copy of the letter," Nick says, holding it up. "It says, 'There will be no charges filed at this time pending further investigation.' *Pending further investigation*, Mr. Simms. That's what we're doing now. I'm getting your version. I want to know your side of the story. Tell me what happened."

"You have a smoke?"

Nick doesn't smoke, but he's prepared. He pulls a Lucky Strike package and small silver butane lighter out of an inner coat pocket and pushes them across the table.

Simms lights up, his blue eyes following the stream of smoke drifting upwards before he focuses on Nick again. "I've never had a homosexual experience. There were times I could have. I was at summer camp once. I was only nine or ten, and this counselor tried something. Well, he didn't try it, he just talked about it, and I said, 'If anyone here ever tried that on me, I'd go right to the camp director.' That was that. He was the photography guy. We were in the darkroom when he started in on it. Boy, did the lights ever go on in a hurry."

"Who turned you out?"

Simms blows out a mouthful of smoke. "What?"

"You heard me."

"No one. No one turned me out."

"You don't want this charge hanging over your head for the rest of your life. I need to know what happened."

"Nothing happened. I never did anything."

"We have too much to drink. Our defenses are down. We meet someone who's attractive. We want to please them. The next thing you know, we're being used. Can happen to anyone, Mr. Simms."

175

"I'm not queer. I don't want anyone ever to say that I am. I'm not. I can get all kinds of women to say I'm not. Lots of women. I've had hundreds of women."

"Let's drop this queer thing for now. Talk about something else."

"Yes."

"Maybe you can help us with another matter then. If you can help us, maybe we can help you. Could you do that?"

"I'm listening."

"You're a smart, talented man. You're a teacher. I've always admired teachers. I wouldn't be here today if my high school teachers hadn't taken an interest in me, encouraged me to make something of myself. So I have great admiration for what you have accomplished, Mr. Simms."

"Thank you."

"How'd you get those scratches on your cheek?"

Simms takes a drag on his cigarette and blows the smoke out. "My cat. I already told the other detective how it happened."

"Other detective?"

"Yes. Lieutenant Cafferty."

Nick glares at the one-way glass and then focuses his eyes on Simms again. "What else did you talk about with Lieutenant Cafferty?"

"How I was the ghost writer for Zeno's books."

"You wrote Malkin's books for him?"

"I did. The only reason he finally put my name in the Ac-knowledgments was because I raised such a stink about it. He finally had to give me some credit, or I would have had a press conference and exposed him for the fraud that he was. He wasn't supposed to change my copy either, not even a comma, without asking me first, but he did."

"Malkin changed your copy?"

"Yes. He changed it. He had no right to change it."

"Is that why you . . ."

"Why I what?"

"Why you killed him?"

Simms' face pales. "I didn't kill Zeno."

"But you were angry with him."

"Yes. But I didn't kill him."

"You know what? If I were in your situation, Mr. Simms, I probably would've done the same thing."

"You're wrong. I'm not a murderer."

"We're in the process of analyzing evidence from the crime scene. Excuse me for a moment." Nick gets up, leaves the room, and walks over to Jake and Avery Arnold, who are watching Simms through the glass.

"What're you doing?" Arnold says. "He's ready to break."

Nick ignores Arnold and stares at Jake. His heart is beating hard in his chest. "Why the hell didn't you tell me you'd talked to Simms?"

"He didn't tell me anything important."

"No? He told you how he wrote Malkin's books for him. How he was upset that he didn't get any credit. That's a motive. I should've known that going into the interview, *partner*. What else haven't you told me?"

"Easy, son," Arnold says. "Simms is ready to crack. Don't get distracted. Get back in there and finish it."

Nick takes a deep breath, trying to control his anger as he faces Arnold. "Give him a few minutes." He picks up a file folder on the desktop containing reports from the Malkin crime scene.

Jake says, "You sure you know what you're doing, Cole?"

"Damn right I do." He gestures with the folder toward the glass and the interview room. "Take a look."

Simms wipes his brow with the palm of his hand and then rubs both palms on his thighs. He looks blankly around the room, places his elbows on the table, and rests his head in his hands.

Nick says, "We've got motive, opportunity, and evidence with the key and those scratches on his face that Simms claims he got from his cat. I checked with the coroner. Malkin had human skin under his fingernails. And Simms' mother was playing canasta at a friend's house the night Malkin went out the window."

"There goes his alibi," Arnold says.

Nick waits another minute before re-entering the interview room, file folder in hand. He remains standing. "Tough way to go for Malkin. Out a window like that. What kind of punishment should we give the person who committed this crime?"

Simms looks up, as if coming out of a trance. "He should go to prison, that's for sure. I don't believe in the death penalty. Thankfully, we don't have it in this state, but prison for sure. Maybe for life."

Nick holds up the file. "In this folder I have the results of our investigation, Mr. Simms. After reviewing it, I have no doubt that you committed the crime."

Simms crushes his cigarette in the ashtray on the table. "That can't be."

Nick sits down again and lays the folder on the table in front of him. "There's absolutely no doubt about how this happened, Mr. Simms. Now let's move forward."

"Could I see the folder?"

"No. There'll be time for that later. Let's focus on clearing this whole thing up. Why did you tell Detective Cafferty that you were home with your mother the night Malkin was killed?"

Simms hesitates. Then he says, "Because I was."

"No. Your mother was out playing canasta with friends. You were all alone. And why were your fingerprints found at the crime scene?"

"I don't know." He thinks for a moment. "Wait a minute. I've been to Malkin's office before."

"How many times?"

"Quite a few."

"And why were you there?"

"We were working on the books. I came to discuss the manuscripts, to update him on my progress."

"You didn't go there for any other reason?"

"No."

"Did you ever go there after hours?"

"Sometimes."

"How did you get in?"

"I have a key."

Nick lays the key he found in Simms' place on the table. "This key?"

Simms stares at it and then at Nick. "Where'd you get that?"

"In your apartment. Where you hid it."

"I didn't hide it."

"You always keep your keys taped to the bottom of a drawer?"

"I only did that after . . ."

"After what, Mr. Simms?"

Simms stares at Nick but doesn't answer.

"After you killed Malkin."

"No, no. I hid it because I was afraid of this."

"Talking to the police."

"No. I was afraid I'd be a suspect. I'd be wrongly accused."

"Let's be honest, Mr. Simms. You hid the key because you didn't want anyone finding it."

"Then I could've thrown it out."

"Why didn't you?"

"Because Zeno has a new manuscript we were working on. I didn't have a copy. I wanted to make sure I'd get it back."

"So you could publish it?"

"Why not? I wrote it."

"Did you plan this out or did it just happen on the spur of the moment?"

179

Simms shakes his head in denial. "I want to see a lawyer."

Nick pauses, rethinks. "Maybe we could cut a deal."

Wary, Simms says, "What kind of deal?"

"So you're angry with Malkin. He's an asshole. We all know that. He changes your words. Gives himself credit that he doesn't deserve. He's holding out on you. You're not getting your cut of the sales as promised. That would upset anyone. You argue. It turns into a struggle. Simms goes out the window. It's an accident. Not your fault. Now we're talking manslaughter, not murder."

"But I'd still have to go to prison."

"You've got no prior criminal record. With good behavior you'll be out in a couple years."

"But I didn't kill Malkin."

"Look, I understand how upset you are, Mr. Simms. Anyone would be. It's hard carrying around all this guilt. Worried that your mother will find out about this Dugout Bar thing. That Malkin was ripping you off and taking credit for your work. You just blew your stack. It happens. Not your fault. We can keep the whole queer thing out of the press. Your mother will never know."

Simms looks up at Nick. "You can do that?"

"Absolutely."

"Two years if I make a deal?"

"I can make that work. You have my word. All you need to do is give me a written statement. What happened? What he forced you to do." Nick slides a piece of paper and a pen across the table. "I'll help you with it, but I probably won't need to. You're the real writer. The one who should get all the credit, aren't you, Mr. Simms?"

He nods his head and picks up the pen.

* * *

Watching through the one-way glass, Avery Arnold smiles. He shakes his head in wonderment and looks at Jake. "The young man has a gift, doesn't he?"

Jake's eyes lock on Arnold's. "I should've done the interview, Cap. I'm senior. Not Cole."

"He needs experience, Jake. Only one way to get it." Arnold looks at the glass again and continues. "Twenty-five years on the job and it's still a mystery. Some of them, you have them dead to rights, and they still find a way to run through the tiniest opening, give you the finger, and they're off to the golf course for the rest of their lives. This one, you lay the groundwork setting it up, sweating the holes in your theory, and none of it matters. Simms would've popped if we'd brought him in the day we heard his name. We just got the motive wrong. A bad edit." He shakes his head in disbelief and says, "Why hold out on Cole, Jake?"

"Don't know if I can trust him."

"You don't build trust by keeping things from your partner. You know that."

Jake *does* know it. But he's still not sure he can trust Nick Cole.

Chapter 22

Kate Dawson parks her Packard Clipper in the lot at McCarthy's Restaurant in St. Louis Park, a suburb west of downtown Minneapolis, and the home of an expanding and more affluent Jewish population that has elected to move out of the city. The long stucco building has crisscrossed windows, giving it an Old English Tudor appearance.

Tommy Banks, head of the Irish Mob, owns the fancy nightclub/restaurant and the liquor store on its northeast corner, despite being a convicted felon who cannot legally own a liquor license. Rumor has it that the IRS went after Banks for back taxes from '37 to '48, but because of the statute of limitations they could only prosecute in the criminal courts for '45 to '47. Banks' attorney advised him to settle, figuring he could get the charges dismissed for $15,000. Banks ignored the advice and hired another attorney.

Two hours ago, Kate phoned Nick Cole and asked him to meet her at McCarthy's after his shift was over. Nick immediately agreed to the meeting, no questions asked, thinking, perhaps, that she's changed her mind about the breakup. But reconciliation isn't why she's requested the meeting.

Through the big picture window over the bar, Kate sees a rock garden and waterfall. She notes that Nick Cole has chosen a private booth in a corner rather than one in the center aisle.

Seated in a booth in the opposite corner are Tommy Banks and his wife. Banks is in his mid-fifties, neatly dressed in a gray chalk-stripe suit and a wide, red-and-black tie with a splashy geometric pattern. A bottle of Coca-Cola sits on the table in front of him. He no longer drinks or smokes and never carries a gun, preferring to work behind the scenes.

He owns or has a share in at least twenty liquor stores, bars, restaurants, and nightclubs. Banks is also suspected—but never charged—of being involved in the December 1933 murder of Conrad Althen, the mob's auditor. The FBI believed that Althen knew too much and was about to squeal. Word is the feds are about to nail Banks for income tax evasion.

Banks is known as "Soft Touch Tommy" for his willingness to help out his friends with loans. But Kate doubts Banks is a "soft touch." When he looks up and stares at her, his close-set eyes are small, piercing black beads that convey pure malice.

Nick Cole takes a swig from his cocktail glass and stands when he sees her coming toward him. He kisses her on the cheek. She notes the disappointment on his face as she slides into the plush, cushy booth on the opposite side of the table.

"Would you like a drink?" he asks with a hesitant smile.

"Gimlet," she says. "Half gin and half Rose's lime juice, please."

Nick gets the attention of a waiter and orders another Scotch and water for himself along with the gimlet.

"How's Homicide?" Kate asks, directing the conversation away from their failed relationship—and any hopes Nick might have of rekindling it.

"Solved my first case," he says in an excited voice.

She waits for more information.

Nick leans across the table and says in a quiet but proud voice, "I can't say much till the DA brings charges, but it involves the murder of Zeno Malkin."

Kate is surprised. "I thought he committed suicide."

"Well, he didn't. I cracked the case and got the confession."

"Congratulations."

"I always knew Homicide was for me." He lifts his cocktail glass in a salute and drains the rest of it in one swallow.

"You work with Cafferty?"

"Sure did."

"He didn't get the collar?"

"He was a step behind." Nick shakes his head. "He's getting old. Either that or he was riding Russ Krueger's coattails for years."

"I wouldn't be too confident, Nicky."

"What do you mean?"

"Cafferty has a lot of experience. Soak it up."

"I will if he levels with me. But he withheld information."

"It takes time to build a relationship."

"Speaking of a relationship . . ."

Kate regrets using the word "relationship." "That's not why I asked you to meet me," she says.

Nick looks deflated, then guarded.

The waiter arrives with their drinks and departs.

Kate sips her gimlet.

"Why the cold shoulder, Katie?"

"It's no use dredging up the past."

"We're not talking ancient history." Nick takes a long swallow of his drink. "So why the hell are we sitting here?"

"I need your help."

He stares at her with watchful eyes. Then he reaches across the table and puts a hand over hers. "Sure, Katie. Anything. Name it."

She resists the instinct to pull away. "It's the cornfield killings. Ben and Davy Roth."

Nick's eyes narrow. "The *Roths*? What about them?"

"Come on, Nicky. You know what happened. Word's going around that Mike Bannister might've murdered them."

He lets out a derisive laugh and removes his hand from hers. "You're not serious."

"Deadly," she says.

"I was there, Katie. I know what happened."

"Did you see Bannister shoot them?"

Nick hesitates, then shakes his head. "What're you doing, Katie?"

"My job."

"And destroy the life of a cop in the process."

"Even if he might've murdered two people?"

"They were just . . ." Nick catches himself.

"Just *Jews*. Is that what you were going to say, Nicky?"

"No. They were criminals. Burglars. They weren't lily white." Nick pauses a moment.

"What?" Kate asks.

"You're just angry with Bannister because he messed up your first trial."

"That has nothing to do with it."

"You sure, Katie?"

She releases a frustrated breath. "So you won't help me?"

"I can't."

She slides out of the booth.

"Where you going?"

"To find someone who can," she says, heading for the exit.

* * *

Jake and Max Hayes are sitting directly behind home plate at Nicollet Park, the Minneapolis Millers' stadium on 31st and Nicollet Avenue. Max is wearing sunglasses to hide the yellowish purple bruises under his eyes. It's a great night for a baseball game. Clear skies. Light wind. The Millers are in first place and are playing the second-place Indianapolis Indians. Jake loves the smell of fresh cut grass, hot dogs, and fresh roasted peanuts at the concession stand, the sound of the catcher's mitt popping with a fastball, the crack of the bat squared up on the baseball. He knows Max loves it, too, especially since the Millers are fighting for the pennant. Managed by thirty-six-year-old former catcher Tommy Heath, the Miller infield is solid with Davey Williams at second, Ray Dandridge at third, Bill Jennings at shortstop, and their best hitter, Bert Haas, at first.

Dandridge, the only Negro on the team, is at bat. Short and stocky and quick as a cat, Dandridge is a natural third baseman and rarely lets a ball get past him. With his solid defense at the hot corner, a batting average over .300, and his eleven home runs and nearly eighty RBIs, he's a candidate for most valuable player honors in the American Association.

"The Giants should bring Dandridge up," Max says, referring to the New York Giants, who have a working agreement with the Millers. "With his skills, it's a crime he's never made it to the majors."

"They say at thirty-seven, he's too old."

"He's flashy. He can still play, Jake. People would pay to see him."

As if on cue, Dandridge rips one into the gap in right center as the capacity crowd of 10,000 roars. The ball hammers off the short fence in right. Dandridge sprints for second and slides in, just beating the centerfielder's throw to the shortstop covering the base.

"What'd I tell you?" Max says with a grin.

When the crowd quiets down some, Jake says, "How you feeling, Max?"

"Better. But I still have occasional dizzy spells. They'll gradually go away."

"Still no recollection of who did this to you?"

Max shakes his head and chews some popcorn. "Don't know if I really want to remember."

Jake is reluctant to press, but he'd love to get his hands— and fists—on the asshole that beat on Max. "What're you working on now?"

Max takes a sheet of paper out of his jacket pocket and hands it to Jake. "Take a look."

Charles Green, president of the Twin City Rapid Transit Co., testified at a Minnesota Railroad and Warehouse Commission hearing that Fred Ossanna, former TCRT general counsel, had proposed creating a slush fund of $20,000 to buy favors and concessions from six or eight city council aldermen. The slush fund was to be raised by kickbacks from gasoline and oil purchases by the transit firm. City council members are considering a special council meeting to determine what course of action they should take in view of the accusations.

"Where's Ossanna now?"

"Word has it he's in Florida."

"Who told you about these kickbacks?"

Max shakes his head. "I give away my sources, nobody will talk to me."

Johnny Kropf flies out, ending the inning, and knuckleballer Hoyt Wilhelm takes the mound for the Millers.

"Have any ideas about what's going on with the TCRT, Jake?"

"Graft. Corruption. Greed."

"I get all that. But there's something else going on."

Jake takes a sip of Coke and gazes down the first-base line toward the stadium entrance with its steeply pitched red tile roof. The entrance sits at the corner of Nicollet Avenue and West 31st Street, which separates the ballpark from the streetcar barns and garages of the Twin City Rapid Transit Company.

"Whatever it is, stay out of it."

Wilhelm has retired the first two batters of the inning when Max says, "I've been thinking a lot about her lately."

"Your girlfriend, Sarah?" Jake says, knowing full well that Max is referring to his mother, Rachel.

"You know."

"Your mother was special."

"Must be my investigation into the restrictive covenants. I was old enough to remember how she fought against those, not just for Jews, but for Negroes, Orientals, whatever group was being discriminated against."

"She was a firebrand."

Max looks squarely at Jake. "You've always been different."

"I'm not perfect. But I try to judge one by one. It helped that I met your mother. Never ran across a Jew growing up in Northern Minnesota, though I'm sure there were some. She clued me in."

"You ever consider dating her?"

Jake avoids Max's gaze and stares at the brightly lit field as Hoyt Wilhelm strikes out the third batter of the inning on a wicked knuckleball that floats out of the strike zone. Then his gaze slides back to Max. "She sure caught my eye. But I doubt your grandparents would've approved, me being a goy and all."

Max is quiet for a time before he says, "I always wondered where she was going on Armistice Day when the blizzard hit."

Jake looks away again and says, "I sure as hell wish she'd gotten there."

* * *

Kate Dawson walks into the Cassius Bar & Café on South Third Street in downtown. The place is filling with a well-dressed, ethnically-mixed crowd. There's a low buzz of conversation, a tinkling of glasses, and a thin haze of smoke in the air. Later in the evening men in tuxedos and women in gowns will listen and dance to jazz in the elegant Bamboo Room, one of

Kate's favorite haunts. She often brought Nick here when they were dating.

Nick once told her that the Chinese On Leong Tong and the Hip Sing Tong mobs, which controlled the biggest gambling pot in all of Minnesota, operated out of the second floor of the bar. They've been operating out of Minneapolis since the early 1900s. The Tongs never cause trouble, so the MPD never has any reason to shake them up.

Anthony Brutus Cassius, the owner of the café, waves from behind the bar when he sees Kate. Brutus, as he prefers to be called, is part of the "Great Migration" of Negroes that began moving from the southern states into Minneapolis in the 1930s. They settled on the Northside, Seven Corners, and the Southside, between East 34th and 46th Streets and from Nicollet Avenue to Chicago Avenue, an area first populated by Swedes and Norwegians.

An outspoken man, Brutus first gained notoriety when he organized a union after discovering Negro waiters at the Curtis Hotel where he worked were making only $17 a month while their white counterparts brought home $75. The union negotiated higher wages and eventually brought a lawsuit against the hotel, winning back pay for its members.

In '37, Brutus opened the Dreamland Café at 38th Street and 4th Avenue, in the heart of the Southside community, at a time when the nicer restaurants downtown were off limits to non-whites. The café was a favored haunt of Negro celebrities, like Lena Horne, who stayed with colored families in the neighborhood during her visits to town because coloreds were barred from Minneapolis hotels.

Then, in '46, Brutus became the first Negro in Minneapolis to be granted a liquor license and the first to get a large loan from a major bank to start a business. Before Brutus received the loan in '46, Negroes were limited to owning barbecues, shoeshine parlors, and barbershops. The club was the first place in downtown Minneapolis where whites and coloreds could openly mingle. A stocky, muscular-looking man, Brutus often uses the contranym "Janus-faced," after the Roman god with two faces, when describing Minneapolis.

"Hello, Miss Dawson," he says, coming over to greet her. "Good to see you again."

"Good to see you too, Brutus."

"Are you meeting Sergeant Cole?"

She shakes her head. "Not tonight. I'm looking for information."

He escorts her to an open table and sits down across from her. "What's on your mind?"

Kate takes a photo out of her wallet and passes it to him. "I'm looking for this man. Sam Witherspoon. He's been suspended from his job on the police force, but the department has no current address."

Brutus peers at the photo and then at Kate. "And you think I know him because he's a Negro?"

"I deserve that. Stupid question. Let me put it to you this way. Sam Witherspoon was involved in the cornfield shooting."

Brutus looks at the photo again, then raises his eyes. "Why was he suspended?"

"Don't know. But it might be because of the shooting."

"Like how?"

"Maybe Sam saw more than he's willing to admit."

Brutus slides the photo across the table to her. "Perhaps he doesn't want to be found."

"I want to help him."

Brutus looks skeptical. "You? How?"

"By saving his life."

"That's awfully dramatic."

"Not if some powerful men in this town are covering something up."

"About what?"

Kate's about to tell him and then changes her mind. "I can't say."

"Yet you expect me to help you."

"You know what goes on in this city, Brutus. And you're not just helping me. You're helping Sam."

"So you say."

Another dead end. Kate begins to rise.

Brutus places a hand over hers. "I never said I wouldn't help you, Miss Dawson." He takes a pen and paper from his coat pocket and jots something down. As he pushes the paper across the table, he says, "Try the Young Brothers' barbershop on 38th Street and Fourth Avenue. Johnny, Sylvester—known as Chubby—and Fred run the place. If Sam Witherspoon is around, they'll know where."

"I appreciate your help."

"I'm hoping no harm comes to Mr. Witherspoon."

"I'll do my best to prevent it."

Brutus's smile is as thin as a knife blade.

Chapter 23

When Kate Dawson walks into the Young Brothers' Barbershop, the Negro customers in the three barber chairs—and the Young brothers standing behind each chair—stare at Kate as if in a freeze-frame.

Kate smiles. "I'm not here for a haircut," she says, holding out the note Brutus gave her.

The barber standing behind the nearest chair tentatively reaches out his hand and takes the note. After reading it, he passes the note to his brother standing behind the second barber chair. He reads it and then passes it to the third brother, who takes a moment to read it and then approaches Kate.

"A woman named Gloria Two Bears lives in the duplex near Franklin and 23rd Avenue," he says in a quiet voice. "She might know where Sam Witherspoon is." He holds out the note.

Kate takes it back. "Thank you."

"You're welcome, Miss . . ."

"Dawson. Kate Dawson. Well . . ." she says, hesitating a moment. Then she smiles, waves, and heads out the door.

Twenty minutes later Kate cruises to a stop along the curb in front of a two-story duplex. She kills the engine and remains seated behind the Packard's steering wheel in a metaphorical darkness, trying to suppress the feeling of desperation that has overtaken her ever since she left Nick Cole at McCarthy's in search of someone who could help her. In the past, she's always found a path around obstacles in her life, though, admittedly, they've been few and far between—at least up to this point in time. She's rarely experienced doubt. Now, she wonders if searching for Sam Witherspoon is a mistake. If word should filter back to Wilson Barlow that she's pursuing the cornfield shooting, she might as well kiss her law career with the DA's office good-bye. A little voice whispers, *You can always work for your father*, but that would be an admission of failure. She blows out an anxious breath, exits the car, and marches up the sidewalk.

She steps onto the front porch and spots Two Bears' name on a small mailbox attached to the wall next to the screen door on her right. The inner door behind the screen is open, and Kate can see a set of steps leading to the second floor. She pulls on the door handle, discovers it's latched, and pushes a doorbell, which triggers loud barking. A moment later, the dog, a big black and tan German shepherd, bounds down the stairs, locks its dark eyes on Kate, and continues barking.

Kate steps back, unsure if the dog can get through the flimsy screen door, and wonders if it does, what it will do to her.

"Quiet, Mato," a woman calls as she comes down the stairs. The voice is soft, but there's strength behind it. The dog quits barking and stares at Kate as if she's a juicy bone.

A full-figured woman approaches the door in a pair of dungarees and a red flannel shirt. Her feet are bare. Her face is round, the nose slightly flat. She has the almond-shaped dark eyes and heavy eyelids common to American Indians. Her skin tone is reddish brown, and her long, thick, dark hair is twisted in a side braid. Kate estimates she's somewhere in her mid-to-late twenties, but hard years have worked her over.

"Gloria Two Bears?" Kate says.

The woman pushes the dog aside with a knee and nods.

"My name is Kate Dawson. I'm looking for Sam Witherspoon."

193

"Don't know any Sam Witherspoon."

"I was told you do."

"Whoever told you that was either lying or mistaken."

"Who you talking to, Gloria?" A man's loud voice carries down the stairs.

Kate glances at Gloria Two Bears, who just looks away. Kate steps closer to the screen door and calls upstairs, "Sam Witherspoon?"

"Who the hell are you?"

"Kate Dawson. I'm from the DA's office. I'd like to talk with you."

"Got nothin' to say to the DA."

Kate looks at Gloria Two Bears. "Sam's in trouble," she says.

Two Bears arches her eyebrows. "And you've come to help?"

Kate notes the sarcasm. "Big trouble," she insists.

"You heard what he said."

"Did you hear what I said?"

"Sam's in trouble."

Kate nods.

Gloria hesitates, thinks about it, and looks upstairs. Then she shoves the dog again with her knee and unlatches the screen door.

"What about the dog?" Kate asks.

"Come, Mato," Gloria says.

Kate peers through the screen door. "Interesting name."

"It's Sioux for Bear," Gloria says, heading up the stairs. Mato follows.

Kate waits a moment, still wary. Then she opens the screen door and walks up the steps and into the small living room, stopping behind Gloria and the dog.

A half-dozen Indian dolls stand on a single wall shelf. Tacked to another wall is a beautiful ivory and scarlet starburst quilt. An empty bottle of Grain Belt beer and an ashtray loaded with cigarette stubs rest on a marred coffee table in front of a beige davenport. A Motorola television with a 12" console and walnut cabinet stands in a corner.

Sam Witherspoon comes out of the kitchen. He's wearing khaki pants and a coffee-stained sleeveless undershirt, and he needs a shave. In one hand is a full bottle of Grain Belt, in the other, a sandwich with a bite taken out of the white bread. Shocked by his disheveled appearance, Kate barely recognizes the man she saw at the awards ceremony one week ago. The extra few pounds around his middle and his sallow complexion add years to his appearance.

"What's she doin' here?" he says to Gloria.

"Why were you suspended from the force, Sam?" Kate asks, jumping in before Gloria can reply.

Witherspoon's upper lip curls in disdain as he plops down on the davenport with a heavy sigh. The dog jumps up on the couch and curls up next to him. "How 'bout I'm everything they hate."

"But you knew that going in."

Witherspoon shrugs.

Kate hustles to an armchair and sits down.

"Bring the lady a drink," Witherspoon says to Gloria.

"I'm fine," Kate says.

"Suit yourself."

Gloria disappears into the kitchen.

"Could there be something else about your suspension, Sam?"

Witherspoon takes a long pull on his beer and thinks the question over, his bloodshot eyes flitting restlessly.

"What happened in that cornfield, Sam?" Kate says, leaning forward.

"Two young men were killed." His eyes slide off Kate and stare at some distant point.

"Did Mike Bannister murder them?"

"Don't know."

"I think you do."

His eyes find hers again. "What's your game, lady? What do you want?"

"You tell me what really happened. Maybe we can help each other."

"Yeah?"

"Yeah. I'll help you get your job back."

He looks away. "I don't want my job back. I just wanna be left alone."

* * *

Late that afternoon Jake is at his desk in the Homicide/Sex Crime pen when he gets a call from Harold Jamison, the coroner.

"Three days ago you were here for Zeno Malkin's autopsy," Jamison says. "You asked about a stiff we ID'd as Abe Fishman."

"What about him?"

"Wife said he wasn't Fishman. Said her husband disappeared years ago. Doesn't know what happened to him, but the guy on the slab isn't her husband. Doesn't know who this guy is."

"How'd you ID him as Fishman in the first place?"

"Driver's license in his wallet."

"Got any idea who this guy is?"

"Ran his prints. Came up as Eli Roth. Did a stretch for bootlegging years ago."

"You talk to Roth's wife?"

"She came down and ID'd him. It's Eli Roth, all right."

* * *

A thin blade of moon cuts a small hole out of the darkness over the city. Heat lightning flashes on the horizon. The air is heavy with the threat of rain. A siren wails. Far away.

Max Hayes has the driver's side window open on his 1940 Chevy, his left arm resting on the window frame. The lightly traveled tar road ahead of him snakes along the high banks of the Mississippi. Through the trees to his left he glimpses the black ribbon of water. He's thinking about the ballgame he attended with Jake—happy that the Millers won—and listening to the Reverend Paul Rader preach a sermon on the radio as he drives.

Paul and his aging father, Luke, are two of the first radio evangelists in Minneapolis. Working out of the Lake Street Tabernacle, their show is broadcast twice a day. The Raders preach that Anglo-Saxons are the true Israelites and that Satan created Jews. They refer to FDR's New Deal as the "Jew Deal." Hitler's actions and the Holocaust during WWII were justified because Jews aren't fit to live. Since World War II ended, they've toned down the anti-Jewish rhetoric and replaced it with an anti-Communist message. Max listens to Luke Rader's rants because they often provide him with ideas for his columns.

Tonight's sermon focuses on an all-too-familiar theme of good versus evil. Godless Communists are the evil outsiders infiltrating the US and undermining the inherent goodness of the country, with the help of atheists and Communist sympathizers, themes championed by Wisconsin Senator Joseph McCarthy. Max isn't a Communist, though he's been accused of being one. But as a Jew he's had plenty of experience with being an outsider.

He turns down the radio and focuses on the headlights illuminating the road and his upcoming meeting with an informant who has information on secret TCRT dealings. Max has a sense that this could break the story wide open. He's eager to share the info with Jake, but not before he has a chance to review it. He wants to make sure the informant is not just blowing smoke. Max's father, Arthur, had a reputation—deserved or not—for bending the truth to suit his journalistic purposes.

A large raindrop splatters on the windshield. Max rolls up the driver's side window. In his rearview mirror he spots a pair of headlights coming up fast behind him. The river road has no shoulder and is too narrow for him to pull over to let the car pass. His speedometer reads 30 mph, plenty fast on this stretch of road. He figures the asshole behind him has his high beams on. Max presses the accelerator and the speed climbs to 35 mph. Still, the headlights are blinding.

A deluge suddenly hammers the windshield. Max switches on the wipers. The car behind crowds his bumper. The rain is coming down so hard that the wipers are having trouble keeping the glass clear. Max squints and leans forward. He slows rounding a sharp curve and lets out a sharp cry. A stalled car directly ahead blocks both lanes. Max slams on the brakes, trying to maintain control of the Ford as it skids to the left on the slick surface. He realizes in a heartbeat that he'll miss the car ahead, but not the tall, thick oak tree along the embankment.

The impact of the ton-and-a-half car slamming into the oak crumples the passenger side door, rips off the hubcaps, and shatters the glass. Max is thrown against the driver's side door and then against the steering wheel. The Ford bounces off the tree and slides through a fence toward the embankment. Dazed, Max fumbles for the door handle as the car rolls on its side and then over and over, down the steep hill, pinning him inside. There's a cacophony of grinding and popping, and finally an explosion as the gas tank ignites. Flames engulf the metal. The last roll sends the car into the river, where it sinks slowly below the surface, extinguishing the flames and leaving a smoky cloud hanging like a pall over the water.

Chapter 24

Darkness has descended upon Jake Cafferty. Hollowed out his insides. He's unable to concentrate on anything for more than a few minutes. He wants to cry, but no tears come. Keeping busy is the best antidote to the looming depression and the temptation to drink. But after a day of wandering around like the undead, he calls in sick.

Max Hayes' body is to be interred in the gravesite between his deceased mother and father at the Minneapolis Jewish Cemetery, the oldest and largest of four Jewish cemeteries located side-by-side near Penn Avenue in Richfield, on twenty acres of what was once farmland. With headstones nestled together in tight rows like tenements, the cemetery is like a desolate city of the dead.

Max's death, much like Rachel's death almost ten years before, is beyond Jake's understanding. Why is he still alive while the two people he loved are dead? It makes no sense. Perhaps Max's death would be easier to accept if there were someone to blame—someone who would afford him the opportunity to exact revenge. But Max apparently lost control of his Ford on a slippery curve. His car slid off the road, broke through a retaining fence, and rolled one hundred feet down an embankment before coming to a rest in shallow water along the river's edge. Two employees of the city's Public Works Department discovered the wreckage the following morning. Still, despite all evidence pointing to an unfortunate accident, Jake has lingering doubts. Maybe it's his detective instincts—or maybe it's something else.

The day is blustery and cool. Clouds veil the sun. Having attended Rachel's funeral, Jake understands that a Jewish burial takes place as soon after death as possible. Because Jews want the body to decompose naturally, embalming is forbidden. Neither the body nor flowers are displayed.

The funeral ceremony at the gravesite is brief and includes the recitation of psalms, followed by a eulogy and a closing prayer. Jake hangs back as mourners then come forward to participate in the filling of the gravesite. Using a spade, each mourner throws three shovelfuls of dirt into the grave. When finished, they put the shovel back in the ground, rather than handing it to the next person, to symbolically avoid passing along their grief to other mourners. As Max's grandfather, Samuel, tosses the last shovel full of dirt on his grandson's grave, his gaze connects with Jake's.

Age and misfortune have softened the old man's eyes. Where once Jake saw only hostility and anger, he now sees pain and despair. Samuel has lost his wife to cancer, his only daughter to a sudden storm, and now his only grandson to a car accident. Jake would like to offer condolences, but "I'm sorry" seems feeble in the face of such tragedy. Besides, the old man has always resented Jake's short-lived relationship with Rachel. In the few times that Jake has run into him over the years, no greeting, no words were ever spoken.

As the Jewish mourners recite the Kaddish prayer, honoring the departed, Jake stands in silence, his eyes drawn down to the information written on the cold marble face of the headstone. Max's name is written in English and Hebrew. Below it is the date of his death in English, and then his birth and death dates according to the Hebrew calendar. As the crowd disperses to spend the next seven days sitting *shiva*, Jake notes that some tombs have small piles of stones on them.

"Visitors leave them to show they have stopped by the gravesite," a woman's voice says.

Jake turns and sees Sarah Weisman, Max's girlfriend. She's wearing a black dress and pillbox hat with a net veil in front of her eyes. "I saw you looking at them," she says.

"I hadn't noticed the stones earlier." Jake offers a thin smile. "How you doing?"

Sarah's eyes fill with tears. She lifts the veil and wipes her eyes with a handkerchief. "Not so good. You?"

"Toughest thing I've had to do since . . ." He pauses. "You know where Max was going that night, Sarah, out on River Road?"

She shakes her head. "I don't. But Max's journal is missing. He always kept it with him. His belongings were returned after the accident, but the journal wasn't there."

"Maybe it fell into the river during the crash?"

"It's possible. But he usually kept it in his briefcase. And that was recovered. I'm going through Max's office. All his previous journals are there, but not the one from this year. If I find it, I'll let you know."

"Thanks."

"Are you coming to the house?"

"I don't think so."

"You should."

Not knowing what else to say, Jake shrugs.

"Lieutenant."

Jake looks to his left and sees Max's grandfather, Samuel, approaching, his cheeks sunken, a kippah covering the few thin white hairs on his head, and a cane in his arthritic hand. He leans forward against the wind, as though it might blow him over.

Sarah reaches out and touches Jake's hands with her own. "Take care." With that she turns and hurries away.

Jake turns to meet the old man. Then, not wanting to cause a scene, he backs away.

"Wait!" Samuel calls in a hoarse voice. "I have something to tell you."

"I'm not here to cause trouble."

Jake is surprised when Samuel takes his hand and says, "Thank you for coming, Lieutenant, and for looking after my grandson. When Rachel died, I . . ." There are tears in his eyes, but a smile of gratitude on his face.

"You're welcome," Jake says.

The old man releases Jake's hand and looks up at him. "A wise man once said that any man can make mistakes, but only an idiot persists in his error."

"Sounds like good advice."

"My grandson," he says, struggling to get the words out. "I want you to know."

"Know what?" Jake asks.

"Max was your son."

Part Three

"... Descend and follow me down the abyss.
I am thy child, as thou wert Saturn's child;
Mightier than thee: and we must dwell together
Henceforth in darkness ..."

—Percy Bysshe Shelley
"Prometheus Unbound: Act III"

Chapter 25

Mike Bannister unracks the Ithaca 12 gauge with his gloved hands and quietly opens the car door. His breath fogs the cold air as he steps out of the car and onto the snow-covered ground. Overhead, above the alley where he's parked, he hears a man and a woman arguing in the unit on the upper level of the wood-frame duplex. He pulls a Colt .22LR from a coat pocket and fires a bullet straight up in the air.

The shot draws a heavy-set man, clad only in boxer shorts, out onto the balcony, where he stands under a single lit bulb, reeling gently. The man looks down and sees Bannister, who fires another round from the .22 revolver, slips it in his coat pocket, and then lifts the shotgun to his shoulder. Steadies it. "Police! Put down your gun!"

"Huh?" The heavy-set man looks puzzled, leaning over the railing.

Bannister thumbs off the safety and fires. The puzzled look is gone. So is the face. The body slams back against a post and then pitches forward over the balcony rail and falls onto the snow.

Sirens scream in the distance.

Bannister quickly pulls an old Iver Johnson .22 revolver from a pants pocket, loads the two spent rounds from the Colt .22LR into the Iver Johnson's chamber, fits the dead man's right hand around the grip to get the prints, and tosses the Iver Johnson beside the body. Then he slides two fresh rounds into the Colt's chamber and pockets it.

He's walking back to his Ford as backups arrive.

* * *

Nick Cole parks in the alley beside two squad cars, their red flashers swirling in the darkness. In the glare of spotlight beams, he sees the body of a black man in a puddle of bloody snow, clothed only in a pair of boxer shorts. Mike Bannister and four patrol officers stand around it. Clouds of condensation blur the cold air above their heads.

Nick looks across the front seat, where Jake Cafferty is slumped against the passenger side door, shoulders hunched. "Wanna stay in the car?"

Unshaven and wearing a hat and rumpled sport coat, Jake sits up with a start.

"You need an overcoat," Nick says.

"I'm fine," Jake says, blowing out a boozy breath.

Nick gets out, buttons his overcoat, and heads toward the body. Jake trails behind, walking unsteadily across the icy alley, his sport coat waffling in the wind.

Looking down at the body, Nick sees that most of the victim's head is gone. "What happened, Mike?" he asks.

"I heard the domestic call on my radio and pulled into the alley. Heard a guy and woman arguing. Stepped out. Vic must've heard me and gone out on the balcony. I saw kind of a glint."

"Then?"

"Ducked back in the car. Got the shotgun. Steadied it behind the car door. I said, 'Police. Put down your gun.'"

"Then what?"

"He pointed a gun at me."

Nick sees a handgun beside the body.

"He fire at you?"

"Damn right."

"How many shots?"

"Two."

"Okay. We'll bag the revolver." To the other cops Nick says, "Go upstairs and find the woman. Then check with the neighbors. See if we have any wits." Turning to Bannister, Nick says, "Take the shotgun, put it on safe, and lean it against my car. Give me your gun."

Bannister slides his Colt Official Police out of his holster and hands it to him.

"Sit in the back of our car. Got it?"

Bannister nods.

Jake, standing outside the circle of men, looks up at the balcony. Then he looks at Bannister. "Balcony light on or off, Bannister?"

Bannister, ignoring Jake, looks back at Nick. "You the lead on this?"

"Answer the question."

Bannister shrugs. "Light was off."

He starts for the detective sedan and stops again when Jake persists, "You sure? Tough to see the 'glint' of a gun with no light and a crescent moon."

"Yeah, I'm sure. Sure you don't need to sleep off the drunk?"

Moving toward Bannister, his fists clenched, Jake slips on a patch of ice and tumbles to the ground.

"You all right?" Nick calls.

Jake, embarrassed, waves him off, struggles to his feet, and brushes off the snow.

Bannister looks at Nick.

"It'll be okay, Mike. Go sit in the car."

"Hey, Cole," says one of the patrol officers, coming out of the duplex. "You'll never believe who the dead guy is."

"Who?"

"Lady upstairs says it's Sam Witherspoon."

Chapter 26

Jake has a hazy memory of the information he and Nick Cole gathered from the scene and their interview with Gloria Two Bears. But he does recall Bannister saying that he saw the "glint" of a gun before he fired. Doubting that Bannister could see much of anything if the balcony light was off, Jake examined the pull switch and filament in the broken bulb just before he threw up in the toilet in Two Bears' bathroom. Cole helped him to their detective sedan shortly afterward. Now, after leaving the scene, he stares blankly out the Ford's passenger side window, clear-headed, but craving a drink. He looks at Cole and says, "Turn left at the next corner."

"What for?"

"Have to see someone about a problem."

"We're not stopping at a bar, Jake."

"Didn't say we were."

Nick hangs a left.

"Keep going," Jake says. "I'll tell you when to turn again."

"Where we going?"

"Don't know the address. Just the location."

"'Bout time you started trusting me, Jake."

Jake glances out the passenger window and then at Nick. "Been married, Cole?"

"Neither have you. What's marriage got to do with trusting your partner?"

"It's about a contract. An even stronger covenant binds cop partnerships. Can I trust this guy with my life? The greatest fear a cop has is having a coward for a partner. One way or another a cop has to be tested. Has to prove himself willing to lay his ass on the line."

Cole rolls his eyes. "I didn't see you at the Bulge. So spare me the lecture."

"Street is a different battlefield, Cole." Jake knows it's the booze talking, but he can't help himself. "When I was in uniform, two guys I thought I knew well, Ty Jorgenson and Eddie Flowers, were on routine patrol when the call came in that there was a botched robbery and shooting at a liquor store at 26th and Hennepin. Eddie went into the store where the shooter was barricaded behind a couple of tables, after taking down the owner and two customers. He and Eddie exchanged fire. Eddie took a .38 slug in the chest and died on the spot. The shooter committed suicide. Ty Jorgenson stayed outside. Never went in, even after backup arrived. Six months later he ate his gun while he sat in his parked car outside the liquor store with the radio turned to the classical music station."

"You sayin' that I'm Ty Jorgenson, that I'm a coward?"

"Don't know till you lay it all on the line."

"Same goes for you, Jake."

"Couple months back, when I was at the morgue for Zeno Malkin's autopsy, body on one of the slabs was Abe Fishman. Gandy dancer killed him with a knife. Week before that I saw you talking to Fishman near the Flame Café."

"Fishman sold booze out of his car. Joe Briggs beat him up one night. I felt sorry for the old guy and gave him a few bucks."

Jake pauses a beat before he speaks again. "Turns out the stiff wasn't Fishman. It was Eli Roth."

"Roth?" Cole says. "Any relation to Ben and Davy?"

"Their father."

"No shit. Why was he using the name Fishman?"

"Don't know. But I aim to find out."

It's nearly midnight. The streets are as cold and bleak as Jake's soul. Without plenty of booze coursing through his blood, the only thing keeping him going is the rage he feels whenever he thinks of Max Hayes' death—and the person he holds responsible.

"Turn right in two blocks," he says.

Soon they're in the warehouse district near Gluek's Bar.

"We're not stopping for a drink, Jake. I know what too much booze can do to you."

Jake looks at Nick. "You talkin' about me or you, Cole?"

"Maybe both. You want to kill yourself, use your thirty-eight. It's quicker. You don't have to drag me and everyone else who cares about you through your slide into the gutter."

Jake puts his hand over his heart. "I'm touched, Cole. Didn't know you cared."

"Shut the hell up, Jake, and tell me where we're going."

"You're not going anywhere. You're dropping me off."

"Where?"

"Here," Jake says, pointing to a large warehouse on the right. "Pull over."

Nick slows and nudges the car to the curb. "What the hell we doing here?"

"My business."

"I'm not leaving you alone."

"You'll do what I tell you to do." Jake opens the passenger side door.

Nick grabs him by the arm.

Jake tries to give him his best cop stare.

Nick lets go. "Everyone loses someone they care about, Jake."

"I'm not everyone. See you in the morning, partner."

"How you gonna get home?"

"I'll take a cab." Jake gets out, steadies himself, and heads for the warehouse entrance.

*   *   *

Nick watches from the car till Jake is inside the warehouse. Light spills from two windows. He starts to drive away, hits the brakes, and pulls to the curb again. The warehouse looks familiar from his time as a beat cop, though he has trouble coming up with why. Then he remembers. Ever since Kid Cann was running illegal liquor during Prohibition, he's kept an office here in an old milling building. Now, curious, Nick shuts off the car engine and steps out.

A gust of wind scatters papers and sharp, biting crystals of snow. Nick tries the door where Jake entered, but it's locked. He steps to his left, cups his hands, and peers through a dirty windowpane. He sees three blurry figures standing by a large desk. The short one has to be the Kid. The tall one has to be Jack Apple. Jake is facing them.

Moments later Jake throws a looping punch at Apple. The punch catches Apple on the shoulder. Jake follows up with a left, but Apple rolls with it. Instead of a solid hit, it's a glancing blow. Off-balance, Jake topples onto the desk. Apple grabs Jake by the lapels and shoves him to the ground. Jake lands on his ass, but he doesn't stay down for long. As he struggles to his feet, Apple digs a right into Jake's gut, doubling him over. Then he drives a knee into Jake's face. Jake goes down hard on his back.

Nick steps away from the window and kicks open the warehouse door, drawing his piece as he rushes in. "That's enough!" he yells, waving the gun at Cann and his enforcer.

The Kid and Jack Apple gaze at him as they would a fly buzzing around their heads.

"Easy," the Kid says. "Nothing to get excited about."

Nick glances at Jake, who's sitting on the floor holding a blood-soaked handkerchief over his nose. "You all right?"

"Been better," he mumbles.

Nick's eyes lock first on Apple, who has a smirk on his ugly face, and then at the Kid, who looks as innocent as a five-year-old. "What's going on?"

The Kid gestures at Jake. "The lieutenant believes that I, or my associate, Mr. Apple, is somehow responsible for Max Hayes' death. We had nothing to do with it. It's been reported as a tragic accident."

"Lots of *accidents* happen around you," Nick says.

The Kid points at the gun. "Wouldn't want another. Why don't you holster your gun before someone else gets hurt?"

"Only person likely to get hurt now is you," Nick says to Cann.

"That a fact?" Apple says, giving Nick his deadeye stare.

Nick's eyes never falter as he shifts his gaze to Apple. "I've heard about you, Jack. You're a real tough guy when it comes to beating up drunks and threatening old people."

"You ain't drunk or old."

"Now, now," Cann says. "No need. No harm done here."

"Speak for yourself," Jake says, struggling to his feet. He glances at the bloody handkerchief and covers his nose again. "I think my nose is broken."

"Nothing but a misunderstanding," Cann says.

Nick glares at Jack Apple. "Wanna take your best shot?"

Apple grins. "Love to."

"This is my problem, Cole," Jake says. "Let's go."

"In a minute."

"Ain't going to take that long," Apple says.

Nick's heart is pumping hard. He holsters his thirty-eight, takes off his overcoat and shoulder rig, and tosses both on the desk.

The Kid says, "Let it go, Detective."

"Get out of the way, Kid."

Cann's face reddens. "Don't say I didn't warn you." He backs away.

Nick moves to his left, away from the desk, on the balls of his feet, both hands up in a boxer's stance, like he was back in the ring.

Jack Apple chuckles and shakes his head. "Okay, pretty boy. Messin' you up is gonna be fun." He moves toward Nick, feinting with his left and then launching a right with enough force to take Nick's head off.

Nick ducks under it, steps to his left, and drives a hard left hook into Apple's right kidney. Apple grunts as his legs buckle. He whirls in anger to face Nick. As he does, Nick snaps Apple's face with two left jabs and follows up with a straight right to his nose. The blow sends Apple crashing against a post. Before he can regain his senses, Nick is on him, hammering Apple's midsection. The air rushes out of Apple's lungs. Nick steps back and lands a quick left/right head combination. Apple's legs turn to spaghetti. He sinks to his knees and falls face first onto the wood floor.

"Not bad, Detective," Cann says. "I could use a man like you."

Nick shakes his right fist, trying to regain some feeling. "I'm not for sale. And don't ever threaten me or my partner again." He slips on his shoulder rig and throws his coat over Jake's shoulders. "Come on."

As they're walking toward the exit, Jake says to Nick, "I could've taken Apple."

"Yeah. You hit him a few more times with your face, I'm sure he would've given up."

"I'm not at my best."

"Haven't been for a while now, Jake."

"I wasn't always a drunk, Cole."

Nick stops and looks at him. "Sure you were, Jake. Sooner you admit it, the sooner you can sober up. For good."

Chapter 27

The next morning Nick Cole takes a seat in front of Chief William Flanagan's desk. Captain Avery Arnold sits in a chair to his left. In the chair to his right is the DA, Wilson Barlow.

"Thanks for taking the time to see us, Chief," Barlow says.

Flanagan tosses the report he's been reading on his desktop. "Mr. Barlow," he says, "do you know how many successful homicide prosecutions there have been of on-duty police officers killing civilians?"

"No, but I have a feeling you're going to tell me."

"Zero."

"But we're not dealing with a civilian. It's one cop killing another cop."

"Witherspoon wasn't a cop," Arnold says. "He was an ex-cop assaulting a hooker and waving around a handgun."

"I stand corrected," Barlow says.

Flanagan says, "You're sure Gloria Two Bears will testify to the assault?"

"Yes. Detectives Cole and Cafferty interviewed her."

"And Witherspoon with the handgun?"

"Not likely."

"Speaking of Detective Cafferty," Flanagan says, "where is he?"

Nick says, "He had a slight accident last evening. He's home recovering."

"Car accident?"

Nick shakes his head, stalling for time, figuring out an answer that won't make Cafferty look even more stupid.

Flanagan cocks his head. "He's drunk again?"

"You mean *still*," Arnold says.

"No," Nick says reflexively. "He fell on the ice, broke his nose. Had to have it reset at Hennepin General. He'll be back on duty soon."

Flanagan eyes Arnold. "I'm worried about Cafferty. He better get his act together soon or . . ." Flanagan ends the thought with a shrug.

Nick jumps in before Arnold can respond. "He'll be fine, Chief. Give him some time."

Arnold shoots Nick a look. Then his expression softens as he faces Flanagan. "Been thinking the same, Chief. We can ease Cafferty out to pasture if need be. He'll still get his pension."

Flanagan nods his head slowly in agreement. "You all know I don't criticize my men when it comes to enjoying a little re-freshment. They're entitled after a day on the streets. But excesses of any kind can lead to immorality and sin, whether it's booze, sex, or gambling. Moderation is key. Wouldn't you all agree?"

They nod their heads in unison.

"Well," Flanagan continues, "we'll deal with Lieutenant Cafferty later. For now, Mr. Barlow, Gloria Two Bears, the lady of the evening, has a rap sheet longer than a giant roll of toilet paper, but nothing in the last year and a half. She's Bannister's snitch. Could Gloria and Bannister have an arrangement?"

"Sure, she might owe him a favor," Barlow says. "But proving it is another matter."

Nick glances at Arnold, waiting to see if the captain says anything. When Arnold doesn't, Nick decides to stay quiet.

Flanagan peers at Barlow. "Do you really think Wither-spoon was standing out on that deck in thirty-degree weather in his boxer shorts carrying a handgun?"

"I doubt if it can be shown it's a throw-down."

"Then you agree it's a throw-down."

"Yes."

"I don't know what's worse," Flanagan says with a frustrated shake of his head. "The niggers up in arms over the Witherspoon killing, or the Hebes still bitching about the deaths of Ben and Davy Roth."

"Who cares if we can prove they're both good shootings?" Barlow says.

"We're already covered with the Roths," Arnold says. "The coroner destroyed the original autopsy report. Mike Bannister is a hero."

"Won't be a hero for long," Flanagan says. "Unless we prove that Witherspoon had a gun and shot at him."

"No witnesses to the shooting," Barlow says. "Two Bears maintains that Witherspoon didn't have a gun. Even if it was a throw-down, Chief, doesn't mean a jury will convict Bannister of murder. Not a cop. Juries are more likely to believe the testimony of police and police defense witnesses. And keep in mind that there's no ironclad standard of what is or isn't an acceptable use of force. It comes down to a judgment call by the officer. The time-tested standard that is virtually encoded in law is that 'I feared for my life.' Bannister's defense attorney will repeat it in every conceivable way during his opening and closing statement."

"Who's the public going to believe, Chief?" Arnold asks. "Some redskin like Two Bears or a decorated police officer?"

"Any fingerprints on the throw-down?"

"Only Witherspoon's."

"We've got a couple of aces in the hole," Barlow says, peering at Flanagan.

"How so?"

"I know who we can get to defend Bannister. And as far as the prosecution goes, I think it's time I gave Miss Kate Dawson an opportunity to redeem herself."

The mention of Kate's name alerts Nick. "Why her?" he says to Barlow without thinking.

"Ever since the Roths were killed, she's been dying to get Mike Bannister in front of a jury. I think it's time she had that opportunity."

"But we don't want her to win," Flanagan says.

"She won't," Barlow says.

"How can you be sure?"

"We'll get Joshua 'Peerless' Jackson to defend Bannister."

"A colored Jew lawyer defending Bannister?"

"It's brilliant," Arnold says.

Flanagan's eyes narrow, his brow furrowing in a questioning look at Barlow. "How you gonna convince Jackson to take Bannister's case?"

"The man has a massive ego. Believe me, it won't be difficult." Barlow looks at Nick. "You and Kate Dawson were an item at one time, weren't you, Detective?"

Nick nods but says nothing.

Arnold says, "Any problem with the plan, Cole?"

At first, Nick searches for ways to defend Kate, some way to get her off the case, save her the embarrassment of another loss. Some reason that would make Barlow change his mind. But now, as he thinks about it, he realizes this might be good for their relationship. She's already lost her first case. If she loses this next one, a higher profile case with even more on the line, she might finally come to her senses. Realize that being an attorney isn't the best choice. Not what she *really* wants.

Nick smiles as he sits back in his chair. "No problem, Captain."

*   *   *

Wearing only a sleeveless undershirt and boxer shorts, Jake Cafferty sits on the edge of his unmade bed, swallowing what's left in the pint bottle of Old Fitzgerald. Finished, he tosses the empty bourbon bottle on the sheets and rubs his eyes with his palms, hoping that the last of the booze will cut the pain in his nose, which throbs with each beat of his heart.

He picks up the vial of medication on the nightstand. Percodan. Prescribed last night by the attending hospital physician. Despite his addiction to booze—and it is an addiction, as Cole bluntly told him—Jake has never taken anything stronger than an aspirin. He's told himself that he doesn't need pills, but truthfully, he's always been afraid that if he takes one, he'll lose complete control of his senses. Even at his worst, he's never had a blackout with the booze or totally forgotten where he's been and what he's done.

Take last night. Jake knows he made a fool of himself falling down in the snow and throwing up in the Indian woman's toilet. *Hey, at least I made it to the can.* The word *can* reminds him of Kid Cann and how he let Jack Apple get the best of him. Embarrassed himself in front of Cole. Got to give it to Cole, though. He handled himself well. More than well. Jake figured he'd be dragging Cole back to the car after Apple handed him his ass. But it's clear that his young partner knows how to use his fists. Cole must've boxed in the service or fought as an amateur. Maybe both. Apple never landed a punch. Jake chuckles, which sends a spike of pain shooting up his nose and into his forehead. Jesus, he needs a drink. He shuffles over to the couch, looking for a pint bottle that might've slipped between the cushions. His gaze is drawn to a headline on the front page of yesterday's *Minneapolis Daily Tribune* and the article underneath it:

JEWISH COMMUNITY RELATIONS COUNCIL CALLS FOR INVESTIGATION INTO THE DEATHS OF BEN AND DAVY ROTH

The executive director of the Minnesota Jewish Council, Samuel Scheiner, today called for an independent investigation into the shooting deaths of Ben and Davy Roth. The two brothers were gunned down in a Richfield cornfield on September 6th after a high-speed chase with police in which shots were exchanged.

Scheiner, who was hired as executive director in 1939, the same year the Anti-Defamation Council incorporated and was renamed the Minnesota Jewish Council, is urging the Minneapolis Police Department to release the autopsy and case reports to the public. "If the police department has nothing to hide, then they should be willing to provide the documentation I've requested," Scheiner said. "It's been two months since Ben and Davy Roth were killed. More than enough time for the department to complete their investigation."

In response, Police Chief William Flanagan is quoted as saying, "Mr. Scheiner is correct. The Minneapolis Police Department has nothing to hide. We'll be more than happy to release these reports to the public once the investigation is completed."

According to Scheiner, the MJC was the first independent statewide agency in the US. His responsibilities include reviewing reports of anti-Semitic incidents and running out-state offices. In his time as executive director, Scheiner has protested anti-Jewish remarks, hate-filled leaflets, and swastika graffiti. He has also exposed attempts by real estate agents, resorts, and employers to subvert anti-discrimination laws, whether by using code words such as "selected clientele," or statements such as "Gentiles preferred." Strategies for dealing with anti-Semitism have included private negotiations, letter-writing campaigns, requests for apologies, threats of boycotts, and tracking letters to newspaper editors.

Prior to 1939 the anti-defamation leagues from around the state, including the Minneapolis chapter, merged into the Anti-Defamation Council of Minnesota, which investigated the state's pro-fascist climate. Local Jewish leaders realized they needed to become permanent after the 1938 governor's race. Supporters of Republican candidate Harold Stassen used anti-Semitic tactics to discredit the Farmer-Labor Party and its incumbent governor, Elmer Benson.

Benson and his predecessor, Floyd B. Olson, both employed Jewish staff. Stassen supporters claimed that the Farmer-Labor Party was "run by Jews." A cartoon used to promote this message, titled "The Three Jehu Drivers," was displayed on posters and billboards throughout the state.

Scheiner told the *Daily Tribune* that "neither the state nor the nation should allow this hateful, anti-Semitic message to rise again. In keeping with the spirit of this message," Scheiner said, "I'm sure the MPD will do the right thing."

Jake tosses the newspaper on the couch. The MPD and Chief Flanagan will do what's best for them, like they always do. He heads for the cupboards and is rummaging through them, looking for a bottle, when someone knocks on his apartment door.

"Who is it?"

"Kate Dawson."

"I'm busy right now."

"Doing what?"

"None of your business, Miss Dawson," he says behind the closed door.

"Got something to show you. Could save your job."

"Didn't know my job needed saving."

"You don't know a lot of things, Cafferty."

"Anyone ever tell you being a smart ass isn't the best way to win friends?"

"Look. I can stand here knocking all day."

Jake lets out a weary breath. "Give me a minute." He pushes the Murphy bed back into the wall, pulls on a pair of pants, and goes to the bathroom, where he stares in the mirror at his stubbled jaw, bloodshot eyes, swollen nose, and matching shiners. *Handsome devil, aren't you*? He brushes his teeth and puts on a wrinkled white shirt.

Kate Dawson knocks again.

"Hold your horses," he mumbles to himself as he unlocks the door and opens it.

Kate enters and then stops abruptly when she gets a look at him, her expression aghast. "What happened to you?"

"I ran into a knee."

"Whose?"

"Jack Apple's. Your ex-boyfriend bailed me out of a jam." Jake shuts the door, trudges over to the kitchenette, lifts the coffee pot off the gas burner, takes off the cover, and gives it a whiff. Not too bad for day-old coffee. He sets the pot back on the stove and lights a burner. "Want some coffee?"

"If it's any good."

"No time to be picky."

"That's for sure."

Jake follows her eyes as she scans the apartment. Newspapers scattered on the sofa. Wrinkled suit coat draped over a kitchen chair. Underwear, shirts, and towels tossed in a laundry basket in a corner. Empty Chinese take-out boxes standing beside an empty bottle of bourbon on the coffee table.

"You could use a housekeeper, Cafferty." She takes a file folder out of her briefcase, slips off her coat, and hangs it on the hat rack by the door.

"Make yourself comfortable."

Kate leans the briefcase against the hat rack and heads for the sofa, brushing aside the newspapers as she sits down.

Jake glances at her before turning his attention to the percolating coffee pot. He reaches for the handle and then pulls his shaking hand back. He stuffs it in a pants pocket and fingers his AA medallion. Sweat dampens his brow. He considers calling his sponsor and then rejects the idea. He needs a drink. Needs it *fast*.

"Let me get the coffee," Kate says, suddenly appearing beside him. "Go sit down."

Jake makes his way to an overstuffed chair opposite the sofa and drops into it. "Mugs are in the first cupboard."

Kate brings him a mug of coffee and sits on the sofa. She takes a sip, makes a face, and sets the mug on the coffee table. "When did you make this? Last week?"

"You don't like it, don't drink it." Jake takes a sip and spits the black mud back into the mug. He looks at her and smiles. "Awful, huh?"

She nods.

"Let's go out. Get something to eat."

"You want booze and not food."

Jake snickers. "What's in the folder?"

"Your salvation."

"From what?"

"From whatever demon is eating you up, Cafferty."

"You're my therapist now?"

"Your friend."

"Yeah. You're my *good* friend."

Kate holds up the folder. "I am. Take a look." She tosses the folder on the coffee table.

Jake hesitates, not sure he wants to see what's in it.

"What're you afraid of, Cafferty?"

He shrugs and reaches for the folder, opens it, and recognizes the autopsy report for Ben Roth. "Where'd you get this?"

"MPD just released it to the public."

Jake scans the summary of Ben Roth's wound.

DESCRIPTION OF GUNSHOT WOUND

Entry: The entry of the gunshot wound is located 12 inches from top of head and 7 inches right of midline. It is a round uniform wound measuring ¼ inch.

Direction: The direction of the wound is right to left.

Path: The path of the wound involves the right anterior chest wall, the right rib #3, right upper lung lobe, pericardium, heart, (right atrium, tricuspid valve, right ventricle)

Exit: None.

Projectile: .38 caliber steel jacket cartridge recovered from right ventricle on 9/15/50 at 8:47 a.m. to evidence safe at 9:08 a.m.

Opinion: The gunshot wound is a perforating, fatal wound due to the extensive trauma to the heart with associated hemorrhage.

Then he reads Davy Roth's autopsy report. The reports are virtually the same. When Jake finishes reading, his eyes lock on Kate's. "What's the problem?"

"I saw the bodies. Saw the teardrop zone of powder and soot above the entrance wounds. They were shot at an angle and from up close. How come that's not mentioned in these autopsy reports?"

"You a coroner now?"

"I'm learning."

"Well," Jake says, searching for a plausible explanation, "I don't know."

"You saw the bodies."

"I did."

"Then you *do* know."

Jake tosses the folder with the reports on the coffee table. "What do you want from me, Assistant DA?"

"Your honest opinion. I've done my homework. You and I both know that blackened teardrop zone indicates an angled near-contact wound. Those boys were shot from behind at close range." Kate leans forward and rests her forearms on her knees. "They were likely murdered."

Jake considers his options for a time—and the consequences. "So now what, Miss Dawson?"

"So now I'm going to prosecute Mike Bannister for the murder of Sam Witherspoon and the shootings in the cornfield. Witherspoon went out on the back balcony in his boxer shorts. He wasn't carrying a gun. The gun found at the crime scene was a throw-down. You were one of the investigating officers. You know what happened to Witherspoon. And you know the Roths were executed." She points to the folder on the table. "Their autopsy reports were written to cover up their murders. I believe Sam Witherspoon saw what happened in the cornfield. Bannister shot Witherspoon to keep him quiet."

"The DA is willing to let you prosecute Bannister?"

Kate smiles. "He expects me to lose."

"Why the charade?"

"If he wants to keep his job, Barlow has to placate the bleeding hearts in the city, especially the Jews."

"And you think you can get Bannister for all three murders."

"I'm going to put Harold Jamison on the stand and get him to admit he falsified the autopsy reports for Ben and Davy Roth. Hopefully, the correct reports are concealed in another folder, if Jamison actually wrote them."

"But you're not trying Bannister for murdering the Roths. This is about Sam Witherspoon."

"The murders are all connected, Cafferty. I know it. I think Witherspoon's murder was a setup. Bannister circles the block.

Gloria Two Bears' door is ajar, so sound carries, but Wither-spoon is too drunk to notice. She starts yelling and screaming and throwing stuff around. That's the signal. Bannister pulls up. Fires two rounds from a throw-down. Calls out Witherspoon. He steps out on the balcony. Bannister blows him away. He's wearing gloves. He gets Witherspoon's prints on the throw-down. Tosses it next to the body and calls for backup."

"How's this supposed to save me?"

"You've been on a bender for the last two months. You're headed for the pasture. You've got one chance to save your job and yourself."

"And you know all this because?"

"It isn't hard to figure out. Look at yourself, Cafferty. Is this how you want to end your career? In a disgraced drunken stupor? I'm sure your ex-partner, Russ Krueger, would be real proud of you now."

"You don't know a damn thing about Russ," Jake says, heat coming into his voice. "And this isn't about saving me or my career, Miss Dawson. Never has been. This is all about you and *your* career."

"Something wrong with doing my job *and* furthering a career?"

"I'm interested in more than justice."

Kate pauses a moment before responding, her eyes fixed on his. "Yeah, Cafferty, you're interested in revenge."

"Same difference."

Kate shakes her head. "I don't think so. One is rational. The other is emotional. You can't seek revenge and then call it justice."

"Call it what you want."

"Was that why you and Nick were bracing Kid Cann and Jack Apple? You blame Cann for Max Hayes' death?"

Jake tries to hide the painful memory behind a well-prac-ticed cop face, but he can tell that she sees right through it. His eyes find the framed photo of Rachel Wagner on the nightstand.

Kate's eyes follow his. "Who's the pretty lady?"

"Someone I once knew."

"You don't just keep a framed photo of *someone*, Lieutenant. Was she your wife?"

"No."

"I could keep guessing, but it'd be easier if you just told me who she is."

"None of your business." Jake waits for her angry response, but Kate only nods her head slowly. Then she appears to recall something. Gazing down at the newspapers scattered on the couch, she picks up a page, looks at it a moment, and turns the page so that it's facing Jake.

The headline on the second page reads:

EDITOR OF *DIRTY LAUNDRY* KILLED IN AUTO ACCIDENT

Just below the headline in a sidebar to the right is a photo of Max Hayes.

Kate rises and walks to the dresser where the woman's framed photo rests. She picks it up and holds it next to the newspaper photo of Max Hayes. Then she looks at Jake. "Striking resemblance between the two, don't you think?" She glances at Jake and then continues. "I could be mistaken, of course, but you'd have to be blind not to see it. You're not blind, are you, Lieutenant?"

Jake shrugs his shoulders like he doesn't know what's happening.

She stares at him and then at the two photos again, her head going back and forth like a tennis ball across a net.

Jake looks out the window at the cold white landscape.

Chapter 28

Kate retrieves a bottle of Coca-Cola from the refrigerator. "Want one?"

Jake nods his head, hoping the sugar will satisfy his craving for booze. "Opener is in the first drawer to your right."

"Thanks." Kate pops the caps on the bottles, takes one to him, and returns to the couch. She drinks and then says, "Tell me about it."

Jake guzzles half the bottle, wipes his mouth with a sleeve, and says, "About what?"

She nods at the framed photo.

"Her name was Rachel."

"How'd you two meet?"

"I was walking a beat in north Minneapolis. Rachel's father owned a butcher shop. I used to stop in there."

"She was Jewish."

"Didn't matter to the two of us. But it mattered a whole lot to her parents. They had someone already picked out for her."

"Arthur Hayes."

Jake nods. "A few months after he was shot and killed in '39, we started seeing each other again. Just to talk. Nothing serious."

"So what happened?"

Jake hesitates.

"Come on, Cafferty."

Jake figures he's got nothing more to lose. "I thought she'd gotten pregnant on their wedding night."

"My God," Kate says under her breath. She looks at Max's photo in the newspaper and then at Jake again. "He's got the same lock of hair that hangs down and curls on his forehead."

Jake nods. "We only made love once. It was a month before the wedding. I tried to get Rachel to call off the marriage. I believe she wanted to." Jake bows his head as he remembers. "There was just too much pressure from her family, especially from her father. I remember when she left my apartment that night, I thought my world had ended. I started drinking. My job suffered. Then I became Russ Krueger's partner. He got me help."

"Rachel never told you Max was your son?"

Jake shakes his head.

"And you never suspected?"

Jake looks at her. "I guess a part of me did. But something kept me from asking Rachel."

"How'd you find out?"

"Max's grandfather told me at the funeral. Rachel's mother found Rachel's diary after she died. She told her husband."

"But they never told you."

"No. But in her last diary entry, Rachel wrote that she was going to tell me."

"How'd she die?"

"Armistice Day blizzard. I rented a cabin up north the day before. She never made it."

"And you blame yourself for her death?"

"Hard to blame Mother Nature."

"On the contrary, if there was no blizzard, you, she, and Max would all be together. Did Max know you were his biological father?"

"Don't think Rachel ever told him."

"Did he suspect?"

"Possibly. Hard to know for sure."

Kate waits a beat before she asks the next question. "Will you help me put Mike Bannister behind bars, where he belongs?"

Despite the resolve in her eyes, Jake says, "You'll never convict him, Miss Dawson."

"Only one way to find out, huh, Lieutenant? And you might as well call me Kate, as long as we're working together."

"Who said we were?"

"I just did."

"You always so confident?"

Kate gestures toward the empty bottle of booze on the coffee table. "Don't worry about my confidence. Can you stay off the sauce?"

Jake finishes off the bottle of Coke and burps. "I've done it before," he says with more confidence than he's feeling. "Just need some motivation."

Kate looks at him for a long moment. "There's one other possible connection we haven't talked about. Suppose Max Hayes' death is connected to the deaths of Sam Witherspoon and Ben and Davy Roth?"

Jake nods but offers no response.

"You're not surprised?"

"I've considered it. But everything points to an accident. And we need a motive."

She smiles and looks relieved. "Good to hear it's *we*."

At least for now, Jake thinks.

"Where do we go from here?" Kate asks.

"You think Nick Cole saw what happened in the cornfield?"

"No."

"How can you be sure?"

"I asked him."

"And he wouldn't lie to you?"

"He's in love with me."

Jake chuckles. "Men in love lie all the time. How does my hair look? Do you like my dress? Do you think I look fat from the back?"

"I'd call those fibs. Lying is a deliberate attempt to deceive."

"You really are a lawyer."

Kate's face twists with irony. "Yeah. You mean the only one wearing a skirt in the DA's office."

Jake chuckles, warming to her. "So we've got the coroner's reports."

"The falsified reports."

"Witherspoon can't tell us anything. And Cole either didn't see what happened, or he's protecting Bannister."

"I don't think Nicky would do that."

Jake shrugs. "Either way, he isn't talking. Neither will Bannister."

"Then what do we do?"

"Might be someone else."

"Who?"

"Ramona Gutierrez. She and her husband own the farm and the cornfield. When I interviewed her, she knew something but wasn't talking."

"So interview her again."

"No. You will."

"Why me?"

"Because she might be more willing to talk to a woman."

"All right. I'll do it."

Jake thinks about their partnership once more before speaking. "This isn't going to be easy . . . Kate. If I go along with you, the risk might be much greater than the payoff."

"You like to gamble, Jake."

"When the odds are in my favor. But the odds are against us. Someone, besides us, has a lot to lose."

"Maybe it's about time they did."

Chapter 29

The following evening after work, the headlights of Kate Dawson's Packard spear the darkness and illuminate the lightly falling flakes of snow. She's on her way to the farm in Richfield owned by Ramona Gutierrez and her husband, Manny.

She turns off Penn Avenue onto a winding dirt road that ends at a double garage. Seeing lights in the window of the farmhouse, she parks and gets out, hunching her shoulders and cinching her coat belt tightly to ward off the cold. As she heads for the house, she glances back at the cornfield where the shooting took place, the field now bare of stalks and covered with a thin blanket of snow. She shivers, not from the chill, but from the image in her mind of the Roths, on their knees, as Mike Bannister coldly shoots both of them in the back.

She knocks on the farmhouse door, waits a few seconds, and then knocks again.

A short man dressed in a flannel shirt and bib overalls opens the door.

"Mr. Gutierrez?"

"Yes," he says with a heavy accent. He has the thick black hair of a younger man, but the creases in his weathered face suggest a man older than his years.

"I'm Kate Dawson with the Hennepin County prosecutor's office. I'd like to speak to your wife, Ramona." Kate removes a card from her purse and hands it to him.

He takes it reluctantly, looks at it, and then at Kate again. "She is not here."

"When will she be back?"

He shrugs. "Maybe a few days. Maybe longer."

"Then she's out of town."

He nods.

"Where?"

He peers at the card again but doesn't respond.

"It's very important that I talk to her, Mr. Gutierrez."

"Is this about the shooting?"

Kate hesitates, not sure she should tell him the truth, but why else would she be here? "Yes. It's about the shooting."

"My wife knows nothing about it." He starts to close the door, but Kate stops it with a hand.

"I could get a court order, Mr. Gutierrez. She wouldn't like that. Neither would you. Where is she?"

He waits a few beats before he says, "Mexico."

"I need the address and phone number."

"Maybe she is not there anymore."

"And maybe both of you could be in a whole lot of trouble if you're not telling me the truth."

"I don't want no trouble."

"I don't either, Mr. Gutierrez." She gives him her best smile.

"Okay. You wait." He closes the door, leaving Kate standing on the stoop.

The wind has picked up, as have the snowflakes, which swirl and dance in the air. Toes beginning to numb, Kate is about to knock again when the door finally opens. Manny Gutierrez hands a small sheet of paper to her on which is scrawled a Mexican address and phone number. "Thank you," she says.

He shuts the door without replying.

Kate hurries back to her car, keys the engine, switches the heater fan to high, and wiggles her toes to regain some feeling. She gazes at the piece of paper in her gloved hand, wondering if Ramona Gutierrez really is in Mexico and if she fled the state to avoid testifying. Both suppositions could be correct—or both could be wrong. In any case, Ramona isn't in town and probably won't be till Bannister's trial concludes, which, if she did see something and is afraid to testify, will be too late. She'll need convincing to return to Minnesota. Kate can subpoena her, but she prefers that Ramona return of her own volition and as a friendly rather than hostile witness.

She stuffs the paper in her purse, shifts the car into gear, and heads down the winding driveway. Most of the snow accumulating on the windshield blows off, but Kate switches on the wipers to clear any remaining patches and to give her an unobstructed view of the road ahead.

Ten yards from Penn Avenue, a car pulls into the driveway, blocking Kate's path. She steps on the brake pedal, raises a hand to shield her eyes from the blinding headlights, and lays on the horn. The car doesn't move. Wondering if perhaps Ramona Gutierrez is returning home, Kate shifts into park and gets out.

As she starts toward the other car, the driver's side door swings open and a man in a trench coat and fedora exits. Kate stops, sensing something isn't right. Shielding her eyes with one hand again, she tries to glimpse his face, but it's impossible in the bright light. Back-pedaling, in a sudden grip of fear, she yells, "Who are you? What do you want?"

The man offers no response—and keeps coming.

Kate turns and runs toward her car. She's fumbling with the door handle when he grabs her shoulder and roughly swings her around. A three-hole ski mask covers his face.

"Leave me alone!"

He slams a hand in her chest and shoves her back hard against the car door. Leaning in close, a hand clutching Kate's throat, his breath smelling strongly of garlic, he whispers, "Stay away from the Gutierrezes," and then gives her ear a lick.

"Go to hell!"

He backhands her across the cheek. "Don't get cute."

Kate sees stars as her legs give out and she slides down the driver's door onto the snowy ground.

Bending over in front of her face, he says, "This is your first and last warning." He kicks her in the side and laughs as he walks away.

Kate lies in the snow. Tears of pain sting her eyes. But her teeth clench in anger.

* * *

Nick Cole sits on a stool at Curly's, a downtown bar named after Monroe "Curly" Shapiro, who along with his brother, Nate, opened the place back in '33. Nick knocks back the last of his Scotch and listens as a woman croons a Buddy Johnson blues ballad entitled "Since I Fell for You." The words resonate with Nick, reminding him of his busted relationship with Kate Dawson, and how Chief Flanagan and the DA, Wilson Barlow, have set her up to fail in the Mike Bannister trial.

It's after ten p.m. when he arrives at Kate's place. She lives in Minneapolis in one of twenty row houses on Milwaukee Avenue. Each is freestanding, separated from its neighbors by a discreet distance but with no fences between them and garages behind. Ten row houses face one another on each side of a landscaped boulevard with a path running down it. Most of the row houses, including Kate's, are A-frames, with lofts for bedrooms, and a main floor atrium in which living, dining, and kitchen areas flow into each other, loosely separated by half walls.

Kate is still in her lawyer outfit—a fitted green skirt and suit coat—when she opens the door. Her auburn hair hangs loose, caressing her shoulders. She looks tired.

"Surprised to see you, Nicky."

He stares at the bruise on her cheek. "What happened to you?"

Reflexively, she touches her cheek with her fingers and says, "Nothing."

"Bullshit. Who hit you?"

"It's late. Busy day tomorrow."

He nods, though he knows she's lying. *Why?* "This won't take long."

She sighs, steps back from the door, and waves him in.

He notices the empty lipstick-printed brandy snifter on the coffee table beside the brick fireplace. "I'll have whatever you're having."

Nick drapes his coat over the back of the print couch and sits down near the warmth of the fire. Kate heads for the mini-bar in a corner. She pours Mouquin brandy into a snifter, walks across the carpeted floor, and hands it to him. Then she sits on the loveseat opposite him, her nylon-covered feet tucked under her.

"Not drinking with me?" he says.

"What do you want, Nicky?"

"Who says I want anything?"

"You didn't come by just to chat. Besides, it's late."

Nick has had second thoughts about throwing Kate to the wolves in the Bannister trial, but he doesn't know how to get her out of it without causing another scene, or letting her know that it's a setup. Still, he needs to try. "I don't want you to make a fool of yourself."

"Well, that's gallant of you. How, exactly, will I make a fool of myself?"

"By prosecuting Mike Bannister."

"He's a crooked cop who murdered Ben and Davy Roth and Sam Witherspoon."

"You don't know that."

"Everyone in town knows it. Your department wants to bury it. Save themselves from embarrassment. Ain't gonna happen."

"They're using you, Katie."

She shakes her head. "Or maybe I'm using them."

"To further your career."

"Yes."

"If this goes wrong, it could ruin your career."

"You'd like that, Nicky, wouldn't you?"

He's taken aback. More by what she knows about him than what she says. "That doesn't make any sense."

"Sure it does. If I fail again, you're right. I shouldn't be a prosecutor. I shouldn't be an attorney at all."

He leans forward, elbows on his knees, eyes locked on hers, brandy snifter held with both hands. "I came here to warn you, Katie."

"Lot of that going around."

Nick pauses before putting it together. "Your bruised cheek?"

"It'll take more than that to get me off this case."

More concerned now, Nick says, "Who did this to you?"

"He wore a ski mask."

"Describe him."

"Big and strong."

"Did he say anything?"

"Told me to leave the Gutierrezes alone."

It takes a moment before Nick recognizes the name. "They own the farm where the cornfield shooting took place."

Kate nods. "Why would someone be warning me to stay away from their place?"

Nick shrugs. "I don't know, unless . . ."

Kate finishes the thought for him. "Unless one of them saw what happened that night?"

Nick shakes his head to clear his thoughts. "But we already know what happened."

"Do we? Really?"

Nick gulps his brandy.

"I can understand why the department is protecting one of their own," Kate says. "What I can't understand is why you've decided to be part of it. Even if Mike Bannister skates on the murder charges, I won't quit. And nothing you say or do, Nicky, will get me to change my mind."

"Suit yourself." Nick stands, grabs his coat, and marches to the door. As he opens it, he turns and says, "We could've had it all." With that he leaves, slamming the door behind him.

Chapter 30

Jake Cafferty has no intention of getting on a plane, so he takes the Milwaukee Road overnight sleeper train, called the *Pioneer Limited*, to Chicago. The six-hour-and-fifteen-minute ride to the Windy City is popular with businessmen because they can sleep while they travel and arrive in Chicago at 7:45 a.m. ready to do a day's business before returning to the Twin Cities that night.

Two days ago, Kate Dawson burst into Jake's apartment with a bruised cheek, a piece of paper with a Mexican phone number and address, and a story about how a masked man had threatened her when she went to the farm looking for Ramona Gutierrez. While serving as a warning to Kate, it also indicated to Jake that they are on the right track. Someone is feeling the heat.

Knowing that Captain Avery Arnold won't approve a paid trip to Mexico City to interview a witness to a shooting he wasn't supposed to be investigating, Jake digs into his savings to purchase the train tickets. He also spends time searching for leverage he can use on Ramona Gutierrez in case she refuses to return to Minnesota and testify. He hops the train on a Thursday after explaining to the captain that he's having dizzy spells from the broken nose and needs time before returning to work. He doubts Arnold believes him.

Jake doesn't sleep much on the train—hasn't slept much at all since the fight with Jack Apple—because he can't sleep comfortably on his back or his side. Sleeping on his stomach is even more uncomfortable.

He catches the Wabash *Blue Bird* from Chicago's Dearborn Station to Union Station in St. Louis, then the Missouri Pacific's *Texas Eagle* for the eighteen-hour trip to San Antonio. The *Aztec Eagle* hauls him from San Antonio to Laredo, Texas, and from Laredo the last 955 miles to Mexico City. After four days of trains and sleeper cars, Jake checks into the Hotel Majestic in the main plaza in the center of Mexico City and, exhausted, sleeps like a baby for six hours—on his back.

* * *

Ramona Gutierrez has returned to paradise. No more ugly people, no more being called a wetback and spat on. Now her home is a villa, with servants and flowers and a swimming pool, not a farm. She's a lady again. Protected. Pampered. An object of respect. Almost veneration. She's only been back in Mexico City for a month, but already she rarely thinks of the uncultured existence she's left behind. When Cafferty called from Minneapolis and asked to see her, she was surprised, too surprised to say no.

She remembers him as a big, burly Irishman with wavy dark hair, who wore suits that always seemed a size too small for him. She doesn't want him in her home. People of her class don't do business with people like Jake Cafferty in their homes, but she *does* want him to be aware of her stature, her position in Mexican society. When he calls from the hotel after arriving in Mexico City, and the maid hands her the phone, she tells him to meet her at the *Hipódromo de las Américas*. The racetrack and site of the Mexican Derby is located about four miles from the downtown district.

"One of our horses will be running tomorrow in the feature race. Go to the clubhouse. Give them your name at the desk, and they will show you to our box."

*   *   *

Situated 7,382 feet above sea level, Mexico City's thinner air is tough on horses. Tough on out-of-shape cops as well. After trudging up a long grandstand stairway, Jake pauses a moment to catch his breath. As cops will do, he assesses the stocky security guard leading him to a private box and concludes that the guard can handle himself.

Ramona Gutierrez is seated with her back to him as he approaches. She's wearing a silk flower-print dress. Her hair is pulled back in a tight bun under a broad-brimmed hat. She has gained some weight, but ampleness is becoming to her. She is a strikingly handsome woman. *"Señora* Gutierrez," he says, smiling broadly.

"Lieutenant Cafferty." Her dark eyes widen in surprise. She gestures at his nose. "Were you in an accident?"

"In a manner of speaking."

"Here in Mexico?"

"Happened in the States. Looked a lot worse a few days ago."

"I thought perhaps . . ." She pauses, then says, "Security is very tight here . . . we live well, but bad things can happen to gringos in Mexico. Security keeps a careful eye on us. Makes sure no one disturbs us, disturbs our lives."

Jake points his chin at the security guard standing at the door to the private box. "I noticed."

"I hope no one else was hurt in this . . . accident."

"No one to be concerned about, *Señora.*" Jake smiles and gestures to the clear blue sky. "Beautiful day for a race."

"It is."

"So who do I like in the feature race?"

"Our horse is Tarry This Night. He's won six of nine lifetime starts and is three for three this year. The race today is nine furlongs, or one and one-eighth miles. He comes from off the pace, and it is a long way from the last turn to the finish, so he has a good shot."

"Long home stretch kills speed, is that the idea?"

"You have done this before."

"I have. Already placed a bet on your horse."

She smiles. "I hope we both are satisfied with today's outcome."

Aware of the double entendre, Jake offers a smile of his own. "I hope so, too, *Señora*. Did you pick the biblical name for the horse?"

"You know your horses and your Bible. Yes. Before his passing, my father bought him at the Keeneland two-year-olds-in-training sale in Lexington, Kentucky."

Jake nods and lets his eyes wander over the crowd. "Don't know the Bible all that well, but I've always loved the book of Esther. Not the first part so much, with the 'Wither thou goest,' but the last part with Boaz and Naomi, where the old man asks her to spend the night." Jake looks at Ramona Gutierrez again. "Tarry this night. Greatest seduction line of all time. Wish I'd had the chance to use it."

Looking not at all embarrassed, she says, "I am a married woman."

"You know that's not what I meant, or why I'm here."

"What I know is that you have wasted your time coming all this way."

"Not if you tell me what happened that night in the cornfield."

"I have already told you."

"I could use some appropriate passages from the Bible here."

"Don't."

"God makes judgments, *Señora* Gutierrez. Everything is not compassion and forgiveness. There's a reckoning, a price for sin. All the flowers and perfume can't blot out the stench. Prancing horses can't hide it."

She turns away from him. "You should not have come."

"I need you to testify, to come back with me. All I'm asking for is the truth."

"I cannot."

"Why?"

She thinks about it for a time before facing him again.

"My husband, Manny, he is ambitious and tireless. He wanted to go to the States to start a new life. His family is not wealthy or part of the society I grew up in. My father did not approve of our marriage. But what could I do?" she says with a shrug. "I fell in love with him. But life in your country is difficult for Latinos, for anyone who is not white. We bought land and horses with money my father gave us. We worked hard. But soon the government will take our land to build more roads. Some law you have gives them the right to do it."

"Eminent domain," Jake says.

"Yes. The government will pay us, but not as much as the land is worth. We cannot win. Once the farm is sold, Manny will join me. After the shooting in our cornfield and the . . ." She looks down at the program in her hand before continuing. "I knew it was time to leave."

"And the *what, Señora* Gutierrez?"

She stares at him without speaking for a moment, then lets out a sigh and says, "A man has threatened us. My husband is in danger."

Jake figures it's the same punk that roughed up Kate Dawson. "Tell me about him."

She shakes her head. "Nothing to tell. Manny said he wore a mask."

"We can protect your husband."

"Meaning the police?"

Jake nods. "Yeah."

"I do not think so."

Murmurs from the crowd draw Jake's attention to the track and the jockeys in their colorful silks. Ten horses in the race, trotting alongside the escort ponies in the post parade before being led to the starting gate. Jake zeroes in on Ramona Gutierrez's horse, Tarry This Night, the big brown colt in the maroon-and-white colors. The gambler in Jake has momentarily switched places with his detective persona as he looks for clues to the horse's attitude. Tarry This Night appears alert and composed and not at all sluggish or nervous. Jake glances at the tote board, where the odds list the horse at 4-1, not a long shot, but not the favorite either. Jake has a Benjamin riding on the outcome. With luck, he'll pay for his round trip with his winnings.

The buzz of the crowd grows louder as the gate crew leads the horses into the starting gates. Everyone's attention focuses on the track. Then the gates spring open and excitement sweeps through the crowd as the horses thunder down the track.

Into the first turn, Tarry This Night settles into fifth place just outside the fourth-place horse that's running along the rail. He holds the position into the far turn as the first five horses increase the distance between the second five. Down the backstretch Tarry This Night moves more to the outside and slips past the third-place horse, two lengths behind the first- and second-place horses that are running neck and neck. Soon the first-place horse, Enlisted, a sprinter, begins dropping back off the pace. Tarry This Night moves into second place, a length behind the leader, Quorum. Tarry This Night's jockey holds the position into the final turn. It's a two-horse race now and the crowd is on its feet, some screaming for Quorum, others for Tarry This Night.

Jake glances at a silent Ramona Gutierrez, whose hands are cupped together under her chin as if in prayer.

Head-to-head, the two horses sprint past the grandstand, their hooves thudding against the dirt track, their jockeys giving them the whip, urging them on. But it's Tarry This Night that pulls ahead. The crowd roars. Jake's heart thumps in his chest. Tarry This Night crosses the finish line a length ahead of Quorum.

Ramona Gutierrez lets out a cry of excitement and raises her hands above her head. She turns to Jake with a wide smile and says, "I told you how he comes off the pace."

"That you did. He's a wonderful horse."

"Would you like to meet him?"

"I would."

"Come to the stables. I'm going to greet some friends. I'll meet you there."

Jake's eyes track her as she leaves the private box. Then, using the little Spanish he knows, he finds the way to the stables.

A groom is walking Tarry This Night and giving him water, making sure he's "cooled out" and his heart rate returns to normal. Then Jake follows the groom and horse to its stall.

A few minutes later, Ramona Gutierrez arrives.

Watching her, Jake remembers that she arranged their meeting so she was mostly seated. Now he realizes why. She has a slight, almost imperceptible limp, more of an imbalance really, as though one side is slightly stronger than the other. It could be just a pelvic tilt, but he thinks it's probably the result of childhood polio. The god-awful disease has been on the rise in the States, infecting mostly kids five to nine years of age. Jake has seen enough of them in wheelchairs and on crutches to last a lifetime.

"Congratulations again, *Señora*," Jake says. "Your horse was clearly the best in the field."

Standing with his head out of the stall, Tarry This Night bobs his head in recognition and then lowers it and leans toward her as she strokes his neck.

Jake's attention shifts back to Ramona Gutierrez. "*Señora*, would you mind if we just talk a bit? You don't have to say anything, just nod."

"Talk all you want."

Jake begins. "Your husband is away the night of the shooting. You're alone in the house, about to retire early, when you hear the commotion in the cornfield. You go to a window and peek out. It's sunset. Okay so far?"

She doesn't nod, but she doesn't challenge his account either.

Jake figures it's a good sign. He continues. "You see two young men get out of a car in a ditch and run into the cornfield."

She nods.

"Then you see four cops arrive and chase after them. Shortly afterwards the young men emerge from the cornfield, followed by a cop. He orders them to their knees and holds them at gunpoint. Am I doing all right?"

Her eyes drift away from his, but she gives a barely perceptible nod.

"What happens next is the cop kills them. They're down on their knees, begging for their lives."

Eyes jittery, she looks away. "I told you, I really did not see it."

"All right, just tell me this. Tell me what Sam Witherspoon, the Negro cop, did."

She inhales a deep breath and releases it slowly. As she regains her composure, her moist eyes look directly into Jake's eyes for the first time. Her eyeliner is smeared, and bright sunlight reveals crow's feet at the corners of her eyes.

"Look at me, Lieutenant. You see the expression on my face. The sadness I cannot hide when I look at you. You are looking at the Negro's face. What he looked like that night—and what I imagine he looks like every night of his life since. Why don't you ask him what he saw?"

She doesn't know, Jake thinks. *Doesn't know that Sam Witherspoon is dead or that Mike Bannister killed him.* "I would ask him, *Señora*. But the Negro cop, Sam Witherspoon, is dead."

Eyes wide, she mutters, "How?"

"Shot and killed by Mike Bannister. The same cop who murdered the young men in your cornfield."

"*Ay, Dios mío.*"

He gives her time to process before he says, "Come back with me, *Señora*. Help me right this wrong."

She shakes her head—but not emphatically, like she's unsure. "God won't judge me for what I did or did not do that night."

"You're more familiar with Him than I am. But we all have to answer for our choices at some point."

She gives him a cold-eyed stare. "You are not an instrument of God. Now go. Leave me alone. Go back to Minneapolis."

"What about your husband? Who'll protect him?"

Her eyes soften. "You won't?"

Jake decides he'll use some leverage to guarantee her return. "I'd like to protect your husband, but it's out of my hands."

"What do you mean?"

"Are you familiar with the Internal Security Act?"

"No, I am not."

"Just passed Congress last September. All Communist organizations have to register with the US Attorney General. There's a control board that investigates persons suspected of subversive activities."

Her dark eyes flare with anger. "*Pendejo cabrón.* My husband is not a Communist."

"I believe you. But there might be some in the department who don't." Jake pauses. "I have a subpoena in my pocket, *Señora*. But it doesn't need to be this way. I'd rather you came willingly."

"You police are all the same. Here in Mexico or in the States!"

"We're not all the same, *Señora*. But as long as men like the thug who threatened you are on the loose, no one, including your husband, is safe. Think about it. Think real hard."

Part Four

"...Many times man lives and dies
Between his two eternities,
That of race and that of soul..."

—William Butler Yeats
"Under Ben Bulben"

Chapter 31

November 27, 1950

The case against Mike Bannister will be tried before Judge Howard Gunderson, who, like most judges Kate Dawson knows, has been appointed to the bench because he's a lawyer who knew a governor. As a state senator, Howard Gunderson supported the governor's legislative program with more enthusiasm and loyalty than necessary from a purely partisan standpoint, earning himself an early retirement from the rough and tumble of elective politics.

As she looks up at him now from below his judicial perch, Gunderson appears to be a large man. But when he steps down from the dais to the level occupied by ordinary mortals, it becomes apparent that only his head and his voice are large. Like many a former legislative water boy, once he has his own show, he runs it with an iron fist. Judge Gunderson does not suffer fools gladly.

In a packed courtroom half-filled with the venire—the sixty prospective jurors called at random from a fair cross-section of qualified county residents—and half-filled with members of the press, the city's elite, spectators, and courtroom gadflies who are lucky enough to grab a remaining seat, the voir dire gets underway.

Judge Gunderson begins by identifying the parties and their respective counsel and by outlining the nature of the case. Then, in the course of explaining the responsibilities to the first twelve prospective jurors, eight men and four women, who have taken their seats in the jury box and have been sworn in, the judge tells a joke. "Someone once said that a jury is twelve persons chosen to decide who has the better lawyer."

While lawyers are compelled to laugh at any attempt at judicial humor, however feeble or inappropriate, Kate also observes the first twelve closely. Two prospective jurors join in the fun. Kate's take on Judge Gunderson's joke is to mark the two laughers as keepers. Her wish list tilts toward upper income types, college graduates, fallen-away Catholics, academics, civil servants, and especially Jews, all of whom who are less sympathetic to cops and more sympathetic to folks shot by cops.

Joshua "Peerless" Jackson, though Jewish himself, wants to keep Jews off the empaneled jury and will use his peremptory challenges to try and eliminate them. But he must be careful. If Judge Gunderson perceives Jackson's peremptories of creating bias, he will, hopefully, overrule.

Because Gunderson wants to protect jurors from the press and public attention, the jury pool is anonymous. The attorneys know where the prospective jurors are from and what they do for a living, but nothing else about them, not even their names.

Kate suspects there is a least one Jew in the first group of twelve, based on his residence on the North Side of Minneapolis and the waves of hostility she senses, directed at Jackson. Surely, the juror knows that Mike Bannister is the cop accused of killing the Roths in the cornfield. What he doesn't know is that Kate suspects Bannister of murdering them. In the eyes of most Jews, Jackson might as well be defending Adolf Hitler. Yet, Kate has to hand it to Bannister. Getting a Jewish lawyer to defend him is pure genius.

Kate figures Jackson will look for a couple of bleeding hearts, based on her observation that liberals seem to have trouble convicting anyone of anything, and those who typically side with the police. His wish list probably includes blue-collar workers, nervous housewives, retirees on fixed incomes, and regular churchgoers, particularly Fundamentalists and Catholics.

Judge Gunderson next asks the twelve prospective jurors a series of basic questions: Has anyone in your immediate family been arrested or been a victim of crime? Has anyone in your immediate family worked in law enforcement? Has anyone served on a trial jury that tried another person for the same or a related offense as the pending charge? Has anyone served on the grand jury that found the indictment or an indictment on a related offense?

A prospective juror who answers yes to any of these questions will be considered biased and removed for cause from this jury pool. There's no limit to the number of challenges for cause. Many times a judge will dismiss a juror before either the prosecution or defense raises an objection.

Both attorneys also have a limited supply of peremptory challenges at their disposal to eliminate a prospective juror. In cases such as the one before the court, punishable by life imprisonment, Minnesota allows the defense fifteen peremptory challenges and the prosecution nine, putting Kate at a disadvantage. For any other offense, the defense has five peremptory challenges and the prosecution three.

Joshua Jackson will use his peremptory challenges to remove anyone from the final twelve jurors with a possible bias against the police. Kate hopes that among the sixty names are one or more who've had a run-in with or hold a grudge against the police department and will vote to convict Mike Bannister, if they manage to slip by the judge and defense counsel.

Voir dire takes a day and a half. Kate carefully uses her nine peremptory challenges. By the time jury selection is over there are four women and eight men seated. Each side has five they like, five they don't, and two they're unsure of. At least one of the men, Kate believes, is Jewish.

Before breaking for lunch, the judge reminds jurors and attorneys that testimony will begin each morning at nine a.m. sharp and continue until five p.m., with a ninety-minute lunch and morning and afternoon breaks of fifteen minutes each.

The whole city is fixated on the trial. Kate feels like she's a Christian about to face the lions in the Roman Coliseum. Opening arguments are bombastic and unrevealing of the evidence that will be presented.

"Miss Dawson," Judge Gunderson says. "Call your first witness."

Kate calls Harold Jamison, the Hennepin County coroner. After he's sworn in, Kate has Jamison describe the nature of Sam Witherspoon's wounds and the cause of death.

"Dr. Jamison, what was the level of alcohol in the victim's body?"

"Point zero six."

"What would that correspond to for a man of Mr. Witherspoon's size and weight in terms of number of drinks he'd consumed?"

"About two ounces of eighty-six-proof whiskey."

"Is that enough to make him intoxicated?"

"Depends on the individual. But from this man's size and weight, I'd say no."

"Dr. Jamison, did you weigh the victim's body?"

"What we had to work with, yes."

"What did the victim weigh?"

"One hundred ninety-eight pounds, eleven ounces."

"What would you estimate was his true total weight at the time of death?"

"I estimate two hundred six pounds, eleven ounces."

"How did you arrive at that estimate?"

"The average human head weighs twenty-two pounds. Mr. Witherspoon had a large head. I estimate it weighed twenty-four pounds. Approximately one-third of Mr. Witherspoon's head was missing when we examined his body."

"And Dr. Jamison, what was the victim wearing at the time of his death?"

"Boxer shorts and a watch."

"Is it customary for people to wander around outside in thirty-degree weather in boxer shorts?"

"Objection. Foundation," Jackson says.

With a disapproving look at Kate, Judge Gunderson says, "Sustained. Jury will disregard. Continue, Counsel."

"Dr. Jamison, was there any other foreign substance on the victim's body?"

"Yes. Shards of glass on the shoulders and what remained of the head."

"Were you able to identify the shards of glass?"

"Yes."

"Please describe your findings."

"I recovered eighteen pieces, all less than one millimeter long, very thin and frosted. Several pieces were curved. I sent a few pieces off to the FBI boys in Washington. They said in their report that they were from a shattered hundred-watt GE light bulb. Pretty standard item."

"Do you have that report with you today?"

"Yes."

"Your Honor, we'd like to have this marked and entered into evidence as state's exhibit number one."

"Has the defendant had a chance to examine it?"

Kate gestures toward the defense table. "Counsel is examining it now, Your Honor."

"Any objections?"

Jackson shakes his head. "No objections, Your Honor."

"Mark it as state's exhibit number one," Gunderson says.

Kate continues. "Is there any way to determine how that shattered glass came to be on the victim's body, Dr. Jamison?"

"Yes. If there was a light bulb directly above him that was shattered by debris from the same blast that killed him."

"Thank you, Dr. Jamison. That will be all I have for now."

"Mr. Jackson?" Judge Gunderson says. "Cross-examination?"

Jackson stands. "Yes, sir. About the drinks, Dr. Jamison, was it possible Sam Witherspoon could have consumed more than two ounces of whiskey if he'd taken the drinks more than, say, an hour before his death?"

"Yes, it's possible."

"Considerably more?"

"All depends on when he drank them."

"Dr. Jamison, you cannot be sure Sam Witherspoon did not fire a gun immediately prior to Sergeant Bannister's returning fire, can you?"

"Objection," Kate says. "Assuming a fact not in evidence. We have no evidence Sergeant Bannister was returning anyone's fire."

"Sustained. Rephrase your question, Counsel."

Jackson nods. "Dr. Jamison, based on your examination, you cannot be sure that Samuel Witherspoon did not fire a gun immediately prior to his death, can you?"

"No, sir."

"Thank you. That's all."

"Your Honor," Kate says, "the state calls Gloria Two Bears."

Once she's sworn in, Kate asks Gloria Two Bears what she does for a living.

"I'm a waitress at the Lodge."

The Lodge is a dump, Kate thinks, *but if you happen to live in Minneapolis and are of the American Indian persuasion, it's about all you have in the way of a place of respite from the cares of the day.* Gloria Two Bears spends almost every evening there, but not to drink. Gloria is a teetotaler and proud of it.

"Miss Two Bears, isn't it also a fact that you work as a prostitute out of the Lodge?"

Jackson rises. "Your Honor, counsel is impeaching her own witness."

"Your Honor," Kate says, "I could've called Miss Two Bears as a hostile witness under the rules, and I will if I have to, but until she indicates otherwise, I would like to treat her as a state's witness."

"Mr. Jackson, you will object now or forever hold your peace. Once we get going, you've waived on those grounds."

"No objection, Your Honor. We'll let it ride."

Kate says, "Have you ever worked as a prostitute out of the Lodge, Miss Two Bears?"

"Yes."

"Thank you. Please describe your relationship to the victim, Samuel Witherspoon."

Two Bears rambles through her long, sometimes professional, sometimes consensual, sometimes loving, sometimes violent relationship with Samuel Witherspoon, and how he had recently moved in with her.

"What was Sam doing for a living?"

"They got him some bouncer jobs, that sort of thing."

"Who are *they*?"

"The Police Federation. Mike Bannister."

"Did Sam ever say why the defendant was getting him jobs?"

"Yes. He said Mike told him that he liked him and wanted to help him, but Sam thought Mike wanted to keep an eye on him, too."

"Why?"

"Because he knew about killing those two Jewish boys in the cornfield."

Jackson jumps up. "Objection! This is irrelevant and highly inflammatory and hearsay. Sam Witherspoon is not here to testify as to what he said."

Kate pushes back her chair and stands. "Your Honor, this is a question of the victim's state of mind, not his veracity. It bears on the motive for the crime here. This whole matter is about a continuing event that began in that cornfield."

"The objection is overruled. This incident appears to be connected to the actions we are considering here. Continue, Miss Dawson."

"Miss Two Bears, are you saying Sam Witherspoon was frightened?"

"Objection," Jackson says. "She's leading the witness."

"Sustained. Jury will disregard."

"Miss Two Bears, were you able to determine the victim's state of mind?"

"Yes. Sam was afraid."

"Of who or what?"

"Mike Bannister."

"Because of the killings in the cornfield."

"Yes."

"All right, Miss Two Bears. Tell us what happened the night Samuel Witherspoon was killed."

"He was in the Lodge, drinking. He motions me to come over. We talk for a while. He says he wants to go back to my place. I say okay. When we get there, I tell him it's the end of the month and I need money for rent. He says let's do it first. I say I need the money first. We get into an argument, and he starts hitting me. I hit him back."

"Miss Two Bears, was Sam drinking a lot when you first met him?"

"Not really. He'd have a few beers now and then, but I never saw him really drunk."

"Was he always abusive to you?"

"No. He was a good man when I met him."

"So he changed?"

"Yeah, he did."

"When did this change in personality come about?"

"About the time of that shooting in the cornfield."

"Objection," Jackson says. "Sam Witherspoon isn't on trial here, Your Honor. What happened months before has no bearing on this case."

Kate isn't ready to establish the clear connection between the cornfield murders and Sam Witherspoon's subsequent murder, but she needs to lay the groundwork. "Your Honor, I'm simply attempting to establish that the victim, Sam Witherspoon, had psychological issues, which I intend to explore with a trained psychologist later."

"I'll allow it, Miss Dawson. But don't stray too far afield."

"Thank you, Your Honor." Kate turns back to Gloria Two Bears. "All right. Let's go back to the night Sam was shot and killed. You were arguing. Sam was drinking. Then what happened?"

"Well, next thing I know, Sam goes outside on the balcony. Then bang, bang, bang. That's all I know. Police are all over the place. Big mess."

"Miss Two Bears, do you know why Sam went out to the balcony?"

"I'm not sure."

"Did someone call his name?"

She shrugs. "I don't think so."

"Did you or Sam hear a gunshot?"

"Might've been a gunshot."

"Did you hear a gunshot, Miss Two Bears?"

"I don't know."

"Either you did or didn't."

"Objection," Jackson says. "Repetitive. Witness says she doesn't know."

"Your Honor, I'm just trying to refresh her memory."

"Overruled. You may answer, Miss Two Bears."

"I heard a shot."

"Was there more than one?"

"Yeah."

"Two? Three?"

"Maybe three."

"You heard three shots?"

She nods. "I think so."

"What was Sam wearing?"

"Underwear. He strips down soon as we get there. He don't like to waste time."

The jurors laugh. The judge admonishes them. "Only one comedian allowed in this courtroom."

After the laughter subsides, Kate waits for a few seconds before asking the next question. "Did you see a gun in Sam's hand?"

"No."

"At any time that evening, did you see him in possession of a firearm?"

"No."

"Not even when he went out the door to the balcony?"

"No."

"At the time he went out, was the door to the back balcony open?"

"Maybe a little. It gets real hot in my place."

Some in the gallery titter but quickly quiet down when the judge glares at them.

"Miss Two Bears, was the light on when Sam went out on the balcony?"

"I don't know."

"Was it on when you came home with him?"

"I think so."

"Could it have been off?"

"Yes, it could have."

"So you're not sure if the light was on or off, are you?"

"Objection, repetitive," Jackson says. "She's asked the same question three times."

"And gotten three different answers, Your Honor."

"Overruled. Continue. Reread the question."

The clerk rereads the question. "So, you're not sure if the light was on or off, are you?"

"No, I'm not sure."

"Miss Two Bears, do you recognize the defendant?"

"Yeah. Officer Bannister."

"How do you know him?"

"He arrested me."

"What did he arrest you for?"

"Prostitution."

"Are you a prostitute?"

"Sometimes I have to do things I don't like to do. Money is hard to come by for Indian people in Minneapolis."

"How many times did Officer Bannister arrest you?"

"Once."

"When was that?"

"Couple years ago."

"More like a year and a half ago, wasn't it?"

"Could be."

"How many times prior to that had you been arrested for prostitution?"

"I don't know."

Kate walks back to the prosecutors' table and picks up a document. "Do you dispute that you have been arrested for prostitution eleven times?"

"That sounds right."

"Your Honor, we would ask to place in evidence this document, the arrest record of Gloria Two Bears, as state's exhibit number two. Copy to defense counsel."

Judge Gunderson looks at Jackson. "Any objections?"

"No objection."

Kate continues. "How many times have you been arrested for prostitution subsequent to the time you were arrested by the defendant?"

"I don't remember."

"You don't remember that you have not been arrested since the defendant arrested you? You don't remember that you have not been arrested for prostitution—or for anything else—in the last year and a half, even though in a seven-year period of time prior to that you were arrested eleven times?"

"I don't remember."

"You don't remember. But you remember Officer Bannister."

"Yeah."

"Okay, Miss Two Bears, do you remember making a deal with the defendant?"

"No."

"Do you remember the defendant telling you that he had done you a favor and that you owed him one?"

"No."

"Do you remember the defendant telling you he wanted you to tell him when Samuel Witherspoon was there?"

"No."

"Do you remember calling the defendant the evening Samuel Witherspoon was killed and telling him Sam was in the Lodge and would be coming home with you?"

"How could I call him? He was in a police car."

"I'll ask the questions here, Miss Two Bears, but this time I'll answer yours. Because he told you where he would be waiting for your call."

"Objection," Jackson says. "Who's testifying here, counsel or the witness? Move to strike."

"Sustained. Jury will disregard."

"The defendant told you where to call him, didn't he?"

"No."

"Do you deny you placed a call to him from the Lodge on the night Samuel Witherspoon was murdered?"

"Objection to the word 'murder.'"

"Sustained. Counsel, you're getting carried away here."

"I apologize, Your Honor. On the night Samuel Witherspoon died with his head blown off by a shotgun blast from defendant."

Jackson jumps to his feet. "Objection! Inflammatory!"

"Sustained. Counsel, I told you to phrase your questions in the proper manner. You are bordering on contempt here."

"I apologize to the court and to the witness, Your Honor. Miss Two Bears, do you deny placing a call from the Lodge to the defendant at Augie's on Hennepin Avenue the night Samuel Witherspoon was shot?"

"I deny it."

Kate goes to the prosecution table and returns with a sheet of paper. She hands it to Gloria Two Bears. "Please tell the jury what you are holding in your hand."

"A piece of paper from the phone company."

"What does it say?"

"It says there was a phone call that night from REgent 8145 to WAlnut 1296 at 11:15 pm."

"Can you identify those phone numbers?"

"No."

"Look at the piece of paper again."

"I'm looking."

"Isn't it a fact that one of those phone numbers is the pay phone at the Lodge, and the other is the phone number at Augie's Bar?"

"It says at the top of the paper that one phone number belongs to Augie's. But it doesn't say that the other number is from the Lodge."

"Okay, Miss Two Bears, we'll have someone verify that later. Your Honor, we'd like to place this document in evidence as state's exhibit number three."

"Any objections?"

"None," Jackson says.

"Your Honor, I have no further questions at this time."

Kate is relieved when the judge calls for a short break. She needs to collect her thoughts before Joshua Jackson's cross-examination.

Chapter 32

"**M**r. Jackson?" Judge Gunderson says after the break.

"Thank you, Your Honor." Jackson stands, adjusts his custom-tailored suit coat, and approaches the witness. Smiling, he says, "Miss Two Bears, are you employed?"

"Yes, I work at the Lodge."

"Doing what?"

"I'm a waitress."

"How long have you been employed there?"

"About two years."

"Your Honor, we would like to place in evidence Miss Two Bear's withholding tax statements and time sheets from the Lodge over the last two years and have them marked as defendant's exhibit number four."

"Any objections?" Gunderson asks.

"No, Your Honor," Kate says.

"What did you do prior to that time?" Jackson asks.

"I prostituted myself."

"Why did you decide to become a waitress?"

"I got tired of being arrested. I was disgusted with myself. I wanted to do something better, something so I wouldn't feel so bad all the time."

"So you became a waitress."

"Yes."

"Do you still prostitute yourself?"

"Sometimes. I have to. Like when I need rent money real bad, but no, not on a regular basis. I quit doing that after Sergeant Bannister arrested me."

"Did Sergeant Bannister say anything to you to encourage you to quit?"

"Kind of."

"What did he say?"

"He said it would go hard on me if he had to arrest me again."

"What do you think he meant by that?"

"I don't know."

"Do you think he meant that he might use physical violence on you?"

"Maybe. I don't know."

"Did you have any sort of deal with Officer Bannister?"

"No. I wanted nothing to do with him."

"Why?"

"He frightened me."

"So you did not call him the night Sam Witherspoon was killed?"

"No. Someone else must've called him. He had lots of people."

"You mean he had people they call snitches?"

"Yes."

"Why would a snitch call him?"

"If someone was doing something at the Lodge. Like drugs. Or prostituting themselves."

"Was anyone prostituting themselves at the Lodge or doing drugs that night?"

"They do that in there every night."

"Every night?"

"Every night I was ever there."

"Miss Two Bears, did you ever see Mr. Witherspoon with a gun?"

"Sure. He used to be a cop. He always had a gun."

"Miss Two Bears, you testified earlier that when Mr. Witherspoon went out on the back balcony, you heard three bangs. Am I correct? You heard three bangs?"

"Three bangs."

"Not one bang? Not two bangs? Three bangs?"

"Three bangs."

"Thank you. That's all I have, Your Honor."

The judge peers at Kate. "Any further questions, Miss Dawson?"

"Yes, just a few," she says, standing. "These bangs you say you heard, can you identify them, Ms. Two Bears?"

"Identify them?"

"What kind of guns they were. Could you tell what they were?"

"One sounded like a shotgun. It made a big noise."

"What about the other one?"

"Could have been a handgun."

"Could it also have been a car door slamming? Your balcony door slamming?"

"Could have been."

"That's all, Your Honor."

"Mr. Jackson?"

"Which came first, Miss Two Bears? The big bang or the other bangs?"

"I don't remember."

"Could the other bangs have come first, before the shotgun?"

"They could have."

"No further questions."

"Miss Dawson?"

"Just one, Your Honor. Miss Two Bears, so the noise, which could possibly have been door slams, could have come after the big bang you identified as the shotgun blast, am I right?"

"Yes."

"That's all I have at this time, Your Honor."

"Mr. Jackson?"

"Nothing more at this time, Your Honor."

"You may step down, Miss Two Bears. You are dismissed, subject to recall. Court is adjourned for the day."

Kate is totally drained. She feels she's gotten most of what she wants from Jamison and Two Bears. She'll call Jamison to the stand again to testify about the deaths of Ben and Davy Roth, *if* Gunderson allows it. If he doesn't, her case—and her brief career as a prosecutor—might be over.

She considered saving the phone call testimony for Mike Bannister, but he'd be ready for it. Kate clearly surprised Gloria Two Bears on the stand today. She doubts the jury bought the business about someone else making the phone call from the Lodge.

Kate *really* hopes to hear something from Jake Cafferty regarding Ramona Gutierrez's testimony. The Mexican woman is the key link in the chain that connects Bannister to three murders. Even if Gunderson allows her latitude, Kate knows that Cafferty must convince Gutierrez not only to testify, but also to testify that she saw Bannister murder the Roths in the cornfield. Without Gutierrez's testimony, Kate doubts the jury will convict. She needs something else, something irrefutable. And she needs it *now*.

If the coroner hasn't destroyed the original autopsy copies for Ben and Davy Roth, she knows the one place where she might find them.

* * *

The corridor leading to the coroner's office at Hennepin County General Hospital is dark. *Good*, Kate thinks. She recognizes Benny Goodman's signature clarinet on the song "Ain't

Misbehavin'" playing loudly on the radio in the brightly lit autopsy suite at the far end of the corridor. She figures Scott, the attendant, is on duty, but she questions whether she can count on him to help again, or if he would keep his mouth shut if he did.

Her heart trips as she makes her way quietly to the coroner's office door, halfway down the corridor, and tries the handle. *Locked.* She didn't expect it to be open but hoped she'd get lucky.

Removing two bobby pins from her hair, she opens up one to use as a pick. She bends the end of the second bobby pin to use as a tension wrench. She works both into the keyhole and the lock mechanism, pushing the key pins flush with the shear line till the driver pins are forced out of the plug, allowing her to rotate and disengage the lock with the tension wrench. She's inside the office with the door closed and locked behind her in less than a minute, whispering "Thank you" to Harry Houdini and the tricks she learned as a child.

She takes a small flashlight out of her purse, flicks it on, and scans the office, the beam moving past a desk and a mimeograph machine, then finally settling on two large file cabinets in a corner. She hurries over to the cabinets and pauses a moment, listening to the muted music on the radio and for any unusual sounds.

Satisfied that Scott hasn't heard her, she opens the first cabinet and eyeballs the autopsy files using the flashlight. They're in alphabetical order. The folders for Ben and Davy Roth are near the end of the row of file folders. She pulls both out, scurries over to the desk, and opens them. The first page in each of the folders is the autopsy summary Wilson Barlow gave her to read when she came to his office. She looks for a second—and correct—report that Harold Jamison should've written, but doesn't find it. "*Dammit!*"

She returns the folders and then, fearing she'll be caught in the office, she turns off the flashlight and shuts the drawer, just as someone fits a key in the office door.

In a panic, her eyes sweep the room. *Shit! Where to hide?* Frantic, she dashes across the room and plants her back against the wall behind the door. As it swings halfway open, Kate holds her breath. Through the frosted glass, she sees the shadow of a man. The radio plays in the background. *If he comes in, I'm finished.*

He stands in the doorway for what feels like *forever*. Kate waits, her mind searching for an excuse as to why she's in here.

Then he takes another step into the room and looks behind the door. "Hi, Kate."

Her heart falls into her shoe. She can hardly get the words out. "Caff . . . Cafferty," she stutters, releasing her breath.

"You know what you're doing?"

She can't get the words out.

He takes her arm. "Better get going." He motions for her to go first.

She skedaddles out the door. Jake turns the lock and closes the door behind them.

"You have a key?"

Jake holds up a set of lock picks.

"Always wanted a set of those," Kate says as they hurry down the corridor.

* * *

Back at her row house, hands still shaking, Kate pours herself a snifter of brandy. "How'd you know I was in the coroner's office?"

"Saw you leaving City Hall and wanted to talk to you," Jake says. "Thought you were headed home. When you stopped at Hennepin General, I tried to stop you, but you were too far ahead."

Kate slumps on the couch and drinks some brandy. "Why stop me?"

Jake settles back in the overstuffed chair. "You didn't think the real autopsy reports were there, did you?"

She shrugs her shoulders and takes another swallow. "I confess I was desperate."

"You were looking in the wrong place."

Kate sits up. "You saw the actual dated and typed reports?"

Jake nods.

"I need the originals, Jake. Where are they?"

"Don't know."

Kate finishes off the brandy and sets the glass on the coffee table, her eyes fixed on his. "They're proof the department is covering up the murders. That'll go a long way in convicting Mike Bannister."

"Really set on convicting him, huh?"

His response surprises her. "Aren't you?"

"Won't bring back the Roths."

"Come on, Jake. Why save Bannister? What's he ever done for you?"

"Not a damn thing. But I keep thinking there's more to these killings than just the cornfield shooting."

"Like what?"

He shakes his head. "Been trying to put it all together, but too many loose ends."

"You said 'killings.' You think there's more than just the Roths and Sam Witherspoon?"

"Possible."

"Who else?"

"Just speculation now."

"You'll let me know if it becomes something else."

Jake nods. "Got anything to eat?"

Never much of a cook, Kate heats two Swanson chicken potpies in the oven while Jake sips a cup of coffee and watches Groucho Marx host *You Bet Your Life* on television. When the potpies are done, Kate brings them into the living room and sets them on a pair of TV trays beside the coffee table. "Sorry. It's all I have."

"Got a stack of 'em in my freezer."

Kate turns down the volume on the TV and settles herself on the sofa. Jake has cleaned up since the last time she saw him in his apartment. The bruises and swelling under his eyes and around his nose have faded, as has her bruise, with the help of some makeup.

They eat in silence for a time before she says, "When did you get back from Mexico?"

Between mouthfuls Jake says, "Late this afternoon."

"Did you bring Ramona Gutierrez with you?"

"She'll be here in a couple of days."

"Jesus. That's not enough time, Jake. I need to prep her. Make sure she has her testimony straight."

"Then don't put her on the stand."

"She's my last witness before the defense presents their case. She's the only one who'll testify as to what happened in the cornfield."

"She admitted seeing the Roths shot in the back. What else do you need?"

"I'm just uncomfortable putting her on the stand without talking to her first."

"The whole trial was a roll of the dice, remember?"

"We're so close to getting Bannister, Jake."

"Then throw the dice and hope they don't come up snake eyes."

"I can't have her testify if I don't know what she'll say. Otherwise, why bring her back here?"

"Because you asked me to."

"Why didn't she come with you?"

"She had some business to attend to."

"You think she'll come?"

"I do."

"And she'll testify honestly as to what she saw?"

He nods.

"And you base that on what?"

"Call it instinct. Call it a hunch. Call it her belief in a higher power. She puts her hand on that Bible, she isn't going to lie."

Kate lets out a frustrated breath. "I don't even know if the judge will allow her testimony or evidence of the cornfield shootings. I left her name off the witness list. Didn't know if you'd find her or if she'd agree to testify. If I call her, Jackson will object. The more I talk about it, the more I think I've got no chance of convincing the judge."

Jake finishes up his meal and dabs his mouth with a napkin. "Howard Gunderson is the judge, right?"

Kate nods.

"Don't worry. He'll allow her testimony and evidence about the Roths' shootings."

"Why?"

Jake smiles. "Little secret we share about the Persian Palms. I'll remind him of it."

"Are you going to tell me what—"

He holds up a hand to stop her from speaking. "Better you don't know."

"What about Ramona Gutierrez's testimony?"

"Done what I can. Up to you now."

*   *   *

After Jake leaves, Kate listens as KSTP newscaster Bill Ingram reads Today's Headlines at 10:00 p.m. Ingram leads off with the retreat of the US 25th Infantry Division and the South Korean 1st Infantry Division across the 38th parallel into South Korea, the troops having been trapped between the Yalu River and the North Korean capital. Ingram then shifts to the Bannister trial. Kate thinks it's stupid for the cops to hitch their wagon

271

to a thug like Mike Bannister, but that's a cop for you. The secret-society-circle-the-wagons attitude is why they're in the court-room in the first place. She knows Bannister murdered the Roths. But without the true autopsy reports and Ramona Gutierrez's testimony, she'll have trouble proving it.

Chapter 33

Jake would rather be watching the trial this morning than sitting at his desk in the Homicide/Sex Division. But because he's on both the prosecution and defense witness lists, he's prohibited from attending the trial until his testimony is finished. So he hauls out the latest edition of the *Minneapolis Daily Tribune* and reads an article about Franklin Simms.

Still awaiting trial on a first-degree manslaughter charge in the death of Zeno Malkin, Simms was assaulted in his Hennepin County jail cell last night. Nick Cole assured Simms that he'd serve only a couple of years if he pleaded guilty, but he could receive up to fifteen years. A nagging doubt about the motive for Malkin's murder is like a strong wind, pushing Jake toward an unknown but important destination.

Looking over at the desk where his old partner, Russ Krueger, used to sit, Jake feels a throb of old music. It's Nick Cole's desk now. Scheduled to testify today in the Mike Bannister trial, Cole is probably waiting in the hallway outside the courtroom. Jake wishes he could watch the interaction between Dawson and her former boyfriend. Appears to Jake that she's had the upper hand in that relationship since the beginning.

Jake sets down the newspaper and picks up the Brazama Gold certificate he found outside Joe Briggs' house. The certificate is wrapped in a plastic evidence bag. Malkin ran the Brazama Gold scam in which a number of investors lost money, creating a laundry list of suspects that had a motive to kill him. Malkin was also connected to Global Enterprises, a shell company in a Vegas building owned by a man named Dominic Cozens. In his conversation about shell companies with Leo Hirschfield, Jake recalls asking himself whom Malkin was fronting for. He'd never gotten a satisfactory answer to his question.

Martin Crenshaw was a stockbroker for Bass, Sterns, and Wheeler. The firm is included in the list of brokerage firms Leonard Lindquist, the chairman of the state Railroad and Warehouse Commission, is seeking information from regarding Twin City Rapid Transit stockholders. Nearly three months ago, Crenshaw committed suicide by jumping into the Mississippi River from the Short Line Bridge. *Or did he*? Jake has never been comfortable with that conclusion either.

He heads for the property room next to the jail on the fourth floor. There he opens a cardboard evidence box and pulls out Martin Crenshaw's suit coat and shoes. The items remind him of another question he never got a satisfactory answer to. Why were Martin Crenshaw's shoes and suit coat found by the side of the road a half-mile from the bridge? Then it hits him. *Son of a bitch*! He repacks the box and hurries to his car.

Snow swirls across the icy asphalt, blown by a blustery, cold wind. A slate gray sky and freezing temperature add to the barren surroundings. According to the odometer, Jake has parked the Ford on West River Road, a half-mile from the Short Line Bridge. Uniforms found Martin Crenshaw's suit coat and shoes here. But Jake doubts they searched the woods. He buttons up his overcoat, puts on his leather gloves, and pulls his hat tightly on his head before exiting the vehicle.

He stands still on the shoulder of the road for a moment, scanning the woods. Except for the evergreens, winter has stripped the leaves from the trees, giving him a clearer view of the area. Only problem is, he doesn't know what the hell he's looking for. Then he realizes it's not his only problem. At least three to four inches of fresh snow cover the ground. And he isn't wearing boots. *Screw it.* He trudges into the snow.

He wanders aimlessly around for twenty minutes, looking for God knows what, his feet turning to blocks of ice. A hot toddy would be perfect right now—if he were still drinking. Cold and frustrated, silently cursing himself for wasting his time, he tromps through the snow toward his car.

Thirty yards from the car and shelter from the cold, Jake steps in a hole and nearly falls over. Stepping back, he stumbles over something sticking out of the snow and almost goes down again. At first, he assumes it's a broken tree branch. But upon closer inspection, he realizes it's a long-handled shovel. Yanking it out of the snow, he notices a clump of dirt frozen on the pointed tip. Curious, Jake uses the shovel to clear away the snow beneath his feet.

It's a hole all right, rectangular. Someone dug here, but why? And why leave what appears to be a new shovel? Jake stares at the hole, back at the road, and then at the shovel in his hand. Martin Crenshaw left his shoes and suit coat on the road and walked or ran to the Short Line Bridge a half-mile away, where he jumped to his death. Turning toward his car, Jake stops in his tracks. Was *Crenshaw* or someone else digging here? Did it happen on the same night that Crenshaw took his life?

Jake stares at the hole once more. Although it's shallow, it has a familiar shape. Jake lays odds that Martin Crenshaw wasn't alone the night he died. Who or what was he running from? And how did he get here in the first place? Jake checked taxicab records. No one from the cab companies dropped Crenshaw here. Someone must've brought him.

Making his way through the snow back to his car, Jake tosses the shovel into the back seat, gets in, and fires up the engine. He lets it run till heat flows from the vents, and he feels some life in his toes and fingers. Then he gets out and scans the pavement.

A car coming toward him honks and swerves by him, the driver offering a one-finger salute. Gusty winds have cleared the road of snow. Jake squats and peers at the black tire marks. They're still readable. He didn't pay much attention to them the day Crenshaw's body was found. Now Jake doubts Crenshaw committed suicide. More than likely he was running from someone, running from his own grave.

* * *

"Counsel, call your next witness," Judge Gunderson says.

Kate says, "The state calls Dr. Walter Gardner."

Gardner is a psychiatrist who serves as a consultant to the Minneapolis PD. He examined Witherspoon in connection with the hearing conducted at the time of Witherspoon's suspension and his subsequent decision to leave the police force.

"And what were your findings, Doctor?"

"Severe depression."

"Symptoms?"

"This was a man who a year earlier was something of a fitness fanatic, a participant in various community outreach and police-sponsored athletic events, a man with good nutritional habits and physical conditioning. At the time of my examination, he was fifteen pounds overweight, drinking heavily, lethargic, unresponsive, disengaged, borderline hallucinatory, borderline paranoiac—in layman's terms, a mental basket case."

"Cause?"

"Any number of possibilities. Physical decline. Pressure of the work. A triggering incident."

"You said 'paranoiac.' Who did he think was after him?"

"I said 'borderline paranoiac.' Who was after him? Everyone. Fellow officers, neighbors, relatives, the newspaper boy who couldn't seem to get the paper all the way up to the front door and left it on the sidewalk every morning, part of a conspiracy to prevent him from learning what was going on in the world. Everyone."

"During your examination, did he mention a specific triggering incident?"

"Yes."

"What did he say?"

"He said that one of the principal reasons he'd become a policeman was because Negroes shouldn't always have to deal with white people as policemen, but that it hadn't done any good, that he'd been a failure."

"The specific incident, what did he say about that?"

"That there was a time when the chips were down and he had a chance to do the right thing, and he'd been a coward. That he'd been afraid to act and as a result let everyone down, including himself."

"That's it?"

"Yes."

"Did you know what he was talking about?"

"I had an idea, but my role is not investigative. It's to evaluate his fitness to continue as a police officer, and in my opinion, there were too many demons. He couldn't handle it."

"What was your idea?"

"Objection," Jackson says. "Speculative. Anyone can make guesses. I'm sure Dr. Gardner reads the same newspapers we all do."

Kate says, "I'm asking for a professional opinion here, Your Honor, not a guess."

"Objection sustained. We're too far afield from an expert opinion here, Counsel."

Kate moves on. "Dr. Gardner, is it your expert opinion that Samuel Witherspoon was a deeply troubled, deeply disturbed man, and that the cause of that disturbance may have been an incident involving police work with particular reference to Jews?"

"Yes."

"Thank you. Your witness."

Jackson rises and approaches the witness stand. "Dr. Gardner, in your expert opinion, could the cause of Samuel Witherspoon's depression have been a personal incident, such as a failed romance?"

"Well, it could have been."

"So your answer is 'yes.'"

"My answer is, it could have been."

"No further questions."

Judge Gunderson says, "Call your next witness, Miss Dawson."

Kate knows she has to call Nick Cole as a witness, and she dreads it. But it's the job, and the job has become her life. She stands. "The state calls Sergeant Nick Cole."

Chapter 34

Nick Cole is in his dress blues. *Of course*, Kate thinks. Cops always get spiffed up for their courtroom appearances. It makes a hell of an impression on a jury. Gleaming metal flashed from the bars on his collar and his badge and name bar, but not from a gun. Witnesses, even cops, are not allowed to have guns in the courtroom.

"Sergeant Cole, please disclose the nature of our relationship." Kate wants the jury to know she isn't hiding anything from them, even though the press has been full of it, and she suspects the jury already knows.

"Okay. We dated for about a year but broke up recently."

"Thank you. Now, Sergeant, please describe your actions on the night Sam Witherspoon was shot and killed."

Nick goes into the usual robotic drone that policemen affect when they're testifying, referring occasionally to the piece of paper he holds in his hands for sticky details like exact times. Standing at her counsel table, Kate glances down at her copy of the same document, the official report Nick filed the night of the Witherspoon incident.

When Nick finishes, Kate says, "Did you touch or handle any of the firearms involved in the incident?"

"I bagged the victim's handgun found at the scene and had Sergeant Bannister give me his handgun. I was wearing gloves."

"Did you handle or touch the shotgun the defendant used?"

"Only to put it in the trunk of my car. Again, I was wearing gloves."

"Was Sergeant Bannister carrying any other guns?"

Nick hesitates.

Kate waits a moment, then asks, "Would you like me to repeat the question?"

"No. Sergeant Bannister was carrying a shotgun."

"Let me rephrase. Was Sergeant Bannister carrying any additional handguns?"

"No, he wasn't."

"How do you know?"

"I . . . uh . . ."

"You didn't ask him, did you, Sergeant Cole?"

"Objection," Jackson says, standing. "Miss Dawson is asking *and* answering her questions."

"Overruled. You may answer the question, Sergeant Cole."

"Uh . . . no, I didn't."

"You didn't search him either, did you?"

"No."

"Did you disturb the body of the victim in any way prior to the arrival of the coroner?"

"No."

"What about your partner, Lieutenant Cafferty?"

"No."

"Did you know who the victim was?"

"Not at first. Most of his face was gone due to the shotgun blast. I knew it was a Negro male is all."

"Did the defendant, Sergeant Bannister, give any indication he knew who the victim was prior to that?"

"No, he did not."

"Did he tell you what happened?"

"Yes."

"What did he say?"

"Objection. Hearsay."

"Your Honor, he's testifying as to the report, which is in evidence."

"Overruled. Continue."

"Well, it's in the report," Nick says. "I can't add too much. Sergeant Bannister was kind of shook up, of course. He says he heard the arguing and sounds like they were really going at it, so he pulled in and started to get out of the car when this guy steps out on the deck with a gun and starts waving it around. He ducks back in the car and pulls out the shotgun. He identifies himself, tells the guy to drop it, and the guy takes a couple of shots at him, so he returns fire. That's about it."

"Did he say whether he called him out?"

"No."

"Did you ask him about the balcony light?"

"Lieutenant Cafferty asked him."

"Did Sergeant Bannister say whether the balcony light was on?"

"He said the light was off."

"How soon after the incident occurred did you arrive on the scene?"

"We were there fifteen minutes after we got the call."

"Had you seen Sergeant Bannister earlier in the evening?"

"No."

"How well do you know Sergeant Bannister?"

"Pretty well."

"Have you ever been involved in other shooting incidents with him?"

"I suppose you could say that."

"One very notorious incident, if I'm not mistaken?"

"Objection," Jackson says. "This is irrelevant."

Kate takes a deep breath. *This is it.* She hopes Jake had time to phone the judge about the "little secret they share." She steels herself and says, "Your Honor, may we approach?"

"Yes. Clerk, sidebar."

Judge Gunderson leans over to hear the two lawyers, who have gathered with the court stenographer at the side of the bench away from the jury. Jackson gets in the first lick.

"Your Honor, Miss Dawson is going to try to smear my client by suggesting that he murdered Sam Witherspoon because of some ancient grudge, something to do with Witherspoon being present when Sergeant Bannister took down two cop killers. This is ridiculous. This is outrageous. That incident was thoroughly investigated by the department, and my client even received an award and promotion as a result of his heroism. The results of that investigation have recently been released to the public."

The judge peers at Kate over a pair of reading glasses. "Miss Dawson?"

"Your Honor, we have ample evidence to support our charge that Sergeant Bannister committed murder. We are going to present that evidence. But I need to establish the motive. That's why I need to explore this prior incident. Sam Witherspoon was going to blow the whistle on this so-called heroism. His death is the conclusion of a continuing event that began with that earlier shooting."

Judge Gunderson ponders this for moment before coming to a decision. "I will allow you to pursue this line of inquiry, Miss Dawson, on the condition that you can tie this to what we're dealing with here. If it becomes apparent that you cannot, I will strike the testimony. Mr. Jackson, your motion is denied, but I will grant a motion for you to strike the word 'notorious.' Nothing has been proven—not yet, anyway—to permit the use of that word."

"I so move, Your Honor. Exception to the ruling on the earlier shooting."

"Exception noted. Continue."

Kate's heart pounds in her chest as she returns to the defense table. Pouring a glass of water from a pitcher, she drinks it slowly, giving herself time to control her excitement and relief. She doesn't want the judge or the jury to see her emotions.

"We're waiting, Miss Dawson," Judge Gunderson prods.

Kate sets down the glass, turns, and gives the judge a smile. "Sorry, Your Honor." She looks at Nick, still seated on the witness stand, and leads him through the killing of the Roths in the cornfield. Her questions tell the story she wants to sell to the jury. Witherspoon caught up with the suspects and was holding them at gunpoint when Bannister arrived. Instead of placing them under arrest, Bannister killed them in cold blood. Witherspoon, watching in horror while two defenseless young men were shot dead as he stood by helplessly, went into a downward spiral from which he never recovered.

So the way it shakes out, Nick Cole and Jake Cafferty were present when the shootings occurred. They could share some of the responsibility for Witherspoon's death. If not planners and instigators of a cover-up, they're accomplices after the fact to murder.

She asks her next question hoping she can use Cole's answer later. "Sergeant Cole, would you describe for the jury the topography of the landscape around the cornfield where the Roths were shot and killed?"

"How do you mean?"

"Is the landscape hilly or flat?"

"Flat."

"So there are no hills or high ground around?"

"No. It's flat as a pancake."

Kate checks her notes and then eyeballs the witness stand again. "Sergeant Cole, do you deny having any foreknowledge that Sergeant Bannister planned to carry out the murder of Samuel Witherspoon?"

"Yes. Definitely. I totally deny it."

"Sergeant Cole, I'm sure counsel for defendant will be sharing with the jury your outstanding record as a member of the Minneapolis Police Department, but before he gets into that, I have one further area I wish to explore with you. Are you a drinker?"

"A drinker? Do you mean do I take a drink every now and then?"

"I mean has your drinking ever gotten you in trouble?"

"With you it has."

There's a buzz. Gunderson silences the gallery with a shake of his index finger.

"But if you mean legal trouble, yeah, once, before I was even on the force, I got a DWI."

"Since then?"

"I've never had a problem."

"Had you had anything alcoholic to drink the night the two suspects were killed by Sergeant Bannister?"

"I don't recall."

Kate pauses. Then she says, "Your testimony is that you don't recall if you had anything to drink that night, correct?"

Nick glares at her. "That's what I said."

"No further questions at this time."

"Your witness, Mr. Jackson," the judge says.

Kate conducted most of her examination from behind counsel's table, as far as she could get from her former boyfriend. Jackson does the reverse, getting so close to Cole as to practically jump into the witness box with him.

"Sergeant, we are going to tell the jury about your career on the Minneapolis police department. Is that agreeable?"

"Yes."

Jackson reviews Nick's record, the fitness reports, the citations, the arrest record, the promotions, and the advanced schooling in police work paid for by the city. "Are you an active member of the Police Federation, Sergeant?"

"Yes."

"Is Officer Bannister also active in the Federation?"

"Very active. He's a board member."

"The Police Federation is currently in a rather heated dispute with the city and the administration of the department, aren't they?"

"Yes."

"Do you think that has anything to do with the reason why we're here today?"

"Objection," Kate says. "Speculative."

Jackson signals the judge. "Approach, Your Honor?"

Gunderson nods. "All right."

The lawyers huddle beside the bench.

"Your Honor, this is just payback for your earlier ruling," Kate says. "This is beyond speculation. It's fantasy."

"Your Honor, if the state can make up motives out of whole cloth, we should be able to have opinions on that subject, too."

"You have a point, Counsel, but let's not take this too far. Overruled."

While frustrated with the ruling, Kate figures Jackson doesn't really expect anyone on the jury to buy his theory. But she knows that jurors leaning towards Bannister's acquittal need a tool to blunt the more plausible motive Kate offered. Jackson is offering them one.

"Sergeant Cole, state's attorney has brought up an incident that occurred months ago in order to establish a motive for my client to have deliberately taken Samuel Witherspoon's life. Your Honor, we have furnished a copy of the recently released Minneapolis Police Department's official report on this incident to the state's attorney, and we would now like to have it marked and placed in evidence as defendant's exhibit number five."

"No objections," Kate says.

"Received. Mark it, please."

"Sergeant, I'm handing you defendant's exhibit number five, and I'm going to refer you to the conclusion of the report dealing with the conduct of the police officers involved."

As Nick reads the leaden bureaucratic prose studded with nuggets like "risk of his own life," "fulfillment of their sworn duty," "best traditions of the Minneapolis Police Department," "commended" and "acted with merit," Kate sees Jackson and Bannister sneaking sly glances at her for signs of despair.

"No further questions at this time, Your Honor," Jackson says.

"We'll break for lunch," the judge says, adjourning the court with a loud gavel. "We'll start again promptly at one thirty."

* * *

Nick Cole is waiting on a hallway bench for Kate as she exits the courtroom through the double doors, briefcase in hand. He's up and in her face before she has a chance to speak. "Thanks for the questions about my drinking," he says, his face flushed. "Nothing like trying to ruin my career."

"This is a murder trial, Nicky. It's not about your career."

"No," he says with a shake of his head. "It's all about yours."

Kate leans forward, bile rising in her throat. "We both know you lied on the witness stand. You were drinking the night you came to see me about our breakup, the night Mike Bannister murdered those two young men in the cornfield. You know what Bannister did. You're protecting him."

Nick breaks eye contact and looks away.

Kate wonders if he just flinched. "You do know what Bannister did, don't you?" she says.

He shakes his head but offers no reply.

"I'll put you back on the stand," Kate says. "You can do the right thing. Put Mike Bannister where he belongs."

"Katie. I'm sorry."

She grabs him by the forearm. *God, I still like this guy.* "I never meant to hurt you, Nicky."

"Seems like that's all you've been doing lately."

"You're right. Maybe . . . after all this is over . . ."

"Maybe what?" he says with an expectant look.

"I care about you, Nicky. I really do. Maybe we could—"

"I wish we could, Katie." His smile is crooked, his eyes misty. With that he turns away and strides down the hallway, moving faster until he's nearly running.

Kate raises a hand to call out to him and then changes her mind. She glances at her watch and heads in the opposite direction.

Chapter 35

Kate's high heels click across the black-and-white Bakelite floor as she enters the Forum Cafeteria on South 7th Street. Light reflects off the glowing chandeliers and etched glass. The aroma of freshly cooked food wafts through the air. The building, with its ivory terra cotta façade and Art Deco interior of black onyx and pale green tiles, is a popular venue for those who shop and work downtown.

Just as she finishes eating, the DA, Wilson Barlow, sits down at the table in a chair opposite her. "Got a minute, Kate?"

Kate checks her watch. "Not much more than that."

"Things going well?"

She nods, wondering what he wants.

Barlow tries a smile, but it's forced. "Glad to hear it." His eyes scan the crowded, noisy room and then come back to her. "You're recalling the coroner to the stand?"

She gets it now. "I am."

"Not a good idea."

She wipes her mouth with a napkin. "Why?"

"If you have information that can hurt the police department and our office, Kate, I need to know."

"Let me get this straight. We're more concerned about our image than we are about solving the murders of two boys."

"Those *boys*, as you put it, murdered a Minneapolis police officer in cold blood."

"So Mike Bannister gets to play judge, jury, and executioner."

"Think about the consequences of what I'm saying, Kate."

"What? I'm going to lose my job if I win this case?"

"I never said that."

"But that's what you're insinuating."

"I'm talking about the coroner's testimony."

"You're not the first person who's warned me off, Wilson."

He raises his eyebrows in surprise. "What're you talking about?"

"A man threatened me the other night."

"Threatened you how?"

"He slapped me around. Warned me to back off."

"Why didn't you tell me this before?"

"Would it have done any good?"

"Did you report it to the police?"

"He wore a mask. I couldn't identify him."

"Nobody threatens my attorneys."

"Isn't that what you're doing now? Threatening me?"

"Christ, Kate, I'm trying to protect you."

"From what?"

Barlow appears to struggle a moment for an answer. "Embarrassment."

"Right. That's what this is all about. Embarrassment."

"No need to get sarcastic, Kate."

"Look," she says, leveling her eyes at him, "the jury needs to know these boys were executed. Not shot while they were running away. Not shot in self-defense. And I believe their murders are directly connected to Sam Witherspoon's murder. Mike Bannister killed Witherspoon because he saw what happened in the cornfield."

"That's all speculation."

"You gave me this case, Wilson, and I'm doing my best to win it."

"Winning isn't the only thing."

"No, it isn't." Kate tosses her napkin on the table, stands, and marches toward the exit.

*   *   *

Kate tries to concentrate on Mike Bannister and the questions she's prepared for the afternoon as she makes the chilly five-minute walk past the store windows decorated with Christmas decorations and back to the courtroom in City Hall. But her conversation with Wilson Barlow keeps interrupting her thoughts. One voice in her head is telling her to forget about recalling the coroner and perhaps save her career, but a second voice, a much angrier voice, urges her to do what she knows is right and the hell with her career. *Easier said than done.*

After the lunch break and when the judge and jury are seated, Kate stands and says, "The state calls the defendant, Michael Bannister, to the stand."

After he's sworn in, she goes through the preliminaries and then moves on to the cornfield shootings, setting up her motive hypothesis again with a series of questions, which Bannister answers by referring to the crime scene report and denying any wrongdoing.

"So if Samuel Witherspoon or anyone present that night were to claim they saw you deliberately shoot Ben and Davy Roth after they had been disarmed, subdued, and were being held at gunpoint, they would be lying, am I correct?"

"Yes."

"You shot them from a distance as they were fleeing."

"They shot at me."

"And you had no reason to silence Samuel Witherspoon forever by taking his life, am I correct?"

"Yes. I liked Sam. I felt bad he was suspended and then quit. I felt even worse about the shooting."

"And you were not aware at the time that the person whom you killed was Samuel Witherspoon?"

"I wasn't."

"All right, Sergeant Bannister. We're now going to go over the killing of Samuel Witherspoon. Before we get started, let me ask, have you rehearsed your testimony with your counsel?"

"No. I discussed it. I didn't rehearse it."

"Where were you earlier that evening before you drove to the alley behind Gloria Two Bears' place?"

"I stopped by Augie's."

"Did you stop to drink?"

"No. I don't drink while on duty."

"Then why did you stop at Augie's?"

"I was waiting for a phone call."

"From whom?"

As Kate expected, Bannister claims the phone call from the Lodge came from one of his snitches, Leon Beauchamp, now conveniently deceased.

"Where were you when you first heard the discussion taking place between Samuel Witherspoon and Miss Two Bears?"

"It wasn't a discussion."

"Answer the question," the judge says.

Kate thanks Gunderson.

Bannister says, "I was in the neighborhood when the ten seventy-nine call came over the radio."

"What's a ten seventy-nine call?"

"Domestic disturbance."

"And you didn't have a partner with you?"

"No. My partner called in sick that night."

"You're assigned to the Morals Squad, are you not, Sergeant?"

"That's right."

"Is it standard operating procedure that a Morals Squad sergeant respond to a domestic disturbance call?"

"I was a patrol officer. I know how dangerous a domestic can be. Being in the area, I thought I could help."

"So you heard the ten seventy-nine call."

"Yes."

"Please continue, Sergeant."

"Well, I turned into the alley behind her place."

"Meaning Miss Two Bears' place."

"Yeah."

"Where was Miss Two Bears' apartment located?"

"You mean the address?"

"No, I mean what floor? How high up?"

"Second floor."

"Was the window on your car open or closed when you first heard them?"

"Closed."

"Yet you were able to hear them, in a moving car, with the car window closed, from inside an apartment above you on the second floor, with the door to that apartment nearly closed, am I right?"

"I could've heard them from two blocks away, the way they were going at it."

"So they must've been quite loud?"

"Quite."

"Even though their voices were so loud you could hear them from two blocks away, you didn't recognize Samuel Witherspoon's voice?"

"I told you, it wasn't just voices, they were throwing stuff around and banging on each other, and yelling and screaming. You don't make out individual voices when it's like that."

"What did you do when you heard the voices?"

"I pulled into the alley and parked behind Miss Two Bears' place, kind of at an angle, partially blocking the alley."

"Why partially blocking the alley?"

"You don't want anyone zipping by taking a shot at you, or blocking the alley behind you."

"Is that standard procedure?"

"I don't know. That's the way I do it. I don't know if it's in a book somewhere, but that's the way I learned it."

"Is it standard procedure to call out someone by name?"

"I didn't call him out. He must've heard the unit pull in because he stepped out on the balcony."

"Were your headlights on?"

"No."

"Why? Wouldn't your lights have illuminated the scene better?"

"Look, he's stepping out on the balcony just as I'm pulling in. I see something in his hand. I'm not going to light myself up like a Christmas tree for him to take a potshot at me."

"You say you saw something in his hand. Was the overhead balcony light on?"

"No."

Kate moves closer to the witness stand, getting in Bannister's space. "You're absolutely sure about that?"

"I'm absolutely sure."

The whiff of garlic stops her for a moment. *The night she was assaulted in front of the Gutierrezes' farmhouse!*

"Do you have a follow-up question, Miss Dawson?" Judge Gunderson asks.

"Yes . . . Your Honor," Kate says, stepping back from the witness stand, collecting her thoughts, getting control of her emotions. "Because if the light on the balcony had been on, Sergeant Bannister, you clearly would have been able to identify Samuel Witherspoon, wouldn't you?"

"Objection," Jackson says. "Speculative."

"Your Honor, we can call an expert if we have to, to testify that if a hundred-watt GE light bulb had been on directly over Samuel Witherspoon's head, then he would be clearly identifiable from where the defendant was standing when he shot him."

"Miss Dawson, you'll have that opportunity. Sustained."

Kate nods and continues. "So Sam Witherspoon was standing in the dark and you could not identify him, am I correct?"

"Correct."

"Then what happened?"

"Well, as I'm stepping out of the car, he shoots at me."

"How many times?"

"Once."

"And what would you estimate was the distance from which he fired?"

"Oh, maybe twenty feet."

"He was a trained police officer, trained in the use of firearms, marksmanship, and he missed entirely at a distance of some twenty feet, right?"

"He *was* a police officer. He sure wasn't at the time. And he was drunk."

"Objection, Your Honor," Kate says. "The medical examiner did not conclude Officer Witherspoon was drunk."

"Sustained. Strike that from the record. Continue, Miss Dawson."

"Then what happened?"

"I ducked back into the car, grabbed the Ithaca, knelt behind the door on the driver's side, rolled down the window, and braced the shotgun on the window sill on the driver's side. I identified myself, and he fired again. Then I fired and it was all over. He pitched over the rail. I took a quick look and saw that most of his head was missing. I went back to the car and called for backup."

"How did you identify yourself to Sam Witherspoon?"

"I said, 'Police, put down your weapon.'"

"Do you think he could have misunderstood you? Sometimes 'Police' might've sounded like 'please,' couldn't it?"

"Look, the guy was drunk, and I said, 'Police' and not something else."

"Your Honor, this is the second time Officer Bannister has referred to the victim as being drunk. That has not been established. I move to strike."

"Sustained. Jury will disregard the witness's characterization but is free to consider other testimony on this subject that has been admitted."

Kate continues. "And you don't have your flashing lights on, so he has no way to identify you from your car, does he?"

"I believe I already explained that. No. He doesn't."

"Then what happened?"

"Like I said, he fired another shot at me, and I took him down with the shotgun. He went over and that's it."

"Why did you go back into your car for your shotgun? Why didn't you return fire with your handgun after he shot at you the first time?"

"I don't really know. I've thought about that. I mean, I could've saved time and all."

"So the former police officer takes a second shot from about twenty feet, misses again completely, not even hitting the door of your car, and you return fire. His head is blown off, and he goes over the rail and falls in the snow?"

"Yeah, that's right."

"After you called for backup, did you go upstairs, see about Miss Two Bears?"

"No."

"Did you touch the body?"

"I looked at it, but he was dead. I didn't do anything else."

"And the gun next to the body was not a throw-down?"

"No, it wasn't."

"So I would be absolutely mistaken if I accused you of planting a gun at the scene to make it appear he shot at you, is that correct?"

"That's correct."

"And he did fire at you at least twice, is that correct?"

"Yeah, it's true," he answers sarcastically.

"Did you touch or handle this handgun in any way?"

"Objection," Jackson says. "Asked and answered."

"Sustained. Move along, Miss Dawson."

"What did you do with your shotgun?"

"I think I was still holding it when Sergeant Cole got there."

Jackson's coaching has not been entirely successful, Kate thinks. Bannister is defensive and belligerent. She's gotten what she wanted. But so has Jackson.

"No further questions, Your Honor."

Judge Gunderson fixes his gaze on Jackson. "Counselor?"

Jackson rises from his chair behind the defense table. Making it clear he feels that Kate has done nothing to damage his client's credibility, he asks Bannister, "Did you murder Samuel Witherspoon?"

"No, sir."

Jackson casually waves him off the stand.

*   *   *

Exhausted, Kate makes a quick stop at her PO box outside her office before heading home for the day. She removes a large manila envelope and carries it into her small, windowless office in which most of the floor space is taken up by cardboard file boxes.

Her mind plays a continuous loop of the final hour of the trial. After Mike Bannister's testimony, she introduced the bloody photos of Sam Witherspoon's body and missing face, despite Jackson's objections. She considered having the other uniforms that were at the scene the night Witherspoon was killed testify but changed her mind. They would offer nothing but support for Bannister's account.

Sitting behind her desk, she opens the envelope and pulls out two documents, scans them, and straightens up. *Jackpot!* After she catches her breath, a smile brightens her face.

She looks up and out her open office door at the empty hall. Talk about a huge favor. Now she just has to convince Judge Gunderson to allow her to introduce the documents as evidence.

Chapter 36

Still upset about Kate's questions while he was on the witness stand, Nick Cole returns to the Homicide/Sex Division late that afternoon. Looking at Jake's unoccupied desk, Nick spots a note stuck on the desk spike. He sidles over and skims it. Curious, he heads for the crime lab.

Nick walks into the lab just as a heavyset, balding man test fires a handgun into a water recovery tank to obtain comparison bullets for evaluation under the microscope. Nick waits for the man to remove his ear covers and then says, "You left a note on Cafferty's desk, Charlie."

"Yep."

"What's it about?"

Charlie glances at a shovel leaning against the wall. "When I see Cafferty, I'll tell him."

Nick follows Charlie's gaze and says, "I'm his partner."

"So I hear."

Nick walks over to the shovel. "Cafferty give you this?"

"Thought you'd know. Being his partner and all."

"I testified in court this morning. Just got back."

Charlie shrugs. "Jake wants the shovel checked for prints."

"Tell you why?"

"Nope."

"How 'bout where he found it?"

"West River Road. Something to do with the Martin Crenshaw case."

Nick thinks on it a moment. "Thought Crenshaw was a suicide."

"Me, too."

*   *   *

The following morning Jake Cafferty stops by Hennepin General, where he finds Franklin Simms recovering from his assault. Simms is lying on his back on a pillow with the sheets pulled up to his chin, a wrist cuffed to a side-rail.

"Remember me?" Jake asks as he sits down on a wooden chair beside the bed.

Simms turns his head and looks at Jake. His blue eyes are vacant. A deep red bruise rings his neck. "I remember," he says in a weak voice, turning his head away.

"I need your help."

Simms stares blankly at the ceiling for a time before a small smile curls his lips.

"Something funny?"

"You," Simms says, focusing his dead eyes on Jake again. "Everyone around here tells me I'm the one who needs help."

"Doctors? Nurses?"

Simms nods. "And shrinks. Especially shrinks. Wanna cure the queer." His words hold a bitter edge.

"You help me, Simms, maybe I can get you out."

He snickers. "Not in the mood for cop jokes."

"Murder is no joke, Simms."

"Then why am I here?"

"You confessed."

"It was a mistake. I was coerced. I'm innocent, and a good lawyer will help me prove it. I've had three of 'em. Had to dismiss 'em all."

"You help me, I'll help you."

"Like I trust the word of another detective."

"I ever lied to you before?"

"I wouldn't know."

"Who else you gonna trust?"

Simms thinks about it for a moment. "What about Detective Cole?"

"I'm the one you need to talk to."

"Before I'm dead, huh?"

"Hard to talk to you if you are."

Simms' eyes hold Jake's, searching for something that indicates he's telling the truth. Finally, he says, "What's the deal?"

"Brazama Gold."

"Already told you, I lost money on it."

"Tell me again. Start with who gave you the tip."

"Zeno."

"You tell anyone else about it?"

"Don't think so."

"Think again."

Simms peers down at his hands folded on the sheet and then back at Jake again. "Mike Bannister."

Jake nods. "Anyone else?"

"No."

"Not Joe Briggs?"

"Didn't know him."

"But Bannister did," Jake mutters to himself.

"What's that?"

"Nothing. Bannister is queer, right?"

Simms nods his head.

"Isn't interested in women?"

"No."

"You sure?"

Simms gives Jake an *Are you kidding me?* look. "Trust me. I'd know."

"Okay. Remember what Bannister said when you told him about Brazama Gold?"

"It better be a good tip—or else."

"Or else what?"

"What do you think?"

Jake thinks Franklin Simms could be as dead now as Zeno Malkin. "That why Bannister was beating you up in the alley outside the Persian Palms?"

"That and because he wanted a blow job and I wouldn't put out."

Jake stands. "Stay alive for a while, Simms. I'll be back."

"I'll believe it when I see it, Lieutenant."

*   *   *

Kate rises from her chair behind the prosecution table and says, "The state calls Sergeant Paul Langseth."

If Bannister is the prototypical street cop, Langseth is the polar opposite: pudgy, rumpled, balding, and bespectacled. He's also a legend in the department as a ballistics expert with encyclopedic knowledge of handguns.

Kate shows him the handgun found next to Sam Witherspoon, asks him to identify it as the one he has examined, and places it in evidence as exhibit number six. Then she says, "Sergeant Langseth, you've examined the handgun that allegedly was fired by Samuel Witherspoon the night he was killed. Could you summarize your findings for us?"

"Sure. It's a six-inch, .22 caliber long-rifle, nine-shot Iver Johnson top break double-action revolver, called a .22 Supershot."

"Let's go over that a bit. I'm not sure we're all as familiar with these terms as you are. First of all, six-inch. What does that mean?"

"The barrel, the part the bullet comes out of, is six inches long."

"Twenty-two caliber. What does that mean?"

"It means the handgun fires .22 caliber rounds. The bullets, the lead part, are two millimeters in diameter."

"What does long-rifle mean?"

"It means the type of case or shell, the brass part that holds the bullet. Long-rifle refers to a shell that is a bit longer than a .22 short or a .22 long in order to accommodate a greater amount of gunpowder. It's a common load, used in both handguns and rifles."

"What's a nine-shot?"

"The cylinder, the part that holds the rounds, can hold up to nine rounds."

"I thought revolvers held six rounds?"

"Well, most do. It's kind of a quality thing. The more shots, the thinner the separation between the chambers in the cylinder and the more likely the handgun will heat up and break down. The better revolvers tend to have five or six chambers."

"We're getting quite an education here. Okay, Sergeant, how about Iver Johnson?"

"Old-time manufacturer. Sells mostly through the big catalog companies."

"How much does it retail for new?"

"Around twenty to twenty-five dollars."

"Pretty affordable?"

"Yes."

"So this is not a quality piece?"

"No."

"How many do you suppose are in circulation?"

"Objection. Speculative."

"Your Honor, may I rephrase?"

"Yes."

"Do you know how many were manufactured and sold?"

"Yes." Langseth pulls out a piece of paper from his coat jacket. "The gun was manufactured between 1928 and 1941, when it was discontinued. It's a very limited production revolver with only 22,650 manufactured. It came in seven- and nine-round versions."

"What are you reading from?"

"Federal government statistics."

"Lieutenant, what's the serial number on this particular handgun?"

"K-15642."

"Can you determine from the serial number when this was manufactured?"

"Yes. In 1930, according to those federal reports I gave you."

"Do all revolvers have serial numbers?"

"No. And some companies reuse the same serial numbers. Colt used the number 776500 on the 1942 Model 1911A1 Military and the 1949 Official Police, which many of the MPD officers carry."

"Okay, now, Sergeant, explain top break, please."

"It means that the cylinder does not swing out from the frame like in most revolvers. You push a release with your right thumb, the gun opens up at the top, and the barrel tilts downward, exposing the cylinder. There's a little spring under the cylinder, so it kind of pops up and the cartridges pop out."

"What's the purpose of this design?"

"Quick load. In some revolvers, single-actions mostly, there's a little gate on the side, and a spring-operated rod so you can push out the rounds, but you have to unload one chamber at a time."

"You said Iver Johnson quit making the gun in 1941."

"Yes. It's inherently unstable. Instead of being a solid one-piece frame, the barrel and the frame are separate. This is a gun that tends to spit lead."

"Why is that?"

"Because they're separate, the cylinder and the barrel don't always align properly, and it doesn't help when you have nine shots and much less margin for error between the chambers. So when it's fired, pieces of the bullet tend to shear off instead of going through the barrel. The Iver Johnson people knew it, too. That's why they only made it in a .22, but even a .22 releases a lot of energy."

"Okay, now what about double-action?"

"It means you can fire just by pulling the trigger. With a single-action, you have to cock it by pulling the hammer back before you can fire."

"What's revolver mean?"

"It means that as you pull the trigger, the cylinder revolves."

"What happens when you pull the trigger on a double-action revolver?"

"The trigger mechanism engages the hammer, which is on a spring. The hammer goes back until it passes a release point, where it disengages from the trigger mechanism, and the spring then propels it back to the frame. As this is happening the cylinder revolves, placing a fresh cartridge directly under the hammer. The firing pin mounted on the head of the hammer strikes the end of the cartridge. This causes the gunpowder inside the cartridge to ignite, converting it from a solid to a powerful gas, which forces the bullet out of the barrel."

"What you've just described is standard operating procedure, right?"

"Right."

"But as you've pointed out, this particular handgun is unusual in several respects, am I correct?"

"Yes."

"In what respects other than those you have already described?"

"The cylinder in the Iver Johnson rotates counter-clockwise. In most other revolvers, the cylinder rotates clockwise."

"Does that affect your findings with respect to the handgun which was allegedly fired at defendant by Samuel Witherspoon on the night Mr. Witherspoon was killed?"

"Yes."

"Were you in the courtroom when defendant testified about being shot at by the victim?"

"Yes."

"Did you hear the defendant say he was fired at twice by Witherspoon?"

"Objection. Leading."

"Sustained. Rephrase."

"What did you hear the defendant say with respect to being fired upon by the victim?"

"That the victim fired at him at least twice."

"Did your examination of the handgun found beside Samuel Witherspoon's body support the defendant's statement that the victim fired on him at least twice?"

"No."

"Why?"

"Keep in mind that a fully-loaded revolver will have a live round under the hammer, but when the hammer is cocked, that live round rotates one position over and the second live round moves into its place to be fired. Thus, the round directly under the hammer of a fully-loaded revolver will be fired last."

"Why is this important?"

"Because, in this handgun, the cylinder rotated counter-clockwise, so that if there were two rounds in the revolver and two rounds were fired—and nobody messed with the gun after it was recovered—the first round would have moved to the left of the hammer when the second one was fired and the second one would stay under the hammer. Officer Bannister testified that Sam Witherspoon fired at him twice before he returned fire. If that's true, there should have been one spent round on the left side of the hammer and one under the hammer. There wasn't. There was a spent round under the hammer and a spent round on the right. That's not correct for this revolver."

"So, in your expert opinion, what do you conclude about the firing of this handgun on the night of Samuel Witherspoon's death?"

"It wasn't fired the way Sergeant Bannister testified."

Kate glances at the jury. Some are taking notes. Just as she hoped.

"Sergeant Langseth, can you explain to the jury what a throw-down is?"

"Yes. An untraceable gun dropped at a crime scene, usually left by an officer who needs to justify a bad shooting."

"Could the Iver Johnson in question be a throw-down?"

Jackson leaps to his feet. "Objection! Speculation."

"Sustained."

"Your Honor," Kate says, "Sergeant Langseth is an experienced police officer and is considered a ballistics expert on handguns."

"Then rephrase the question, Miss Dawson."

"In your *opinion*, Sergeant Langseth, could the gun in question be a throw-down?"

"Yes, I believe it is."

Kate steals another glance at the jury. Their eyes are riveted on the witness stand. "In your opinion, Sergeant Langseth, how did two .22 caliber bullets end up in the wrong position in the Iver Johnson's cylinder?"

"The Iver Johnson was an old, cheap gun. In my opinion, it's unsafe to fire. I believe Sergeant Bannister fired two shots in the air from a backup .22, making it look like Witherspoon fired at him. He then gets the throw-down, the Iver Johnson, and takes the two spent shells from the backup .22 and puts one under the hammer in the Iver Johnson cylinder and one on the *right* side of the barrel, thinking that the cylinder would rotate on this gun the same way it does on his .38 Colt Detective Special, the standard gun for many detectives on the MPD. Of course, Colt doesn't rotate the same way as the Iver Johnson.

Sergeant Bannister should've put one of the spent shells in the cylinder on the left side and one under the hammer, because Iver Johnson rotates counterclockwise, to the left."

"Thank you." Kate looks at Jackson. "Your witness."

Jackson stands. "Would you tell us again, Sergeant Langseth, what type of revolver Sergeant Bannister was carrying the night Sam Witherspoon was shot?"

"A Colt Detective Special."

"And what caliber of bullet is the Colt Detective Special chambered for?"

"A .38 caliber bullet."

"And the Iver Johnson fires a .22 caliber, correct?"

"Yes."

Jackson walks over to the exhibit table. "Your Honor, if I may, I would like to examine this handgun, but to tell you the truth, these things make me kind of nervous. Could we ask the bailiff to make sure it isn't loaded?"

"Certainly."

The bailiff checks it out and hands the Iver Johnson to Jackson, who holds it pointing downward with his finger outside the trigger guard. "Sergeant Langseth, if I recall correctly, you testified that the gun couldn't have been fired the way Sergeant Bannister described in his testimony because of the position of the bullet casings in the cylinder, am I correct?"

"Yes. I said that, assuming the gun was not tampered with after it was recovered."

"Ah, not tampered with. You also, I believe, testified that you heard Sergeant Bannister's testimony with respect to the firing of the gun, am I right?"

"Yes."

"Then you heard him testify that a total of two shots were fired at him, right?"

"Right."

"Is it possible that someone who fired two shots at Sergeant Bannister could also have wanted to fire three shots at him?"

"Yes."

"In fact, it's possible, isn't it, based on the testimony you heard, that Mr. Witherspoon was in the process of trying to shoot Sergeant Bannister for the third time, when he himself was shot?"

"It's possible."

"Sergeant Langseth, you say this is a double-action piece, am I right?"

"Yes."

"Now, if I'm not mistaken, a double-action piece can also be fired single-action, can it not?"

"Yes."

"And when you fire single-action, you pull back the hammer with your thumb, and then you pull the trigger?"

"Doesn't have to be with your thumb, but that's the usual way if you're going to fire single-action," Langseth says.

"And in the process of pulling back the trigger with your thumb, you hear a kind of click, click, click as you go through various, shall we say, stages of engagement between the hammer and cylinder, is that correct?"

"Yes."

"And on the second click, the cylinder free wheels, doesn't it?"

"Yes."

"So Samuel Witherspoon could have been pulling back the hammer and got as far as the second click, getting ready to take that third shot at that very instant when he was hit, right?"

"It's possible."

"Sam Witherspoon loses control of the gun. It falls out of his hand. And then . . ." Jackson pulls back the trigger two clicks with his right thumb. Then with his left hand, he spins the cylinder, which rotates freely for several seconds and stops.

"Round and round she goes, and where she stops, nobody knows." He doesn't wait for an answer. "Thank you, Sergeant Langseth, that will be all."

"Redirect, Miss Dawson?" Judge Gunderson asks.

Kate stands. "Sergeant Langseth, how many empty .22 cartridges did you find in the Iver Johnson?"

"Two."

"So Sam Witherspoon wouldn't have attempted to fire a third shot, would he?"

"Objection," Jackson says. "Speculation."

"Sustained."

"In your opinion, Sergeant Langseth, would Sam Witherspoon attempt to fire a third shot if he knew there were only two bullets in the chamber?"

"No. He would not."

"Thank you. No further questions, Your Honor." Kate sits down.

Judge Gunderson looks at the defense table. "Mr. Jackson?"

Jackson stands. "In your opinion, Sergeant Langseth, is it possible that Sam Witherspoon thought there were more bullets in the chamber?"

"It's possible. But—"

"That will be all, Sergeant Langseth. Thank you."

Chapter 37

Kate knows that Jake Cafferty is a practiced witness who has testified in scores of criminal trials. But she also knows that his drinking might impact his testimony. After a lunch break and after he's sworn in, she gets right to the point. "Did you conduct an examination of the scene the night Sam Witherspoon was shot?"

"Yes, I did."

"And in the course of that examination, did you examine the light fixture on the balcony where the victim was standing at the time he was killed?"

"Yes."

"And are you aware that the defendant, Sergeant Bannister, testified that the balcony light was off at the time he discharged his shotgun?"

"Yes."

"On the night that Sam Witherspoon was shot, did you ask Sergeant Bannister if the balcony light was off?"

"Yes."

"Do you recall how he answered?"

"He said it was off."

"Based on your examination of the balcony light, could you determine whether the light was in fact off when the shot was fired?"

"Yes, I could make a determination."

"How were you able to make that determination?"

"By examining the filament of the light bulb in the light fixture after I arrived at the scene."

"When was that?"

"About ten minutes after we ID'd the body."

"Had anyone else examined the fixture prior to that time?"

"Not that I'm aware of."

"How did your examination enable you to determine whether the balcony light was on or off when Samuel Witherspoon was shot?"

"When a light bulb is broken while the light is turned on, the gas inside it reacts to the oxygen in the atmosphere, turning the filament black. If a light bulb is off when the bulb is broken, the metal in the filament, at most, turns a light gray, because the gas in the light bulb is cool and doesn't react to the oxygen."

"Based on what you have just testified to as to the chemical reactions that take place in broken light bulbs, could you tell us whether the balcony light was on or off when it was broken?"

"It was on."

"How did you determine that?"

"The filament was black and curled up. It had burned up. The light was on when Sam Witherspoon was shot."

The courtroom buzzes and then quickly settles under the judge's glare.

Kate continues. "Lieutenant Cafferty, did you subsequently conduct another examination of the scene?"

"Yes."

"What was the purpose of that examination?"

"To determine if someone walking or standing on the balcony under the light with the light on would be identifiable to someone standing in the alley."

"When was this examination conducted?"

"Actually, it was conducted twice. Two weeks after the shooting at one a.m. in the morning, same weather conditions, and then again two nights after the first time."

"How did you conduct that examination?"

"I had an officer walk back and forth under the light and also stand under the light."

"What were the results of your examination?"

"The person would be clearly identifiable."

"What do you mean 'clearly identifiable'?"

"That you could easily determine who it was that was on the balcony if you were in the alley where Sergeant Bannister says he was standing."

"Thank you. Your witness," Kate says to Jackson.

Mike Bannister's face has turned to stone, but Jackson never changes expressions. Chipping away at the tiny openings, he manages to get Jake to admit that if Witherspoon turned off the light when he stepped out onto the deck, and the shots were exchanged immediately afterwards, the gases in the bulb might not have had time to cool completely, and the burned filament might have been darker than light gray. Jackson also gets Jake to admit that Negroes might be a little harder to identify in the dark under hundred-watt light than white folks.

Then Jackson says, "You're an alcoholic, are you not, Lieutenant?"

"Objection," Kate says, rising out of her chair.

"Your Honor," Jackson says, "Lieutenant Cafferty is a member of Alcoholics Anonymous."

"Overruled, Miss Dawson."

Kate figured Jackson would raise questions about Jake's drinking, as she raised questions about Nick's. She hopes the damage inflicted won't hurt her case or prejudice the jury.

"Thank you, Your Honor." Facing the witness stand, Jackson says, "Lieutenant Cafferty, had you been drinking the night Sam Witherspoon was shot?"

"I might've had a drink."

"Just one?"

"Not sure if it was more."

"So you could've had more."

"Could've."

"Isn't it true that you were so drunk that you fell in the snow, Lieutenant?"

"It was icy. I slipped."

"Did anyone else at the scene slip and fall?"

"Not that I remember."

"So you're not sure if you had more than one drink, Lieutenant. You don't remember anyone else slipping and falling. Do you remember throwing up in Miss Two Bears' bathroom?"

"I had a touch of the flu."

"Is that so?"

"Is that a question?"

Jackson looks at the judge.

Gunderson says, "You know better than that, Detective."

"Sorry, Your Honor."

"Given your lapses of memory, Lieutenant," Jackson says, "isn't it possible that your recollection of the filament in the light bulb that evening might also be hazy?"

"No. I remember it was black."

"You're sure?"

"Objection!" Kate says. "Asked and answered."

"Sustained. Move on, Mr. Jackson."

"No further questions, Your Honor."

"Redirect, Miss Dawson?" the judge says.

Kate stands, determined to avoid further questions about Jake's drinking. "Detective Cafferty, where was the switch for the balcony light located?"

"At the head of the stairs."

"So someone leaving Miss Two Bears' apartment would've had to pass under the light to get from the apartment to the light switch to turn it off, is that correct?"

"Yes."

"And then, if they were to be showered by fragments from the light bulb, they would have had to be under the light, wouldn't they?"

"Yes."

"Detective Cafferty, who was on the balcony when you were conducting your subsequent examinations as to whether someone was identifiable under the light?"

"My partner, Sergeant Cole."

"What race is Detective Cole?"

"White."

"Thank you. Your witness."

Jackson gives it another go. "If someone were to leave Miss Two Bears' apartment and walk across the balcony to turn off the switch, how long would they be under that light?"

"A couple of seconds."

"Even less than that, wouldn't you say?"

"No, because they would be visible the entire time they were walking across the balcony. That's the whole idea behind a balcony light, so you can see where you're going in the dark."

"And are you claiming that at one a.m. in the morning, a Negro male, crossing under a hundred-watt light bulb for a second, would be identifiable to someone standing in an alley twenty feet away?"

"To a trained police officer, yes."

"How about to a trained police officer pulling an eight-thirty-p.m.-to-six-thirty-a.m. shift for the third night in a row, maybe a little tired, maybe not quite as attentive as he should be?"

"Sergeant Bannister should've been able to identify Sam Witherspoon under those circumstances. We try not to send out people when they're exhausted or overstressed."

"Try not to?"

"That's right."

"Thank you. No further questions."

"Miss Dawson?"

"Just one question, Your Honor. Detective Cafferty, isn't it a fact that Sergeant Bannister was sufficiently alert to avoid two bullets, if there were in fact two bullets, and to take down Sam Witherspoon with a head shot?"

"Objection. Leading. Argumentative. Move to strike."

"Sustained. Jury will disregard. Miss Dawson?"

Kate doesn't mind the objection. She got her point across to the jury. "I have nothing further, Your Honor."

"All right, Detective Cafferty, that will be all. You may step down. Miss Dawson, call your next witness."

Chapter 38

When Kate notified the Hennepin County coroner that he'd be testifying again, Harold Jamison was more resigned than surprised, as he was when Kate showed him the two conflicting autopsy reports he'd written for the Roths.

Jamison has a good reputation. Cops respect him. He's nearing retirement and wants to keep his reputation intact. But someone, Kate believes, pressured him into writing a second—and phony—autopsy report on Ben and Davy Roth. She's anxious to learn who that someone was.

When he's settled in his chair on the witness stand, Kate asks her first prepared question. "Dr. Jamison, did you perform the autopsies on Ben and Davy Roth?"

"Objection," Jackson says, standing. "My client is not on trial for the deaths of the Roths."

Judge Gunderson swivels his chair and faces the defense table. "We've already discussed the possible connection between Sam Witherspoon's death and the Roths, Mr. Jackson. The horse is out of the barn. We're not revisiting it. Overruled."

"Thank you, Your Honor," Kate says. She figured Jackson would object and hoped the judge would respond appropriately. Emboldened now, she repeats the question. "Dr. Jamison, did you perform the autopsies on Ben and Davy Roth?"

"Yes," Jamison says.

"And you wrote the autopsy report for both based on your examination of the bodies."

"Yes, I did."

Kate picks up a folder on the prosecution table. "Your Honor, may I approach the witness stand with a document?"

"Go ahead, Miss Dawson."

Kate walks to the defense table and gives Jackson a copy. Then she approaches the witness stand, where she hands a copy to Jamison. "Doctor, could you identify this document for the court?"

Jamison adjusts his glasses and says, "It's a copy of the autopsy report for Ben Roth."

"That's your signature at the bottom of the report, correct?"

"Yes, it is."

"So you wrote it."

"Yes."

"Please read the date for the court."

"September 8, 1950."

"Thank you. Now, Dr. Jamison, please read the underlined sentences for the court."

Jamison clears his throat. "The entry of the gunshot wound is located 12 inches from top of head and 7 inches right of midline. It is a round uniform wound measuring ¼ inch. The direction of the wound is left to right." He returns the report to her.

"Thank you, Dr. Jamison."

Kate returns to the defense table and gives Jackson a copy of the second document. Then, at the witness stand again, she hands Jamison a second document and asks him to identify it.

He clears his throat once more and says, "It's a copy of the autopsy report for Ben Roth."

"That's your signature at the bottom of the report, correct?"

"Yes."

"So you wrote it."

Jamison hesitates.

"That's your signature, isn't it, Dr. Jamison?"

"Yes."

"Please read the date for the court."

"September 7, 1950."

"So it's dated one day before the previous autopsy report you just read."

"Yes, it is."

Jackson leaps to his feet to object and immediately requests a sidebar.

"We'll discuss this in my chambers," the judge says. "The jury and court personnel will remain in place while I confer with counsel."

Kate follows Judge Gunderson and Jackson through the half gate into the clerk's corral, which gives them access to the hallway behind the courtroom leading to the judge's chambers. Once there, the judge sits down behind his desk, his back to a wall of law books. Kate takes a side-by-side chair next to Jackson. The court reporter sits on a stool to the judge's right, her steno machine on a tripod in front of her.

Gunderson names all those present for the record and proceeds. "All right, Miss Dawson. I assume Mr. Jackson is objecting because this is the first time he's seen this second document."

"Thank you, Your Honor," Jackson responds.

"Miss Dawson?" Gunderson says.

Heart pounding in her chest, palms sweaty, Kate says, "Your Honor, I received these copies of the autopsy reports for Ben and Davy Roth last night."

"And how did you receive them?"

"Anonymously, Your Honor."

"Of course," Jackson says, his voice laden with skepticism.

"They were in an unmarked envelope in my PO box outside my office."

"Convenient," Jackson says.

"That will be enough of the sarcasm, Mr. Jackson," the judge says.

"I've had no chance to look them over," Jackson complains.

"Let me see the copies you were about to show Dr. Jamison," Gunderson says to Kate.

She hands him the two conflicting copies of Ben Roth' autopsy.

Jackson is out of his chair and behind Gunderson in a flash, reading over the judge's shoulder.

When he finishes reading, Gunderson hands the reports back to Kate without asking Jackson if he's finished. "You should've notified defense counsel that you planned to introduce conflicting reports and provided him with copies, Miss Dawson."

"There wasn't time, Your Honor. I apologize. I never intended to blindside defense counsel or the court."

Judge Gunderson gives her a hard look. She's certain he realizes the importance of this information and how vital it is to the prosecution's case.

"Your Honor," Jackson says, "I need time to review this new information and to prepare an adequate response. If we could quit for the day, I—"

"You could take the rest of the day, all next week, and beyond," Judge Gunderson interrupts, "and still not come up with an adequate response. It appears to me—and to you as well, Counsel—that the good doctor may have falsified documents. The jury needs to hear this information." Gunderson turns toward Kate and gives her another stern look. "No matter how it came into the prosecutor's procession. So let's get back out there and continue with the trial."

Kate tries to let out a breath without anyone noticing, but Jackson does. He glares at her before they follow the judge out of chambers and back into the courtroom. When everyone is settled again, Gunderson says, "Continue, Miss Dawson."

"Now," Kate says to Jamison, still seated on the witness stand. "Please read the underlined sentences."

Jamison stares at the report a moment before he begins reading softly.

"Excuse me, Doctor. Could you read louder, please, so the members of the jury can clearly hear you?"

Jamison clears his throat again and reads more loudly. "The entry of the gunshot wound is located 12 inches from top of head and 7 inches right of midline. It is a round uniform wound measuring ¼ inch. There is a wide, teardrop zone of powder, soot, and seared, blackened skin above the entrance wound. The direction of the wound is right to left and downward." Jamison holds out the report to her as if it's toxic.

"Hold onto the autopsy report a moment, Doctor. I'm confused. I'm sure the jury is as well. Because the words 'a wide, teardrop zone of powder, soot, and seared, blackened skin above the entrance wound,' and 'the direction of the wound is right to left and *downward*,' were not written in the first report you read. Were they?"

Jamison lowers the report to his lap. "No."

"Yet you've indicated to the court that each is the autopsy report for Ben Roth, have you not?"

"Yes."

Kate leans closer to the witness stand. "Dr. Jamison, which report is correct? Keep in mind that you're under oath."

Jamison drops his head in resignation. "This is the correct report."

"The one you have in your hand."

"Yes."

"There are two similar reports for Davy Roth as well, am I correct?"

"Yes."

"Dr. Jamison, why did you write differing autopsy reports?"

Jamison hesitates.

Kate looks at the judge.

Gunderson says, "Answer the question, Doctor."

Jamison lets out a long breath and says, "I was instructed to."

"By whom?"

Jamison raises his head, locks eyes with Kate, and says, "Chief William Flanagan."

The courtroom goes nuts. Judge Gunderson gavels furiously. "Quiet or I'll clear the courtroom!" he bellows. It takes a while before order is finally restored and the judge nods at Kate. "Continue, Miss Dawson."

Kate thanks him and turns her attention to Harold Jamison again. "Why did Chief Flanagan instruct you to change the autopsy reports for Ben and Davy Roth?"

"He was worried about negative publicity for the department."

"You mean if the correct report was released to the public."

"Yes."

"Let's go back to that report, Dr. Jamison. You concluded that the direction of the fatal gunshot to both Ben and Davy Roth was angled downward, based on the wide, teardrop zone of powder, soot, and seared, blackened skin above the entrance wound."

"Yes."

"Does the presence of powder, soot, and seared blackened skin indicate a distant or close shot, Dr. Jamison?"

"Close."

"So when Sergeant Bannister testified earlier that he shot the Roths from a distance while they were fleeing, that wouldn't be possible based on the wounds they received, would it?"

Jamison shakes his head. "No. They were shot at very close range."

Kate returns to the prosecution table and consults her notes before continuing. "Earlier in the trial, Sergeant Cole testified that the landscape around the cornfield where the Roths were shot is, and I'm quoting here, 'flat as a pancake.' So if the trajectory of each bullet was downward, Sergeant Bannister would have to be standing over them, wouldn't he?"

Jackson rises. "Objection, Your Honor. Speculation."

Kate peers at the judge and spreads her hands, as if the objection makes no sense. "Your Honor, Dr. Jamison has had years of experience examining gunshot wounds. He's already written and testified that the angle of the gunshot was downward."

"Objection overruled. Please continue, Miss Dawson."

"Thank you, Your Honor. My question for you, Dr. Jamison, is how could the shots that killed both Ben and Davy Roth be downward?"

Jamison looks at Kate for a moment before he answers. "Well, they would have to be shot while kneeling or lying face down."

A murmur rolls through the courtroom.

"In other words, Dr. Jamison, the Roths were executed."

The murmur becomes a roar.

Jackson bounds out of his chair. "Objection!" he hollers. "The question should be stricken from the record!"

"Sustained," Judge Gunderson shouts, hammering the gavel.

"No further questions for this witness," Kate says, having made her point. On her way back to the prosecution table she glances at Mike Bannister, who glares at her. *If looks could kill.* She shifts her gaze to Joshua Jackson and his suddenly pale complexion. He's staring straight ahead with a blank look on his face.

Once order is restored and the courtroom has quieted, Judge Gunderson instructs the jury to disregard Kate's question. Kate doesn't mind. The question could be stricken from the record, but not from the minds of the jurors.

The judge looks at the defense table. "Your witness, Mr. Jackson."

Jackson doesn't answer at first, so the judge prompts him again. "Mr. Jackson?"

Jackson turns his head slowly and looks at the judge. "No questions for this witness, Your Honor."

Gunderson eyes the clock on the wall. "We'll recess for the day and begin promptly at nine tomorrow morning." He reminds the jury to keep an open mind about what they heard and saw during the day. He tells them to avoid newspaper, TV, and radio reports on the trial, and not to discuss the case among themselves or with others. Then he sends them back to the Andrews Hotel, where they are sequestered.

*   *   *

Early that evening Kate waits for Jake Cafferty at Charlie's Café Exceptionale. Seated in the oak-paneled dining room, she watches as he approaches the table with a smile on his face and sits down in a chair across from her.

"Good day, huh?" he says.

"The best so far. All I need is Ramona Gutierrez's testimony to put Mike Bannister away for the rest of his life." Kate orders the President cocktail, a mix of orange, lemon, and gin, finished with a dash of grenadine; Jake orders a club soda with a twist of lime. She smiles at him when he places his drink order.

"I haven't had a drop since you showed up at my apartment."

"The same night I gave you the falsified autopsy reports for Ben and Davy Roth."

Jake nods.

"Any idea how the original reports ended up in my PO box?"

"None at all."

"Guess I just got lucky, huh, Jake?"

"Lot to be said for luck, in cards and in life."

Kate pauses a moment. Then she says, "Where did you get the originals?"

Jake levels his gaze on Kate and gives her a half-smile. "From Jamison. When I talked with Arnold about the gunshot wounds in the Roths, and realized he and the DA were shit-canning the investigation and autopsy results, I had Jamison make me a copy of each."

"He must've known he was risking his career if this ever came out."

Jake nods. "A few people still have some integrity."

Kate releases a frustrated breath. "Dammit, Jake. Why hold out on me all this time?"

"Three reasons. One, I didn't know the DA's office would prosecute Bannister."

"What about after I told you I was prosecuting him?"

"Jamison is a good man. Didn't want to put him in a tough spot if I didn't have to."

"And the third reason?"

"If I gave you the original autopsy reports before the trial, you would've had to show them to defense counsel. Who knows what might've happened to Jamison?"

"You think he would've been killed?"

Jake shrugs. "Who knows? Might've just retired early and gone on an extended vacation out of the country. Either way, you would've tipped your hand."

"But what if Gunderson hadn't allowed the original reports to be presented as evidence?"

"The judge is no fool. He knew I was working with you. And he'd hate to lose on appeal."

The waitress arrives with their drinks.

Kate takes a long sip of the cocktail and then dabs her mouth with a napkin. "I'll have to put Ramona Gutierrez on the stand tomorrow morning. Have you heard anything?"

"No. But she promised she'd be here."

Kate bites her lip. "I'm running out of time. And I've got two problems. The rules of evidence require that both the prosecution and defense complete their discovery exchange no later than thirty days before the start of the trial. I didn't know if you'd find Ramona Gutierrez, or if she'd testify if you did, so she isn't on the witness list."

Jake raises his glass of club soda. "Like not listing the autopsy reports."

Kate nods. "But I should've listed her anyway. That's my mistake. Jackson will strenuously object when I call her to the stand. Judge Gunderson won't be pleased either. But I think I've got a way around him."

"And the other problem?"

"The only way I can properly prepare is to understand what a potential witness knows, and how that witness will respond under the pressure of questioning. The old adage 'Never ask a question at trial you don't know the answer to' applies here. Presenting a witness at trial without knowing the specifics of the witness' testimony, and how they will react under cross-examination, is courting disaster."

Chapter 39

The following morning, Judge Gunderson says, "Miss Dawson. Do you have any further witnesses before the state rests?"

Kate turns in her seat at the prosecution table and looks at Jake sitting in the first row of the gallery directly behind her.

He leans forward and whispers, "Ramona Gutierrez called me from Chicago. She'll be here by one."

"Dammit, Jake, that's not good enough," Kate says in a voice louder than anticipated.

"Miss Dawson?" Judge Gunderson says. "Time is wasting. Any more witnesses?"

"Can you stall?" Jake asks quietly.

"Maybe." Kate turns and faces the judge. "Yes, Your Honor, just one. The state calls Ramona Gutierrez."

Jackson leaps to his feet, waving a sheet of paper in his hand. "Objection, Your Honor! She's not on the witness list."

Gunderson swivels his chair toward Kate. "Miss Dawson?"

"Ramona Gutierrez just arrived in town, Your Honor. We haven't had time to inform defense counsel."

Judge Gunderson orders the jury to remain seated. Then, standing, he says, "My chambers. Now."

Once inside the judge's chamber, Gunderson sits behind his desk, the court reporter to his right. Kate and Jackson take seats in front of his desk.

"We're on the record," Gunderson says. "Miss Dawson?"

"Your Honor, the farm in Richfield where Ben and Davy Roth were shot and killed belongs to Mr. and Mrs. Gutierrez. Mrs. Gutierrez is the only eyewitness as to what occurred in the cornfield that evening besides the officers involved. As such, her testimony is the lynchpin of our case."

Jackson lets out an audible sigh. "If I may, Your Honor?"

Gunderson nods. "Go ahead, Counsel."

"Your Honor, the name of this witness should've been given to the defense weeks ago."

"We hadn't located Mrs. Gutierrez weeks ago," Kate responds. "And when we did—"

"Who's 'we'?" Jackson asks.

"Lieutenant Cafferty and myself."

"Cafferty located Mrs. Gutierrez?" the judge asks.

"Yes, Your Honor. As I previously stated, had I known that she would be found, I would've let defense counsel know immediately."

Judge Gunderson leans back in his high-backed chair and swivels side-to-side as he thinks about it. "This could be compelling testimony, though it comes rather late, Miss Dawson. Still, I believe it's testimony the jury should hear."

Kate feels the tightness in her chest loosen.

"I will allow it," the judge continues, "but the defense needs time to prepare."

Yes! Kate thinks, nearly jumping out of her chair. *Exactly what I was hoping for.*

Judge Gunderson looks at her. "You wanted to say something, Miss Dawson?"

Swallowing her excitement, she says, "I'm happy to give Mr. Jackson time to prepare."

"Good," Gunderson replies. "When we go back out there, I'm going to break for the morning. We'll return after lunch."

"Your Honor," Jackson says.

Judge Gunderson holds a hand up. "That should be enough time. Any further questions, Mr. Jackson?"

Clearly frustrated, but resigned to the judge's decision, Jackson shakes his head.

"Then let's get back out there so I can dismiss the jury for the rest of the morning."

* * *

At 1:20 p.m., ten minutes before the trial reconvenes for the afternoon, Ramona Gutierrez, her husband, Manny, and Jake Cafferty exit an elevator near the courtroom.

Kate, waiting anxiously in the hallway, hurries toward Ramona Gutierrez, her hand outstretched. "*Señora* Gutierrez, I'm pleased to meet you," Kate says, trying to see the woman with first impression eyes to gauge how a jury will react to her.

Gutierrez is wearing a black, worsted wool suit coat with bracelet-length sleeves, long black gloves, and matching slim skirt. On a chain around her neck is a silver cross with the crucified Christ. *Not bad*, Kate thinks. *A little too much makeup, a little too much of the Great Lady about her, but she has a certain vulnerability behind the façade. Plus, the religious cross will add credibility to her testimony.*

Kate shakes Manny Gutierrez's hand. "Good to see you again, *Señor*."

In his double-breasted zoot suit, Manny Gutierrez looks smaller than Kate remembers. She gestures toward an empty bench in the hallway and then sits to the couple's right. Jake remains standing in front of them.

"You've traveled a long way, *Señora* Gutierrez. I appreciate it."

"The lieutenant promised to protect us."

"And he will, won't you, Jake?"

"I'll do all that I can."

Not exactly the guarantee Kate hoped for, but she moves on. "Have you ever testified in court before, *Señora*?"

"No."

"Then before we begin, I must insist that you be completely honest and tell me the truth. Do you understand?"

She nods but doesn't speak.

"Finding justice for the two murdered young men is important. But not telling the truth has serious consequences."

"I am not a liar, Miss Dawson. *Creo en Díos*. I believe in God. When I place my hand on the Bible, it is my sacred duty to tell the truth."

"Then you're aware you'll be under oath."

"Yes."

"Tell me what you saw that evening in the cornfield, *Señora*."

"I saw the policeman shoot two young men."

"So you did see the shooting."

She nods.

"Were the young men running away?"

"No. They were on their knees with their hands behind their heads."

Kate shoots a look in Jake's direction, but his eyes are focused on Gutierrez.

"Was the black officer present when the shootings happened?" she asks.

"Yes. He was watching."

Kate releases a breath of relief and checks her watch. Five minutes. *Time to decide. She has to take the chance.* "Lieutenant Cafferty will lead you into the courtroom, *Señora*. Your husband can sit beside the lieutenant directly behind the defense table. Before I question you about the shooting, I'll ask you to tell me a little about your background. Are you both US citizens?"

"Yes."

"Okay. I need to go now. Follow Lieutenant Cafferty." Kate gives him a hopeful look.

Jake nods.

Kate returns to the prosecution table just as Judge Gunderson enters and requests that the jury be brought in.

When they're settled, Gunderson says, "Your witness, Miss Dawson."

"The state calls Ramona Gutierrez to the stand."

All eyes shift to the back of the courtroom as Jake escorts Ramona Gutierrez down the aisle. She stares straight ahead, a proud, confident woman, as Jake opens the gate in the rail separating the gallery from the counsels' tables and lets her go the rest of the way on her own.

When she's seated on the stand, Kate begins by asking her about her background. Ramona Gutierrez explains how her grandparents became citizens of the US after the 1848 Treaty of Guadalupe-Hidalgo ending the Mexican-American War. What was then Northern Mexico eventually became California, half of New Mexico, most of Arizona, Nevada, and Utah, and parts of Wyoming and Colorado. Mexicans living in the annexed territory were given the choice of relocating to Mexico's new boundaries or receiving American citizenship. Her grandparents chose the latter. Her father and mother, both born in Nevada, lived and worked there for many years, raising their three children before moving to Mexico City to race horses. Ramona joined them, which is where she met her husband, Manny. He, too, had been born in the US but chose to live and work in Mexico. After their marriage they returned to the States and purchased the farm in Richfield, hoping to raise horses as her family did in Mexico City.

"So both you and your husband are US citizens."

"Yes."

Kate then brings Ramona Gutierrez around to the night in the cornfield when the Roths were shot and killed.

"You were home alone that evening, Mrs. Gutierrez?"

"Yes. My husband was out of town."

"What first alerted you that something was going on in your cornfield?"

"I heard car doors slamming and men yelling."

"Then what did you do?"

"I went to the living room window and pulled back the curtain."

"Tell us what you saw."

"Two men came running out of the corn."

"What happened next?"

"A man was chasing them."

"Then what happened?"

"He yelled at the two men he was chasing to stop. The two men raised their hands."

"Go on."

"The young men were standing with their hands over their heads, very frightened."

"Objection," Jackson says. "The witness can't know their state of mind."

"Sustained," the judge says.

Kate rephrases the question. "Could you see the expression on the young men's faces?"

"Yes."

"How would you describe their expressions?"

"Frightened."

"Continue, Mrs. Gutierrez."

"The police officer had the two men get down on their knees and clasp their hands behind their heads. Then the young men said something to the officer."

"What did they say?"

"I'm sorry. I couldn't hear."

"Go on."

"The officer . . . how you say, *frisk* them?"

"That's correct, Mrs. Gutierrez. What happened next?"

"The officer found a gun on one of the men."

"What did he do with it?"

"It was very strange."

"How do you mean?"

"He pointed the gun at the cornfield and fired a shot."

Kate hesitates, unsure as to her next question. "The policeman fired the gun he'd taken off the young men into the cornfield?"

"Yes."

"At what?"

"I don't know."

"How many shots did he fire?"

"One. Then I heard two more shots."

"Who fired them?"

"I don't know. But I believe the shots came from the cornfield."

"Please continue, Mrs. Gutierrez."

"The Negro officer came running out of the cornfield."

"Then what happened?"

"I thought the Negro officer was going to arrest the two men. But then the white officer, he shot the two boys in the back. One right after the other."

"The defendant shot them." Kate points to the defense table. "Sergeant Bannister?"

"No," Gutierrez says with a shake of her head. "The other one shot them."

"The Negro officer?" The instant Kate asks the question she realizes she's made a mistake.

"No. *Him*." Ramona Gutierrez points to Nick Cole, standing in the back of the courtroom near the double doors.

"Sergeant *Cole*?" Kate blurts, aghast.

"I don't know his name, but he shot them."

The courtroom is in an uproar. Gunderson bangs his gavel like he's pounding the Golden Spike for the Union Pacific.

Kate feels like she's been punched in the stomach. Air rushes out of her mouth. There's a loud rushing inside her head, as if seashells are pressed against her ears. The courtroom spins. Her knees wobble. About to faint, she grabs the railing in front of the witness stand for support.

Her eyes meet Nick's for just a moment before he bolts out of the courtroom.

She always sensed there was more, much more, to the killings in the cornfield than Nick told her, but she denied herself the right to pursue it. She owed him that much. Yet in her heart of hearts she never believed that he could do such a thing. Never believed that he was capable of cold-blooded murder. She questions her own judgment now, her ambition. She was wrong about Nick. Has she been wrong about her career as well, about everything in her life?

It finally quiets down.

Kate pauses a moment to regroup. She glances at the defense table. Jackson and Bannister are smiling. Bannister's five cop buddies sitting in the first row of the gallery behind the railing are giving him thumbs up and slapping each other on the back. Kate can't bring herself to look at the members of the jury, but she knows what the verdict will be unless she can come up with a plausible explanation quick. Otherwise, Mike Bannister will walk on all three charges of murder. And her short career will end in bitter disappointment and embarrassment.

"Sidebar, please, Your Honor," Kate says.

"Granted."

Standing beside Jackson, Kate says, "Your Honor, when this witness came here and was willing to testify, she said a police officer shot and killed the Roths. And I assumed—"

"Assumed what, Miss Dawson?" Judge Gunderson asks, peering down at her.

"That Mrs. Gutierrez was talking about . . ." Kate doesn't finish her sentence, realizing she'll paint herself into another corner.

"Was there something else, Miss Dawson?"

She tries to make sense of the scrambled thoughts in her head. "Yes . . . Your Honor. It's now clear Mrs. Gutierrez is hostile to the state's case. I ask permission to cross-examine her under the rules. If I am not allowed to do that, Mr. Jackson here will simply waive his right to cross-examination and we'll never have the opportunity to question her testimony."

"Your Honor," Jackson says, "I have an obligation to protect my client's interests. I can't be required to challenge a witness who appears to be supportive of my client's innocence."

"Miss Dawson," Judge Gunderson says, "in the interest of justice and of getting to the bottom of this matter, I will permit you to treat Mrs. Gutierrez as a hostile witness and cross-examine her under the rules. Your objection is overruled, Mr. Jackson. Continue."

Kate pours a glass of water from the pitcher on the prosecution table and drinks half of it before approaching the stand again.

"Mrs. Gutierrez, what happened after the young men were shot?"

"Another officer in uniform came out of the field. The police officer you identified as Sergeant Cole said, "You did it, Mike. You can make sergeant on this.""

"By Mike, you mean Sergeant Bannister?"

"Yes." She points to the defense table. "Him."

"You were able to hear as well as see all of this?"

"The window was open some. The officer you called Sergeant Cole was yelling."

"Did Sam Witherspoon witness this?"

"If he's the Negro officer, yes."

"Did you hear him speak?"

"No. I don't believe he spoke."

"Then what happened?"

"The officer you said is Sergeant Cole collected the other officer's gun. The one called Mike Bannister. Shortly after that, a fourth officer ran out of the cornfield."

"Was he wearing a uniform?"

"No. But the others seemed to know him."

Kate figures the fourth man was Jake Cafferty. "Mrs. Gutierrez. Are you sure the man who shot the boys isn't sitting at the defense table?"

"No," she says.

"No, he isn't or no, you're not sure?"

"I thought the officer on trial was the one who shot the boys. I did not realize until I came to the witness stand that . . . "

"Mrs. Gutierrez," Kate interrupts before she can finish, "so you're confused as to who actually shot the two boys, aren't you?"

"Objection!" Jackson says, bounding out of his chair. "Counsel is impeaching her own witness."

"Your Honor," Kate says. "You agreed to let me cross-examine the witness."

"I did, Miss Dawson. But I didn't agree to let you badger her. So be careful. Overruled."

"Thank you, Your Honor." Kate turns to Ramona Gutierrez again. "You're not sure who shot the boys, are you, Mrs. Gutierrez?"

With one hand, Ramona Gutierrez clutches the cross hanging on the chain around her neck. "As God is my witness, I'm sure."

Chapter 40

Jake spotted Nick Cole leaving the courtroom a moment after Ramona Gutierrez testified that Cole and not Mike Bannister shot the Roths in the cornfield. Jake sidestepped out of the crowded aisle and went after Cole, but by the time he got to the hallway, Cole had disappeared. Now Jake doubts Cole went back to the Homicide/Sex Division, but he hustles there anyway. When that proves to be a dead end, Jake phones Cole's apartment. No answer. He hurries to Avery Arnold's office. Arnold's door is open when Jake arrives. He's talking on the phone.

"Something you need to hear, Captain," Jake says. "Now."

Arnold raises his index finger, indicating it'll be a minute.

Jake taps a foot, waiting.

Arnold answers, "Uh-huh," three times to whomever he's speaking to.

When he hangs up, Jake zips into the office, declining Arnold's offer to sit down in the chair facing the desk.

"What's so goddamn urgent?"

Jake tells him.

Arnold's eyes hold Jake's for a long, silent moment. "The witness must be mistaken. Sergeant Cole? A murderer?"

"Then he should be here, Captain, explaining himself."

"Have you tried his apartment?"

"Didn't answer his phone."

"Get over there and check. Let me know what you find."

"We should send out an APB."

"Were my instructions not clear, Lieutenant?"

Jake shrugs. "All right. You have an address?"

"You don't know where your partner lives?"

"We're not that close, Captain."

"That's a shame."

"Probably not."

Directions in hand, Jake drives to Cole's apartment and parks. He holds the entry door for an older lady carrying groceries. Then he's up the stairs, knocking on Cole's apartment door. No answer. Jake uses his lock picks to break in.

The place reminds him of his own dumpy apartment. Detective Special in hand, Jake looks around. An open suitcase rests on the couch. Clothes strewn. Dresser drawers open. A half-empty bottle of Jack Daniel's sits on the coffee table. Cole is ready to hightail it out of town.

Jake uses the phone to call Avery Arnold. "Cole's suitcase is packed, but he's in the wind, Cap."

"Couldn't be far. Keep looking."

Jake hangs up, holsters his piece, and searches for information indicating where Cole might've gone.

He finds an old copy of the *Intelligencer Journal* of Lancaster, Pennsylvania, folded in a drawer. The banner headline and article describe Cole's WWII exploits and his family. Jake's impressed. Cole was a true hero. He had guts. Throwing his career and future away by murdering the Roths makes no sense.

About to toss the paper into a drawer, a name catches Jake's eye. *S.S. Orbita. Where have I heard that name before?* Then he recalls his visit to Esther Roth's home. *Cole's parents arrived on the same ship as Eli and Esther Roth. Did the families know each other?*

* * *

The lights are on in Esther Roth's ramshackle farmhouse when Jake pulls into the dirt driveway and knocks on the front door.

"Hello, Mrs. Roth," he says, holding up his badge wallet when she opens the door.

"Already talked to a detective about my dead husband."

"I'm not here about your husband's murder, Mrs. Roth."

"Then what?"

"If you have a few minutes."

"Six o'clock news on the radio said your partner murdered my boys." Her voice is flat.

Jake pauses. Then he says, "Yes, he did, Mrs. Roth. I'm sorry about that."

"Not sorry enough to come to their funeral."

"I'm trying to find Sergeant Cole, Mrs. Roth. Maybe you can help me."

"How?"

Jake gestures toward the door.

She sighs, unlatches the screen door, and leads him to the kitchen table. Jake sits down opposite her at the Formica table.

She picks up the half-empty bottle of Grain Belt in front of her. "Want one?"

"No thanks."

She takes a swig, sets it down, and waits for him to speak.

"The detective assigned to your case said your husband was impersonating a man named Abe Fishman. Fishman and your husband were bootleggers when Fishman was killed in an accident. His body was never found. Your husband assumed his identity. Have any idea why he was using Fishman's name?"

"My husband had some trouble with the law. Guess he wanted a fresh start."

"You never saw or heard from him after he disappeared?"

"No. I thought he was dead."

Jake intends to explore the possible connection between Nick Cole and Eli Roth, but in doing so, he'll raise some questions she'll want answers to.

"Did your husband ever mention a man named Nick Cole?"

"No."

"You and your husband were immigrants from Germany."

She cocks her head. "How'd you know that?"

"I have my sources," Jake lies. "I understand the two of you came over on the *S.S. Orbita*."

She glances in the direction of her bedroom. When her eyes come back to Jake, they're as hard as stones. "You were snooping in my bedroom dresser."

"I was looking for information."

She stands. "You should go."

Jake remains seated. "I need your help."

"Why should I help you? The police killed my sons."

"Your sons killed a police officer."

"I'll never believe that."

"I didn't kill your sons, Mrs. Roth. Give me a few more minutes. Please."

She hesitates and then sits down again. She drinks some beer.

"When you and Eli arrived from Germany, did you come directly here to Minnesota?"

"We spent five years in Pennsylvania."

Jake leans forward. "Was it in Lancaster County?"

She nods. "Yes."

"Did you or your husband know a Joseph and Hannah Cole from Lancaster County?"

She thinks a moment. "We knew a couple named Joseph and Hannah. Met them on the ship from Germany. But their last name wasn't Cole. It was Kohn."

Chapter 41

Dirty Laundry
January 8, 1951
POLICE CHIEF RESIGNS AMID SCANDAL

By
Sarah Weisman

Four years to the day that William Flanagan accepted the job as chief of police in Minneapolis, he has resigned. Flanagan, implicated in the scandal to cover up the murders of Ben and Davy Roth, maintained that he had not directed the Hennepin County coroner to falsify autopsy reports indicating that MPD Sergeant Nicholas Cole executed the two young Jewish men in a Richfield cornfield as they fled police officers. "Rather than attempting to defend myself against these outrageous charges, I have elected to resign and return with my family to my home town of Boston," Flanagan said. When asked to respond to Flanagan's denial, retired Hennepin County coroner Harold Jamison declined to comment.

The murders of Ben and Davy Roth touched off a firestorm among the Jewish community in Minneapolis, which ultimately led to Flanagan's resignation. Samuel Scheiner, head of the Minnesota Jewish Council, called the murders "a tragic result of hatred and bigotry." Scheiner urged members of all religious faiths "to seek common ground and understanding in order to combat the intolerance of minorities that exists in this city."

Sergeant Michael Bannister, implicated in the deaths of Ben and Davy Roth, was cleared when an eyewitness identified Sergeant Cole as the triggerman. Charges that Bannister murdered his former MPD partner, Samuel Witherspoon, were also dropped. Cole has disappeared. A warrant has been issued for his arrest.

Former captain of the MPD Homicide/Sex Crimes Division Avery Arnold has been appointed acting chief. In a speech at City Hall, Arnold promised to "rid the city of its criminal element" and "to create an atmosphere of transparency between the department and the public." Having heard this promise before from politicians and MPD officials, this writer remains skeptical.

The cloud of depression that has hung over Jake since Max Hayes' death worsened during the holidays, especially after the revelation that Nick Cole murdered the Roths. On top of that, all charges against Mike Bannister were dropped. Jake's been tempted more than once to drink again, despite the support he gets at AA meetings.

The *Dirty Laundry* article written by Max's girlfriend, Sarah Weisman, who has taken over the magazine, offers Jake Cafferty a ray of hope. Flanagan is gone. Jake never cared for him anyway. He's more comfortable with Avery Arnold and knows he can work with him. Sgt. Mike Bannister is another story. In his last act as chief of police—and as a "fuck you" to the city and the department—Flanagan assigned Bannister to the Homicide/Sex Crimes Division. No way Arnold can reverse it without a union uproar. Many in the department view Bannister's promotion as a just reward for the DA's wrongful attempt to convict him of murder. Work keeps Jake busy now. Keeps his mind from thinking about all the things in his life that have gone wrong.

But it's the crime lab's fingerprint analysis report on the shovel Jake found in the woods off West River Road that gets his investigative juices flowing again. He checks his watch. He's meeting Kate Dawson for lunch at the Nankin Café. He hasn't seen or talked to her since the Bannister trial. She wasn't enthused when he called and offered to buy her lunch. Jake figures she's keeping a low profile and is probably as depressed as he is. Maybe the fingerprint report will cheer her up.

* * *

Kate Dawson takes the elevator up to the 11th floor of the Roanoke Building on South 7th Street, where her father's law office, Dawson, Donnell, Goodman, and Reed, is located. Her father's secretary, Sally, greets Kate warmly. She's worked for him for twenty years. Sally takes Kate's coat, hat, and gloves. "Your father is expecting you." Kate follows her down a hallway to her father's office and waits while Sally knocks once and holds the door open for her.

Paul Dawson stands and comes out from behind his desk as Kate enters. "Katherine," he says with a smile. She's shocked when he hugs her before planting a kiss on her cheek. Gesturing toward a leather couch and coffee table at the far end of his office, he says, "Please, sit down."

If Kate is jealous of Wilson Barlow's office, her father's is nearly twice as large and even more expensively decorated, with plush burgundy carpet and heavy mahogany furniture. There's money to be made in corporate law.

When they're comfortably seated, her father says, "Would you care for something to drink?"

"Thank you. But I'm fine."

"You were down the last time I saw you at Christmas."

"What do you expect?" she replies, her voice rising. "Sorry," she says quickly. "I didn't mean to—"

"It's perfectly understandable, Katherine. I hope you're feeling better now that you've had some time to reflect."

"That's why I'm here."

"Oh?" he says, cocking his head.

Kate takes in a breath and releases it. "After giving it considerable thought, I'd like to come and work for you."

He nods his head slowly and says, "Is that so?"

"Yes. I think you've been right from the beginning. I'm not cut out for criminal law, at least on the prosecution side of it."

"Have you talked with Wilson Barlow about your decision?"

"Not yet. I wanted to talk to you first. See if there's even an opening at the firm."

"There's always an opening here for you, Katherine. If you want it."

"I do."

"You're sure?"

"Yes."

Paul Dawson stands and walks to his desk, where he lights a cigarette with a gold-plated lighter. He peers out the wood blinds on the windows overlooking the city for a moment and then turns to face Kate, resting his backside on a corner of his wide desk. "I think you're making a mistake, Katherine."

Kate is surprised. "What? I thought you wanted me to work for you."

"I do. But not under these circumstances."

"What circumstances?"

"You know perfectly well what I'm talking about. You've lost a couple of cases. So what?"

"So what? How can you say that?"

"You've never been a quitter, Katherine. Don't start now."

"It's not just that I lost the cases. It's that the police department has blindsided me twice."

Paul Dawson puffs on his cigarette, contemplating, before crushing it out in the ashtray on his desk.

Kate waits, still trying to get her head around her father's change of heart.

"I know it's especially hurtful that your ex-boyfriend lied to you," he says at last.

"It's more than the lie, Father. Nick Cole embarrassed me. Made me look like a fool. And so did my own witness, Ramona Gutierrez. I should've known what she was going to say."

Her father returns to the couch. Sitting beside her, he takes her hand in his. "Barlow won't fire you."

"No. He's waiting for me to quit."

"Don't give him the satisfaction."

"Easy for you to say."

"Listen to me, Katherine. You didn't notice, but I was in the courtroom during the Mike Bannister trial."

"You were?"

He nods. "Not for all of it, but for enough of it to see that you were going to win the case against Bannister. You were terrific. You've got all the makings of a fine litigator. I'm very proud of you."

Kate tears up. She looks away, giving herself a moment to get control of her emotions. This isn't how she thought the conversation would go. Once again she's caught off guard. But this time it's in a good way.

"Think on it a bit, Katherine. If you still feel the same way six months or a year from now, you're more than welcome to join the firm. I'd be proud to have you."

Tears running down her cheeks, she slips her arms around her father and squeezes him tight. He squeezes back.

*　　*　　*

Jake is surprised to see Kate Dawson waiting for him when he arrives at the Nankin Café. He removes his hat and overcoat, tosses them onto the seat cushion, and slides into the booth across the table from her. "Kate."

"How are you, Jake?"

"Getting along. You?"

She manages a half-smile. "I'm prosecuting DWIs and low-level marijuana busts."

"Barlow's gift for losing the Bannister case?"

"Of course."

"But he won't fire you."

She shakes her head. "Wouldn't look good. Firing the first female in the DA's office. Hell, maybe I deserve it."

"Don't sell yourself short."

"It's hard not to."

"Don't plan on quitting?"

"I considered it. First time in my life I ever have. My father talked me out of it."

"Good advice." Jake pauses a beat and then says, "A stock-broker named Martin Crenshaw supposedly committed suicide last August by jumping off the Short Line Bridge into the Mississippi."

"I remember reading about it. Wasn't he Douglas Crenshaw's son?"

"He was. But what you didn't read was that his shoes and suit coat were found on the side of the road a half-mile from the bridge. I uncovered a shovel thirty yards off the road in the woods."

"What's the connection?"

"I stumbled into a partially dug hole near the shovel." Jake shows Kate the fingerprint reports on the shovel he found.

Kate scans them. "Whose prints?"

"Joe Briggs and Mike Bannister. I believe they were digging a grave for Crenshaw. When he took off, they chased him and either threw him off the bridge, or Crenshaw jumped trying to escape."

Kate perks up. "Can you prove it?"

"Not yet . . . but I'm getting close."

Kate's quiet for a time, her expression lost in thought.

"What is it?" Jake asks.

"I prosecuted a guy the other day for marijuana possession. Name was Ronald Crennan. Busted a few years ago for the same offense. In looking for his file, I came across a file for Virginia Crenshaw."

"Really? What was she arrested for?"

"Marijuana."

"Recently?"

"A year ago. She was at a party where guests were smoking dope."

"How'd she plead?"

"Not guilty. Her daddy hired a high-buck lawyer. Judge ruled there was no probable cause to search the apartment. Case got tossed."

"You recall who the arresting officer was?"

"Who else? Mike Bannister. Mean anything to you?"

"Not sure." Jake makes a mental note to check the file.

"What're you going to do now?"

"Rattle Bannister's cage."

Kate leans forward, her forearms on the table. "I'd still love to get Bannister."

"Won't make up for everything."

"It'd be a start," she says.

*   *   *

Nick Cole keeps meaning to leave town. Keeps waking up with a hangover. If Cafferty hadn't gotten to the apartment so quickly, Nick might be in Chicago now, living in a good hotel, establishing another ID, instead of sitting on a filthy cot in a stinking cage hotel with nothing but the clothes on his back. Dreams shattered. Nothing left now. No chance—if he ever had one—with Kate. Doesn't blame her. Trying to nail that bastard Mike Bannister. Doing her job. Too bad Cafferty found the wetback in Mexico. Bannister might've gone down for Witherspoon's murder and Nick would've skated, still a hero.

He's been running for over a month now since the Bannister trial, moving from place to place till his beard and hair grew out. He's settled in the Victor Hotel, a twenty-five-cent-a-night flop, just another anonymous, bearded face among the gandy dancers, winos, and drunks of Skid Row. Not even the messiah to the men on Skid Row, Johnny Rex, recognizes him.

When they run out of money, Rex gives them credit for booze. First of the month the men's checks are sent to Rex at the liquor store. He takes the money owed him and gives the rest to the men. Never cheats them. But Nick isn't giving up his cash— or his Colt Official Police .38. All he has left.

Flophouse walls made of plywood and tin. Nails to hang clothes. Ceiling nothing more than chicken wire with a bare bulb hanging through it. Nick's cage has a single bed with a metal frame, a small dresser with an attached mirror, and a small table. Stinking toilets, stale cigarette smoke, rank odor of unwashed men: the smells linger in Nick's clothes and nostrils, stick in his throat. Eating in Skid Row slop joints, where coffee is ten cents. Add two boiled eggs, bread, and butter for thirty-five cents. Better than eating in the missions where all you got was a cup of coffee, stale bread, and margarine after enduring an hour of homilies and hymns.

Not what he worked for, trained for, got an education for —all of it gone in a heartbeat, an impulse. He had to make sure Bannister took credit for the cornfield killings because of the angle and proximity of the two shots. In case things went south. He thought the autopsy reports would be permanently buried.

Never figured Kate would get the originals, or that the Gutierrez woman saw what happened. He's trying to protect himself from who he really is. From who he'll always be. He hadn't planned to ice the Jews. But he couldn't take the chance that they knew about his past, that old man Roth had told his sons. He criticized Cafferty for drinking, but Nick always knew he too had a problem with alcohol, and with ambition.

Nick pulls the .38 from his pants pocket and stares at it. *Do it*, he thinks. *It's the only way out. Or is it?*

Chapter 42

Late that afternoon, Jake's thinking about his recent conversation with Kate Dawson, which reminds him of a mental note he made at the time. He leaves his desk in the Homicide/Sex Crimes pen and heads for the Records and Identification room, where he pulls the thin file on Virginia Crenshaw.

Virginia Irene Crenshaw, W.F., DOB 11/9/20, pot bust, 178 Nicollet Island East, 7/22/49, RO M. Bannister

Jake reads it again to make sure that Mike Bannister was the reporting officer and made the bust. *Something else, though. Something about the address. I've been there*! He returns the file to the cabinet and heads for his Ford.

A cold snap sharpens the darkness as he drives to the Crenshaw mansion on Park Avenue. Christmas decorations still hang on the light poles and on the doors and in the glowing windows of many of the homes. With a fresh coat of snow covering the ground, the avenue looks like a picture postcard. But sharply pointed icicles hang from the gutters, and underneath the soft, fluffy snow, sheets of ice slick the sidewalks. Footing is treacherous. Jake treads lightly up the steps to the front door and rings the bell. Every exhalation leaves a tiny cloud in the air.

Virginia Crenshaw answers, dressed casually in a pair of wide-legged black trousers and white crewneck sweater. "Jake," she says with tight smile. "What brings you out on a cold night like this?"

"Your brother."

Her eyes skitter, guarded, before she composes herself. "Please. Come in."

She hangs his overcoat and hat in a closet and leads him into a living room the size of his apartment. Logs crackle in the fireplace. A grand piano rests near one wall. A half-empty martini glass sits on the antique coffee table. Large tufted sofas straddle the coffee table fronting the fireplace. She sits in one, he the other.

"Can I get you something?"

"No, thanks."

"What about my brother?"

"Your father might want to hear what I have to say."

"He isn't well."

"Hope it isn't serious."

"At his age, everything is." She finishes off her martini, gets up, and heads for the cellaret built into a sideboard on the opposite wall. She mixes another martini, adds an olive, and returns to the couch, her eyes leveled at his. "So? About my brother?"

"First tell me how much money your father lost in Zeno Malkin's Brazama Gold scheme."

She picks the olive out of her drink and chews it, the light hardening in her eyes. "I don't know what you're talking about."

"I think you do."

Her gaze holds Jake a moment, then slides off and settles on the martini glass. "What does Brazama Gold have to do with my brother's death?"

"Your brother was a stockbroker. He saw an opportunity to make a boatload of money on Brazama Gold and convinced your father to invest. But the whole thing was a hustle. Your father, along with others, lost money. Some took the loss hard."

Her eyes focus on him again. "And you believe someone killed my brother because of it?"

"How much did your family lose to Malkin?"

Reluctantly, she admits, "Enough that it hurt."

"Figured it had."

"If Marty was murdered, then you must have a suspect."

Jake says, "Tell me about Mike Bannister."

She gives her head a shake, as if coming out of a trance. "Bannister killed my brother?"

"I never said that."

"Not in so many words, but—"

"He's worked security for you."

"Yes. You saw him at my father's birthday celebration."

"First time you've used him?"

"No. He and another officer handled security for my father from time to time."

"What officer?"

"The one who was killed."

"Joe Briggs?"

"Yes. Officer Briggs."

"Did Avery Arnold suggest using them?"

"I haven't a clue. My father hired them. He hired other officers as well."

Jake nods but doesn't reply.

"The trial," she says. "Do you really think Bannister killed Officer Witherspoon?"

"A jury didn't."

"I'm not asking the jury."

Jake considers asking her about the pot bust that Bannister arrested her for, but he figures he's said enough and stays quiet.

"Are you planning to arrest Bannister for my brother's murder?"

Jake stands. "Gotta prove it first."

Clenching a fist, she says, "You get him, Jake. Get him good."

*　　*　　*

Later that evening Jake attends a party at Gluek's celebrating Mike Bannister's promotion to the Homicide/Sex Crime Division. The noisy bar and restaurant is filled with cops and brass, including the new chief, Avery Arnold.

Arnold slips an arm around Jake's shoulders. "Surprised to see you here, Jake. But pleased nonetheless. Better to let it slide. We all have to get along."

Jake hasn't come to "get along" or to congratulate Bannister. "Think Bannister feels the same?"

"Ask him."

"I will. Congratulations on your promotion."

"Right time and place, Jake."

"Yeah. Too bad Flanagan left us with Bannister."

"Look at it this way. Staffing Sex Crimes is always a problem. Too much free pussy. Have to rotate the personnel every six months so no one gets too comfortable with it. Don't like to use married guys because the wives hate it, and it leads to divorces."

Jake wonders if nights working Sex Crimes contributed to Arnold's divorce.

"Unmarried guys are best even if you know what they're gonna do. Job comes with free booze, too. Have to enforce the liquor laws in illegal after-hours bars," Arnold says with a wink. "Mike Bannister is good at it."

Someone calls Arnold's name and waves the chief over. As Arnold walks away, he cautions, "Stay out of trouble, Jake."

Jake is already looking for Bannister. He spots him holding court with a group of four near the bar, none of whom Jake recognizes. Talking loudly, laughing, and holding a bottle of Hamm's beer in one hand, Bannister is the center of attention. Jake moves closer to the group, directly in Bannister's field of vision.

Bannister pauses in mid-sentence and stares at Jake. "Well, well. If it isn't Lieutenant Cafferty," he calls, breaking into a crooked grin. "Come to help me celebrate."

The cops facing Bannister turn and look at Jake, animosity evident in their faces and tense body language. They part as Bannister steps forward and then slowly surround Jake, as if waiting for Bannister's command, for the trigger that'll set them off. Jake looks around for Avery Arnold but doesn't see him. Finally, Bannister says, "Buy you a drink, or are you still on the wagon?"

"Still on the wagon," Jake says.

Bannister laughs. The men do the same, breaking the tension. A few purposely bump into Jake as they return to the bar.

"Must've been tough for you to stay clean after that trial fiasco, huh?" Bannister says.

"Talk to you a minute, Mike?"

"We are talking."

"Private."

Bannister narrows his eyes. "About what?"

"Let's step over there," Jake says, nodding at an empty space in a corner.

Bannister hesitates and then follows. When they're out of earshot of the others, Bannister says, "What's so important you had to interrupt my party?"

"Fingerprints."

"Huh?"

"Yours and Joe Briggs'. A shovel I found you left by the side of the road not far from the Short Line Bridge. What were you and Briggs doing out there last August?"

"Don't know what you're talking about."

"Looks to me like you and Briggs either threw Martin Crenshaw off the bridge or forced him to jump."

"You're crazy, Cafferty."

"Enjoy your short stint in Homicide, Bannister. You won't walk away from this one."

Chapter 43

January 10, 1951

Saturday morning, 12:30 a.m., Jake pulls another dog-watch. *Just as well. Can't sleep anyway.* Getting out of his chair, he goes to the coffee pot across the room and pours a fresh cup as his phone rings. Hurrying back to his desk, he grabs the phone before it quits ringing.

"Homicide. Cafferty."

"I need your help, Jake."

Voice is familiar. "Miss Crenshaw?"

"I just shot Mike Bannister."

*   *   *

Thirty-five minutes after Jake gets the phone call, the Crenshaw mansion is crawling with crime lab personnel. Jake stares at the chalk outline on the living room floor in front of the sideboard, where Bannister fell. He was barely breathing when they rolled him out on a stretcher, a bullet wound in his chest. Prognosis poor. Shot with a Colt Vest Pocket .25. It's a cute, deadly little weapon. Jake bags the gun, gives it to one of the crime lab personnel, and heads for the library, where Virginia Crenshaw and her father are waiting.

Dressed in a blue silk negligee and gown, she's sitting stiffly on a leather couch, a lacy handkerchief clutched in her hands, eyes red and swollen from crying. An ugly swelling marks her left cheek. She looks up at Jake as he enters. On the end table is a shot glass and an open bottle of Jack Daniel's. Douglas Crenshaw is sitting in his wheelchair beside her, dressed in pajamas and a bathrobe.

Jake wheels a swivel chair out from behind the desk and sits down in front of them, notebook and pen in hand. "Ready to talk now?"

She sniffles and nods once.

"Go easy, Lieutenant," the old man cautions.

Jake says, "Tell me what happened."

"It . . . wasn't . . . my fault, Jake," she stutters.

Douglas Crenshaw touches her shoulder. "Of course it wasn't, my dear."

"Mr. Crenshaw," Jake says. "I need to hear from your daughter."

Douglas Crenshaw sets his mouth in a hard line and nods.

Jake again focuses on Virginia Crenshaw. "Go on."

Wringing the handkerchief in her hands, she casts her eyes downward.

"After our conversation the other night concerning my brother's murder, I thought about what you said."

"And what was that?"

She raises her eyes level with his. "About Mike Bannister. If he was in some way responsible for Marty's death."

"I see."

"I called him and—"

"How'd you know Bannister's number?"

"I gave it to her," the old man says. Then, raising his hands in surrender, he adds, "Sorry to interrupt, Lieutenant."

"Go on, Miss Crenshaw."

"Well, I called and asked him flat out if he knew anything about my brother's death. He got very mad and hung up."

"And what time was this?"

"Around eleven."

"Late for a phone call, isn't it?"

"I tried earlier and couldn't get him."

"Then what happened?"

"An hour later, as I'm getting ready for bed, the doorbell rings."

"Bannister."

"Yes. I told him to go away, but he forced his way in."

"So you didn't let him in?"

"Absolutely not."

"Was anyone here besides your father?"

"No. He was upstairs. Bannister grabbed me by the arm, dragged me into the living room, and threw me down on the couch. When I tried to get up, he slapped me, hard." For emphasis she gingerly touches the bruise on her cheek.

Jake writes the information in his notebook. "What happened next?"

"We argued. He became physical again. Tried to rip my clothes off and rape me. I broke away and drew the gun."

"He tried to rape you?"

"Yes."

"You had the gun on you?"

"Yes," she says matter-of-factly. "When you hear a knock on your door at midnight, you can never be too careful. I certainly couldn't count on my father for help."

"How long have you owned the gun?"

"It's not mine. It's my father's. He's had it for years."

"That's correct," the old man adds.

"What happened after you drew the gun?'

"I told Bannister to leave and if he didn't, I was calling the police. He laughed and said he *was* the police. Then he said . . ." She hesitates and stifles a sob.

"He said what?"

"He said my brother pissed in his pants before he jumped from the bridge." She shakes her head and casts her eyes downward, as though it's impossible to believe. Then she wipes her eyes and looks at Jake. "He came at me, tried to take the gun away and . . ."

"And what, Miss Crenshaw?"

"And it went off. I didn't mean to shoot him. I was scared. I panicked. I didn't know what he was going to do. I mean, if he had gotten the gun from me . . ." She buries her face in the handkerchief and sobs.

While he waits, Jake gets it all down in his notebook. When she's done crying, he says, "Anything else you can tell me?"

"That's all I remember." She looks like she's about to start crying again. "It's all so terrible."

"Do you think my daughter will need a lawyer, Lieutenant?"

"Up to you, Mr. Crenshaw. But at this stage, it looks pretty cut and dried. Bannister broke in, threatened and assaulted your daughter. She shot him in self-defense."

"Yes. That's exactly how it happened," the old man says.

"I'll station an officer outside the house for tonight. You'll need to come to the station in the morning to make a statement."

"Thank you, Jake," she says. "I knew I could count on you."

*   *   *

After interviewing Virginia Crenshaw, Jake drives to Minneapolis General to check on Mike Bannister. He's hooked to a ventilator to help him breathe, bullet still lodged in his chest, too close to the heart to attempt surgery till he's stronger. Internal and external bleeding stopped. Prognosis critical.

Back at his desk in Homicide, Jake types up a search warrant for Mike Bannister's address and takes it to the night judge at City Hall for a signature. It's 3:30 a.m. when he arrives at Bannister's place, located on the bottom floor of a duplex on Humboldt Avenue in South Minneapolis. Jake finishes his cup of strong coffee and tosses his cigarette out the car window. He's running on a nicotine and caffeine high now.

Using his lock picks to enter through the front door, he hits a light switch and does a quick walk-through. It's a one-bedroom with a living and dining room, small kitchen, and one bathroom. Basement has a washer and freezer. Bannister's clean clothes are hung in the closets. Jake searches the closets and Bannister's suit coats and pants pockets. Then he checks under the mattress, bed, and in the desk drawers. *Bingo!* Underneath a stack of papers, he finds a hardback journal with "NOTES" embossed on the cover.

Jake gets a much-needed boost. He opens it. Then he gets an ache in his heart when he confirms that it's Max Hayes' missing journal. *Son of a bitch.* Jake's tempted to drive back to the hospital and pull the cord for Bannister's ventilator out of the wall. Smother him with a pillow. Was Max's *accident* staged? Jake needs answers, but Bannister is unconscious, maybe already booked on the graveyard express.

Jake sits on the edge of the bed, weighing the notebook in his hand. *Why did Bannister keep Max's journal?* Max has done him a favor by writing the dates on each entry, beginning with January 1, 1950. Jake quickly scans each page. There are few personal entries. Most of the entries are reminders dealing with his work, but not all of them. Jake pauses on a September entry written after he and Jake attended the Minneapolis Millers game. Under the section labeled "Ballgame," Jake reads a note that Max has written:

> Asked Jake about my mother. Said he doesn't know why she was driving up north on Armistice Day, the day of the blizzard. Think he's hiding something. Will press next time I see him.

Did Max suspect I was his father? No way to ever know. Jake grimaces and turns to the last journal entry:

Will finish latest article on TCRT kickbacks after meeting tonight with T.D. He's promised to provide more information on those involved in scheme. Corruption runs deeper than initial suspects. MB likely involved.

Jake re-reads the journal entry. *There it is. M.B. Mike Bannister. But who's T.D.?* Only one snitch he knows with those initials. Back in his car, Jake guns it, the wheels slipping on the icy road, the back end fishtailing before he regains control, and the Ford races down the street.

* * *

Four thirty a.m. Jake hightails it to the Parkway Motor Court on Hiawatha Avenue and Minnehaha Parkway, where Teddy Doss has been staying since his prison release. Next to the Canteen Café and easily identifiable by the tall totem pole in the parking lot, the motel is open 24 hours, 365 days of the year. Jake badges the desk clerk and asks for Teddy Doss' room number and the master key. When the desk clerk hesitates, Jake grabs him by the tie and gets in his face.

Two minutes later Jake unlocks the door to Doss' room and barges in. Doss, half-awake, sits up in bed. Jake kicks the door closed and flips the wall switch.

Doss squints at Jake. "What the hell?"

Jake hauls Doss out of bed and slams him against the wall, knocking the wind out of him. "I want answers, Doss! And I want 'em now!"

Doss, struggling to catch his breath, slides down the wall onto his rear end. He brings his knees up and leans forward till he's breathing normally again.

"Come on, Doss!"

Doss looks up at Jake. "Answers to what?"

"Who killed Max Hayes?"

"Who's Hayes?"

Jake pulls his .38 out of the shoulder holster and jams it in Doss' mouth. "I want answers. Now!"

Doss mumbles loudly and bobs his head.

Jake pulls the gun back.

"Okay! I know Hayes!"

"Then you know he was on his way to see you the night his car went off West River Road and into the Mississippi."

Doss looks up at Jake again, his eyes wide. "I didn't have anything to do with him getting killed, Jake. I thought it was an accident."

"Why was Max meeting you?"

"Cop came to see me that day."

"What cop?"

"Big guy. Blond. Wavy hair."

"Mike Bannister."

"Yeah."

Jake glares at him. "I'm waiting."

"Okay. So Bannister tells me to call Hayes. Tell him I've got information on the TCRT scandal. Tell him to meet me near the Short Line Bridge. That's all."

Jake wonders if Bannister's plan was to take out Max like he and Briggs took out Martin Crenshaw. Maybe Bannister changed plans when the rain started. Made it look like an accident. Max loses control and goes off the road. Otherwise, Max might've ended up in the grave Bannister and Briggs dug for Crenshaw.

Doss starts to get up.

Jake rests the sole of his shoe on Doss' chest. "Stay down, Teddy. Tell me what you know about the TCRT."

"They operate the streetcars."

"And?" Jake pushes the barrel of the gun into Doss' forehead.

"They're tearin' up the rails, sellin' off the steel."

"Tell me something I don't know."

"Minneapolis Iron & Steel. They got a contract with the TCRT."

"What's the scam, Teddy?"

"Not sure."

Jake whacks Doss across the cheek with the gun.

Doss covers his head with his hands.

Jake realizes that anger has gotten the best of him. He needs to think clearly. He lowers the gun. "Your best guess."

Doss peeks up at Jake. "Kickbacks."

"Keep talkin'."

"I hear things, you know. Can't say how accurate the information is."

"Gimme more."

"Okay, Jake." Doss uncovers and leans back against the wall, looser but still shook. "So the new investors who control the TCRT sell off assets for less than market value in exchange for payoffs."

"From Minneapolis Iron & Steel."

"Right. The streetcar system disappears, replaced by hundreds of General Motors diesel buses. Taxpayers foot the cost of the conversion. The investors and Minneapolis Iron & Steel make out like bandits."

"You involved in any of this, Teddy?"

"No," he says, waving his hands in surrender. "I got nothin' to do with it."

"Tony Rizzo in on it?"

Doss nods.

Given Rizzo's history of kickbacks, Jake figured he'd be involved.

"Look, Jake, don't let Bannister know I told you anything."

"Bannister is in Minneapolis General with a bullet in his chest. Likely won't survive."

"Oh, man. Who shot him?"

Jake ignores the question. "Who else is part of this?"

"That's all I know, Jake. Honest."

Jake squats and looks Doss in the eyes. "Keep your mouth shut, Teddy. And put some ice on that cheek."

* * *

Jake heads for his apartment and a few hours of shut-eye before he's up again. He showers off the night smells, then has a shave, a change of clothes, and a breakfast of scrambled eggs and fresh coffee. By 11:00 a.m. he's back behind his desk in Homicide, smoking a Camel and typing his summary report on the Bannister shooting and the statement Virginia Crenshaw has just given him. Looking more composed and without her father, she gave a straightforward account that matched what she'd told him the previous evening.

Jake re-reads what he's typed. No errors. Report is neat and clean, just like the Bannister shooting. Except the shooting isn't clean. Not in Jake's mind. Leaning back in his chair, he's considering his next move when his desk phone rings.

He crushes out his cigarette in the ashtray on his desk and picks up the receiver. "Homicide. Cafferty."

"Hello, Jake."

Jake bolts upright in his chair, heart racing. "Calling to turn yourself in, Cole?"

"I am. But you gotta come and get me. Don't trust anyone else. I know too much."

"Where?"

"Scrapyard. Minneapolis Iron & Steel. By the big side door."

"I'll be there."

"Alone, Jake."

"Wait for me." Jake hangs up and pulls his Detective Special. He checks the chamber, re-holsters it, and opens the desk drawer. He grabs a handful of cartridges and shoves them in a pants pocket. Then he heads for his Ford.

Chapter 44

Jake steps out of his car at the Minneapolis Iron & Steel Company and scopes the scrap yard. The arm of a heavy-duty material handler sweeps across the snow-packed ground, its enormous claw-like grapples releasing a load of twisted metal onto a pile that rises forty feet. A metallic tang hangs in the cold air, and he hears the shriek of shattering steel over a thudding backbeat of mangled appliances that a crane drops into the pile—food for a nearby shredder. Among the items in the heap are steel rails that once made up the streetcar tracks of the Twin City Rapid Transit Company.

Jake senses something is off the moment he spots a bearded, disheveled-looking Nick Cole, both hands in the pockets of his overcoat, standing near the side entrance, where streetcars are rolled along a track and through a huge open door into the plant to be stripped down.

Jake cautiously approaches. *Why here? Why now?* He stops beside a steel barrel filled with snow and ice, ten feet from Cole. "Couldn't understand why you murdered the Roth brothers, Cole. Were you wound too tight? Over-excited? Did the murders have something to do with your war experiences or your breakup with Kate Dawson? But the murders weren't about any of that. They were about Eli Roth."

Cole hesitates and then says, "What about him?"

"He and his wife, Esther, came over from Germany on the same ship as your parents. Even lived in Lancaster County for a time. Eli Roth, a.k.a. Abe Fishman, was blackmailing you, Cole. He knew your surname was Kohn. Knew you were Jewish. You couldn't take the chance that his sons knew. Why you killed 'em. Switched guns with Bannister. Probably planned to kill Eli Roth till some gandy dancer saved you the trouble."

As Cole is about to speak, a car speeds into the yard to his left, tires splashing through ruts filled with water and slush. The driver slams on the brakes near Cole and gets out. It's Avery Arnold. The chief glances at Jake and then walks toward Cole. "Seems you have some explaining to do, Sergeant." Pulling a gun out of his coat pocket, Arnold points it at Cole.

"Easy, Chief," Jake says. "Let's take him alive."

Turning to face Jake, Arnold aims the gun at him.

"Sorry, Jake," Nick says.

Jake puts the rest of it together now. The words Ramona Gutierrez said she couldn't hear that night in the cornfield. Why he had his doubts about the Roths killing Joe Briggs. "Before you shot the Roths, they told you Arnold set up the burglary and killed Joe Briggs, didn't they, Cole?"

Nick stays silent.

Jake's eyes meet Arnold's. "Cole blackmailed you into a promotion."

Arnold waves the gun. "Doesn't matter, Jake."

"Afraid it does." Jake shifts his eyes to Nick. "Was murdering the Roths worth it, Cole?"

"Should've let it go, Jake."

"Couldn't."

"Makes you a good cop."

"What does it make you, Cole?"

"Come along with us, Jake," Arnold says.

Jake looks around, considering his options. "No chance," he says. "You're gonna do it, do it here. While I'm looking you in the eyes."

Nick turns to Arnold. "Maybe there's another way, Chief."

Arnold chuckles. "Sure there is. You take the rap for the Roths, go down for murder one. I go down for Joe Briggs' murder. We both spend the rest of our lives taking it up the ass in a double-bunked prison cell. That how you want to spend your golden years?"

Nick shakes his head.

"But now that you mention it, Sergeant, there might be another way." Arnold turns and shoots Nick Cole point blank in the chest.

Nick's eyes blanch with shock as he drops to his knees, tries to say something to Arnold, and then falls face first into the mud.

Arnold pivots in Jake's direction, ready to fire again.

Jake isn't there. Crouched behind the steel barrel now, Detective Special in hand, he peers around the barrel and fires a round in Arnold's direction. But the chief is on the move, running toward the lone streetcar at the far end of the scrap yard.

Jake starts after him, hesitates, and then rushes over to Nick. He finds a weak pulse. *No time to look for a phone.* "Hang on, Cole," he says.

Arnold has a twenty-yard lead. Jake figures he'll seek cover behind the streetcar and set up for a clean shot. *Which leaves me out in the open.* Jake looks for cover. To his left is the huge forty-foot pile of metal scraps. He darts behind it and keeps running. Arnold can't see him now, but he can't see Arnold either. No more than five seconds, Jake counts, before he reaches the end of the scrap pile.

He stops to catch his breath, cursing his lack of conditioning, and peeks out from behind the scrap pile, trying to locate Arnold's position. Arnold helps him out by firing a round, which cuts the air beside Jake's ear. Ducking behind the scrap pile again, Jake mentally counts. *Two shots.* Unless Arnold has more ammunition with him, he'll be out of bullets soon. But only one of the four remaining needs to hit its mark.

Arnold has positioned himself in a window at the far end of the streetcar. Still panting, heart thudding, Jake sees the crane operator running toward the plant entrance, away from the gunfire. He doesn't see Arnold in the streetcar when he looks again. Could be on the move. *And here I stand.* Jake sucks in a mouthful of air and releases it. *What the hell?* He charges out from behind the scrap pile, firing one and then a second shot in the direction of the streetcar, hoping to draw Arnold out.

Surprised that he's not dodging bullets, Jake keeps running till he reaches the far end of the streetcar. Climbing up the steps into the car, gun pointed ahead of him, his eyes search for Arnold. A bullet splits wood beside him. Chips gash his face.

Jake crouches, spins, and returns fire. He can't see Arnold or where the shot came from. Then he spots him hightailing it toward the back entrance of the plant. Scrambling down the streetcar steps, Jake legs it across the yard after the fleeing chief. Once inside the plant, he ducks into the shadows and pins himself against a concrete wall.

The factory is bathed in a red glow. Molten steel bubbles in giant cauldrons. A crane hoists a ladle to the top of a tall vertical boom caster and pours the molten steel into a giant vat. There's a strange buzzing sound, like electricity arcing a pair of wires. The heat is intense. If hell exists, Jake thinks, it might resemble the enormous blast furnaces that turn tons of junked cars, old appliances, streetcar rails, and other scrap into new steel. Everything about the plant is hot, loud, and dangerous—even without Arnold trying to kill him.

Sweat gushes on Jake's brow. He feels like he's melting. He strips off his trench coat and scans the plant floor and the catwalk above him. With all the noise, no one pays attention to him. Moving forward, he doesn't hear the shot that sends a bullet ripping into the wall beside him, scattering cement particles.

Jake sees the flash of Arnold's fedora on the catwalk. He opens fire. One, two, three shots. No hits. He reloads and clambers up a set of metal stairs leading to the catwalk.

A curtain of steam from the molten steel obscures his view. Cautiously, he moves ahead, one hand on the railing, following his gun, his eyes fixed on the path ahead, his face dripping perspiration. As he passes through the thin curtain of steam, he realizes there's no sign of Arnold. Jake picks up speed, trotting and then running along the catwalk. When he reaches the stairway at the far end of the building, he bends over, hands on his knees, to catch his breath. A flicker of movement. Jake straightens up, levels his gun—too late.

Avery Arnold steps out of the shadows at the base of the stairs and fires.

The round catches Jake in the left calf, knocking him off balance. He fires wildly as he topples forward and plunges down the metal stairs, landing hard on his back at Arnold's feet. He's lost his fedora but held onto his gun. Weakly, he raises it, but Arnold kicks it out of his hand.

Straddling Jake, Arnold shows his teeth in a mirthless smile. "You let your anger over Ben and Davy Roth get to you, Jake. Shot your partner after you found out he murdered them, then tried to kill me when I intervened. I had no choice."

Mouth open, eyes unfocused, blood running down his calf, Jake chuckles and says, "Fuck you."

Arnold cocks his revolver.

"You were in on the kickbacks, Chief," Jake says, hoping to prolong the inevitable.

"Man has to live," Arnold says with a shrug.

"You, Bannister, Tony Rizzo, and Zeno Malkin. You killed Briggs because he wanted a piece of the action."

"So long, Jew-lover." Arnold smiles and takes aim.

Jake refuses to look away, braces for the impact. When the shot comes, he jerks in anticipation. Then. No bullet. Confused, he sees that Arnold is still gazing down at him, but his eyes are glazed. Blood spills from his mouth. He wheels and fires at something behind him.

Nick Cole, on his knees, the front of his shirt soaked red with blood, smoke leaking from his gun barrel, returns fire. He and Arnold both go down pulling triggers.

Jake lies still a moment, his heart thumping in his chest. Then he raises his head. He rips away part of his pants leg and looks at his wound. It's a through and through. Didn't hit the femoral artery. He won't bleed to death. Lucky.

He rolls on his side, gets to his knees, and makes his way to Arnold. Glass eyes. No pulse.

When Jake gets to him, Cole's breath is shallow. Blood drains from his mouth. Jake cradles Cole's head.

Nick coughs and squeezes Jake's arm. "Didn't want it . . . this way . . . Jake."

"In the end, you did the right thing. All that matters now."

"Katie," he says, a pleading look in his eyes.

"I'll make sure she knows," Jake says, but he's talking to a dead man.

Chapter 45

Dirty Laundry

January 12, 1951

WANTED COP KILLED IN GUN BATTLE WITH POLICE

By
Sarah Weisman

Sergeant Nicholas Cole, wanted in connection with the murders of Ben and Davy Roth, was shot and killed yesterday in a gun battle with MPD Detective Lieutenant Jake Cafferty and Police Chief Avery Arnold. Cafferty was wounded and Arnold tragically killed in the exchange of gunfire.

The shootout took place at the Minneapolis Iron & Steel scrap yard. Cole had been hiding out at the Victor Hotel in Skid Row. He phoned Cafferty, requesting that the lieutenant meet him at the scrap yard, allegedly to turn himself in. Cole then ambushed Cafferty, severely wounding him in the leg. Chief Arnold arrived on the scene and confronted Cole. Both men sustained fatal wounds in the ensuing gunfight.

Avery Arnold was recently promoted to chief after the resignation of William Flanagan. A twenty-year veteran of the MPD, Arnold will be buried with full honors at the Lakewood Cemetery in Minneapolis. His ex-wife, Carolyn, and his two young daughters and son survive him.

CITY OF STONES

Detective Lieutenant Cafferty is expected to fully re-cover from his wounds and return to active duty.

Chapter 46

February 20, 1951

Jake Cafferty sits in an overstuffed chair in Gloria Two Bears' living room. Outside of a slight, temporary limp, he's recovered from the gunshot wound to his lower leg. He's not happy that the new chief covered for Avery Arnold and declared him a *hero*, but it fits with the positive narrative the department feeds to a public starved for good news.

Gloria Two Bears is seated on the couch. Her waist-length black hair hangs loosely down her back. She's lost weight since the trial. In her burgundy sweater, blue jeans, and fringed moccasin boots, she's more relaxed than Jake remembers.

"Wanna cup of coffee, Lieutenant?"

"I'm good."

"You said on the phone you wanna talk about Sam."

"That's right."

She raises her eyebrows in expectation.

"Something troubles me about his murder."

"Mike Bannister is dead," she says. "Finally paid for his crime."

"He did."

"Then what's the problem?"

"Motive," Jake says. "Why would Bannister kill him? Sam saw Nick Cole kill the Roth brothers in the cornfield, not Bannister. Had to be another reason Bannister wanted Sam dead."

"Don't know," she says.

"I think you do."

Her eyes narrow with suspicion.

"You were Mike Bannister's snitch. You knew he had a temper. Knew he was queer. Maybe you told Sam."

"I never did."

Thinking about it, Jake says, "No, I don't believe you did tell Sam. But you told Bannister that Sam knew he was queer."

"Why do that?"

"Because if Bannister kills Sam and gets convicted of murder, he's out of your life. That's why you testified Sam had no gun."

"He didn't."

Jake nods. "But that's not what Bannister wanted you to say on the witness stand. And now that Sam is dead, you collect his pension and Social Security."

"But we wasn't married."

"That a fact?" Jake takes a sheet of paper out of his suit coat pocket, unfolds it lengthwise, and holds it up. "Copy of your marriage certificate. Seems you're Mrs. Gloria Two Bears Witherspoon. Married by a justice of the peace in Dakota County not too long before Bannister killed Sam."

"Where'd you get it?"

"Stored in an envelope in a cardboard box with the rest of Sam's belongings when they cleaned out his MPD locker. He probably kept it there in case something happened to him. Sounds like he didn't have much trust in his new bride."

"I looked out for him after he lost his job. Took him in. Sam owed me," she says, her voice rising.

Jake slips the certificate into an inner pocket and stands. "Don't think he owed you his life."

Chapter 47

February 26, 1951

Jake Cafferty pulls his unmarked Ford over to the curb along Park Avenue in front of the Crenshaw mansion. He lets the engine and the heater run while he smokes a cigarette and waits for Frank Morris from the Fraud/Theft Division and two black-and-whites to arrive.

Yesterday, Jake was sitting in the lobby of the Radisson Hotel, waiting for Dominic Cozens to appear. True to his word, Leo Hirschfield called Jake to let him know that Cozens was in town. Working out of Las Vegas, Cozens funnels the kickbacks from Minneapolis Iron & Steel into the shell company Zeno Malkin created. With Zeno Malkin, Avery Arnold, and Mike Bannister all dead, Jake wants to know who's now in control of the funds siphoned from the sell-off of TCRT steel. Jake's instincts tell him that Cozens hasn't left Vegas and come to Minnesota in February for the weather. He's here for another purpose.

At 11:35 that morning Cozens exits an elevator in the Radisson lobby and heads for the entrance to the hotel. A short, stocky man with slicked-back black hair and a widow's peak, he walks bow-legged, like he spent his youth riding horses.

While the doorman hails a cab for Cozens, Jake heads for his unmarked parked out front. He follows Cozens to the Minneapolis Iron & Steel building, where Cozens meets with Tony Rizzo. Jake arrests them. Then he and Frank Morris brace the two men. After Cozens and Rizzo are locked up, Jake heads for the mansion.

Now, Morris and two black-and-whites park behind Jake's Ford. Jake shuts off the engine, signals Morris and the uniforms to remain in their cars, and makes his way to the mansion's front door, where he rings the bell.

Virginia Crenshaw's face reddens when she opens the door. "Jake." She forces a smile, but makes no attempt to let him in.

"We need to talk," he says.

She hesitates as her eyes drift toward the black-and-whites and unmarked cars parked at the curb. "I've got company, Jake. Could we make it another time?"

"Afraid not," he says. He pushes the door fully open and steps inside as she moves out of his way.

"Don't be rude, Jake."

He looks at her for a moment before replying. "Rudeness is the least of your worries." He heads for the living room, Virginia Crenshaw trailing behind. Franklin Simms is seated on the tufted sofa, facing Jake. Douglas Crenshaw sits in his wheelchair beside him.

Simms, a half-filled champagne glass in his hand, looking like he's seen a ghost, stands and offers to shake. "Hello, Lieutenant. Didn't know you were coming."

Jake ignores him.

Simms withdraws his hand.

Douglas Crenshaw says, "I think you should leave, Lieutenant."

Jake grins. "And miss the party?"

Virginia Crenshaw sits on the other sofa and gestures at the champagne bottle on ice in the silver-plated server on the coffee table. "I'd offer you some, but you don't drink."

"What're you all celebrating?"

"I'm out on bail," Simms says.

"So you and Virginia are friends."

"Actually, we've known each other for some time, haven't we, Ginny?" Simms says.

She nods and sips Champagne from her glass.

"Ever since that pot bust at your place on Nicollet Island in '49?" Jake asks. "Or was it before that?"

Simms' mouth twitches nervously. There's a moment of dead silence before he says, "Ah, yes. An unfortunate incident."

The old man says, "You have no business here, Lieutenant."

"Wrong. Your friends Tony Rizzo and Dominic Cozens are locked in separate cells at City Hall. First rats off the *Titanic*."

"I don't know what you're talking about, Lieutenant."

"Sure you do. Ever since you lost money on Zeno Malkin's Brazama Gold hustle, you've been funneling kickbacks from your buddy, Rizzo, through a shell company in Vegas."

"I resent that insinuation."

Jake ignores him and continues. "What I don't know is who's controlling the account now that Zeno Malkin is dead. But I've got an idea." Jake looks at Simms.

Simms, still standing, glances at Virginia and her old man and then sits down.

Jake leans against the piano. "With the Korean War going on, the price of steel is high. Zeno Malkin set up a shell company in Las Vegas with the help of Cozens. Profits from the TCRTC sell-off are being funneled into the shell company, then kicked backed to the TCRTC investors. Avery Arnold took a percentage from that. Martin Crenshaw worked for Bass, Sterns and Wheeler, one of the brokerage firms Leonard Lindquist and the Railroad Commission are investigating for refusing to turn over the names of investors in the Twin City Rapid Transit Company. Arnold had Briggs and Bannister kill Crenshaw because he knew about the TCRT kickbacks through Zeno Malkin. Tony Rizzo was a friend of Malkin. They set up the kickback scheme.

"As Malkin's ghostwriter, Mr. Simms, you were privy to his scams and schemes. Especially the kickbacks he and Rizzo had set up with the sell-off of the TCRT rails and streetcars.

Makes no sense to kill Malkin if his name is the only one on the account. Rather than do another long stretch in a 6' x 8' prison cell, Mr. Cozens was happy to tell me your name is on the account, Simms."

"Have it all figured out, don't you, Jake?" Virginia Crenshaw says.

"Pretty much. Bannister was the cop who busted the pot party at Simms' place. I figure you told him about the kickback scheme. He wanted in. Got the DA to drop the pot charges. Bannister told Arnold and Briggs about the kickbacks. Arnold thought the group was getting too large. So he killed Briggs and set up the Roths to take the fall. Arnold had Bannister kill Malkin. You saw an opportunity to get rid of Bannister. Enlarge your piece of the pie."

"He attacked me, Jake. Tried to rape me."

Jake shakes his head. "Your handsome friend Mr. Simms here knows Bannister was queer. He assured me that Bannister wasn't interested in the opposite sex, right, Mr. Simms?"

Simms reaches for his glass of Champagne on the coffee table and chugs it.

"I'll take that as a 'yes.'" Turning his attention back to Virginia Crenshaw, Jake says, "You set up Bannister and then killed him."

"You can't prove that."

"Probably not. But you and your friends are going down for fraud and tax evasion. Leonard Lindquist and the Railroad Commission will be anxious to hear the details."

"I killed the son of a bitch," Douglas Crenshaw says.

"Father, don't—"

The old man shushes her with a wave of his hand. "Bannister told me he killed my son. Laughed about it before I shot him. My daughter offered an alibi for me. Virginia has nothing to do with the kickbacks or Bannister's death. I won't let her go to jail for something I did."

Jake's eyes hold hers, searching for anything that indicates her father is lying. "That true?"

She hesitates and then nods.

"Wish I could buy it."

She stands. "It is true, Jake."

"What do you plan on doing, Lieutenant?" the old man asks.

"I'll let my colleagues, Leonard Lindquist, and the feds figure it all out. Enjoy the Champagne. It'll be a long time before you taste it again." Jake tips his hat and backs toward the door.

"Hold it, Lieutenant."

Jake recognizes the Colt Vest Pocket .25 caliber in Douglas Crenshaw's hand. His heart kicks into second gear. He considers going for his gun and then rejects the idea. He'll be dead before it leaves his holster rig.

"Father, no!" Virginia says.

He hushes her once more.

"How you gonna explain my murder, Crenshaw?" Jake asks.

"I have friends in the department."

"Fewer every day."

Virginia Crenshaw steps in front of Jake, her back to him, facing her father. "I won't let you do this, Father."

"Move out of the way, Virginia."

She steps toward her father and extends a hand. "Give me the gun."

"Move, Virginia!"

She's between Jake and the old man now, blocking his view. Jake pulls his gun and steps to his right. He has a clear view of the old man in the wheelchair. "Drop the gun, Crenshaw! Now!"

As Crenshaw shifts his aim, his daughter cries, "No!" and dives for the gun.

Crenshaw fires.

Chapter 48

Dirty Laundry

March 7, 1951

SEVERAL CHARGED IN KICKBACK SCHEME

By
Sarah Weisman

Minneapolis city councilman Tony Rizzo, along with Minneapolis resident Franklin Simms, and Dominic Cozens of Las Vegas, Nevada, have been charged in connection with a money laundering and kickback scheme involving the dismantling of the Twin City Rapid Transit Company.

The indictment states that Rizzo's Minneapolis Iron & Steel company got all TCRT scrap metal for "grossly inadequate or, in some cases, no consideration."

As a result of subpoenas delivered last fall to six brokerage houses: Paine, Webber, Jackson and Curtis; Harris Upham & Co.; Bache & Co.; Thomson and McKinnon; Francis I. du Pont & Co.; and Bass, Sterns, and Wheeler, requiring the firms to turn over the names of their customers who bought the stock, it was revealed that mobsters and their family members now own shares in the Twin City Rapid Transit Company.

Isadore Blumenfeld was identified as owning 600 shares of common stock. Mrs. Blumenfeld was revealed as owning 1500 shares of preferred stock in her name worth more than $50,000. James Aune of Paine, Webber, Jackson, & Curtis, who bought 2,000 shares, is suspected of purchasing the stock for Isadore Blumenfeld, aka Kid Cann.

Thomas W. Banks deposited 2,000 shares of TCRT Co. stock at the bank as collateral, and the loan was outstanding in his name. While the stock was held as security for the loan, it was transferred to H. H. Banks, the Nebraska retailer.

Jeremiah Murphy (president of McCarthy's St. Louis Park Café) bought 1,000 shares. Murphy's stock was used as security on a loan. H.H. Clark, a director who owns 2,000 shares, and Reta Banks, corporation secretary and wife of Tommy Banks, gave the authority. The café borrowed $5500 to help purchase the 1,000 shares. Harold Banks, brother of Tommy Banks, also owns 2,000 shares.

Chairman Leonard Lindquist of the State Railroad and Warehouse Commission, investigating crime ties to TCRT, said, "Activities of this new stockholders' group, both before and after taking control, give good reason to fear that it has exploited the transit company for improper purposes and that the good citizens of Minneapolis will foot the bill for millions of the cost of the conversion from streetcars to buses."

Epilogue

March 11, 1951

Mostly cloudy day. Not a lot of sun. Jake Cafferty kneels in front of Max Hayes' tombstone and scans the inscription.

> But O for the touch of a vanished hand
> And the sound of a voice that is still.

He remembers standing beside a row of mourners assembled at Max's funeral to offer the *mitzvah of nichum avelim*, comfort to the bereaved, when he overheard a woman explaining that the lines on Max's headstone are from an Alfred Lord Tennyson poem.

Now Jake whispers the words, wishing he'd said them before. "I'm your father, Max. You are my son." Jake listens for a moment to a whisper of wind. Just wishful thinking.

Then a shadow falls across the tombstone. Jake reaches for his gun as he wheels around.

"Don't shoot," Kate Dawson says, raising her hands.

Jake stands. He relaxes and holsters his gun.

"Heard I'd find you here," she says.

"Every Sunday."

She gestures at the tombstone. "It wasn't an accident."

Jake shakes his head. "No, it wasn't."

"Why was he killed?"

"Because he wouldn't leave it alone."

"The TCRT."

"Yeah. Arnold and Bannister thought Max might be on to the kickback scheme."

"Arnold? The department never said he was involved."

"And they never will."

Kate nods. She looks around the cemetery and at Jake again. "Haven't talked in quite a while. Came to see you at the hospital, but you were sedated."

"Got the card and flowers. Thanks."

"So how're you doin'?"

"Surviving. You?"

"The same."

"All you can do sometimes."

"Till things get better."

Jake shrugs. "Haven't always found that to be the case."

Kate offers a tentative smile. "Have you talked to Virginia Crenshaw?"

"Not since her father's suicide. Last I heard she'd sold the mansion on Park Avenue and gone off to Europe."

"You believe she wasn't involved?"

"Don't know for sure. But it's possible."

Kate lets out a breath and asks, "Why'd Nicky do it?"

Jake wonders if he should reveal that Nick Cole was Jewish, that his determination to hide his ethnicity led him down a dark and deadly path. But Jake sees no point to it now. Both Cole and Bannister, pretending to be someone else, willing to do anything to keep their secret from an unaccepting society. Jake doubts it'll ever change.

"Lots of reasons," he says. "Anger. Alcohol. Ambition. The Roths told Cole how Arnold set them up before he killed them. Cole used the information to blackmail Arnold into an immediate promotion to Homicide. When it came out at the trial that he'd murdered the Roths, Arnold decided to get rid of Cole and take me out at the same time. Thanks to Cole, it didn't work out that way."

Her hand goes to her mouth. She steps back. "'Thanks to Cole'?"

"Arnold had the drop on me in the scrapyard, Kate. Cole killed him. Saved my life before he died."

"I didn't know."

"Now you do."

She tries a smile. "Thanks for telling me."

"Last request Cole had before he died."

She nods and brushes a tear off her cheek. "What a waste."

"Murder usually is."

Kate nods in understanding. She looks into Jake's eyes for a time before she says, "Got somewhere to go after you leave here?"

"Nowhere in particular. What'd you have in mind?"

"Not sure. Maybe play it by ear."

Jake smiles. Then he bends over and adds the stone in his hand to the dozens of stones on the concrete base of Max Hayes' tombstone.

Acknowledgments

The authors wish to thank those who contributed to the writing of this novel. Chief among them is the late Russ Krueger, whose generosity in sharing his stories and experiences during his 25 years as a police officer and detective lieutenant in the Homicide Division of the Minneapolis Police Department provided great insight into the time and places mentioned in the novel.

Thanks also to former Minneapolis Police Sergeant David Niebur, who headed the MPD Decoy Squad and went on to become chief of police in three different cities, including chief of the Cicero, Illinois police department, where he helped send many of the last remnants of the old Capone mob to prison.

The authors gratefully acknowledge the information provided by the archives of Minnesota Historical Society, video and audio recordings from Minneapolis Public Television and Minneapolis Public Radio, and from James Eli Shiffer's excellent book, *The King of Skid Row*. Thanks to Lee Mosher for providing the research on Elizabeth Knapp Owens.

Many thanks to trusted readers Abigail Davis, Linda Donaldson, Lorrie Holmgren, Jenifer LeClair, and Peg Wangensteen. Special thanks to Chuck Logan for all his time and suggestions that helped shape the characters and story. Thanks to our excellent editor Jennifer Adkins and to our designer Rebecca Treadway for the outstanding cover.

Finally, we wish to thank our wives, Martha and Gail, for their love and support.

Authors' Note

The fictional character of Kate Dawson personifies the women who blazed the trail for others in a profession dominated by men before passage of civil rights laws forced law firms to admit women into practice. Though Kate was hired in 1950 as the first woman prosecutor in Hennepin County, the actual first woman prosecutor in the Hennepin County Attorney's Office was Elizabeth Knapp Owens. She was the only woman graduate of the University of Minnesota Law School in 1924 and was appointed assistant county attorney in 1925 by governor Floyd B. Olson. She resigned her position in 1942 to enter private practice. She died in Maple Plain, Minnesota on February 7, 1963.

Author Bios

Christopher Valen is the award-winning author of the literary novel *All the Fields* and seven police procedurals featuring Colombian-born St. Paul Homicide Detective John Santana: *White Tombs*, *The Black Minute*, *Bad Weeds Never Die*, *Bone Shadows*, *Death's Way*, *The Darkness Hunter*, and *Speak for the Dead*. Christopher resides in Minnesota and Arizona with his Colombian-born wife, Martha. To learn more, visit his website at www.christophervalen.com.

Dan Cohen has served as president of the Minneapolis City Council and the Minneapolis Planning Commission. He is the author of *Undefeated*, a biography of Hubert Humphrey, a dozen children's mini mysteries, a history of Breck School, and *Anonymous Source*, a personal memoir of his successful United States Supreme Court lawsuit. He is a graduate of Stanford University and Harvard Law School. He lives in Minneapolis with his wife, Gail, also a Stanford graduate.

AN INVITATION TO READING GROUPS/
BOOK CLUBS

I would like to extend an invitation to reading groups/book clubs across the country. Invite me to your group and I'll be happy to participate in your discussion. I'm available to join your discussion either in person or via FaceTime, Skype, or the telephone. (Reading groups should have a speakerphone.) You can arrange a date and time by e-mailing cjvalen@comcast.net. I look forward to hearing from you.

Not Sure What to Read Next?
Try these authors from Conquill Press

Jenifer LeClair
The Windjammer Mystery Series
Rigged for Murder
Danger Sector
Cold Coast
Apparition Island
Dead Astern
www.windjammermyseries.com

Chuck Logan
Fallen Angel
Broker
www.chucklogan.org

Brian Lutterman
The Pen Wilkinson Mystery Series
Downfall
Windfall
Freefall
Nightfall
www.brianlutterman.com

Steve Thayer
Ithaca Falls
The Wheat Field
The Leper
www.stevethayer.com

Christopher Valen
The John Santana Mystery Series
White Tombs
The Black Minute
Bad Weeds Never Die
Bone Shadows
Death's Way
The Darkness Hunter
Speak for the Dead
www.christophervalen.com
For more information on all these titles go to:
www.conquillpress.com